Irish author **Abby Green** ended a very glamorous career in film and TV—which really consisted of a lot of standing in the rain outside actors' trailers—to pursue her love of romance. After she'd bombarded Mills & Boon with manuscripts they kindly accepted one, and an author was born. She lives in Dublin, Ireland, and loves any excuse for distraction. Visit abby-green.com or email abbygreenauthor@gmail.com.

USA TODAY bestselling author **Natalie Anderson** writes emotional contemporary romance full of sparkling banter, sizzling heat and uplifting endings—perfect for readers who love to escape with empowered heroines and arrogant alphas who are too sexy for their own good. When not writing, you'll find her wrangling her four children, three cats, two goldfish and one dog… and snuggled in a heap on the sofa with her husband at the end of the day. Follow her at natalie-anderson.com.

THEIR ONE-NIGHT RIO REUNION

ABBY GREEN

REVEALING HER NINE-MONTH SECRET

NATALIE ANDERSON

MILLS & BOON

First Published in Great Britain 2022
by Mills & Boon, an imprint of HarperCollins*Publishers* Ltd,
1 London Bridge Street, London, SE1 9GF

www.harpercollins.co.uk

HarperCollins*Publishers*
1st Floor, Watermarque Building,
Ringsend Road, Dublin 4, Ireland

Their One-Night Rio Reunion © 2022 Abby Green

Revealing Her Nine-Month Secret © 2022 Natalie Anderson

ISBN: 978-0-263-30075-8

03/22

MIX
Paper from
responsible sources
FSC™ C007454

This book is produced from independently certified FSC™ paper
to ensure responsible forest management.
For more information visit www.harpercollins.co.uk/green.

Printed and Bound in Spain using 100% Renewable Electricity
at CPI Black Print, Barcelona

THEIR ONE-NIGHT RIO REUNION

ABBY GREEN

MILLS & BOON

I'd like to dedicate this to Margaret.
For forty-one years—most of my life—
she has been woven into the fabric of my existence
like no one else. She has taught me, guided me,
nurtured me, loved me as her own and brought me
into her family like a fierce Mama Bear. She has brought
me immense joy and happiness, and none of this would
have been half as much fun or as satisfying without her.
Thank you, and I love you.

PROLOGUE

A year ago, Cristo Redentor Church, Rio de Janeiro

ANA DIAZ WAS late to her own wedding. Which was entirely to be expected for a normal wedding. But this wasn't a normal wedding. This was an arranged marriage between two of Brazil's elite families.

She was the pawn in a deal between her media mogul father, Rodolfo Diaz, and billionaire tech entrepreneur Caio Salazar. His full name was Caio Salazar de Barros, but he had turned his back on his family fortune and dynasty some years before and struck out on his own, building his own empire.

However, his association and name, even without 'de Barros', was still very potent currency. Hence the marriage match. Her father needed Caio Salazar for a business deal and Salazar needed a wife, because apparently he was under pressure to project a more settled and conservative image in order to expand his business into Europe and globally.

Ana could understand why—he had cultivated quite the reputation as a playboy. Always staying within the bounds of respectability—just—but leaving no one in any doubt that he was—according to breathless accounts in the gossip columns—a masterful lover of beautiful women, while also enjoying all the trappings that came with unimaginable wealth and success.

Ana could appreciate that that kind of reputation would only take one so far on a global stage. Two things had persuaded her to agree to the marriage. One, she'd manage to secure her beloved younger brother's future, and two, the marriage was to last only for one year.

Clearly that was all the time Salazar could bear to indulge in putting forward a less hedonistic persona.

The prenuptial agreement had stated that she would be required to attend social events with her husband, helping to promote his desired re-branding as a re-formed married man. Ana was to do everything to make their union believable by appearing devoted. Connected. *In public.*

Behind closed doors, however, she would not be expected to keep up the act. She'd been assured of her own private rooms and space. Days off when not required for public duties.

The only ambiguity had been the omission of anything specific about marital relations *in the bedroom.* Her heart palpitated at that thought and a cold sweat broke out over her skin. Not because she feared the prospect or didn't find her fiancé attractive. Quite the opposite.

From the moment she'd laid eyes on Caio Salazar in her father's house, when he'd first come to discuss business some weeks ago, he'd branded himself onto her consciousness in a way that was seriously disturbing.

Tall and dark, with a leanly muscular build, he was undeniably handsome. His thick dark hair was kept short, but long enough to frame a hard-boned face. Dark brows lay over deep-set eyes and an aquiline nose that more than hinted at his impeccable lineage, all the way back to the Portuguese *conquistadores* of Brazil. His mouth was sculpted and firm. Sensual. His jaw was hard and more often stubbled than not. His eyes were dark. He oozed an arrogant potent sexuality that made his playboy reputation only too easy to believe.

She'd watched him covertly when he'd come to meet with her father in a series of secret meetings, arriving on each occasion without an entourage—unheard of in the company her father usually kept. Uncoiling his tall, lean body from a low-slung sports car, wearing faded jeans and short-sleeved polo shirts, he'd clearly felt no obligation to adhere to formality, which had intrigued and thrilled Ana in equal measure. It was very seldom she saw anyone exhibit such loucheness around her father.

She'd been surprised to find herself reacting to him so forcefully. She'd never imagined she'd find such an obviously handsome playboy type attractive—especially when he was a product of the same very privileged and cynical world as all of the men she'd grown up with: her father and older brothers.

Her younger brother, Francisco, was different. Vastly different. Which was why she loved him so much. Enough to enter into an arranged marriage.

But something about Caio Salazar had called to her before she could deny it or stop it. On a very deep, base level, where she hid all her insecurities around her inexperience with men. Or, more accurately, her *zero* experience.

Growing up in a house surrounded by men had led to Ana hiding herself away, disguising her femininity, fading into the background. Without a mother and sisters, she'd always felt like an outsider among her peers in school—left out of some essential feminine mystery she should understand but didn't. Together with her natural introversion, it was the reason why she was still untouched at the age of twenty-two, on the verge of walking down the aisle to meet her husband, who might or might not expect to demand his conjugal rights.

She knew that if Caio Salazar did demand his conjugal rights it would be purely because it was a formality, maybe even a legal necessity, so she couldn't back out of the marriage prematurely. *Not* because he would want to. Because she wasn't remotely his type. He favoured tall, leggy models who resembled racehorses, not women of average height, with unfashionable curves and a severe lack of sense of style.

As if hearing her thoughts, her father, who had been on his cell-phone all this time, finally finished his conversation and joined her in the vestibule of the church.

His cold dark gaze, even today, when he was giving her away, raked her up and down. 'You look like an old maid in that dress. Do you want Salazar to decide he's making a huge mistake?'

Ana fought down the anger and the heat of self-consciousness. She'd deliberately chosen this dress because it effectively covered her from neck to toe and shoulder to wrist. She'd wanted to send out a strong signal that she was not to be considered a sexual pawn as well as a marriage pawn. Because right now the thing she feared most was the humiliation of her husband-to-be's realisation that she was as predictably and helplessly in his thrall as every other woman on the planet. That she wanted him with a burning desire that shocked her as much as it dismayed her.

The one meaningful interaction she'd had with Salazar up to now—a mere four weeks ago—flashed into her head. Her father had hauled her in front of the man and presented her like a brood mare to be inspected.

Salazar hadn't even looked at her father when he'd said curtly, 'Leave us.'

If it had been another situation Ana might have appreciated the comical sight of Rodolfo Diaz being ordered out of his own reception room. But her father was nothing if not cunning and smart, and he'd known that Salazar agreeing to take his troublesome only daughter off his hands was too good a prospect to mess up, so he'd swallowed his outrage and left them.

Ana had been incandescent with rage at the thought that she was going to be passed from father to husband like a medieval chattel. But Caio Salazar had just looked at her for a long, unnerving moment before saying, 'Do you want to see the world, Ana? Because that is what I'm offering you. I'm taking my company global. All I need is a wife who will stand by my side, unobtrusive and complementary, for one year.'

A little stunned at his candour, and at the fact that he wasn't trying to flirt to persuade her, Ana had taken a moment to gather her wits and push down the residual anger—and, surprisingly, the dart of hurt that she didn't merit even the most rudimentary charm offensive from a renowned playboy.

She'd been terrified he'd notice how being in such close proximity to him was affecting her, and she'd responded tartly, 'Blow-up dolls are very sophisticated these days. You might save yourself a lot of time and money by procuring one for your convenient marriage.'

His dark eyes had flashed at that. The evidence that she'd managed to surprise him had been a small comfort.

He'd drawled, 'Ah, but a blow-up doll hasn't been brought up to navigate the upper echelons of society the way you have, Ana. Everyone wants something…

so what is it that you want, or need, that would make this arrangement more…palatable?'

And that was why she was doing this.

For her little brother and ultimately—she couldn't deny it—for herself. For her own freedom.

Ana looked at her father now and bit out, 'If you delay us any longer it won't be because of *me* that Salazar decides to renege on this deal.'

Her father scowled, but nodded to the attendant, who sent a signal to someone, and Ana heard Mendelssohn's "Wedding March" start. She steeled herself as the doors opened and looked down the long aisle to where the tall figure of the man she was about to marry stood. A total stranger, and yet one who had already got under her skin in a way that was seriously disturbing.

CHAPTER ONE

Today, Rio de Janeiro

'MR SALAZAR?'

Caio Salazar turned around to see his solicitor putting some papers down on the wide oak table with little pointed stickers indicating where to sign.

He held out a pen. 'These are the final signatures required for your divorce papers.'

Divorce. Caio Salazar took the pen and sat down.

He had never intended to get married. It hadn't been part of his plans. Not after witnessing his parents' toxic mess of a marriage. He was lucky. He had older brothers who had borne the burden of inheriting the legendary Salazar de Barros wealth and industry, leaving Caio free to strike out on his own and unshackle himself from the yoke of his family, losing 'de Barros' en route.

The success of his self-made business had put paid to any rumours that he wouldn't survive without his family's help. He'd not only survived, he'd become one of Brazil's top net worth individuals, rivalling his own family's dominance single-handedly, leaving him free to live an independent life, beholden to none.

He'd made the most of it at first—cultivating quite the reputation as a playboy rebel, cutting a swathe through Brazil's legendary nightlife and most beautiful women, which had been fun but admittedly had had more to do with irritating his old man than sating his own appetites.

In truth, that life had begun to lose its appeal some time ago. Caio had felt increasingly as if he was going through the motions, living down to a reputation he'd created that no longer served him or amused him.

When his forays into Europe and North America had started falling flat, among rumours that his reputation was too volatile, Caio had realised he was in danger of ruining everything he'd built up. And there were plenty of people waiting to see him take a very public fall from grace.

He wouldn't give them the satisfaction and he wasn't that self-destructive. And so he'd considered the unthinkable—the fastest route to turning his reputation around—a solid marriage to a suitable woman.

Which was why, almost a year ago to the day, he'd married the daughter of one of Rio de Janeiro's most prominent families, taking everyone by surprise.

The marriage had been a serendipitous by-product of a deal with Rodolfo Diaz. The media mogul had a daughter he'd wanted to see married off and Caio had needed a wife. The fact that she came from a suitable background and a similar lineage to Caio had been a bonus. It would make the marriage look even more authentic.

However, Caio had only agreed to think about the union once he'd met with Ana Diaz. Their first meeting hadn't been auspicious. An unfashionably long veil of dark hair had obscured her features and loose clothes had drowned any view of her body. Of average height, she hadn't made much of an impression.

But then her father had taken her chin in his fingers and tipped her face up, and her hair had fallen back to reveal a pretty heart-shaped face, pale, with dark arching brows. Her soft mouth had been set in a mutinous line. Her dark brown eyes had flashed with defiance as her father had spoken to Caio, and she'd pulled away from her father and said angrily, 'I'm not a chattel to be passed around between men.'

In that moment, bristling with tension between father and daughter, Caio had recognised that there was a very real danger that she would provoke her father to violence. He'd smelled it like a metallic tang in the air. He'd known it because he'd smelled it before.

It had impacted him right in his gut, even though she was a complete stranger.

Before he'd had time to analyse his reaction, he'd decided that he would marry her. He'd asked her father to leave them alone to discuss it, and she'd turned that barely concealed fury on him.

To Caio's surprise, even though the woman had been as non-descript as a student, something had pulsed to life in his blood. He'd told himself it was just confirmation that he was making the right decision to save his reputation and move his business forward.

He couldn't have contemplated a marriage of convenience with one of his lovers. That would have spelled disaster and drama. No, marrying a total stranger—albeit one from the right family and background—would be perfect. When they divorced she would be a very rich woman. No harm, no foul.

He'd assured himself that it had nothing to do with the protective instinct aroused within him when he'd sensed the violence in the air from her father. Or the disturbing physical reaction that he'd dismissed as an aberration as soon as it had happened.

And so, just over a year ago, their wedding had been discreet and conducted with little fanfare. It had caused a flurry of interest at first, but that had died down quickly. After all, strategic marriages between the offspring of Brazil's wealthiest families happened all the time.

And today, the divorce was an equally understated affair.

In many regards the marriage had been a complete success. Ana had travelled the world with him as he'd taken his company global, opening offices in New York, London and Bangkok. With a wife by his side, he'd been accepted among the business community and society without question, because he was no longer a playboy threatening to leave a storm of headlines in his wake as he bedded his way through Europe and North America.

In fact, much to Caio's surprise, he'd found that he'd been singularly *un*-enticed by any of the women who had made it very clear that they were available. He'd discovered that having a wife was no deterrent in that regard.

Caio looked across the room at the back of the woman who stood in front of one of the floor-to-ceiling windows that showcased a jaw-dropping view of the financial district of Rio de Janeiro, early-morning sunlight making the tall buildings sparkle and shine.

His wife no longer had unfashionably long hair. Now it was cut much shorter, into a bob that brushed her shoulders and framed her face. A face that he hadn't fully appreciated when they'd first met. A face that had revealed its beauty in such a way as to mock Caio daily for having first assumed she was average.

She wore a little make-up now, expertly applied, highlighting dark, long-lashed brown eyes framed by naturally arching brows. Her light olive skin was flawless. Her nose had a slightly patrician bump. But it was her mouth that he'd grown more and more fixated by: soft and naturally pouting, it sometimes gave her an air of intense vulnerability and sometimes, more recently and disturbingly, an air of something much closer to sultry, almost provocative.

The shapeless clothes she'd favoured when they'd first met were long gone. Today she wore a designer slim-fitting black trouser suit paired with a grey silk shirt and black high heels, drawing attention to her slender ankles. Discreet jewellery. Even in heels, she was still a full head shorter than him.

A low cough alerted him to the fact that his solicitor was still waiting for him to sign the papers.

What the hell was wrong with him?

This marriage had always been destined to end today, and Caio had achieved exactly what he'd set out to achieve a year ago. Ignoring the knot of resistance in his gut, Caio signed the papers and handed the pen back to his solicitor.

Ana Diaz Salazar heard the sound of a pen moving over paper behind her. Her husband…signing their divorce papers. Next, it would be her turn. So why wasn't she more impatient to get this divorce signed, sealed and delivered?

She'd stood in this very same spot just over a year ago, when she'd come here to sign the prenuptial agreement. Then, as now, she fancied that she could almost see all the way to where the early-morning surf would be foaming up onto the famous Copacabana beach.

She longed to be there now. It was her favourite time to be on the beach—early, before it became packed with fellow Cariocas. Or, better yet, to be there with her beloved younger brother Francisco. Except he was many thousands of miles away, in Europe. Where she'd be heading too, this afternoon, on a one-way plane ticket, as a newly divorced millionairess—thanks to the very generous settlement from her husband. A settlement that would have been even larger if she hadn't insisted that she didn't feel entitled to the money.

She waited for a feeling of excitement to grip her at the thought of flying to Europe with enough funds to start a new life but, much to her irritation, any sense of excitement was tempered with frustration. Regret. Unfinished business. *Unrequited desire*, whispered a sly voice in her ear.

She slammed a lid on that incendiary notion. She'd come far too close to humiliating herself, trying to get her husband to notice her in recent weeks, as if in desperation as their divorce date had come closer. The inconvenient desire she'd felt for him at the start of their marriage had only grown stronger, as if to mock her daily. Like a thorn under her skin. A constant reminder that she was weak.

Thank God they were divorcing today and she would be able to put some distance between them with her dignity more or less intact. He would never know how much she wanted him. Because he'd never really noticed her.

'Mrs Salazar? We're ready for you to sign.'

Ana tensed. *Mrs Salazar*. Not for much longer. She would be Ana Diaz again after this. She could feel her husband's eyes on her back. But was he even really her husband if they hadn't consummated their marriage?

They'd lived together, yes, and they'd travelled—*a lot*—and had attended events as husband and wife, but apart from that contact had been minimal.

Business associates probably spent more time together. Knew each other more intimately. Except…she did feel as if she knew her husband intimately. On a level that was very secret, where she'd watched him avidly, discovering that he was a man far different from the one she'd first judged him to be.

Caio had become too intriguing for Ana's liking and when intrigue was packaged with physical attraction… Her feelings for him now added up to something she didn't even want to articulate.

'Ana?'

His deep voice cut through the chatter in her head and made the tangle in her gut knot even tighter. She took a deep breath and turned around, steeling herself for her husband's effect on her.

But even steeling herself didn't work. Her blood leapt and her pulse-rate tripled. She worried that his image would be permanently etched onto her brain. And his dark eyes that weren't completely dark. They had golden flecks up close that made them look molten. She knew because she'd seen them turn molten one night…

They'd moved around so much in the past year that it had become normal for her to feel a little disorientated when she woke at night in a new place—a hotel suite or one of Caio's residences. That particular night she'd been walking sleepily back into her bedroom after getting a glass of water and a sound had made her look up. She'd registered too late that she hadn't returned to her room. It was Caio's, and he'd been emerging from a cloud of steam, obviously having just taken a shower in the bathroom.

The incendiary sight before her had glued her feet to the spot. He had been entirely naked. Drying his hair roughly with a small towel. Dark olive skin still damp. Gleaming.

In that moment Ana had understood why sculptors created works of art dedicated to the male form. His chest was a hard and broad expanse, covered in a light smattering of dark hair, muscles bunching and moving as he'd dried his hair. A dark line of hair dissected the well-defined six-pack of his abdomen before disappearing into the thicket of hair that cradled the very essence of his masculinity. Lean hips and powerful thighs. Long legs.

But she hadn't been able to take her eyes off that most potent part of him. Even at rest it had been impressive.

A heavy, tugging ache between her legs had made her press her thighs together, as if she could contain the longing. And then the hand holding the small towel had dropped, obscuring her vision. Only then had she been able to break out of her trance and her stricken gaze had met his. And that was when she'd noticed for the first time how his eyes could look…molten. Not just dark and frustratingly unreadable, as she'd often told herself, but actually…hot. Hotter than the sun.

She'd fled.

'Ana?'

His voice jerked her out of the past and back into the present. Those dark brows were drawn together now. That sensual mouth was tight. She would have expected him to be more relaxed. He was getting rid of the wife he'd married only to further his business interests. He could go out now and take any number of beautiful women to bed and slake his lust—because she knew he hadn't taken any lovers during their marriage. He'd respected their sham marriage vows. And that had only confused her even more.

She blinked. 'Yes, I'm ready.'

She dragged her gaze away from his and looked down at the table, where her solicitor was pointing to the dotted line and handing her a pen, saying, 'The last signature, Mrs Salazar. This will complete the paperwork.'

Ana took the pen. It felt unbearably heavy. She bent down and noticed that her hand was trembling. Angry with herself for reacting like this to an event that she'd anticipated since the day she'd agreed to marry this man, she scrawled her name and the pen dropped out of her nerveless fingers.

Done.

The marriage of convenience she'd entered into with the utmost reluctance was now over and it hadn't been what she'd expected it to be at all. It had been…something else entirely…

CHAPTER TWO

CAIO WATCHED AS Ana straightened from signing her name. She looked...agitated. Biting her lip. His insides twisted with helpless reaction. He tensed against it and reminded himself that the sooner she was gone, the better. His reaction to her was just a build-up of sexual frustration after a year of celibacy.

But no other woman has interested you, pointed out a mocking voice.

Caio ignored it.

He'd got what he needed out of the mutually beneficial arrangement and it was time to move on. He'd go out tonight, arrange to meet one of his ex-lovers who'd made it very clear throughout the last year that she was available if he so desired...

Yet right now it was hard even to recall what she looked like. And the thought of going through the charade of wining and dining and indulging in inane conversation was suddenly very unappealing.

Slightly disgusted with himself, Caio wondered if a year of domesticity—even if it had been a charade—had somehow rewired his brain?

You could have seduced Ana, taunted another voice.

Caio's mouth firmed into a tight line. Seducing her had not been an option. She was a virgin, and she'd been so terrified on their wedding night that he would force her to sleep with him that she'd tried to run away. He'd assured her that he wouldn't touch her during their marriage, because he didn't sleep with innocents.

And he still didn't.

Time to move on.

The chief legal advisor looked first at Ana and then at Caio. She said, 'Once the decree is signed off by the court, the divorce will be final. That will happen within the next twenty-four hours. But essentially, as of this moment, you can consider yourselves divorced.'

Ana swallowed past the obstruction that had appeared out of nowhere in her throat. She forced herself to say, 'Thank you.'

The legal advisor cracked a small smile. 'I just wish every divorce was as amicable and respectful as yours—it would make life a lot easier.'

Ana's face grew hot, and she avoided Caio's eye. It was pretty much common knowledge that her marriage to Caio Salazar had been one borne out of a business arrangement between Caio and her father, even if Caio *had* made sure the final decision was hers.

The legal team were starting to file out of the office now, talking in low voices, and the sound of their chatter broke Ana out of her reverie. She reached for her bag on the table and Caio walked over to join her. All the tiny hairs on her body vibrated with awareness. She didn't like the wrenching sensation in her gut. She gritted her jaw. The sooner she was out of his disturbing orbit the better.

'My driver is outside to take us home.'

Home. Ana wanted to reject the notion that Caio's Rio de Janeiro penthouse apartment had been a home to her, but in fact it had become more of a home than her own had ever been, and the thought of never seeing it again made her feel acutely vulnerable.

She shook her head. 'Thanks, but my flight to Europe leaves in a few hours. I'm going to go straight to the airport.' She forced down a dart of inexplicable guilt and looked at him. 'It's not as if we need to pretend any more, do we?'

He looked at her intently. A muscle ticked in his jaw. She could see the golden flecks in his eyes so clearly now, and wondered why it had taken her so long to notice them. Maybe because she'd avoided looking at him directly for a long time. Scared of his effect on her. And maybe because for many weeks after they'd married she'd still been crippled by the lingering humiliation of her father completely exposing her.

When he'd found out that she'd agreed to the marriage, Rodolfo Diaz had boomed in his loud voice, 'Excellent! And let me assure you that you are getting a wife not only of impeccable breeding but also one who still has her virtue intact. How many twenty-two-year-olds can claim that in this day and age?'

Ana still burned at the excoriating memory a year later. She'd wanted alternately to throttle her father and to disappear about a thousand feet under the earth. But Caio hadn't appeared shocked. He hadn't been remotely interested in whether or not Ana was innocent, as she'd found out on her wedding night. Just to compound her humiliation.

Eventually Caio responded, breaking Ana out of her painful reminiscences. 'What's your plan when you get to Europe?'

Ana said, 'I've rented an apartment near Francisco for six months. I can figure out where to go from there.

I've arranged for my things to be put in storage until I know where I'll be long-term.'

Caio's expression was impossible to read. Even now. He clearly couldn't care less that she was leaving—he was just being polite, making it appear as if her imminent departure wasn't something he'd been waiting for for weeks. It made something rebellious and volatile bubble up inside her—a need to see that polite façade crack.

But before Ana could say something—anything to try and provoke some last reaction—there was a sharp rap on the door, and they both looked around to see Caio's chief of security, Tomás, who organised the discreet security detail that followed them both daily. He looked serious, and apologised for interrupting so precipitately.

Tomás acknowledged Ana and then addressed Caio. 'Mr Salazar, we have a situation and it's serious.'

'What is it?' Caio's voice was sharp.

The man answered, 'It's a kidnap threat, and it's very credible. They're here, in the city right now, highly organised and motivated. We need to extract you and Mrs Salazar straight away and remove you to a secure location.'

Ana felt that now wasn't the time to point out that technically she was no longer Mrs Salazar. She wasn't overly shocked at this news. Growing up as a Diaz, daughter to one of Brazil's wealthiest businessmen, she had never known what it was to live without the threat of violence or kidnap. Security had been a constant feature of her life, and in many ways she'd grown used to it.

She took a step forward, feeling slightly panicky that there might be a delay in putting Rio de Janeiro and Caio and all the disturbing things he made her feel, behind her. That was more of a threat.

'I'm due to fly to Europe this afternoon—surely I'll be safe there?'

Tomás looked at her, and he was grimmer than she'd ever seen him. 'Mrs Salazar, we have it on good authority that two of the kidnappers are on your flight and have plans to snatch you once you're through Customs in Amsterdam.'

Ana gulped.

Tomás looked at Caio. 'And they are planning a simultaneous operation with you here, Mr Salazar. They are going to substitute your driver with one of theirs, so that they can take you to a location and inform you of the kidnap of your wife and lay out their demands. They're not planning on freeing you until their demands are met.'

A cold finger traced down Ana's spine at the thought of Caio being put in danger.

The man continued. 'They've been operating for some time, and they're wanted by every security agency in the world. They're the same gang who kidnapped the daughter of Federico Falluci in Italy and got a massive ransom.'

Ana went even colder. She'd heard about that. The little girl hadn't spoken for months afterwards.

'This is the first time they've managed to track the gang down and discover who they're targeting next.'

Ana shook her head. 'But we're divorced...or as good as...what worth have I to them?'

'They will have been observing you for months by now. They only go after targets they know will do whatever it takes to retrieve the victim and pay the ransom.'

Before Ana could respond to that, Caio addressed Tomás, 'So what's the plan?'

Ana turned to face him. 'What's the plan? The plan is that I go to Europe today. They've targeted the wrong people!' The thought of Caio caring enough to bankrupt himself to save her was almost laughable, except Ana didn't feel like laughing.

The security man was shaking his head. 'I'm afraid that's not possible, Mrs Salazar. The special security forces are involved now. This is bigger than you or us. We have organised a safe location for you both to go to, but you need to leave immediately. Staff have prepared essential items for you.'

Ana looked at the man. 'Go where? For how long?'

'I'm afraid I can't tell you that. You'll find out when you get there. As for how long? At least twenty-four hours. That's the window of time we have to catch this gang, before they realise they're being watched.'

Her head reeling at this abrupt turn of events, Ana repeated faintly, 'Twenty-four hours…?'

CHAPTER THREE

EVERYTHING BECAME A blur of activity after that. Ana and Caio were taken down to the basement of the building in a staff elevator and put into the back of a non-descript, shabby SUV with blacked-out windows. They were instructed to lie down until told otherwise and Ana complied, suddenly more frightened than she'd ever been by the sheer level of security that had sprung up around them. Some of the men were wearing full protection gear and holding massive guns.

She lay down on the back seat, turning her head to one side, and Caio had no option but to cover her body with his. Far from getting away from him, she was now closer to him than she'd ever been.

The vehicle started to move—up a ramp and presumably out onto a side street.

She was burningly aware of Caio's body over hers. Her bottom was cupped by his hard thighs and that memory of his naked image filled her mind.

She gritted her jaw. *Not helping.*

His hands were beside hers on the seat, laughably bigger than hers. His scent filled her nostrils, heady and masculine. She could feel the heat of his body through his clothes.

He generally erred on the side of being casual, working in an industry that wasn't renowned for conforming at the best of times, but today she'd been surprised to see him wearing a dark three-piece suit. A dark blue tie.

The only other time she could recall him wearing a three-piece suit—apart from their wedding—had been the day she'd signed the prenuptial agreement. It had completely intimidated her the first time around. The suit had made him look remote and like a stranger. But today... All she'd been able to see was the man under the suit. A man full of many more contradictions that she could have ever imagined. A man she'd come to respect.

And more.

The suit was a reminder that he was one of the richest self-made men in Brazil. After ostracising himself from his family and rejecting any inheritance he was due a long time ago, he'd sold his first start-up to one of the big Silicon Valley companies for many millions at the tender age of twenty-four. And since then he'd only become more successful. Everything he touched turned to gold.

Ana had always wondered about why he'd turned his back on his family, but whenever she'd broached the subject Caio had firmly diverted the conversation. Fair enough. She didn't particularly relish discussions about her family either. They had that much in common.

'Okay?'

Caio's breath near her ear made Ana's heart-rate pick up. If she turned her head to the other side they'd be face to face. Closer than they'd ever been. He hadn't even kissed her on their wedding day, apart from a perfunctory peck on the mouth at the priest's nudging. And yet it had burned.

She nodded. 'Fine.'

She could sense that he was resting his weight on one arm, so as not to crush her to the seat, but Ana felt a pulse throb between her legs and a skewering sensation of need. She'd fought the desire she felt for this man for so long, but now it felt as if it was breaking loose. Like a swollen river bursting its banks. She *wanted* to be crushed under this man. She wanted to feel all that lean and steely strength around her. *In her.*

She bit her lip. *This* was why she'd booked a flight out of Rio de Janeiro as soon as she could. She felt as if her control around this man had been fraying for a long time, and she'd been veering into dangerous territory recently, wanting to provoke a reaction—as if she needed to prove to herself once and for all that he saw her as merely a by-product of a business deal.

A deal that was now going to be prolonged for another twenty-four hours in a secret location…

Tomás's voice came from the front of the vehicle. 'You can sit up now, Mr and Mrs Salazar, it's safe.'

Suddenly Caio's heat and weight were gone. Ana felt ridiculously bereft. She sat up slowly. They seemed to be driving into some kind of small airfield with a hangar nearby.

Tomás said, 'We weren't followed, but we took a circuitous route just in case. The helicopter is waiting here. If we'd taken you from the roof of your building it would have raised suspicions.'

'Won't they be suspicious when we don't come out of the building? When I don't get on the plane later?' Ana pointed out.

Tomás's eyes met Ana's in the mirror. 'There's a plan in place, Mrs Salazar, and that's all I can tell you. You'll find out more if it's successful.'

Ana shivered. *If* it was successful.

As if sensing her sudden trepidation, Caio took her hand. She looked at him, surprised by the contact. 'Nothing will happen to you, I promise,' he said.

Ana swallowed. For a moment she could almost imagine that there'd been something fierce in his voice. But then Caio abruptly let go of her hand, as if aware that he'd transgressed their tacit agreement only to touch in public. For the purposes of a marriage that no longer existed.

The SUV came to a stop and Ana saw the helicopter, its blades circling slowly outside the hangar. Staff waited along with more men in dark clothes with guns.

They were escorted to the helicopter under strict surveillance. She got in first, followed by Caio, and before she could take a breath she was strapped in, headphones on, and they were lifting up into the sky with a little wobble.

Ana gripped her armrests and after a few minutes looked down and saw Rio de Janeiro sprawling along the coast, early-morning sunlight glinting off tall buildings. The slightly misty outline of the famous Cristo Redentor statue dominated the top of the Corcovado mountain, arms outstretched.

Soon they were high above the Atlantic Ocean, leaving the coastline behind, and Ana could see nothing but a vast expanse of dark blue water. After about fifteen minutes the helicopter started circling an area. Ana looked down, and at first she could see nothing. But then she saw it: a tiny jewel of an island, rocky and lushly green, with a wide sandy beach and dense foliage. Waves broke and foamed against the shore. What looked like a sprawling villa sat in the cleared centre, and as they descended she could make out a huge pool set in lush, manicured grounds. There was also a pier, and a yacht bobbing in the water.

It was as if someone had plucked what Ana imagined to be a fantasy island out of her head and planted it here in the middle of the ocean.

They landed on a clear expanse of lawn, not too far from the villa, which Ana could see was artfully camouflaged with lush foliage so that it almost seemed to emerge fully formed from the landscape. Definitely the work of an architect—and a renowned one at that, she guessed.

When they got out, they were met by an efficient woman in a uniform of black trousers and crisp white shirt, saying, 'Welcome to Ilha Pequena. I'm Estella, the estate manager.' As she walked them to the villa she explained that the kitchen was stocked with enough provisions for a week.

Ana stopped in her tracks. *A week?*

Estella showed them around the open-plan airy villa, with its wide, deeply varnished floorboards. It was decorated with the kind of understated elegance that only serious money could buy, and yet it was also charmingly lived-in. Ana had the sense that, whoever's home this was, it was very much loved and enjoyed, not treated like a museum, in spite of the very expensive art she recognised on the walls.

She spotted bowls for dog food and water in the kitchen. She could imagine a family here…children running in and out of the French doors that opened out from the kitchen/dining area to the lawn…and the image made a dart of longing pierce her gut, exposing her.

She'd told herself long ago that happy families were pure illusion. Maybe for other people who lived simpler lives, but not for people like her. All her tender fantasies had been blasted apart the day her mother had walked out of the family home, abandoning her husband and children, and so Ana had always been very careful not to allow herself to imagine even for a second that she could have something she'd never even experienced.

But in spite of everything she knew, the fantasy persisted, deep inside her, like a stubborn illicit stain. A dream of a happy family like the ones she saw on TV. Or in the movies. Or in books. She'd always loved the image of Tiny Tim and his loving, humble family from *A Christmas Carol*—she'd read that story over and over to her brother Francisco when they were younger.

Ana turned away from the view and castigated herself. *Pathetic.*

They were shown next into a luxurious but obviously lived-in lounge, with huge comfortable couches and armchairs, where a projector was set up, along with a state-of-the-art smart TV and music system. Also on the ground level was another more formal lounge, a library, a study, a gym and a dining room.

Upstairs there were numerous bedrooms, most of them closed off—Ana guessed they belonged to the children—and a master suite.

'These two bedrooms are free for you to use,' Estella said, indicating two rooms on opposite sides of the corridor. She opened the door on the left. 'I put you in here, Mrs Salazar, I hope it'll be sufficient?'

Ana realised that she'd grown so used to being shown into her own separate room that she didn't even wonder any more what people might think.

That whole side of her marriage with Caio had been handled with discreet efficiency. When not in the apartment in Rio, they'd either been in apartments belonging to him around the world, or hotel suites with enough rooms for people not to know what their sleeping arrangements were.

The door opened into a pretty bedroom suite dressed in cool whites and blues. A vast four-poster bed dominated the room, and there was an en-suite bathroom with rolltop bath. There was a dressing room, and a balcony terrace, overlooking the back gardens. She could see the ocean and hear the waves lapping against the shore. It was more than *sufficient*.

When Ana looked inside the dressing room she was surprised to see the clothes she'd packed for Europe hanging up or folded neatly onto shelves, alongside clothes she'd never seen before. 'But…how?'

Estella said, 'Essential items were picked up for you both from your apartment and sent out with me on the first helicopter trip, along with other supplies. They thought it best to alert you only at the last minute, in case anyone found out about the plan. The other clothes are here for guests' use. Feel free to help yourself to anything that makes you more comfortable.'

Ana balked a little as the full enormity of the operation to get them out of Rio and to this place sank in. She asked, 'Who owns this estate?'

'Luca Fonseca. He was prepared to give you the use of the island as I believe he knows Mr Salazar.'

Ana looked at Caio, who was nodding. 'We go back a bit. He was one of my first investors.'

Estella was continuing, 'The island estate was bought for his wife as a wedding anniversary present some years ago.'

Something twisted inside Ana at this mention of one of Brazil's most famous couples. They were famous not only for being who they were—Serena Fonseca, née DePiero, was the daughter of an infamous and disgraced Italian tycoon—but also because they seemed to be genuinely in love and conducted a very happy private family life with their three children and their extended family.

Fêted and adored by the press, the blonde beauty and her handsome Brazilian husband were rarely spotted, which only added to their allure. And with hideaway private islands like this to escape to, Ana could understand how they stayed under the radar.

Estella was showing Caio into his bedroom across the hall. Similar to Ana's, it differed only in colour scheme, being decorated in shades of dark grey and white, set off beautifully against the same very simple floorboards that ran through the entire villa. Artisanal rugs added softness and pops of colour against the otherwise muted interiors.

Ana followed Caio into his dressing room, to see him indicate to where one of his tuxedoes was hanging up. 'I don't think I'll be needing this.' His tone was dry.

Estella shrugged. 'Best to be prepared for every eventuality. Please, feel free to explore all you want and make yourselves at home. I have to return to Rio de Janeiro.'

'You're not staying?' Ana didn't like the tinge of panic in her voice. But she was nervous of being alone in this idyllic and totally unexpected place with Caio. Especially when her emotions were so close to the surface.

Emotions? Who was she kidding? It was her desire she was afraid of.

The woman shook her head. 'No, unfortunately I have work to do for Mr Fonseca. You'll have everything you need, and your protection team will be keeping watch from security boats stationed around the island for as long as they're needed.'

Ana went back into her bedroom and looked out to sea from her small terrace. Sure enough, she could see a boat on the water, and then another at a distance. She breathed out a shaky breath, wrapping her hands around the terrace railing, and tried to absorb the fact that an hour ago she'd been on the mainland, newly divorced and about to head to the airport to start a new life.

Now what?

CHAPTER FOUR

CAIO STOOD ON the terrace outside the open-plan kitchen and watched the helicopter take off, the loud *thwack* of its blades fading as it sped over the ocean back to the mainland. He pulled absently at his tie, feeling constricted. He was still reeling at the speed with which they'd been despatched here.

All he could see in his mind's eye, though, was Ana's huge brown eyes filled with shock. Her face so pale. Not out of fear. Out of shock that she wasn't getting away from Caio fast enough.

He still couldn't believe she'd booked a flight out of Rio that very day. Couldn't she even bear a few more days in his company? It made a mockery of his sense that their relationship had reached a level of *simpatico*. Understanding. Mutual respect. Friendship.

Clearly he'd misread it. Badly.

He heard a sound behind him and turned around to see Ana. She'd taken off her jacket and the top button of her shirt was undone. She was barefoot, hair a little tousled, as if she'd run a hand through it. He could see the curves of her breasts through the thin material encased in plain white. Lace? Or silk?

His blood quickened and grew hot, but he'd become a master at disguising her effect on him. She was looking at him warily. It made the heat in his blood surge even more.

'You had no inkling of this?' she asked.

He shook his head. 'I can understand their logic in not telling us till the last moment, in case we accidentally tipped the kidnappers off that we knew.'

'Do you think they'll get them?'

'My security firm is the same one used by Luca Fonseca—that's presumably how he was approached about using his island. And considering his level of zeal when it comes to protecting his family, together with the involvement of the special forces, if they can't catch them then I don't know who can.' He couldn't help adding with a slight bite to his voice, 'Don't worry, I'll have my assistant book you on the next available flight to Europe as soon as we get back to Rio. I know you're eager to leave.'

A flare of pink appeared in Ana's cheeks. She lifted her chin. 'I would have thought you'd be pleased to get your life back. You only married me for a business deal.'

'You married me to secure your brother's freedom and future, as well as your own,' Caio reminded her. 'So you got something out of it too.'

She immediately looked chastened. 'Yes, I did get something out of it—and so did Francisco. We're both grateful for that.'

He clenched his jaw. 'I didn't mention that to ask for your gratitude.'

'I know. And you have treated me with the utmost respect. What could have been a nightmare scenario was...*not*.'

'You mean the bit where you thought I was going to demand my conjugal rights on our wedding night?' He still smarted to think that she'd been so averse to the idea of sleeping with her husband that she'd tried to run away.

Ana's cheeks flushed. 'We hadn't covered that in the prenuptial agreement. I didn't know you... I didn't know what to expect. What *you* would expect.'

She bit her lip, as if to stop more words spilling out. Caio wanted to know what she was holding back but she stayed silent.

He sighed. 'I can't blame you, after meeting your father. It was only natural you'd fear that I was similar.'

'I wasn't scared of you.'

Caio looked at Ana and saw the defiant set of her chin. It made his mouth want to quirk. He could recall only too easily how pale she'd been that night, when he'd found her trying to open a staff entrance door to the apartment. She'd changed out of her wedding dress and had been dressed in jeans and a loose top. Her hair, long and silky, had been tumbling over her shoulders and down her back...

He folded his arms and regarded her now. 'Where were you even planning on going?'

Caio hadn't asked her that question at the time. Why now?

Ana prickled self-consciously under his gaze. It reminded her too much of the sense of exposure she'd felt when she'd stood beside him on their wedding day in her very plain, long white dress overlaid with lace. The dress that had made her look *'like an old maid'*, as her father had stated so memorably.

She'd thought it was a good idea, sending a strong signal to Caio not to view her as anything but a convenient wife, but standing beside him she'd felt hideously frumpy and out of date.

The indiscreet whisperings of the stylist to the hair
and make-up team hired to get her ready had come
back to haunt her.

*'This man is Brazil's sexiest playboy...is she delib-
erately trying to turn him off?'*

Ana had fought the urge to turn around and inform
the woman that that was her plan precisely.

She'd always told herself she didn't care what people
thought, but when they'd arrived at the church and everyone had turned to look at her, including Caio, she'd
never felt more exposed. She'd felt as if everyone was
judging her and finding her lacking. She'd never been
more acutely aware of the fact that not even her own
mother had found her lovable enough to stay.

Those few steps down the aisle had been the longest
of her life, but she'd found to her surprise that Caio's
gaze had searched for hers and held it the whole way
down. As if he was silently commanding her to think
only of him and nothing else. And for that moment she
had thought of nothing else.

But then, up close, he'd been so intimidating—re-
splendent in a steel-grey morning suit, clean-shaven,
hair swept back—and all her self-consciousness had
surged back. She'd burned with embarrassment. And
awareness.

By the time they'd returned to Caio's apartment that
evening Ana had been a bag of jangling nerves, exhausted after a long day of meeting more people than
she'd met in her lifetime. Seriously wondering if she'd
made a huge mistake.

She really hadn't known what Caio would expect
after her stunt with the wedding dress, and she'd imagined him appearing in her bedroom, demanding to
consummate their marriage. She'd even thought that it

might be a legal requirement. She'd imagined the humiliation of his finding out that she really *was* a virgin. That her father hadn't lied.

Not to mention the humiliation that she wanted him. So...she'd panicked.

She'd changed and packed and found the staff entrance to the apartment. And then Caio had appeared behind her, divested of his wedding waistcoat and tie, top button of his shirt open.

'Ana? Where the hell are you going?'

She'd turned around, gripping her small case. She'd felt very young and very foolish. And vulnerable.

Caio's hands had been on his hips, effortlessly drawing attention to the leanness of his waist. She'd swallowed painfully before saying, 'I don't know what you're expecting, but I won't sleep with you.'

That dark, impenetrable gaze had swept up and down, humiliating her even further, because she had known exactly how she must look while Caio had oozed male sophistication. And then she'd realised in that moment, with bone-chilling horror, that she'd got it all wrong. This was not a man who would lower himself to take an unwilling wife. He would have sophisticated, experienced mistresses for his needs.

As if reading her mind, he'd said coolly, 'I don't know what *you* are expecting, but I don't sleep with virgins, Ana. You're quite safe from me, I assure you. This marriage will not extend to the bedroom. It's a business agreement, for one year, as stipulated in the prenuptial agreement.'

He'd reached for the door then, and opened it onto a plain corridor, bright with harsh emergency lighting and leading to stairs down to the lower levels.

'By all means, leave if you want to. I'm no gaoler.

But if you do, I can't promise that your father will keep to his end of the agreement and allow your brother to pursue his art studies in Europe.'

Drowning in embarrassment, Ana had remembered why she'd married Caio in the first place. For her brother. So he could get away from their family's toxic environment and follow his dreams.

She'd used her hair to try and hide her burning face as much as possible. 'I'm not going anywhere.'

Caio had simply shut the door again and said, 'Goodnight, then, Ana. Sleep well.'

He'd walked back into the apartment and Ana had battled with wanting the ground to open up and swallow her whole and the gut-punching realisation that he didn't want her, and how that felt like a jagged piece of glass between her ribs.

And now, a year on from that night, one thing was crystal-clear: she needn't have worried about unwanted or wanted advances from her husband, because he wouldn't have touched her if she'd begged him to.

'Ana?' Caio prompted, frowning.

Ana struggled to recall what he'd asked. *'Where were you even planning on going?'*

She shook her head. 'It doesn't matter now.' She needed to escape from that incisive gaze. As lightly as she could, she said, 'I think I'll explore a little, and change into something more comfortable.'

'I'll see what provisions we have and prepare some lunch.'

'Don't worry about me,' Ana said quickly. 'I can look after myself.'

Caio unfolded his arms and slipped the shades resting on his head down to cover his eyes. 'Suit yourself.'

He turned and walked back inside the villa.

CHAPTER FIVE

IMMEDIATELY ANA FELT churlish and childish. It had taken the full year for her to emerge from her shell and feel she could stand with this man in public and not stick out like a sore thumb. But right now she felt as gauche as she had on their wedding day.

She cursed herself. It was going to be a very long twenty-four hours. But surely with a vast villa and sprawling grounds between them they could keep their distance?

Ana made her way down to the lawn, past the vast pool, its surface barely rippling in the light breeze, towards the beach.

She told herself she was being paranoid to think for a second that Caio cared if she ate with him or not. No doubt, in his mind, this whole security threat was just an unfortunate speed bump on the road to getting his life back to normal. Ana could well imagine the legion of beautiful women lining up, waiting to entice Brazil's hottest newly minted bachelor back into their beds. He'd undoubtedly already lined up a woman to celebrate his first night of freedom with—except now he was stuck here.

Ana reached the beach. Wide, pristine, empty. The Atlantic Ocean was calm today, but she could imagine that it would be breathtaking on a stormy day, lashing the beach and swirling around the island.

But her mind wasn't on the view. It was on Caio. He'd seemed surprised that she was insisting on leaving Rio today. And almost… Ana shook her head. No way had he been *hurt*. He didn't care for her. But then, a little voice pointed out, he didn't *not* care for her.

She sat down on the sand, under the shade of a palm tree. The sun was merciless even at mid-morning at this latitude.

A memory resurfaced. She'd been married to Caio for about two months, and they'd been in Bangkok for the launch of Caio's South East Asian office, staying in a stunning penthouse hotel suite with views over the Chao Phraya river as it snaked its way through the teeming Asian city.

The sights, sounds, smells and sheer humidity—Ana could recall the sensory overload as if it was yesterday. It had been the first time her hair had felt like a heavy, thick burden, and she'd vowed there and then to chop it off at the first opportunity.

That had been the start of her metamorphosis from being a tomboy who'd hidden behind her brothers all her life into her own woman. *Seeking Caio's attention had also been a motivator.* Her conscience pricked. Yes. She had wanted to lure his eye, not liking how invisible she felt when she stood beside him in public…

But she didn't want to think about that now.

One evening Caio had returned to the hotel suite from a business meeting to find Ana pacing up and down, so full of rage and a sense of helplessness that she wasn't even aware she'd been crying.

'What is it? What's happened?' he'd asked.

She'd been so angry she hardly been able to speak.

He'd made her sit down, given her a glass of water, and then she'd explained that her father had reneged on his agreement to send her younger brother to art school in Holland.

It shouldn't have surprised her that her father was capable of that, but it was the reason she'd agreed to marry Caio Salazar. Caio had asked her what she wanted in return for marrying him, and he'd promised to extract an agreement from her father that he would not stand in the way of Francisco's dream to attend art college.

Caio had gone very still and left the room for a long moment. When he'd come back his tie had been off, and his jacket gone, shirt open. He'd poured himself a whiskey and said, 'Call your brother tomorrow and let him know he's still going to Holland. Nothing will stand in his way again.'

That had been the first time Ana had seen a different side to Caio and felt some sort of kinship. She'd had a strong sense that he was almost as angry as she that her father had reneged on the agreement. It had made her wonder about Caio's relationship with his own family... only his mother had come to their wedding...

After that night, Ana had become more and more aware that the image of man she'd thought Caio was—a jaded playboy pretending to reform for the sake of his ambitions—was not truly reflective of the man she was coming to know.

For instance, he'd never seemed to mind that his life was suddenly devoid of loud thumping nightclubs and glamorous premieres. The events they'd attended had been on the more sedate and serious side.

He'd proved himself to be nothing like the men she knew—her father and older brothers. And, contrary to his infamous persona as a louche playboy, he'd either been the most discreet man on the planet or he'd embraced a year of domesticity and celibacy, showing a far more introverted side than the world at large would have expected of him.

She knew better than anyone how the press could magnify a situation and turn it into something lurid. Like when her mother had walked out on her family.

She'd left because she was bored. She'd felt she'd done her duty, providing an heir and some spares. And so she'd left. It had been devastating to Ana, to realise how little her mother loved her, and the rest of her siblings. Her father hadn't been under any illusions—it had been an arranged marriage, after all. But his pride had been wounded.

The press had had a field-day, painting a melodramatic picture of a woman seeking love and solace with a younger and even richer man. Ana knew that it hadn't been a lack of love driving her mother—it had been dissatisfaction and boredom—but they'd spun it into something else entirely, the truth being too prosaic and cynical.

Ana shook her head, as if that could clear the toxic memories. She refocused on the memory of Caio coolly taking her father to task for not following through on his agreement.

Now she felt even more churlish for not joining Caio for lunch. She should go back.

She stood up, took a few steps, and stopped. Maybe she was better just to avoid him... After all, when this was over and they returned to Rio she wouldn't see him again. So why bother to make any effort now?

You just don't want him to find out how much you want him, whispered a mocking little voice.

Ana was making a face at herself when she heard a

sound and looked up to see a vision of masculine perfection, largely naked but for a short pair of snug swimtrunks, striding out from the trees onto the beach, a towel slung over his shoulder, shades covering his eyes.

He might as well have been naked for all the trunks barely covered. They only drew attention to the perfect curvature of Caio's muscular buttocks.

The breath stopped in Ana's throat. She must have made some sort of gurgling sound, because Caio glanced at her but didn't seem surprised she was there. He said, off-handedly, 'I figured it's best to swim before eating. Join me if you like.'

Ana was no more capable of joining Caio than she was of moving. She managed to garble something about seeing to lunch and stumbled backwards, unable to take her eyes off the acres of gleaming olive skin moving smoothly over taut muscles.

Oblivious to the nuclear explosion happening inside Ana, Caio threw the towel and sunglasses down on the sand and launched himself into the water, arms scissoring powerfully through the waves.

The cooler confines of the open-plan kitchen were no comfort to Ana's hot and prickling skin, which had nothing to do with the sun and everything to do with Caio's little exhibition back there.

She paced the space; the tiles were cool underfoot but provided no relief. Anger rose. Did he have no idea how that might affect her? Seeing all that naked flesh on display? Seeing the prominent bulge at the front of his shorts that left little to the imagination?

Her face flamed. Not that she needed her imagination for that. She'd seen him in the flesh.

This really was peak humiliation. Proof that she

made so little impact on him that walking around in front of her half-naked was the equivalent of being in a locker room full of guys at his gym. Not that he went to a gym, because he had his own gym, but—

Ana scowled and shook her head. *Not the point here!*

The point was that she affected him so minutely that she could have been sunbathing naked on the beach for all he'd have noticed her as being a breathing, sexual woman. A woman who had hidden her responses to him so well that he now saw her as little more than furniture.

And who was to blame for that? Not Caio. Much as it pained her to admit it. He didn't fancy her. Simple as that. And brutal as that.

She stopped pacing. She felt constricted in her clothes now. The silk shirt was clinging to her skin and the trousers digging in at her waist.

On an impulse she went up to the bedroom suite and looked at the clothes.

She noticed for the first time that there were evening dresses in the guests' section. A glimmering opulent royal blue caught her eye. She reached in to pull the dress out. It was silk, and slippery through her fingers. It was stunningly simple but devastatingly sexy. A halter-neck design, with a deep vee in the front, almost down to the navel.

Ana's skin grew hot at the thought of wearing this in front of Caio, of baring so much skin.

She'd been growing more adventurous with her dresses of late, in a shameful and fruitless attempt on her part to see if she had any effect on him at all. She'd worn a red dress to a recent event. Very simple, with spaghetti straps, a chiffon overlay had hugged her torso tight and criss-crossed over her chest with the beaded material exposed over one breast as a contrast, drawing the eye. It had had a thigh-high slit.

She'd drawn lots of eyes that night, but every time she'd sneaked a glance at Caio his jaw had been like granite and his face expressionless. His lack of reaction had made her feel reckless. Volatile. But when they'd returned to the apartment that night he'd said something about working and disappeared into his study to make calls—presumably to the other side of the world, where they were just waking up.

Her volatility had drained away. How could she have forgotten that her primary role in his life was to enhance his career?

Not that she could blame him—it wasn't as if she'd ever been under any illusions in that regard. In their world, a strategic marriage was part of the natural order.

But that reckless feeling was back now, rising inside her. Dangerous. Maybe it was the knowledge that they were divorced. And on a desert island. In the middle of the sea. Nowhere to go and nothing to lose.

Except your dignity.

Ana ignored the voice, even though she knew in her heart of hearts that, as volatile as she felt, she didn't really have the nerve to put herself out there. To really test the waters. As much as she'd love to unsettle him as he unsettled her. As much as she wanted him to look at her with the same hunger she felt.

But then he hadn't even looked at her differently after her transformation at the hands of London's finest stylists and beauty technicians.

As if she needed *that* humiliating reminder…

CHAPTER SIX

AFTER BANGKOK THEY'D gone to London. The first event they'd attended there had been in the glittering ballroom of one of London's most iconic and luxurious hotels. By then Ana had been feeling more comfortable with Caio in social surroundings, while also becoming more and more aware that she was drawing looks not because she was stylish, but because she didn't fit in with all the other sleek and fashionable women.

When she'd overheard a woman say, not so discreetly, '*That's* his wife? I thought Brazilian women were meant to be sexy and beautiful? She looks like she's just been released from a convent...' Ana had made an appointment the following day for a makeover in the hotel salon, knowing full well that her motivation stemmed more from a desire to please Caio than any bitchy gossips.

After a day of being primped, plucked and styled to within an inch of her life, Ana had waited nervously for Caio that evening to meet her in the reception room of the suite before going to a charity gala dinner. She'd been wearing a strapless black cocktail dress so form-fitting that she'd constantly felt like tugging it up over her chest, or down over her knee. Heels so high they'd made her eyes water.

But that dress hadn't been the thing making her feel naked. It had been her hair. Or the lack of it. It was the first time she'd had it cut substantially in her life. Because from the day her mother had left she'd used it as a shield to hide behind. To hide her grief. Her anger. Her burgeoning sexuality. Her vulnerabilities.

But now it was gone. Now it feathered lightly over her shoulders where only hours before it had fallen down to the middle of her back. And at any minute Caio was going to appear...

And then he had. Looking at his cufflinks. Not at Ana, where she'd stood trembling.

Finally, he'd looked up, saying, 'Ready?'

His dark eyes had narrowed on her and Ana's pulse-rate had sky-rocketed.

After a long moment he'd said, 'You look different.'

Ana had thought of how she'd reacted when she'd seen herself in the mirror a short time before. She hadn't looked like herself at all. Or she had. But a much sleeker version. Her eyes had looked huge. Her lips red.

The hair stylist had said, mock severely, 'It's criminal you've hidden this face for so long. You are stunning.'

Ana had smiled weakly, feeling exposed, but also a fluttering sense of hope that maybe now Caio would look at her with interest. Sexual interest.

Except he hadn't looked at her with sexual interest. He'd looked at her with an expression she couldn't read. He'd looked tense. A muscle had pulsed in his jaw.

Ana had swallowed her disappointment and said, 'I got my hair cut...consulted with a stylist about some new clothes.'

Sounding almost accusing, Caio had said, 'You're wearing make-up.'

Ana had said defensively, 'Not a lot, actually.'

The make-up artist had said to her, 'You really don't need much at all…just enough to emphasise those big eyes and your mouth. You know, women spend a fortune to get lips like yours…'

Feeling hurt at the thought that Caio had somehow preferred her when she'd been hiding behind her hair and wearing unflattering clothes, Ana had said testily, 'If you don't think I look okay—'

But he'd cut her off, saying stiffly, 'You look…fine. We need to leave or we'll be late.'

And that had been that.

Caio's less than thrilled reaction to her transformation.

But over the months, in spite of Caio's reaction, Ana had grown in confidence and had found that she preferred a kind of timeless elegant style. The stylist she'd worked with in London had become a friend, and Ana had used her expertise to help her find outfits for various events, working with her remotely.

But now…

Ana let the liquid silk of the beautiful blue dress slip out of her hand. It was good that she'd remembered Caio's reaction to her transformation. No matter how reckless she might feel, it didn't change the fact that he wasn't interested.

She went to her own clothes and pulled out a pair of worn cut-off shorts and a T-shirt. It wasn't as if he'd even notice if she put on that dress anyway, so why bother?

She hadn't worn clothes like this for a long time now. Being married to Caio had morphed her into someone different. *Or someone more herself?* It was a persona she hadn't been comfortable with at first, but now it felt more familiar to her than her old tomboy self ever had.

Leaving her feet bare, Ana went down to the kitchen, relieved to see that it was empty. Caio must still be at the beach. She saw that he'd taken some things out of the fridge—the makings of a salad. She took it upon herself to put the ingredients together, mixing up a light lemony vinaigrette and chopping up tomato, avocado, cucumber, adding some nuts and grapes.

She warmed some crusty bread in the oven, and nearly jumped out of her skin when a deep voice said from behind her, 'Changed your mind, then?'

Ana whirled around to see Caio standing a few feet away, wearing faded jeans and a T-shirt. Like her. His hair was damp. He must have come back and taken a shower. How long had he been there? Why hadn't she heard him?

She looked down. Bare feet like her. Except his were about seven sizes bigger than hers. He was big all over.

A wave of heat exploded in her belly. Her brain felt fuzzy. 'Changed my mind...?'

He gestured to the kitchen island. 'Lunch.'

Ana looked at the salad blankly for a moment before her brain switched back into gear. She affected a little shrug, as if she hadn't just had a brain meltdown just because Caio was in the room. It was as if a layer of protection had been ripped off her skin here on this island.

'I figured I might as well start getting it together. Unless you had something else in mind?'

He shook his head, looking at the salad. 'This is exactly what I envisaged, but I wouldn't have put it together as well as this. You have a real talent. I never did ask where you learned to cook...'

Ana had not been expecting that. Over the year, when they'd been in Rio de Janeiro, and if there hadn't been a function to go to, Ana had got used to letting the chef go and cooking herself. At first Caio hadn't joined her, but as time had passed it had become habitual for them to share meals.

Caio settled on a high stool on the other side of the island and picked up the lone grape left in a bowl, 'You know, I only recently realised that it was you cooking those meals and not the chef. I thought he was leaving food for you to heat up.'

Ana cut up rough hunks of bread, hating it that she still felt self-conscious under Caio's inquisitive gaze. 'I learnt how to cook because I knew it would annoy my father. He was horrified at the thought of me doing anything remotely domestic or manual, and as my life pretty much revolved around irritating him as much as I could…' She trailed off, realising that she must sound like a petulant teenager.

She busied herself carrying the salad in a bowl over to the kitchen's dining table.

Caio followed with the bread and asked, 'Would you like some wine?'

That dangerous flash of recklessness gripped her again. 'Sure.'

She grabbed some sparkling water and glasses, watching as Caio took a bottle of chilled white wine out of the fridge and brought it over. He pulled out the cork with an ease and dexterity that really shouldn't be sexy, but even that caused a spiking of need deep inside Ana.

When it was poured, she took a gulp of wine in a bid to try and cool her wayward hormones. It had to be just a heightened reaction to the adrenalin of the morning—that was all.

The dry, crisp taste of the wine slid down her throat and went straight to her head. Probably not the best idea around Caio, who was taking a sip of his own wine, the glass looking very fragile in his big hand.

She mixed up the salad with two spoons and said, 'Help yourself.'

Caio heaped salad onto his plate and drizzled some olive oil over his bread. He said idly, 'You really hate your father, don't you?'

Ana almost choked on her mouthful of food and had to swallow carefully. 'It's that obvious?' she joked.

Caio shrugged. 'I saw it the day we met, and since then you've made little or no effort to see him.'

Ana took another sip of wine, put her glass down. 'I can't say I feel any great affection for him, no. Me and my younger brother were superfluous to his requirements. My only value to him was as a marriageable asset. I have enough older brothers to ensure the family legacy is taken care of.'

'You and your younger brother are obviously close.'

She nodded, immediately feeling protective. 'Very. There's only a year between us. I was six and he was five when our mother left.'

This was said with as little emotion as possible. Ana hated it that even now the memory of watching her mother pack and leave without a backward glance was still so vivid. She felt raw.

'What about you?' she asked. 'Only your mother came to the wedding—you're not close to the rest of your family?'

Caio's face tightened for a moment and then he said, 'Like you, I was considered superfluous to requirements. My father and mother…it was an arranged marriage.'

Aren't they all? Ana wanted to say, but didn't.

Caio didn't seem inclined to elaborate on his parents' marriage beyond that.

'How old were you when you left home?' she asked.

He looked at her. 'Eighteen.'

'That's when you dropped your father's name?'

He nodded. And then he said, 'Surely you could have left too?'

Ana shook her head. 'I wouldn't have left Francisco on his own.'

'Does he know you agreed to our marriage to secure his freedom?'

Ana felt like squirming. How had they strayed into this territory when for the last year they'd managed to keep their conversations light and superficial? But here, on this island, it was as if all normal operations had been left back in Rio.

Ana huffed out a breath. 'He knows. And he only agreed to go to Europe once he knew the marriage was strictly business and only for a year.' She looked at Caio, feeling defensive. 'He would have done the same for me.'

Caio's lips twitched at the corners. 'I don't doubt it.'

Ana put a forkful of salad in her mouth in case she said anything else or invited the conversation into more personal territory. She'd known that Caio had a very tenuous connection with his family, and even without him elaborating on details, it sounded like it had been a very similar situation. People still whispered and gossiped about her mother's abandonment of her family, and the subsequent bitter divorce, even though it had happened years ago. Ana had never heard any gossip about his family. Presumably they'd been more careful because they were involved in politics.

But then his mother hadn't abandoned her family

like Ana's had. Was it better for a mother to be a martyr to an arranged marriage or selfish enough to leave for her own happiness? She and Caio were products of each scenario, and she realised now that it might not have necessarily been better if her mother had stayed. She recalled meeting Caio's mother—she'd seemed very fragile, brittle. Like a shadow of a former self.

Caio put down his fork and it made a slight metallic sound against the plate, breaking Ana out of her reverie. She wasn't remotely prepared when he asked, 'Was it really so bad that you had to leave Rio today?'

CHAPTER SEVEN

ANA NEARLY CHOKED on her food. She swallowed carefully as she let his question sink in. Why did she feel so guilty and defensive?

Caio was looking at her. Waiting. Her impression of him being hurt because she was so eager to leave returned. But that couldn't be right.

She wiped her mouth with a napkin. 'No, not at all. Like I said... I didn't know what to expect at first, but as the year went on we...' She trailed off. *Became unlikely friends.*

Caio's face was expressionless. She was beginning to understand that this didn't necessarily mean he didn't feel anything. A little muscle pulsed by his jaw.

She said with a rush, 'I thought that you wanted to get your life back as soon as possible.'

'Did I make you feel unwelcome?'

Ana wanted to squirm. The problem had been *her*, not him. 'No. It wasn't that. At all. I wasn't expecting that the marriage would turn out the way it did.' She looked at him 'We got on,' she said, surprising herself.

'I thought so. We worked a room well together.'

A flush of warmth that had nothing to do with desire bloomed in Ana's chest. At first she'd been so awkward on Caio's arm. Felt out of place. Which was ironic given that they'd been in the milieu she'd been born to command as her own. But she'd spent so much time rebelling against the etiquette and social lessons her peers had lapped up, she'd felt about as prepared as an alien visiting earth for the first time.

But gradually, with a discreet guidance from Caio that Ana could appreciate now, she'd grown more adept. She thought of how with the subtlest of touches and glances, silent commands or needs had been communicated between them, fostering a sense of unity that she hadn't fully appreciated until this moment.

'We did work a room well together,' she had to admit grudgingly. She gave a small shudder, 'Remember those couples who'd obviously just had a blazing row and were forced to smile and act as if everything was okay?'

'When it patently wasn't? No, thanks.'

'You never wanted to get married for real, then?' She'd always just assumed that once he had all his ambitions met he would settle down.

'After what I've seen? No way. Happy marriages don't exist. It's fantasy.'

Ana agreed with Caio intellectually, but deep in her gut told another story. She wanted to ask him what he had seen, but reticence held her back.

He continued before she could work up the nerve to speak, saying, 'That's why a marriage of convenience worked so well for us.'

'I can remember the tension between my parents after massive arguments,' Ana observed. 'Moments before a dinner party. And theirs was an arranged marriage.'

Caio took a sip of wine. 'Ah, but children complicate things.'

She hid a dart of hurt to think of how she and her

siblings obviously hadn't complicated things enough to make her mother stay.

Ana pulled a knee up and rested her foot on the chair, wrapping her arms around her leg. She felt emboldened enough by Caio's candour to ask, 'You never wanted children?'

For a split-second Ana could have sworn she saw something like yearning cross Caio's face, as if she'd caught him off guard. But then it was gone.

'No. I didn't see enough of good, positive parenting to be able to pass it on. It wouldn't be fair.'

Not sure where her doggedness was coming from, Ana said, 'But what's the point, then, of building up a business in your own name, if you can't leave it to anyone?'

Caio's focus narrowed on her face. She grew warm.

He said, almost chidingly, 'Having children is no guarantee that they'll want to follow in your footsteps. Not one of my brothers is really interested in the family business but they had no choice. It was accept it or lose your inheritance.'

Ana murmured, 'And you took the latter option?'

Caio said, 'I was lucky to be able to. The pressure wasn't on me.'

Ana had a sense, though, that even if the pressure had been on him he would have gone his own way. Nothing would have stopped him. He was too strong to be bent to anyone's will.

'Do *you* want children?' Caio asked.

Ana's insides clenched. Her dream was too secret and fragile to articulate. Instead, she prevaricated. 'Like you, I didn't exactly grow up with good role models.' She looked around the kitchen area and said, 'But I think this place, this island, is an example that it can exist for some people.'

Caio shrugged and took another sip of wine. 'Who knows what Luca Fonseca's marriage is like...? I'd bet it's not as idyllic as you think.'

His persistent cynicism rubbed along Ana's nerve-endings. 'This place feels *real*. It's not for show. It's for them.'

Caio's mouth quirked. 'Don't tell me you're a closet romantic?'

CHAPTER EIGHT

ANA'S HEART STUTTERED. She was exposing herself.

She sprang up from the chair as if stung and started clearing the plates. 'Don't be ridiculous. I know better than anyone that fairy tales don't exist. That's why I agreed to marry you—to extract as much leverage as I could.'

She took the plates over to the island and put them down with a clatter. She felt brittle all of a sudden.

'So if your aim was to extract as much leverage as possible, why didn't you fleece me for all that you could get?'

Ana turned around and put her hands behind her, wrapping her fingers around the edge of the marble countertop. Caio had angled his chair to face her, his big body sprawled with elegant insouciance, the wine glass between his fingers. He was enjoying this. Damn him.

'Because I'm not mercenary. If I've learned anything about our lives, our world, it's that money doesn't buy happiness. Fulfilling personal dreams does. Finding your freedom does.'

'So what *are* your personal dreams? You've facilitated your brother's, but what about yours?'

Ana's face grew hot again. She wanted to escape this conversation that seemed determined to stray into territory more personal than she'd shared with Caio in a whole year. It was as if the divorce and being sequestered on this island had ripped away any need to tread carefully around each other. It was as exhilarating as it was terrifying.

She lifted her chin and pushed down the sense of exposure. 'I want to get a degree.'

Caio looked at Ana. He'd never seen her look so fierce. Well, he had—the night she'd agreed to marry him if it meant she could guarantee her brother the future he wanted.

Her fierceness made his blood simmer, while also catching at his chest. She reminded him of a cornered kitten, all at once defensive and proud. She looked a little wild. Undone. Reminding him of the girl he'd first met. Prickly. Combative. Distrustful. He was fascinated by her reaction.

'So what do you want to do a degree in?' he asked.

She shrugged, her face pink now. 'I've always wanted to do an English degree. In England.' She blurted the last bit out, then said in a rush, 'But I'm not remotely cut out for university. No woman in my family has ever gone to university.'

Caio felt a surge of anger on her behalf. 'Why would you think you're not suited to it?'

'Because I was never academic. I barely scraped through my exams each year. As my father liked to tell me, paying for my education was a waste of time and money.'

Caio shook his head. 'I bet he didn't say that to your brothers.'

Ana smiled, but it was tight. 'Of course not. They

weren't the brightest either, but he made sure they got degrees from the best North American universities.'

Caio sat forward. 'Ana, I can guarantee you that you're brighter than all your brothers put together. I've met them. I know what I'm talking about.'

A surprised giggle escaped Ana's mouth and she put her hand over it. The movement lifted her T-shirt, revealing a sliver of flat belly above her shorts. Caio's mouth dried. He dragged his gaze up again, over the swells of her plump breasts under the thin material. He could see the outline of her very plain bra. She shouldn't be arousing this raging fire inside him, but she was.

He met her gaze. It was serious now. She took her hand down and Caio looked at her mouth. Provocative. Lush. Why on earth hadn't he tasted her when he'd had a chance? He couldn't fathom it now.

'Anyway,' she said, 'there's not a hope that I'd get accepted on the basis of my exam results. It's a pipe dream.'

Caio made a noise. 'Don't be so defeatist. You could apply as a mature student, and lots of universities accept students based on their current aptitude and desire to do a course, more than past results.'

'I'd only accept a course on that basis, I wouldn't want to buy my place just because I can.'

Caio felt a spike of admiration at Ana's evident pride and desire to prove herself. He'd met very few people like her in his world. Most of them were only too eager to catch a free ride or take advantage of their wealth and influence. But not Ana.

Her integrity mocked his habitual cynicism. It made him feel weary. It made him conscious of this place- Ana was right—this island and villa oozed a kind of peace and contentment he'd never felt in a home before.

It caught at him, made him wonder about another type of existence where you were born into a world where legacy, ambition, greed and cynicism weren't the natural order. Where something else was. *Family.* Unconditional love. Acceptance.

Caio mentally shook his head to dislodge those rogue ideas. He'd been born into an extremely privileged world and, while he'd made his own way in the end, he'd be delusional not to acknowledge that he'd still achieved much of his success off the back of who he was. He didn't need warm and fluffy family values. He needed his wits and his business acumen.

Ana turned away from him and his gaze caught on her shapely bare legs. Toned and slim. The bottom of her shorts was just short enough to give a hint of her buttocks. High and curved.

A solid knot of need tightened in his gut. It was bizarre, this attraction. It had been there from the moment he'd seen her, if he was honest, and she wasn't remotely his type. He'd always gone for women who were taller. Women whose expressions were as carefully schooled as his. Women who were experienced… who knew the game.

Ana was the very antithesis of all that.

Caio broke out of his reverie when he saw Ana pick up the plates again. He put down his glass and stood up to help her, reaching for them and saying, 'Here, let me do that.'

Ana turned around and wasn't expecting Caio to be right behind her, hands outstretched. It all happened so fast it was a blur. But, mortifyingly, she knew even in that moment that it was his proximity that caused it.

The plates toppled out of her suddenly unsteady hands and fell to the floor, smashing to pieces.

She immediately bent down and put out a hand to pick up part of a plate. She felt a sting in her finger.

'Leave it—you've cut yourself.' Caio's voice was sharp.

Before she knew which way was up, Caio had his hands under her arms and was pulling her up, then lifting her into his arms to step over the smashed debris to the sink.

'Your feet are bare too,' she protested weakly, rendered insensible by the fact that she was pressed close to his chest and it felt so broad and hard. His arms were like steel bands around her.

'I'm fine.'

He put her down by the sink and Ana had to lock her knees to stop herself crumpling like a doll. Blood was oozing from the top of her finger. Caio had her hand in his and was putting it under running water.

'I need to make sure there's no splinter.'

He was gentle, but thorough. Ana could hardly breathe, but she managed to say, 'Since when did you know so much about first aid?'

His face tightened. 'Let's just say it was a skill I had to learn.'

Suddenly Ana went still, as something occurred to her. Had there been violence in his family?

Caio shut off the water and said briskly, 'Keep your hand raised while I look for a plaster. It's not a deep cut.'

He turned away to open a cupboard and pulled out a box with the universal symbol for first aid on the side. It was well-stocked, and full of things Ana wouldn't have known how to use, but Caio found the plasters and caught her hand again.

But then he stopped.

Ana looked down to see a fresh bead of blood on her finger. Caio said in a rough-sounding voice, 'I need to clean it first.'

But he wasn't moving. He was just looking at her. Ana couldn't look away. His eyes held her captive. They were molten again, like when she'd seen him naked.

She hadn't imagined it.

He moved then, tugging her back towards the tap, but she said, 'Wait, I can do it.' Acting on instinct, she lifted her finger and put the tip into her mouth, sucking it clean.

The air contracted around them. Caio's eyes weren't molten any more. They were burning. She took her finger out of her mouth and held it up, pink and moist. No blood.

They were so close that if Ana moved an inch forward the tips of her breasts would come into contact with Caio's chest. Heat suffused her whole body and made her feel both energised and incredibly languorous. Something had just shifted between them, and it was monumental. She was afraid to say a word in case she broke the spell. It thrummed in her blood like a drumbeat.

He wanted her. *He wanted her.*

But even as that thought registered, and a surge of excitement and exhilaration made her limbs tremble, Caio broke eye contact and took a step back. He caught Ana's hand again and deftly wrapped a plaster around her finger before she could take another breath. She felt dizzy at the speed with which he'd gone from hot to cold. It almost made her think she'd imagined it— *but she hadn't.* She'd seen it, *felt it.* Could still feel it in her blood.

Caio was avoiding her eye now. He said briskly, 'I'll clean this mess up. You should put some shoes on until I get all the shards.'

Ana felt too unsettled to argue. She left the kitchen and went up to her bedroom, pacing up and down, jittery. She *had* seen it...felt it. There had been something between them. It was as if a veil had been pulled back for a moment and the depth of Caio's desire had been revealed and it was actually...overwhelming.

And yet he'd shut it down. Clearly giving her the option of pretending she hadn't noticed.

Her mind raced—how long had he felt like this?

Ana took a deep breath. If she wasn't imagining this, and if Caio did want her, then this was huge. She was pretty certain she hadn't been as adept as he when it came to hiding her desire. How could she have been? Compared with him she was...*a virgin.*

Ana sat down heavily on the bed. Maybe the thought of initiating a novice just didn't appeal. Not to a man as experienced as him. He would want a lover who knew exactly how to give him what he desired in the shortest amount of time possible. After all, he had told her in no uncertain terms that he didn't sleep with virgins, and clearly that had overridden any desire he felt.

Ana thought of a lurid piece of gossip she'd read when he'd first appeared at their house to do business with her father. Two women—famous supermodels— had sold their story of a steamy night spent with Caio Salazar, mentioning breathlessly how insatiable he'd been and how they'd never experienced such pleasure...

How could she compete with two supermodels and a threesome? But then they weren't here...and she was. And, unless she was very mistaken, Caio had been as celibate as she for this last year.

Which meant that surely his level of control wasn't all that strong? Even if she was a virgin?

That heady recklessness gripped her and this time she didn't try and stop it. Caio wanted her. She was sure of it. They were alone on this island for twenty-four hours. Less, actually. They'd already been here for a few hours. No distractions. No interruptions. Nothing to lose.

Things were very clear to her now. Time was running out and she did not want to be a virgin when she left this island to embark on her new life. And she wanted Caio Salazar, her ex-husband, to be her first lover.

Wanting him and trying to hide it had become a daily battle. But she didn't have to battle it any more. Not if she seduced him.

The thought was so audacious that a semi-hysterical giggle rose up Ana's throat. She put a hand over her mouth to try and contain it.

Serious again, she took her hand down. Caio would not make it easy for her. For whatever reason, he'd kept to his vow for the year, and he hadn't touched her beyond what had been required in public. She would have to work to seduce him. And maybe it would be humiliating if he had stronger control than she gave him credit for.

But…was her dignity really so important? She'd never have to see him again after this night.

She needed to challenge him. To know for sure.

Before she lost her nerve, Ana got up and went into the dressing room. She wasn't even sure what she was looking for, but when she saw it she knew that it was perfect.

CHAPTER NINE

CAIO FELT UNEASY. There was a prickling awareness under his skin. *Ana knew.* She'd seen his hunger because, standing that close to her, he hadn't been able to hide it. The control he'd clung to for months now was snapping and fraying.

All he could see in his mind's eye were those huge brown eyes as she'd sucked the tip of her finger into her mouth. Like a practised seductress. Which he knew she wasn't because, unless she'd employed the stealth of a secret service agent, she was still the virgin she'd been on her wedding night. It had taken him every ounce of effort not to replace her finger with his mouth and tongue, delving deep into the sweetness he'd been dreaming about.

Except the word 'dreaming' was too benign. They were hot, sweaty and X-rated sleeping hallucinations. And, even worse, they'd become fantasies of being the first man to possess her fully. To see her face flush and her eyes grow wide when her first orgasm hit.

Stupid, Caio castigated himself now, in a bid to try and cool his body down. She might be a virgin, but a woman of her age would have fooled around at least, and would have been brought to orgasm many times. Even by her own hand.

Heat fused his brain at the thought of Ana pleasuring herself. *Deus!*

He ran a hand through his hair. He'd cleared up the detritus of the broken plates. He felt edgy. Restless. *Frustrated.* They were mere hours into their enforced confinement on this island and he was losing it already.

He went out through the French doors that led out to the sloping manicured lawn. The pool glinted invitingly.

Caio thought about diving under the water again— anything to try and cool the heat in his blood. But he'd just eaten. *Not a good idea.*

He heard a sound from behind him, and with a feeling of intense trepidation turned around.

When Caio took in the view before him the first thought in his head was that he would never, as long as he lived, erase this image from his brain.

Ana's heart was pounding. So much for aiming for nonchalance. Suddenly she felt very exposed.

Not hard, considering that she was wearing precisely three small triangles of white material that were held together at the front, at her midriff, by a silver and diamond-encrusted circlet, and at her neck by a halter-neck fastening. Dangling from the silver circlet at her midriff, a delicate diamond chain circled her waist. Wedge sandals elevated her a few precious inches.

Not even the sunglasses she wore could protect her from the shock emanating from Caio's rigid body as he turned to look at her. Shock…and also scorching heat. Ana could feel it lick over her skin in little tongues of sensation.

She hadn't imagined it.

Exhilaration coursed through her blood.

She'd tied a short diaphanous wrap around her hips

in a bid to preserve some modesty, but she knew well that it only highlighted the scantiness of her outfit.

She'd plucked a random book off the shelf in the den and held it up now as evidence. 'I thought I'd lie by the pool for a bit.'

'It's after midday…the sun is high.'

There was a rough quality to Caio's voice that made her skin raise up into goosebumps.

'I've put on sunscreen. I'm not careless. And I'm planning on lying in the shade.'

She walked towards Caio, her legs feeling embarrassingly shaky. He watched her with such a brooding expression on his face that she was glad she was wearing sunglasses.

She skirted around him. 'I'll just dump my things and come back for a drink.'

'What would you like? I'll bring it out.'

Ana desperately wanted to emulate Caio's usual lovers and say something sophisticated like, *A glass of champagne, darling* or, *A cocktail, of course. I'll let you decide.* But she was no hardened drinker at the best of times, and in this current mood and climate, alcohol would not be her friend.

'A sparkling water is fine.'

She walked down to the pool, aware of Caio's gaze burning into her very bare back. From behind, she knew that it would look as if she wasn't wearing anything but briefs and that piece of wispy material. And the diamond chain.

By the time she got to the pool she all but fell onto a lounger. She could barely keep it together under Caio's gaze—what would it be like if he actually touched her? Kissed her?

He appeared now, striding across the lawn towards

her with a glass of water, looking like a very stern waiter. A very sexy stern waiter.

She hurriedly arranged herself in as languid a fashion as possible, as if this was entirely habitual for her and not a desperate attempt to seduce her ex-husband.

She could sense him standing beside her and after a moment she stirred, as if she'd had her eyes closed, and pushed her sunglasses onto her head. 'Sorry, I didn't see you there.'

She reached out for the glass, but Caio held it aloft. His jaw was tight. Ana's hand dropped.

'What are you up to, Ana?'

She was determined not to let the fact that she was so obviously acting out of character put her off. She widened her eyes the way she'd seen hundreds of women do when talking to Caio. Her presence had never made any difference.

'I don't know what you're talking about.'

He sat down abruptly on the lounger beside hers. She noticed that he kept his gaze up. He put the glass down on the table between them.

He waved a hand towards her. 'What's…this?'

A spark of fire lit up Ana's insides when she thought of her reaction to him on the beach earlier. 'Swimwear, Caio. I'm sure you've seen a vast array on plenty of women in your lifetime. It's no more or less revealing that what you yourself were wearing earlier, when you took your swim.'

A strangled sound came from Caio's throat. Then, 'I've seen you wearing swimwear before, and you usually prefer one-pieces.'

Do I, now? thought Ana, as that rebellious spirit filled her. She sensed a desperation in Caio.

She sat up on the lounger and put her hands behind

her, so that her chest thrust forward a little. 'Technically, this is a one-piece…with bits cut out.'

The effort it was taking for Caio not to let his gaze drop to take in the plump swells of Ana's high, firm breasts, threatening to burst free from the minuscule pieces of material covering them, was making sweat break out on his brow.

He had been around women a long time. With older brothers who'd been a target for status-climbing socialites, he'd seen a lot, and had been initiated himself at a young age. For years now women had ceased to do much more than spark a modicum of interest in him.

That had been another factor in why a marriage of convenience to Ana Diaz had appealed. The thought of not having to play that tiresome game for a while. But right now he realised he'd made a huge error of judgement—because, contrary to his assumption that marriage to her would be a break, his awareness of her had been a constant, growing thing, and right now it was all he could see and feel.

He was consumed.

He'd been an arrogant fool and now he was paying for it.

She asked pertly, 'How is this different to what you were wearing earlier when you went for a swim?'

Heat was melting Caio's brain. He shook his head. 'It's different.'

She snorted. 'Typical double standards.'

Caio opened his mouth, but he realised that he didn't want to speak. He wanted to stop the words coming out of Ana's mouth by crushing it under his, and then he wanted to pull aside those excuses for pieces of material and feast on her breasts until she was writhing against him with need, and then he wanted to explore between her legs to see how responsive she was—

Suficiente!

Caio stood up abruptly. He felt dizzy with the strength of need coursing through his blood. 'Of course you can wear what you want.'

He turned and took a couple of steps, but then Ana said from behind him, 'Wait.'

He didn't turn around.

'What I wear shouldn't bother you… Unless it bothers you because…' There was silence, and then Ana said in a rush, 'Because maybe you want me.'

CHAPTER TEN

ANA'S HEART WAS pounding so hard she was sure Caio must be able to hear it. He still had his back to her. She thought he might just ignore her, walk away. The ultimate humiliation. But then he turned around slowly.

Every line of his body was tense. She'd never seen his face so stark. His eyes were dark and unreadable from here.

'Ana...'

She held her breath.

'This isn't about me wanting you. You are a beautiful woman. Very desirable. I'm not made of stone. Of course I'm...aware of you...'

All she heard for a long, dizzying second was *'very desirable'*. He thought she was desirable. Beautiful. Ana couldn't breathe.

'...not going to happen.'

Ana blinked. She'd missed whatever Caio had been saying due to the rush of blood to her head. 'What's not going to happen?'

He gestured with a hand between them. 'This. Us.'

'Why not?'

Caio's jaw clenched. 'Because it's not a good idea. We were married. We had a relationship.'

Ana stood up. 'You do realise how crazy that sounds?

If anything, it's stranger that we didn't consummate the marriage.'

Caio's gaze narrowed on her face. 'You made it pretty clear on our wedding night that you weren't interested in consummating the marriage.'

Ana flushed when she recalled her feeling of panic that Caio would realise how much she wanted him. 'That's not fair. I told you I had no idea what kind of person you were. What you'd expect.'

A look of disgust flashed across his face. 'I've never forced a woman to do anything against her will, and I wasn't about to start when we got married.'

Ana bit her lip. This wasn't going at all the way she'd envisaged. 'No, I know. And I never thought you were capable of...*that*.'

'What was it, then?'

Ana looked at Caio. She was practically naked. She had nowhere to hide. She took a breath. 'I was afraid you'd realise how much I... I fancied you. That it would be...humiliating.'

Caio shook his head. 'I wouldn't have humiliated you.'

A memory popped into Ana's head. 'I was certain you didn't want me. That you were immune to me. At that cancer charity benefit last month you were so tense. You could barely touch me. I thought it was because you couldn't wait to see the back of me.'

That had been a low moment for Ana—the realisation that Caio must be counting down the days to when he was free again. Free of this arrangement with his convenient wife.

But he shook his head, his mouth tight. 'Definitely not immune.'

Ana's pulse tripped. She lifted her chin. 'So why

not…now?' *Was he going to make her beg?* 'We're two consenting adults. No one needs to know. I know I'm not your usual type, if that's what you're—'

Caio put up a hand. 'I have a type?'

Ana lifted a shoulder. 'Tall, skinny… Beautiful.'

'There's no comparison,' Caio said abruptly.

This really wasn't going well. Ana wished she had a long voluminous cardigan to wrap around her body. 'I know. You don't need to remind me of that.'

Caio took a step towards her. She looked up.

'No, I didn't mean it like that.' He stopped and ran a hand through his hair. 'I meant that you shouldn't compare yourself with women like that. You are so much more than them. You are sexy in a way that they could never be.'

Sexy. Suddenly Ana's self-consciousness drained away. Her mouth was dry. 'You do want me.'

He looked at her. Glared at her. She was filled with a fizzing, buoying sense of vindication.

'Ana…dammit.' He stopped. 'I won't lie to you. Yes, I want you. I'd have to be devoid of all my senses not to want you. But it's not happening.'

The fizzing deflated a little.

'It's because I'm a virgin, isn't it? I know you're much more experienced…that it takes threesomes to engage your interest—and I can't offer you that. Well certainly not here… There's only us on the island—'

'Whoa, wait—what? Threesomes?'

Ana shut her mouth. She was babbling.

Caio was looking at her as if she had two heads. 'What are you talking about?'

A wave of embarrassed heat rose up from her toes to her face. 'There was a piece online…about you and two supermodels…'

Another look of disgust flashed across Caio's handsome features. 'They put that story out there because I declined their very *un*-tempting offer to have them both pleasure me simultaneously. They were trying to boost their profiles. The piece disappeared once my legal team threatened to sue for defamation.'

'Oh...' Ana's voice was small. But she couldn't stop the small burst of relief she felt in her solar plexus to hear that he wasn't into performative sexual situations. Talk about intimidating...

'"Oh", indeed,' Caio said. Then, 'Look, there's no point making things complicated. We've got one night together and then we get on with our lives.'

Ana folded her arms across her chest. 'That's precisely my point. It doesn't have to be complicated.'

'Ana, look, it's not that simple. You're not experienced—'

'And I won't ever be experienced with that kind of attitude.'

Caio's eyes flashed. 'I will not be your first lover. I'm not the kind of man who is anyone's first lover. I'm not kind, considerate, gentle...and that's what you deserve.'

I don't want kind and considerate! Ana almost growled out loud.

'That's ridiculous,' she said instead. 'You were inexperienced once. You must have slept with a virgin before.'

Caio shook his head. 'Never. I'm not interested in that kind of emotional responsibility. In case it's escaped your notice I signed up to a marriage of convenience purely to avoid emotional investment. To focus on business.'

Ana recognised the obdurate look on Caio's face. She sat back down on the lounger and shrugged lightly. 'Fine.'

His expression went from obdurate to suspicious. 'Fine…?'

Ana sat back and stretched her legs out. She closed her eyes, crossing one ankle over the other. 'I'm not going to beg, Caio. I'll fix something for dinner around six p.m., okay?'

He said nothing for a moment, and then, 'Okay. See you then.'

Ana kept her eyes closed until she was sure Caio had gone back up to the villa. Then she opened them. *Fine*? No, it was not fine. She sat up straight. The memory of that night a month previously at the cancer charity benefit was still vivid. It was the night she'd worn that red dress. The one she'd felt sexy in. The one she'd hoped would provoke a reaction from Caio.

Except he'd been stony-faced and tense all night. Literally almost flinching if she touched him.

They'd actually left the event early, and hadn't exchanged a word on the way home, when usually they would chat idly about the people they'd met, or Caio would ask her what her opinion was of certain people or conversations they'd had.

When they'd reached the apartment he'd disappeared into his study. She'd assumed that it was because, contrary to turning him on, she was actively turning him off. And that with every effort on her part to make him notice her she was only driving him further away.

But it hadn't been that. It had been because she *had* been getting to him. He just hadn't wanted to admit it or act on it.

She'd hadn't fully acknowledged until now how rejected she'd felt that night. And hurt. Because over the previous months it had really felt as if they'd become a unit—not a conventional one, granted, but a unit. Supportive. Respectful. Almost…friends.

But since that night last month they'd been careful to avoid each other. Ana had felt humiliated to think that she'd actually hoped Caio might find her attractive. That she'd put so much effort into transforming herself into a sleeker version of herself when she'd never had a hope.

That was why she'd booked a one-way ticket to Europe for the day of their divorce. She'd wanted to leave Rio ASAP and put Caio and her humiliating crush behind her.

But now everything had just flipped one hundred and eighty degrees.

Caio wanted her.

She was a complete novice in more ways than one, and especially when it came to the art of seduction. But he wanted her. That was all she needed to know.

CHAPTER ELEVEN

CAIO PACED BACK and forth in the den, with the French doors open and leading out to the opposite side of the garden to where Ana was.

She wanted him.

And she knew he wanted her. For a man who'd never held back from pursuing a woman he wanted before, this was novel territory. Up until now there'd been an unspoken agreement between them not to rock the boat. As soon as she'd appeared in that excuse for a swimsuit the boat had started to sink in choppy waters.

But he assured himself he was doing her a favour by not indulging in this mutual lust. He might not have slept with a virgin, but he'd been one once. And he'd learnt a valuable lesson at his first lover's hands.

He'd momentarily confused sex with emotion after that first experience with an older woman. He'd blurted out afterwards, 'I want to see you again.'

She'd turned around and looked at him with pity and said, 'No, you don't. You think you do, but this is just sex, *carinho*, you'll soon learn…don't worry.'

And she'd left.

He'd felt as if his heart had been cut out of his chest. But she'd been right, of course. He had soon learnt, and he hadn't made the same mistake again.

He wasn't about to subject Ana to a similar devastating revelation. Not after they'd spent a year together, getting to know one another and developing a mutual level of trust. In a way, she was the first real friend he'd ever had, and this was something he was only really appreciating now—how entwined their lives had become without him even realising it.

He thought back to when they'd returned to Rio de Janeiro after their tour through Europe. Next, they'd been headed to North America. But for a few weeks Caio had caught up with business in Rio. He'd got used to coming home in the evenings and finding Ana cooking, not realising at the time that she'd cooked the food herself from scratch.

For a man who was allergic to any notion of domesticity he'd found it surprisingly appealing, and they'd settled into a routine of sharing dinner and chatting about inconsequential things. They'd watch a movie together, or a documentary, both of them sharing similar interests—which Caio had subsequently blamed for lulling him into a false sense of security.

One day Caio had found himself postponing a meeting so he could get back to the apartment in time for dinner and he'd gone cold inside. At what point had they crossed some invisible line to turn this marriage of convenience into something that had begun to resemble a real marriage?

Boundaries had already been crossed. He wasn't about to cross the final one now. No matter what she did to provoke him. He could resist. He had the benefit of experience and wisdom gained from painful experience.

'What are you making?'

Ana was careful not to show her reaction to Caio's reappearance. She hadn't seen him since she'd been on the lounger. Admittedly, once the adrenalin had worn off, she'd enjoyed a couple of tranquil hours dozing and swimming and reading.

She'd returned to the villa to put on a thigh-skimming sundress after peeling off the swimsuit. So much for enflaming Caio to the point that he couldn't help himself. But she hadn't lost heart. Not yet.

She looked up, feigning surprise. 'Oh, there you are. If we weren't on an island, I might have suspected you'd left.'

He made a face. 'I was in the study, looking up some news sites to see if there's any mention of us or the kidnappers.'

Ana's hand stilled. For a moment she'd forgotten about the outside world. This island was like a bubble. 'Is there?'

Caio shook his head. 'No, nothing. I can't make any calls or send any electronic messages in case they're intercepted. We just have to hope that things are going according to plan for the security team. So...' he said.'What are we having?'

Ana continued stirring the sauce. 'Chicken in a white wine sauce with some fresh vegetables.'

'Sounds good. I'm going to take a shower...'

Caio turned and left the kitchen and Ana watched him go, her eyes on his tall, rangy body. Broad shoulders tapering down to slim hips, tight buttocks and long legs. In many ways he was still an enigma, even though she felt as if she'd got to know him on a level that most others didn't. Due to sheer proximity for a year. You couldn't help but pick stuff up—habits, behaviours— after spending so much time travelling together and sharing a living space.

The only thing they hadn't done was share a bedroom. *Yet.*

'Wait!' she called out just as he was disappearing.

He stopped and turned around.

She said, as nonchalantly as she could, 'I thought we'd make a bit of an effort tonight.'

'Effort?'

'It'll be our last dinner together.'

'Are you expecting me to wear black-tie?'

The thought of him in a tuxedo, even though she'd seen him in one hundreds of times, made her heart pump. 'You don't have to go that far.'

He shrugged. 'Okay.'

When Caio had disappeared, Ana stopped stirring and took a breath at the thought of staging a grand seduction. She considered not going through with it. Did she really want to try and fail to entice one of Rio's most renowned lovers? But something stubborn within her refused to give in. To admit defeat before she'd even tried.

Before she could lose her nerve, she finished preparing the food and then took off the apron and went up the stairs to her bedroom suite. She took a shower herself, luxuriating in the powerful spray and steam, liberally applying the very expensive-smelling soap.

When she was out, wrapped in a towel, she surveyed the clothes. The deep shimmering royal blue dress caught her eye. She reached out but didn't touch it, suddenly filled with a sense that if she wore it she would never get over the humiliation of rejection. Instead, she pulled out a dress in a dark golden colour. Off the shoulder, it hugged her body all the way down to below her knee. It was sexy, but understated. After appearing all but naked in front of Caio earlier, she wanted to aim for sophisticated elegance this time.

She dried her hair—so much easier now that it was about twelve inches shorter than it had been—and put on a light layer of make-up. She still wasn't overly confident doing her own make-up, but she pushed aside her insecurities.

After putting on a pair of strappy gold sandals, she took a deep breath and went back down to the kitchen. There was no sign of Caio and she felt ridiculously nervous. She put the apron back on over her head and went to check the chicken in the pan and start cooking the vegetables.

She took out a chilled bottle of white wine and two glasses—which she almost dropped onto the tiled floor when she looked up and saw Caio standing in the doorway, wearing not quite a full tuxedo but a black suit and a white shirt, open at the neck.

His hair was damp. She could smell his scent from a few feet away, spicy and earthy. Masculine. *Deus*. She was like an animal in heat.

'Need a hand?' he asked.

She held out the bottle and glasses for fear she would drop them. 'Open the wine, please? The table is set out on the terrace. The food won't be long.'

She was aware of Caio finding a bottle opener and pulling the cork. Carrying the bottle and glasses outside. When the food was ready, she took off the apron and arranged the chicken and vegetables on two plates, then carried them outside to the table, aware of Caio's eyes on her. The balmy sea breeze skated over her bare shoulders and she could feel her nipples getting hard under the stretchy material of the dress.

He said, 'This looks amazing. Your skill with cooking really is a testament to how much you dislike your father.'

Ana retorted, 'You should see my *boeuf bourguignon*.'

The minute the words were out of her mouth she realised that Caio would never see it or taste it. The sudden reminder of impending loss was like a knife between her ribs. But he was right—this wasn't about emotion. She'd come to respect him and trust him. That was all. Nothing more. Apart from epic levels of lust and desire.

Tonight was it. No fear. No regrets.

She was sorry she hadn't gone all out and worn the blue silk dress now. At least if she was going down, it would be in style.

She sat down and Caio handed her a glass of wine. She saluted him before taking a sip, relishing the crisp, dry taste that exploded on her taste buds.

He took a bite of the chicken and made a sound that connected directly with Ana's lower body, sending a wave of heat right through her core. Great. Now her appetite had fled. For food.

'Good?'

'Delicious.'

Ana forced herself to eat, barely noticing the way the succulent creamy chicken almost melted on her tongue. When she'd swallowed, she said, 'I was thinking earlier that it must be amazing here when there's a storm.'

Caio sat back and looked around. The sound of waves lapping against the beach could be heard in the distance. 'Yes, it would be. It's so exposed.'

Like she'd been earlier. Except she refused to feel embarrassed about that.

Caio ate some more and then asked, 'So what's your plan when you get to Europe? Are you going to apply to university? You should, you know.'

Ana felt insecurity rise. 'I'm not sure. I'll stay in Amsterdam for a while with Francisco and maybe get a job.'

'You don't need to work.'

Ana gave Caio a look. 'Do you really see me settling for a leisurely life of shopping and coffee mornings? I loathe shopping, and I never did fit into the socialite crowd.' She held up her neatly manicured hand to demonstrate. 'I never got false nails. If that's not proof, I don't know what is.'

'You're too intelligent for shallow chit-chat and false nails.'

A burst of pleasure caught at Ana's chest. 'Well, I don't know about that...'

'I do,' Caio said, pouring himself more wine and topping up her glass. 'You were always more interested in the conversations that were meant to exclude you and not remotely interested in the conversations that were meant to include you.'

Ana rolled her eyes. 'It's all so sexist and boring. Why do the women have to talk about the latest social events and who is marrying who and who's having a baby and who's not and who's getting divorced...?'

'We got divorced.'

There was an edge to Caio's voice. Maybe to remind Ana of the status quo and to leave it alone?

She decided to ignore it. 'Maybe they're talking about us now.'

'I've no doubt they are.'

'I mean, it wasn't exactly a secret that ours wasn't a love match.'

Caio made a snorting sound. 'Apart from our island hosts—who, I will agree, seem to have pulled off the urban myth of a happy marriage—none of those marriages are love matches. They're all business transactions.'

Ana looked at Caio. 'Did your marriage to me bring you the business dividends you wanted?'

His gaze narrowed on her, as if suspicious of her motives. She felt reckless again.

'It certainly did. It gave me the sheen of respectability I needed to expand globally and, in turn, I think you'll agree that it's given you your freedom. And your brother's.'

Ana lifted her glass. 'Yes, it has. But maybe my freedom isn't all that I want. Maybe I want more.'

Caio tensed. 'Ana…' he said warningly.

She neatly deflected whatever he was going to say by standing up and saying, 'Dessert? Coffee?'

She needed coffee to counteract the way the wine was making her feel languorous. She needed all her wits about her.

'Sure,' Caio said, his gaze still narrowed on her.

Ana took their plates into the kitchen and prepared a tray with two small strong coffees and two perfectly prepared *brigadeiros*—a traditional chocolate sweet that both she and Caio loved.

She brought the tray out and handed Caio his coffee and one of the sweets.

She sat down and he surprised her by saying, 'Thank you for dinner. It was a nice idea to celebrate our last evening together. I wish you well, no matter what you decide to do, Ana.'

Now Ana looked at Caio suspiciously. He sounded utterly urbane. Reasonable. Telling her without telling her that he had no intention of muddying the waters of their last night together.

She lifted her coffee towards him in a salute. *'Saúde.'* The coffee was tart—the perfect accompaniment to the sweet. She sat back in her chair and looked at Caio. 'You asked me what my plan is when I get to Europe... Actually, I know the first thing I want to do.'

'What's that?' Caio took a sip of coffee.

'Lose my virginity.'

Caio choked on his coffee. Ana pretended not to notice. She lifted a shoulder. A bare shoulder. And said, as innocently as she could, 'Well, if you're not interested then I need you to tell me all I need to know about finding the right person. I'd prefer to avoid a bad experience, if I can.'

CHAPTER TWELVE

CAIO STRUGGLED TO get his breath back after Ana's bombshell. *'Well, if you're not interested... I need you to tell me all I need to know...'* That was pretty much all he'd heard.

Not interested? *Madre de Deus*, it was all he could think about. Peeling that dress off Ana's supple body and feasting on her bare flesh until she was flushed and pliant, begging him to sheath himself inside her...

He shifted in his seat, glad of the table that hid his body's rampant response since he'd seen her in that dress, clinging to every curve and line of her body.

She'd never looked more alluring than she did right now, and it made him think of that evening in London when she'd appeared before him, hair chopped and transformed into a vision of beauty that had short-circuited his thought processes for long seconds.

Up until that moment she'd effectively hidden herself from scrutiny, with her long hair and by choosing clothes that didn't flatter her shape. Caio had put it down to lack of confidence, and perhaps the influence of growing up without a mother figure or sisters.

The first time he'd actually seen the shape of her had been on their wedding day, when she'd come to him dressed head to toe in lace, like a bride from the last century. But that night in London she'd been in a slip of a black cocktail dress that had looked as if it was defying gravity, clinging to her chest and thighs, and Caio's first reaction had been one of a man from the last century. He'd wanted to tell her to change immediately into what she usually wore—the kind of clothes that had helped him maintain the illusion that she wasn't as beautiful as she was.

She had the kind of beauty that crept up on you and slapped you across the face for underestimating it. And he'd been as stunned as if someone had slapped him. But then he'd realised that his reaction was ridiculous. Told himself he should be embracing the fact that his wife had discovered her inner style and beauty maven. Her face had been revealed, its spectacular bone structure no longer hidden by a fall of silky hair. Eyes huge. Mouth…

Caio had said something to her then. He couldn't even remember what. He'd just had to get them out of there before she saw her effect on him.

But then he'd started noticing men noticing her. And the women, sensing a rival. It had made him feel protective and…possessive. *Jealous.* Yet he'd managed to keep a lid on his control—mainly by focusing on work to the extent that he was too exhausted to think about much else.

But now control was just a word…and Caio wasn't sure if he even understood the meaning of it any more.

Ana suddenly stood up, and Caio had to fight to keep his gaze up. She said, 'Actually, there's a dress… I'd like your opinion on whether or not it'd be suitable for a date…'

'Ana—'

But she'd turned and gone back inside, disappearing

before Caio could stop her. He gulped back the last of his coffee, but it wasn't helping the itchy feeling under his skin or the fire in his blood.

He stood up, restless. The sunset had somehow come and gone unnoticed and dusk was falling, bathing the grounds in a lavender hue. The birdsong of the night was starting up. It was an idyllic scenario, if only Caio could feel relaxed enough to appreciate it.

Right now, he knew he'd only feel relaxed again when Ana was on a plane and there was some serious mileage between them. Although, much to his chagrin, he wasn't even sure if that would do it. She'd embedded herself under his skin and in his blood so indelibly that he feared there was only one way to exorcise her...

Disgusted with himself, and wondering uneasily what the hell Ana was up to, Caio shucked off his jacket and went into the study/library, where he'd noticed that Luca Fonseca had a drinks cabinet full of the kind of whiskey that had aged in a barrel over many, many years in an Irish distillery on the edges of a misty mountainous lake. Perfect.

He helped himself to a measure from a bottle that was already open and swallowed it in one. He'd hoped the heat might eclipse the other heat in his blood, but so far it didn't seem to be helping.

He'd told Ana on their wedding night that he didn't sleep with virgins, and no matter how alluring she was he would not be tempted. Their marriage might be over, but he knew instinctively that seducing Ana would bring about the kind of emotional complications he'd spent his life avoiding, after witnessing the emotional minefield of his own parents' marriage.

He would resist. He had to. They only had a few hours left. How hard could it be?

Caio had just poured another shot when he heard a sound behind him and turned around. Earlier, when Ana had appeared in the swimsuit, his first thought had been that he would never erase that image from his mind. Well, it had just been erased and replaced.

And now he had a second thought: *I'm a dead man.*

Ana faced Caio across the expanse of room with every cell in her body mustering up the last of her courage. She hadn't noticed it getting dark outside. The low light threw out a golden glow and put everything into shadow. Including Caio's expression. Maybe it was better that she couldn't see his reaction.

She'd changed into the blue silk dress, and the way it skimmed her body made her feel as if she could be naked. The deep vee cut between her breasts almost to her navel. The dress was pretty much backless.

She'd put her hair up in a haphazard bun in a bid to try and cool her flushed face and neck as much to be artful, and tendrils fell down around her face.

She only realised in that moment that she'd forgotten to put shoes on. She was barefoot, and the dress was pooling around her feet because it was too long for her.

Suddenly she was overcome with self-consciousness, and she was about to turn around and flee when Caio said in a strangled-sounding voice, 'What in God's name are you trying to do to me, woman?'

Ana went still. He sounded tortured. She took a step forward and suddenly Caio's face was revealed. It was stark with the same look she'd seen earlier by the pool, and it made her heart skip a beat and her pulse trip at the same time.

It looked like…hunger. The hunger she felt too.

Some of her confidence—admittedly blind confidence—came back. When she spoke her voice was husky with desire and nerves. 'I'm wondering if this is a bit over the top for a first date? When I go to seduce the man who will be my first kind and gentle lover?'

Caio made a sound halfway between a laugh and a snarl. 'I can guarantee you that if you wear that dress, the man won't be kind or gentle. He'll have one thing on his mind.'

Ana took another step into the room. 'Maybe that's a good thing. After all, for my first time I want it to be about just one thing.'

'Do not say it, Ana.'

She lifted her chin. 'Sex?'

Ana saw Caio's hand tighten so much around the glass he was holding that his knuckles turned white. A sense of exhilaration gripped her. She was getting to him.

She held out a hand. 'Can I have some of that, please?'

Caio seemed stricken, frozen in place. But after a few seconds he held the glass out and said, 'Be my guest. I'll pour another one.'

Ana took the glass from him, noticing how he was careful not to let their fingers touch. Even so, she felt the crackle of electricity between them.

This was so on.

Caio turned away to pour himself another glass and she could see the play of movement in his muscles under the thin material of his shirt. He turned around and she lifted her gaze.

Caio raised his glass and took a deep swallow. Ana took a more measured sip from her glass, a little thrill going through her at the knowledge that her lips were probably touching where Caio's had. The golden liquid slid down her throat all too easily, leaving an oaky aftertaste and the burn of alcohol.

'Why does it have to be me?' he asked.

Because I don't want anyone else to touch me for the first time.

It was a visceral, almost violent response. Deeply emotional on a level she hadn't allowed herself to acknowledge before. But it had to be Caio. The thought of leaving this place, of not having known his touch, was suddenly terrifying.

Not that she could articulate all of that to him. So she said, 'Because I know you. I trust you. And I want you.'

But Caio was as immovable as a statue. A trickle of ice went down Ana's back at the very real prospect that Caio's control was strong enough to withstand all her very rudimentary attempts to seduce him. She'd laid herself completely bare and now he was going to reject her.

The picture of her mother walking away without a backward glance swam into her mind's eye, along with the memory of rejection, and the pain of abandonment. Except this time, she'd set herself up for the spectacular fall.

Ana could have been a queen in that moment. She was so dignified. Caio was used to women being direct, but not in such an emotionally honest way. That took guts. He felt humbled by her.

And in that dress…

He felt his final wall of resistance crumbling to dust. But before he could articulate anything he saw her chin dip a little, and some of her bravado falter. She put the glass down on a table beside her and looked at him. He could see the way her expression was closing in. Becoming unreadable. Her body tensing.

'Look, Caio, I'm not going to beg you—you're probably right...this would be a mistake. Let's just forget about it, okay?'

She turned as if to leave, showing her bare back to Caio, her skin luminous in the soft light, the sensual curve of her spine giving her an air of vulnerability. A great roar of possessiveness rose inside him. Feral in its intensity. Maybe earlier he would have taken her cue and packed his lust away in ice, told himself it was for the best that she'd come to her senses, but it was too late now.

'Wait a minute.'

She stopped. But didn't turn around.

'You're giving up so easily?'

She turned now, eyes flashing. It sent another roar through Caio's blood. This woman was his and no one else's, and he would be the first to awaken her. The thought of another man touching her made him feel violent. How had he ever thought he could resist her?

'I'm not a masochist, Caio. I've made it clear I want you to be my first lover but I think you're just enjoying toying with me.'

He shook his head. 'Come here, Ana.'

'You come here.'

The bravado was back.

He put his glass down and crossed the distance between them. He had an awareness of just how petite she was up close. Bare feet. But underneath the bravado he could see uncertainty. It pierced through the fire in his blood to send something alien to his gut. A need to reassure.

He put a finger under her chin and tipped it up. 'Are you sure about this?'

She said nothing for a long moment and Caio's pulse tripped. A cold weight lodged in his gut. What if she was regretting her decision? What if she wanted to change her mind? What if she was toying with *him*?

Suddenly he felt exposed.

Even though it killed him, he said, 'Ana, of course it's okay if—'

She lifted up a hand and put a finger to his mouth. She shook her head. 'What I was going to say was, would you just shut up and kiss me? Please?'

CHAPTER THIRTEEN

ANA COULDN'T QUITE believe she'd said those words. Up close, Caio was a lot more intimidating. Had he always been so big? They'd spent time in close proximity during social events, but never like this...in an intimate setting. It felt illicit. His finger under her chin was their only physical contact, but their bodies were almost touching.

He looked serious. 'This is one night. Tomorrow we go our separate ways.'

She nodded. 'What happens on the island, stays on the island. I get it.'

She would have agreed to anything. She couldn't take her gaze off Caio's mouth. She was barely aware of his hands cupping her face, tilting it up even more. Every cell and nerve in her body vibrated with a fine-tuned awareness as Caio's head dipped and his mouth met hers. It was silk and steel all in one moment. Heat and fire.

For a breath, everything was suspended. And then, under subtle pressure from Caio, Ana opened her mouth and he took the kiss from heat and fire to white-hot incineration.

For a moment she couldn't cope with the rush of sensation. It was overwhelming. Desire pooled between her legs, making her pulse throb. Her breasts were pressed against Caio's chest and her hands gripped his arms tight, as if that might help her stay afloat.

Caio pulled away. Ana opened her eyes. She felt light-headed. Dizzy.

'Okay?'

She nodded. Her mouth felt swollen, even after just a few seconds.

'Just breathe, Ana. We'll take it slow...okay?'

A fire rushed through Ana. Not slow. Not now. She'd been waiting all year for this. Forever. 'Not slow. *Now.*'

She pressed her mouth to his jaw and found the buttons of his shirt, undoing them with clumsy fingers. She reached his mouth again, and even though she knew her moves were inexpert Caio made a little sound in his mouth and put his hands on her hips, drawing her close again.

She could feel the press of his arousal against her belly and it made the heat between her legs gush even more. Mouths clinging, she let him taste her so deeply she could barely think. She caught his tongue and nipped gently, delighting in how his hands tightened on her hips and then moved around, one hand cupping her buttocks, squeezing her through the slippery silk of the dress.

She'd opened the last button on his shirt. She pulled back and pushed his shirt open, her eyes widening on his broad and tautly muscled chest. It was a thing of divine masculine beauty. She lifted her hands and traced her fingers over his skin reverently. Explored a nipple. She wanted to taste it with her tongue, but was suddenly shy.

Caio shrugged off his shirt. He led Ana over to a chair and sat down, tugging her onto his lap. She fell

into the cradle of his hips, grateful that she didn't have
to stand on shaky legs any more. Heat and steel surrounded her. Caio's chest bare under her own skin.
She looked at him hungrily. Couldn't believe this was
happening.

She reached out and traced the firm line of his mouth
with her finger. He caught it. She looked at him. He took
her finger into his mouth. A skewer of need arrowed
right down to her groin when she felt the sucking motion
on her flesh, and she squirmed slightly on his lap. His
eyes flared and suddenly Ana couldn't breathe. They
were burning with golden fire.

He pulled her finger out. 'I want to see you.'

Ana whispered, 'Okay.'

Caio found the hook at the back of Ana's dress. He
undid it and the silky material fell away from her chest
to reveal her bare breasts. Suddenly self-conscious, she
instinctively wanted to put an arm up to cover herself,
but Caio stopped her.

'You're beautiful. I've dreamt of seeing you like
this…bared for me…'

Ana's heart quickened. He'd wanted her too. They'd
both wanted each other. It gave her a sense of urgency.

She leant forward and pressed her mouth to his again,
an unknown emotion clutching at her chest. Caio's hand
was on her bare back, and as they kissed his other hand
explored her breast, circling and cupping her plump
flesh, coming closer and closer to the straining hard
tip of her nipple.

When his palm closed over her breast, she drew back
sucking in a breath. Caio squeezed her flesh, trapping
her nipple between two fingers. Then he took his hand
away and bent his head towards her, blowing on her

flesh lightly before surrounding that peak in moist heat. Sucking on her hard flesh.

Ana's hands were on his head, in his hair, gripping him. She was breathing fast, struggling to comprehend and deal with the sheer exquisite pleasure coursing through her entire body just from his mouth on her breast. She couldn't quite compute how such a simple act could feel so...life-changing.

He lifted his head and smiled. It was wicked. He knew exactly how he was making her feel. She scowled and put her hands on his shoulders, shifting her body so that she was straddling his lap, looking down at him.

Caio's hands went to her hips, holding her firm, and he took merciless advantage of his position to subject her other breast to the same torture. Ana's head fell back. She wasn't even aware that her hips were making small circling movements on Caio's lap, instinctively searching for a deeper connection. For *more*.

He pulled her dress up over her thighs and then slid a hand between them, his fingers finding her underwear and tugging it to one side.

Ana stopped moving. Her pulse was heavy and loud. She looked at Caio, caught in the beam of those molten gold eyes. His fingers explored between her legs, where the secret folds of her flesh hid the extent of her desire...but not for long. Caio opened her up and she saw the flush of colour on his face when he felt for himself how much she wanted him. The heat of her lust made his fingers wet as he massaged her flesh, stroking up and into her in a rhythm that took her by surprise, especially when at the same time his thumb flicked the solid nub of flesh where all her nerve- endings were quivering and straining for release.

Ana's thighs gripped Caio's tight. She came up to

give him more room, her hands like claws on his shoulders as she moved up and down on his fingers, his hand, as he stroked her to her first orgasm. She didn't even know what was happening until she fell over an edge she hadn't seen, falling down and down into a spiral of such intense pleasure that she shook in the aftermath, in awe.

She felt as if she should be embarrassed, but actually, in that moment, she felt a very strong sense of feminine power.

She collapsed forward onto Caio's chest, her face in the crook of his neck. His hand was still between them, on her pulsating sensitised flesh. His other hand was on her back, moving up and down in a curiously tender gesture.

His hand stopped. He said, 'Did you never…? I know you're innocent, but I thought you would have…'

Ana's belly contracted. Now she did feel embarrassed. She pulled back. Caio took his hand from between her legs. She shook her head, avoided his eye. 'No… I didn't… I was in a house surrounded by men. It didn't feel very private.'

Caio found her chin and tipped it up so she had to look at him. 'You're very responsive, *carinho.*'

'Is that a bad thing?'

Caio quirked a smile. 'No, it's something rare…it's a good thing.'

'But what about you? You didn't…' She felt a blush rising up over her bare skin.

Caio shook his head. For a second he looked as if he was in pain. 'Don't worry about me. But we're not going to continue here. Not for your first time.' Ana didn't want to move in case they broke the sensual spell. But Caio was saying, 'Wrap your arms around my neck.'

She did, and he stood up, pulling her legs around his waist. He walked her through the silent villa like that, and up the stairs and into his bedroom.

The doors were open, curtains fluttering in the warm breeze. But Ana barely noticed. Caio placed her on the bed. Her dress was pulled down to her waist and ruched up to her thighs. She didn't care. She felt languorous and sated and lethargic. But as she watched Caio bring his hands to his trousers, open them and pull them down, taking his underwear with them, revealing his naked body, she suddenly didn't feel lethargic any more.

She came up on her elbows, mesmerised by that stiff column of flesh. She dragged her gaze up to Caio's face, suddenly feeling out of her depth. How could she pleasure a man like this, who had already experienced so much pleasure with women far more experienced than her?

'Caio... I don't know what to do... What if I can't...?' She trailed off as he moved over her on the bed, resting on his hands.

He said, 'You don't need to think about anything. Just lie back and let me show you how it's done, hmm?'

Ana collapsed back onto the bed, every cell in her body pulsating with fresh need and desire. Caio was enormous over her, a naked warrior, and right at that moment she was prepared to surrender everything to him.

CHAPTER FOURTEEN

CAIO HAD NEVER seen a more erotic sight. And he knew it had nothing to do with a year of sexual abstinence and everything to do with the woman laid out on the bed before him. There was no other woman for him at that moment, and he had the strangest sensation—before he pushed it way down—that there wouldn't be again.

Dark hair was spread around her head and her cheeks were flushed. Chest bared, her plump breasts pouted towards him, tempting him to taste her all over again. The curve of her waist and the flare of her hips made his fingers itch.

The blue silk still pooled around her body. Caio reached for that first, tugging it down and off. She lifted her hips towards him, and the sweet, musky scent of her desire caught him off guard for a moment.

When he'd explored her body, and found how ready she was for him, it had taken all his restraint not to position her over his lap, free his body from its confinement and bury himself so deep he would find immediate relief. But the fact that she'd never orgasmed before had caught at him in a way he hadn't expected. Making him feel protective. Possessive.

Now all she wore was her underwear. A flimsy lace

thong. Caio dispensed with it easily. The cluster of dark curls over her sex made his straining flesh even harder.

He came down on his knees by the bed and pushed her thighs apart, exposing her glistening folds. *Deus.* He wasn't even sure if he could indulge in this when his body was screaming for release. But he had to make sure she was ready.

Ana's head came up. 'Caio?'

He said, 'Shh…just lie back…trust me.'

She let her head drop back. He put his hands under her hips and tugged her easily towards him. She was so petite. So delicate. Yet strong. He'd felt the strength of her body in its climax, and he had to admit that he'd never really noticed another woman's climax so acutely before.

He pressed kisses along the inside of her thighs, his hands under her buttocks. He could feel her starting to tremble as they had an effect on her, saw her hands close into fists on the bed.

The scent of her was intoxicating. He lifted her a little towards him and blew on her heated flesh before placing his mouth there, licking his way to the centre of her body and that sensitive cluster of nerves that responded under his ministration. Her whole body tensed for a moment, before she let out a little hoarse cry and lifted her thighs, as if she needed to contain the pleasure ripping through her body.

He drew back. He was shaking with the need to sheath himself inside her. He was almost ready to do it. But Ana was looking at him with wide eyes, and he could see that she needed more, even after coming for a second time.

She was looking at him so hungrily he almost threw caution to the wind, for the first time in his life almost forgetting—but at the last second he remembered, and cursed softly.

'What is it?'

Caio stood up and went to the bathroom, 'Protection.'

He came back and unselfconsciously rolled the protective sheath along his length, even that motion almost tipping him over the edge. Ana was exactly as he'd left her. Her chest lifting up and down with her uneven breaths. Legs spread apart. Right at this moment he didn't know how he'd resisted her for so long.

A warning bell rang in his head. He did know, but he didn't want to think about it now, because they'd gone way past the point of no return.

He said gruffly, 'Move back a little.'

She did so, her breasts bouncing with the movement. Caio almost groaned aloud. She was going to kill him. He was sure of it. But he would die happy. He was sure of that too.

He came down over her, careful to shield her from his full weight. He said, 'It will hurt a little, but it should ease…'

'I'm okay…just…please, Caio…'

She bit her lip, and that small, innocent movement pushed him over the edge of his control. He came closer and took himself in his hand, placing his erection at the entrance of her body, where she was still slick and hot. And hopefully ready… Because it was taking a restraint he hadn't even known he had to go slowly.

Caio felt Ana's resistance when he breached her body, saw the momentary flash of discomfort on her face. He almost stopped, but she reached up for him and wrapped her legs around his hips. 'Don't stop, I'm okay. Please.'

Gritting his teeth against how insanely good it felt

to sink into her tight embrace, Caio felt small beads of sweat on his brow as he buried himself inside her. They were both breathing harshly. And they hadn't even started. Caio pulled out again, and then eased back in, feeling Ana's body gradually loosen its tight grip, hearing her breathing grow faster as the timeless rhythm took over.

Ana's body was pliant around him. He could feel the sharp tips of her breasts against his chest. Usually when he made love to a woman he didn't lose himself completely. There was a part of him that stayed aloof. In control. All of that was gone here. Caio was only aware of the slick slide of his body in and out of Ana's, and the tension growing at the base of his spine as he fought to hold back until he felt her body climax around his.

Caio was almost on the verge of not being able to hold the rush of release when he felt Ana's back arch and an infinitesimal moment of stillness before her paroxysms of pleasure made her body contract powerfully around his, precipitating the strongest climax Caio had ever experienced.

Ana didn't know how long she'd been out. She only knew, as she slowly regained consciousness, that she would never forget the onrush of pleasure that had broken her apart into a million pieces and put her back together but in a new way.

She wasn't *her* any more. She'd been altered.

The orgasms Caio had unselfishly lavished upon her before they'd made love couldn't possibly have prepared her for the ultimate pinnacle of pleasure. So much pleasure. And he'd denied himself this for a whole year?

Ana became aware of movement. Sounds. Running water. She cracked open an eye. It was dark outside now. Low lights were burning in the room. The bed was empty.

And then Caio appeared in the doorway of the bathroom. There was a cloud of steam behind him. He was bare-chested and wearing a pair of sweatpants, slung low on his hips. Ana's over-sated body tingled in response, and she felt hot when she thought of how she'd wrapped her legs around him, begging him to go deeper, harder...

She'd become someone unrecognisable. Or the person she was meant to be. *With him.* Except all that was too late. It was over. It had never really started. This was just...an indulgence.

She pushed aside the sudden melancholy that gripped her as Caio came over and sat down on the bed. Ana felt shy. Which was ridiculous.

'How are you feeling? Are you sore? I'm sorry... I tried to be gentle, but I'm afraid I—'

Ana sat up, pulling the sheet up over her chest. 'No, it was fine. It was...perfect. I had no idea it could be like that. I'm sure for you, though, it must have been a bit...boring.'

She let her hair swing forward, hiding her face a little. An old habit. Caio reached out and put it behind her ear in a gesture that made Ana's heart thump. She felt raw in this moment. Exposed. But she forced herself to look at him.

He took his hand down. 'It was not boring, *carinho.* Trust me.' He looked as if he was about to say more, but then he stood up abruptly and said, 'I've run you a bath. You'll be a little sore, and I think you bled a little.'

Now Ana was mortified. She lifted the sheet and looked down to see spots of blood. Her face burned. 'I'll change the sheets.'

'I'll take care of that. Come and take the bath before it gets cold.'

He handed Ana a robe and she let the sheet drop so she could slip her arms into it, moving from the bed and trying to be as blasé as possible, as if she did this all the time. She imagined Caio's regular lovers paraded around naked without a care.

She belted the robe and tried not to acknowledge how the thought of Caio's ex-lovers and future lovers made her feel.

The bathroom was fragrant with a mixture of musky rose and something much earthier and more masculine. The bath was luxurious and filled almost to the brim.

Ana closed the door slightly, her face burning anew when she spotted Caio stripping the sheet off the bed. She pulled her hair back and put it into a rough knot then let the robe drop to the floor and stepped into the bath, wincing a little as the hot water came into contact with sensitive muscles and the skin between her legs.

The hot, fragrant water seeped into her body and made her feel even more boneless. She wanted to run her hands over her body where Caio had touched her.

Licked her. Nipped at her flesh. Sucked her.

Ana groaned, and resisted the urge to bury her head under the water. She felt a pang to think of how Caio hadn't been in the bed when she'd woken. What had she expected? To be wrapped in his embrace and that he would be whispering sweet nothings in her ear? He'd made it abundantly clear that this was a purely physical thing. One night only.

Except the only problem was that Ana already knew once wouldn't be enough. Not nearly enough. They had one night. She would have to make the most of it.

CHAPTER FIFTEEN

CAIO STOOD IN the kitchen, at a loss for a second. He knew what the problem was. His brain hadn't started functioning normally again yet. Sex with Ana had literally fried his brain. Rewired it.

He'd never lost it so completely like that. To the point where he'd lost any semblance or illusion of control. So much so that when he'd managed to surface, and had extricated himself from Ana's embrace and when she hadn't woken, he'd spent long minutes just watching her.

Her lashes had been so dark and long on her cheek. Mouth swollen from his kisses. Marks on her pale skin from his hands, mouth, stubble.

Horrified at his reaction because he never usually mooned over lovers after sex, he'd left her sleeping on the bed and filled the bath. And now she was in the bath, and all he wanted to do was go up there, haul her out, and bury himself inside her all over again. And again.

He cursed himself. He should have listened to his instincts when they'd told him that touching Ana would not be like touching another woman.

But then he castigated himself for such a notion. He hadn't had sex in a year. He'd never slept with a virgin before. Those two things combined were bound to make it feel...different. *Amazing.*

He heard a noise from behind him and turned around to see Ana hovering in the doorway, looking endearingly uncertain and also sexy as hell in the thin robe now belted at her waist and falling to mid-thigh. Her hair was wavy from the steam. Need skewered through him like an arrow, straight to his groin, before he could stop it.

'Are you hungry?' he asked abruptly.

Ana blinked. 'Yes, starving.'

She blushed, obviously thinking of how that appetite had come about, and Caio had to avert his gaze for fear he'd lose any ability to be civilised.

'Sit down. I'll make us an omelette.'

Ana came in and perched on one of the tall chairs on the other side of the island, and watched Caio break eggs into a bowl. He never usually felt self-conscious under a woman's gaze, but he did now.

She said, 'I've never seen you cook anything before.'

Caio glanced at her, and to try and keep himself busy, and not touch her, he poured a glass of wine and pushed it towards her. She took a sip. He took a gulp from the glass he'd poured himself.

He said, 'My repertoire is severely limited. Eggs, I can manage, but nothing more complicated.'

'Why did you ever need to cook?'

'When I left home, I'm ashamed to admit that I suddenly realised my food wasn't going to be prepared daily by a chef. So for a couple of years I lived on variations of eggs and takeout and street food.'

'When you were building your business?'

He nodded.

Ana asked, 'Did you really have no support from your family?'

Caio shook his head. 'My father disinherited me the day I left. I'd betrayed the family code.'

'How did you survive?'

'At first, with difficulty. I had some savings—the money I'd made from doing coding work for a tech company who'd seen a project I'd done at high school. I lived on that, stayed in hostels...getting odd jobs here and there. In my free time I pursued my own work, gradually building it up enough to seek investment... and that's pretty much it.'

Ana made a snorting noise. 'A modest way of describing a journey that led you to inventing a way to pay for products online that is now the most used online payment system on the planet, and to becoming a self-made billionaire by the age of twenty-five.'

Caio poured the egg mixture into a hot pan and looked at Ana. His mother was the only member of his family who had ever acknowledged his achievement. It felt strange, hearing it told to him by someone who wasn't a potential investor or a woman trying to feign interest.

There was no need for games with Ana—apart from the stunt she'd pulled just a few hours ago, which had led to the most mind-blowing sex of his life...

He shook his head, as if he could dislodge that assertion. He'd had sex like that before...he was sure he had. Even if he couldn't quite remember where or with whom...

In a bid to divert his mind and his libido from dangerous territory, Caio put the cooked omelette under the grill for a couple of minutes and commented, 'I know your mother wasn't a part of your family for long...why did she leave?'

Ana put down her wine glass and it clattered a little

against the marble of the countertop. She avoided Caio's eye. When she spoke her voice was clipped, unsentimental. 'She'd had enough of my father's controlling ways. She figured she'd done her duty and so she left. She's married again now, with no children to complicate things.'

Caio noted that she'd echoed his words from earlier. 'Do you ever see her?' he asked.

Ana shook her head and took a sip of wine. Caio noted the slight tremble in her hand and his insides clenched.

'That's why Francisco and I are so close,' she said. 'We only had each other. And then, once he revealed he was gay, I became even more protective of him.'

'You were his mother?'

Ana shrugged minutely. She glanced at Caio. 'I guess…in a way.'

Caio flicked off the grill and got some bread. He said, 'That's rough, not having your mother, but I admire her for doing what my mother didn't have the guts to do.'

Ana frowned. 'What do you mean?'

Caio put his hands on the countertop. He'd never told anyone about this. He suspected not even his brothers knew. He looked at Ana. 'My father is a tyrant, not unlike yours. He's also violent.'

Ana sucked in a breath. 'Earlier, when you tended my finger, you said something and I thought… Was he violent with you?'

'Casual stuff when me and my brothers were small— a clip around the ear, stuff like that. But once we got big enough he knew he had to curb his urges to lash out. But my mother…she was an easier target.'

Ana looked shocked.

Caio said, 'The day your father brought you to meet me, to discuss our marriage—'

Ana made a sound. 'That's a diplomatic way of putting it.'

Caio's mouth quirked, and then he grew serious again. 'I thought he was going to hit you when you stood up to him.'

'My father was never violent, but there was always the threat of it in the air. Especially once he found out about Francisco. But he never touched him.'

Caio said, 'The threat of violence can be almost as bad as the act… I managed to persuade my mother to leave with me after one incident. A bad one. She refused to go to the police. But at least she left. We went to a hotel. For one night. When I woke in the morning she was packed to go home. She said she couldn't do it. Couldn't walk away from the only life she knew. That she'd grown to love him in spite of their marriage being arranged and his behaviour. So she went back. But I never did.'

Ana said carefully, 'I think it took huge guts for her to leave, and maybe to go back too. Being a woman in that world is not the same as being a man. Maybe she really felt she had no other option.'

'Perhaps,' Caio conceded. 'I hadn't thought of it like that.'

'Because you're a man,' Ana pointed out dryly.

He made a face. Then, 'Whatever her reasoning, if that's what love is—something born out of something so dysfunctional—then I want no part of it.'

Ana went very still inside, watching as Caio took the omelette out from under the grill and divvied it up onto two plates with some crusty bread.

'If that's what love is...then I want no part of it.'

Suddenly, as if the last piece of a jigsaw was slotting into place, Ana saw Caio as if for the first time. She truly understood him now. Understood his willingness to enter into a marriage of convenience. All to avoid any emotional connection or entanglement.

And she got it. She came from the same cynical, emotionally barren world. Her own mother had walked out on her sons and daughter to pursue her own happiness. Ana knew she would never get over the awful sense of abandonment, confusion and loss she'd felt watching her mother get into a car and drive away.

And yet a small part of her had stubbornly refused to wither and die. Her relationship with Francisco had proved to her that there was such a thing as unconditional love. Deep inside was still a tiny seed of hope that one day she would find a way to heal from that awful sense of loss by finding a love to prove that all was not cynical and barren. To prove that she wasn't worth abandoning.

Except she'd failed at the first hurdle. Because she knew something else now. Something she couldn't keep denying to herself. And maybe making love with Caio had forced it to the surface, leaving her no way to hide from it any more.

She loved him. She'd fallen in love with him in fits and starts since the moment she'd laid eyes on him and had assumed the worst of him. *She loved him.* And after what had just happened... She knew no other man's touch would ever come close.

'Eat up while it's hot.'

Caio pushed a plate towards Ana. In spite of everything her stomach rumbled, reminding her of just how mortal she was. Seizing on the distraction from too-disturbing revelations, Ana took a bite of the fluffy tasty omelette and made a sound of appreciation. 'This is *good*.'

Caio affected nonchalance. 'I told you—eggs, I can manage.'

Ana's appetite battled with the huge ball of emotion expanding in her chest. In spite of the painful things they'd just been talking about she'd rarely seen this lighter side of Caio, and it was...intoxicating.

She took another sip of wine and a bite of omelette. They ate in companionable silence until Caio pushed his own plate away. He was looking at her intently. Ana swallowed, her appetite for food suddenly supplanted by another growing hunger.

'How are you feeling? Sore?' he asked.

Ana blushed. 'I'm fine. The bath was...nice. Thank you.' It had been thoughtful. As had his lovemaking. He'd been constantly making sure she was okay. Giving her two spectacular orgasms before showing her that they had only been the precursor to the main event.

If he'd been a careless lover, intent on finding his own pleasure, it would have made it easier to tell herself she was being ridiculous, that she was confusing emotions with sex... But he wasn't. And she wasn't. She was in so much trouble. But there was no going back now. She couldn't put the genie back in the bottle. And right now she didn't want to.

'That's good,' he said.

'What's good?'

Caio came around the island and swivelled her chair

around so she was facing him. All she could see was his bare chest…remember how it had felt crushed to hers…

She looked up.

'That you're not too sore… Because we only have one night, and I have no intention of wasting it.'

CHAPTER SIXTEEN

'WE ONLY HAVE one night, and I have no intention of wasting it...' Ana looked up at Caio. Suddenly she felt fearful. She'd thought the same thing herself only moments before. She'd actively seduced Caio for this purpose. But now she had cold feet. She hadn't counted on how making love with him would break her open, exposing a deep seam of need and emotion.

She knew the smart thing to do would be to call a halt now. She would meet someone else who didn't make her feel so...raw. *Wouldn't she?* she wondered a little desperately.

But she knew it was too late for that. This night would ruin her—*was* ruining her—for anyone else. And yet she also knew that she couldn't resist what Caio was offering. For one night only she would gather up these precious pieces of experience and pleasure so she could hold on to them like a miser.

He reached for her robe and opened the belt. Ana's breath quickened. She was totally naked underneath. He pulled the robe apart, baring her. Her skin prickled under his gaze, nipples tightening into stiff little buds.

She could see the pronounced bulge under his sweatpants and wanted to explore him, but before she could do anything so bold Caio lifted her wine glass and held it close to her breast, before tipping it slowly so that a trickle went over her breast and nipple.

She gasped at the cold sensation against her warm skin. Caio cupped her breast and bent down, his hot mouth closing over the peak as he sucked and licked her flesh clean of the sweet drink.

Ana was clutching his head, biting her lip to stop crying out, even though no one would hear them.

Caio pulled back and stood up, eyes dark and golden. 'I want you…'

Emboldened by the evidence of how much he wanted her, and wanting to seize as much of this night and experience as she could, Ana slipped off the chair, her legs feeling distinctly wobbly. She got down on her knees before him and put her hands to his pants, where they hung low on his slim hips.

Immediately she saw the flare of desire in his eyes, even as he put out a hand and said, 'Ana, wait…you don't have to—'

'I want to.'

She curled her fingers under the edge of the material and slowly pulled the pants down. They caught for a moment on Caio's erection, and then it was free. Thrusting from the thicket of hair at its base. Boldly masculine and potent.

Ana was fascinated. Veins ran along the underside of the shaft and moisture beaded at the tip. She put a thumb to the bead of moisture and then licked it. The essence of Caio. Obeying some instinct she'd never possessed before, Ana wrapped a hand around Caio's length. It felt hot under her palm and fingers, the skin silky, slipping over the steely hardness underneath.

She looked up at him, and the tortured look on his face, stark with need, made her feel invincible. She hardly heard his sharp intake of breath when she put her mouth around him, exploring intently, tasting every inch of him.

His hands were in her hair and his hips started to jerk, and then he took his hands from her and before she knew what was happening pulled her up. He looked wild. He lifted her into his arms before she could protest, kicking his pants aside, taking her upstairs and back into the bedroom.

Ana, sprawled on the newly made-up bed, looked up at Caio as he stroked protection onto his length. It was still wet from her mouth, and for a second she lamented that she wouldn't feel him skin on skin—but all that was forgotten, and she sucked in a deep breath as he seated himself inside her in one smooth, fluid and devastating movement.

'Okay?' he said gruffly.

Ana nodded and gripped his arms. 'Make love to me, Caio.'

He did, slow and deliberate, taking her to the edge over and over again, delaying the rush of pleasure, until she'd wrapped her legs around him and was begging, 'Please, Caio... I can't take it...'

'Okay, *amada*, get ready...'

And then he drew out, before seating himself so deeply again that Ana was instantly engulfed in wave after wave of pleasure so intense that she almost regretted begging for release. Because this much pleasure... No one could withstand it.

Caio was still moving, seeking his own climax, sending Ana hurtling over the edge again as he stiffened against her and came, his big body jerking against hers for a long moment until, at last, the storm passed and Ana slipped into a pleasure- induced coma, her inner muscles still clamping around Caio's body, deep inside hers.

In that moment, just before she slipped into blessed darkness, she felt a profound and deep sense of peace.

Caio knew he should move. Normally after making love to a woman he had a clawing and urgent need to put space between them. But the same instinct he'd felt after making love to Ana for the first time was back. And this time it was impossible to resist. Primarily because he wasn't sure he had any bones left in his body.

Ana was curled into his side, one leg thrown over his, her hand resting on his chest, fingers spread out. Soft breasts pressed against him. Her breath feathered over his skin, deep and even.

Caio's hand moved over hers, to lift it so he could move. But instead he felt his fingers curl around hers. A siren song was calling to him just to lie there, not to fight the bone-deep pleasure coursing through his veins and arteries like soporific nectar.

He didn't want to look at what had just happened and how amazing it had been. How unprecedented. How she'd taken him in her mouth like a sorceress and had almost tipped him over the edge there and then, exposing him for being weak. For not having the control to withstand the inexpert ministrations of a woman who had been a *virgin* up until a couple of hours previously!

She might have been inexpert, but her effect on Caio had been all too devastating...

Caio assured himself that this was different. Ana knew the score. She was starting a new life in Europe and he would get on with his life, capitalising on the fact that he was now globally renowned and vastly more successful than he had been a year ago. Ana had been good for business. She'd fulfilled her duty. And he'd given her what she wanted: safety and security for her beloved brother.

All in all, a very successful business deal. And now this—the explosive fulfilment of mutual desire. He would never wake at night again, aching to know what she would feel like underneath him...around him. Now he knew.

And yet as he slipped under the veil of darkness, unable to fight the pull, knowing that gave him no sense of peace. Only the prickling sensation that the more he had of her, the more he would want.

When Ana surfaced to some kind of consciousness she felt boiling hot. Gradually she opened her eyes and realised that she was plastered to Caio's chest, all but clinging on like a monkey, one leg thrown over him as if to stop him escaping.

Except she couldn't escape either—not that she even wanted to—because his arm was firmly and heavily around her, plastering her to his side. She held her breath in case she woke him, revelling in the sensation of all that heat and muscle and sinew under her skin.

But as if he could hear her thoughts Caio opened his eyes and zeroed in on Ana before she could even attempt to put some very necessary defences in place.

'Hi.'

'Hi.'

Such an innocuous word after a storm. Her voice was gravelly. Hoarse from shouting. Begging.

Ana buried her face in Caio's shoulder, but that only brought her mouth into contact with his skin. She resisted the urge to press kisses there. To lick him. Her face flamed when she thought of how she'd wantonly got on her knees before him and taken him into her mouth as if she did it all the time. As if it wasn't her first time.

'What?' Caio tipped her chin up.

Emotion, unbidden, caught at Ana. *She loved him.* A man who oozed cynicism and self-reliance. Who didn't need anyone.

'Is it always like…this?' She hated herself for asking, for revealing her vulnerability, but too much had been stripped away. Literally.

Caio tensed under her. She was expecting him to say, *All the time, and actually usually it's better*, and she braced herself for humiliation. Exposure. But then he said, 'No. It's not. This is…rare.'

Ana pulled back marginally, dislodging Caio's arm. 'You've experienced this before?'

Caio pulled his arm free. 'No…of course not. Because each encounter is unique. But I know how overwhelming it is the first time.'

Ana took her leg down from where it was flung, far too close to an area of Caio's anatomy that fascinated her. She rested on an elbow. 'Tell me about your first time.'

Caio lay back and looked at the ceiling. Ana resisted the urge to let her eyes drift up and down his spectacular body. She felt the stirrings of a resurgence of desire. *Already.*

'It's really not that exciting.'

'Tell me anyway.'

Caio sighed. He looked at Ana, almost scowling. 'I don't do this, you know.'

'Do what? Talk?'

'Talk after sex.'

'Why?'

'Because it tends to send mixed messages.'

'Such as that you might actually like a woman you slept with?' Ana tried to hide an amused smile.

'Something like that.'

'You don't have to worry about me getting mixed messages—after all, I practically had to hit you over the head and drag you up to my lair to make love to me, so it's not as if I'm under any illusions.'

She said the words lightly enough, but they felt heavy in her gut.

Before he could respond to that, Ana said quickly, 'Anyway—your first time. What was it like?'

'Mind-blowing.'

Ana immediately hated his first lover with a passion that scared her.

Caio said dryly, 'But you have to remember that men are simple creatures. It wouldn't have taken an awful lot to blow my mind at sixteen years old.'

Ana felt marginally mollified. 'Who was she?'

'A friend of one of my brother's girlfriends. She'd come to a party. She was older than me. I think she'd have preferred to be with one of my older brothers, but he wasn't interested. She found me lurking in a corner, watching the party, and took me to a private space and…initiated me.' He continued with a thread of self-disgust in his voice. 'The worst thing was that afterwards I was so awed and pathetically grateful. I thought I loved her. I followed her and told her I wanted to see her again. She humiliated me.'

Ana's hatred at the thought of his first lover turned to pity. She said, 'That wasn't nice.'

'No, it wasn't. But she did me a favour, really. She could have strung me along and made a much bigger fool of me than she did. I learnt my lesson early.'

'What lesson was that?'

But Ana already knew.

Caio turned and looked straight at her. 'Not to confuse sex with love.'

Ana opened her eyes wide and sat up, clutching the sheet to her chest. She made her lips tremble a little, 'You mean, you don't love me now, Caio? But what we just did…what just happened…it was so special—'

Caio moved so fast she didn't have time to think or speak. She was pinned under his big body, one leg between hers, another part of his anatomy stirring back to virile life, and he said, 'Very funny. I was a young, nerdy and naïve sixteen-year-old. You know a lot more than I did.'

Ana moved against him suggestively and wound her arms around his neck. 'I'm not sure I entirely grasp the concept—I think you need to show me again.'

Caio didn't need any encouragement. His mouth claimed hers with a ferocity that almost blanked her brain, but not quite. Because she knew she might have fooled Caio into believing that she was more savvy than he'd been at sixteen, and that she wouldn't be so naïve as to confuse sex with emotion, but she hadn't fooled herself.

CHAPTER SEVENTEEN

WHEN ANA WOKE AGAIN, she was alone in the bed. It was still dark outside, which added to the sense of timelessness and also comforted her. It made her think of Romeo and Juliet, and Juliet's insistence that it was the nightingale they heard as dawn approached after their night together, and not the lark.

Ana scowled at herself. She wasn't usually given to flights of literary fancy, no matter how much she wanted to go to England and study literature.

She stretched luxuriously, revelling in all the new aches and twinges in her body...the tenderness between her legs. She felt decadent, and she focused on that rather than anything more emotional.

There was no sound from the bathroom, so she slipped into the robe on the floor and went in search of Caio, not really caring if she seemed needy. They had one night and she wanted him again.

Forever. She blanked that thought out.

All was quiet downstairs; the kitchen was empty. Then she heard a sound from the area of the study/library, where she'd confronted Caio in the blue dress. That felt like an aeon ago now. She felt like a different person.

She stopped in the doorway. Caio was standing much

in the same place as he had been the last time. At the drinks cabinet with his back to her. Except his back was bare this time and he wore those sweatpants again. And, if she wasn't mistaken, she thought she could see the faint marks of her nails on his back.

He turned around. 'I tried not to wake you.'

I'm glad I woke.

Ana didn't say that. She just shrugged. 'I don't think you did. I woke and you were already gone.'

He held up a glass. 'Drink?'

'Sure.'

Ana sat down in a big chair and curled her legs underneath her, accepting the glass that Caio had had in his hand. He poured himself another.

She sniffed it, and the scent made her nose wrinkle and caught at the back of her throat. She'd been too nervous previously to wonder what she was drinking. 'What is it?'

'The same as before—a very expensive Irish whiskey.'

Ana looked up. 'Won't Luca Fonseca mind?'

Caio tossed back the golden liquid in one gulp. 'I'll replace it.' He poured himself another shot and took a seat in a chair just a few feet away.

She arched a brow. 'We survived a year of marriage but now I'm driving you to drink?'

Caio looked at his ex-wife. She was driving him to something. A kind of insatiable insanity.

Even now, after the last time—after he'd been sure that he was done, that his body could not possibly take or generate more pleasure—all he could see was her, sitting in that chair looking so innocent, her legs tucked up under her delectable body.

The robe gaped slightly, showing a tantalising curve of breast. He didn't have to see the puckered nipple to imagine it and know how it would taste, stiffening into a hard bud against his tongue.

When he'd woken a short time before it had been to find himself entwined with Ana again. He'd looked out of the window and felt both perversely relieved and frustrated that there was no sign of the dawn.

He'd come down here to put some distance between them and try to drown out the ever-present hum of desire in his body with the burn of alcohol. It was as if a switch had been flicked and he couldn't switch it off again. For the first time since they'd arrived on the island he felt claustrophobic. But it was an inner claustrophobia. A sense of wanting to get away from himself. Irritating and disconcerting.

Ana, oblivious to the maelstrom happening inside Caio, took a sip of the liquid. She made a little face. 'It burns…and it's smoky. Earthy. I like it.'

'It's peaty, from the bogs.'

'I've never been to Ireland.'

'You can go now. Nothing stopping you.' *Deus.* He couldn't string a sentence together.

'Maybe I will.'

The thought of Ana going off to explore the world on her own suddenly made Caio feel a mixture of things. Rudderless, and also panicky.

'What are you going to do with your newfound freedom?' Ana asked, slicing through the heat in Caio's brain.

He frowned. 'Work.'

Ana rolled her eyes. 'Apart from that.'

Caio felt a bit stupid. What else was there besides work and the transient release of tension and frustration with a beautiful woman? Except that hadn't appealed for some time now. A year, to be precise. And after tonight… He didn't want to think about that…

Before he could formulate a response, Ana asked, 'Why didn't you just marry one of your lovers or a mistress? You wouldn't have had to deny yourself for a whole year.'

Caio welcomed the kind of talk that defused some of the heat in his blood. And a chance to remind Ana, in case she needed it, not to expect that this night meant anything more than the physical.

'Because I needed a marriage where there was no risk of emotional entanglement. A woman who understood the parameters. If I'd married a lover, no matter what I'd said, she would have hoped that it meant more…and no lover has lasted longer than a couple of weeks. I have a short attention span.'

Or he'd *had* a short attention span. Caio hated the suspicion that his brain had effectively been rewired in the last year. The past few hours.

'Why me?'

Caio shrugged, careful to keep his expression neutral, not wanting her to see that his decision to marry her had been born out of far more complicated reasons than he'd ever really acknowledged.

'Your father wanted to do a business deal.'

'So I was just an added bonus.'

Caio shook his head. 'An integral part. You came from the right kind of family…you understood—*understand*—our world. And once you knew what I expected of you I could see that you weren't averse to the idea.'

'No,' she conceded. 'Not when you explained what you needed.'

Ana raised her glass towards him. 'Here's to a business arrangement successfully executed.' Then she said, 'My father would have done the deal with you anyway, even if you hadn't married me.'

Caio shrugged. 'Perhaps. The truth is that he needed me more than I needed him.'

'I bet he hated that.'

Caio recalled the barely concealed aggression of Rodolfo Diaz. 'He'd done his research on me. He knew that my personal life was beginning to damage potential business prospects. He knew I wanted to expand globally. When he mentioned you, and the prospect of marriage, I couldn't help but consider that it was serendipitous.'

Ana smiled, but Caio could see it was brittle.

'And so the perfect sacrificial virgin was handed to you on a platter?'

Caio took a sip of his drink and shook his head, 'There was nothing sacrificial about you, Ana. You were in control of the situation the whole way. You stood up to your father that day...you angered him.'

Ana's eyes flashed at the memory. 'I *was* angry with him.'

'You put yourself in danger.'

Ana looked at Caio. 'I told you he was never violent...'

'I think you pushed him over a line that day. I saw it in him. Remember, I've seen it before.'

Ana frowned now. 'With your mother...?'

Caio nodded.

Ana shook her head. 'I don't think my father would have actually struck me...'

But even as Ana said those words it was all too easy to imagine a scenario where Caio had walked away from the deal and her father had lashed out for the first time. The longer she'd been single and in his house, the more of a burden she'd been.

But she hadn't been able to leave until she'd known Francisco would be safe.

Caio was grim. 'I saw it in him that day.'

Ana focused her attention on Caio again. She frowned. 'So are you saying you offered to marry me to protect me?'

Caio said nothing and Ana's words hung in the air. She'd meant them flippantly but now they felt heavy as their meaning struck home.

She untucked her legs and sat up straight. 'My God— that's it, isn't it? You married me out of some sense of duty. To protect me. Not because I was a suitable candidate, but because you pitied me. You saw me as a potential victim, like your mother. You couldn't save her, so you tried to save me. When you didn't even know me.'

Ana put down her glass in agitation as it sank in. She'd always harboured a very secret hope that somehow Caio had seen something in her that had compelled him to ask her to marry him. Fresh humiliation scored at her insides. Would she ever *not* feel humiliated on some level by this man?

'Ana, wait. It wasn't—'

But she stood up, cutting him off, not wanting to hear some platitude. It all made sense now. And she knew, after a year of living with him, that he had an ingrained sense of integrity and decency. He might have wanted her for what she could bring to the marriage, but he'd also wanted to save her.

She went to walk out, but Caio leaned forward and caught her hand. 'Ana, wait.'

She stopped. Even that small contact made lust surge.

It was too new. Too raw. She pulled free and looked at him. He was sitting forward on the chair. His jaw was stubbled. Suddenly all her feelings for him were too jumbled to make sense of. Right now he looked like the louche playboy he'd been before they'd married, before he'd wanted to clean up his reputation.

All she'd done here tonight was allow him to scratch an itch before he went back out into the world a free man with a clear conscience—because she'd *begged* him to make love to her, to take her virginity, and also because he'd saved her from her father.

She felt sick.

Caio stood up. 'Ana—'

Panicked by the thought that he'd touch her and scramble her brain even more, she got out a strangled-sounding, 'No!' and fled from the room. Straight out into the garden.

It was lit up with solar-powered lanterns. She went blindly down towards the beach, attracted by the sound of the waves, needing to put space between her and Caio. It was clear and still, and the moonlight lit up the beach almost as brightly as if it was day. Ana sucked in a deep breath. She hated it that Caio had pitied her. She didn't want to evoke someone's sense of duty. She wanted to drive someone—*him*—mad with lust and passion.

And she thought she had.

But the truth was that it had taken a year for him to see her as a woman. To want her. And who was to say that his desire hadn't been fuelled by sexual frustration, compounded by being stuck on an island?

The past few hours, which had felt so wondrous and revelatory, now felt cheap.

She heard a sound behind her. She couldn't bear for

Caio to see her vulnerability, so she turned around and pasted a smile on her face. 'Sorry, I went down a rabbit hole for a moment. I'm quite tired now… I'm going to bed.'

She went to walk past Caio, who was just a couple of feet away, and tried desperately not to notice his bare chest, or the way the sweatpants hung so precariously low on his hips.

'Ana, please. You have it all wrong—'

She put up her hand. She really didn't want to hear an explanation. 'It's fine, really. Look, we both know this was just a reaction to extreme circumstances, right? I wanted to get rid of the burden of my innocence before going to Europe, and you've taken the edge off a year of celibacy. We both got what we wanted. We'll be out of here in a few hours. Hopefully. I need to get some rest now.'

Caio watched Ana walk back up to the villa in her short robe. He wanted to stop her and talk to her, but something held him back. His conscience. What could he say?

He turned around and emitted a curse. He hated that she'd come to the conclusion she had, but maybe it was for the best. She was right. In a few hours they would be leaving this place. They'd be moving on with their lives. No matter how good tonight had been…it was over now. It wouldn't help to go after her and try to articulate things he could hardly articulate to himself.

CHAPTER EIGHTEEN

AN HOUR LATER, Ana was still tossing and turning in the bed. After a lifetime of sleeping alone, she now felt the lack of Caio's body like a missing limb. Pathetic!

Angry with herself for allowing her emotions to control all logic, and for allowing herself to fall for someone who was so inappropriate for her, Ana got out of bed. In spite of very little sleep, she felt full of pent-up energy. And sexual frustration. Caio had awoken a need in her that she feared would never be assuaged.

The prospect of that made the sense of desperation even more acute. She needed to do something to defuse the turmoil and tension in her body. Usually she'd go for a run. Or a swim. She thought of the pool, but it was too...calm. She needed something more elemental.

Where the hell was she going?

Caio couldn't sleep, and was standing on the small balcony outside his bedroom. He'd just been contemplating numbing the clamour in his head and the sexual frustration in his blood with more whiskey when a movement had caught his eye and he'd seen the slim shape of Ana, robe belted tightly around her waist, walking down the garden towards the beach—again.

Before he could stop himself, Caio went out to follow her.

When he got down to the beach, it took his eyes a minute to adjust. He couldn't see her. All he could see and hear was the pounding foam of the waves. And then he saw her discarded robe and a couple of other items. He picked them up. A delicate lacy top and matching pyjama bottoms.

It made him think of that moment when he'd come out of the shower into his bedroom—they'd been in some city…he couldn't remember which now—and he'd looked up to see Ana standing in the doorway, staring at his body as if she'd never seen a naked man before. Transfixed.

He'd known she was a virgin, but it hadn't really impacted on him until that moment just how innocent she was. And, if he was honest, that had been the moment when she'd burrowed under his skin and lodged herself there like a briar. He hadn't been able to get her huge eyes out of his head. How awed she'd looked. And then how mortified.

She'd never mentioned it. And neither had he. But a very subtle tension and awareness had come into the air between them after that night.

He looked out to the sea. He couldn't see anything. For a second he felt fear. Panic. She wouldn't possibly—? But then he saw the methodical stroke of arms in and out of the water as she swam parallel to the shore and relief made him feel like a fool.

Had he really considered that she was upset enough to do something drastic? When, as she'd told him herself, she was delighted to have been relieved of her virginity so she could go and enjoy her new solo life in Europe?

Caio's emotions swirled into a volatile mix, and without thinking about what he was doing he strode into the sea.

The first inkling Ana had that she wasn't alone was when she was unceremoniously hauled up by two big hands under her arms. She inadvertently swallowed sea water and spluttered, tried to clear her eyes, but of course it could only be one person. *Caio.*

When she saw him he looked fierce. His hair was wet, plastered to his head. Eyes burning. Ana realised she was standing up, the water waist-deep for her and up to Caio's thighs, where his sweats were moulded to his body.

He shouted, 'What the hell are you doing? You could have drowned out here on your own.'

Anger at him for making her *feel* so much, and for finding her in a private moment when she'd been seeking some peace, made her shout back. 'I'm perfectly safe! I'm a trained lifeguard and my brother and I used to go swimming in the sea regularly at night.'

'There's a perfectly good swimming pool here.'

'I wanted something more,' Ana lobbed back, feeling reckless. Feeling she had nothing to lose.

Dangerous.

'What if you'd got cramp? Or drifted out to sea?'

'I'm sure the security boats would have picked me up.'

'Ana… *Deus.*'

Caio let her go abruptly and Ana swayed against a wave. The current was dragging her back to shore. She was naked. As if he'd just registered that fact, Caio's gaze drifted down, over her breasts to her belly, where the water lapped against her skin. Back up.

'You regularly swim naked?'

'Not with my brother, no. But I figured I was safe here.'

'Unless you're giving the security men a show.'

Ana subjected him to an appraisal. 'Then we both are.'

His sweatpants were all but clinging to his hips, moulded to every taut muscle and one in particular. Even now, in the cold sea, he wanted her. Desire surged through Ana's lower body. She felt elemental. She wanted to punish Caio, except she couldn't remember for what, exactly.

A wave caught her at that moment and sent her off balance. She fell against Caio and he almost fell back too, grabbing her arms to steady her. Her breasts brushed his chest. Electricity crackled between them.

Without saying a word, Caio took Ana's hand and led her through the shallows and out of the sea to the beach. Still without words he let her go, and peeled off his sodden sweatpants.

They were both naked. Alone on this beach, on an island in the middle of the Atlantic Ocean. And suddenly nothing mattered. Nothing but forgetting about everything else but *this*.

Ana didn't know who moved first, but they were in each other's arms and their mouths were fused within seconds, tongues tasting and thrusting deep, hearts pounding.

Caio pulled Ana down so that he was on his back and she was straddling him. She needed him as she needed air to take her next breath.

Acting completely on instinct, she rose up and found him with her hand, positioned herself above him. Bracing herself with her hands on his wide chest, she slowly sank down onto his hard body. Caio's hands went to her hips and he let her dictate the pace as she got used to the sensation, rising up and down, until another more primal rhythm took over.

They were both wet, salty, covered in sand. Locked in their own intense storm. It gathered around them, growing and growing, until Caio held Ana's hips still so that he could pump up into her body.

She cried out and arched her back as ecstasy ripped through her and threw her high. The waves of pleasure were slowly receding when Caio pulled free from sensitive muscles and she felt the hot release of his own climax on her skin.

She collapsed onto his chest, spent. Skin hot…sticky. Her hair was wet. Caio's hand drifted up and down her back. Cupped her bottom.

One minute she'd been in the sea, letting the steady motion of swimming bring her back to some semblance of calm and equilibrium, and now…

Caio somehow managed to move them both and lifted Ana into his arms.

She protested weakly. 'I can walk, you know.'

'Shh…'

She spied the detritus of their clothing. 'Our clothes…'

'I'll get them later.'

Ana giggled. She felt drunk. 'What if they get washed out to sea and end up on Copacabana Beach?'

It felt so nice, being carried against Caio's chest, her arm looped around his neck. But then she saw something over Caio's shoulder, and the languorous heat in her blood cooled a little.

'What is it?' Caio's chest rumbled against her.

She shook her head and turned away. But it was too late. She'd already seen it. The faintest of pinks on the horizon. The dawn, heralding a new day. *The end*.

'Nothing, it's fine.'

But it wasn't fine. She didn't care about the revelations of before right now—she just cared about eking out as much time as she could with Caio.

She closed her eyes against the sight of oncoming reality and pressed her mouth to Caio's jaw. He was carrying her through the villa now, and up to his bathroom. He put her down and reached into the shower to turn it on, the space quickly filling with heat and steam.

He drew her in and she stood against the wall under the spray. She'd never felt so lax. So boneless.

Caio lathered up some shampoo and said, 'Close your eyes.'

She did. He turned her around so that she was facing the wall and put his hands in her hair, massaging and soaping the sea and the sand out of her hair. Her head fell back as he rinsed it away. Soapy suds sluiced down her body and she felt Caio move closer behind her. His erection pressed against her and she wanted to turn around. But an arm had snaked around her torso, holding her upright.

One hand found her breasts, massaging and kneading, trapping her nipples between two fingers. Ana whimpered. His other hand went down, over her belly and over the curls between her legs, gently pushing her thighs apart so that he could find the slippery and hot centre of her desire.

Again. Already. Forever.

Ana made another noise as Caio's fingers delved deep into her sensitised muscles. It took only a couple of strokes for her to fall over the edge again, shuddering against him helplessly. Even as she thought she couldn't possibly take any more she knew that this was better than remembering what had upset her earlier.

Caio turned her around and she looked up at him. He

was magnificent. A warrior. He lifted her so that she rested back against the wall and said, 'Hook your legs around me.'

She did so, and Caio held her safely, with awesome strength, as he stroked his way into her body. Skin on skin. It felt amazing. And just when Ana thought she couldn't possibly experience another ounce of pleasure, Caio proved her wrong.

It was fast and explosive. He pulled free of her body just as her muscles clamped tight around him, and he shouted out an unintelligible word as his own climax ripped through him. It was an awesome sight, to see this man's entire body convulse with pleasure as he held himself in his hand and allowed his essence to drain away.

Ana felt shell-shocked. Hollowed out.

Caio turned off the water and wrapped her in a towel, rubbing her dry and putting another towel around her head. He towelled himself dry and then took her into the bedroom. She fell onto the bed and fell into an instant dreamless sleep.

Caio watched Ana sleeping on the bed. He felt as if an earthquake had just ripped through his body, leaving nothing but rubble in its wake. He'd never experienced a night like this, when the minute after climax he'd wanted to take Ana again. And again.

He turned away from the bed and towards the French doors, which were open. He saw what she had seen. The dawn creeping over the horizon, bringing the new day with it. He saw the lights on the security boats bobbing on the water around the island.

It was over.

The rubble inside him turned to ash. Ana thought

he'd married her out of an impulse to protect her because he hadn't been able to protect his own mother. And clearly that bothered her. He got it—no one wanted to be perceived as a victim. But he didn't perceive her as a victim at all. And he hadn't then.

But what he *had* felt wasn't worth mentioning, because it wouldn't amount to anything. Tonight had been…extraordinary. But it was just sex. Mind-blowing sex. He and Ana had had a business agreement for a year, and they'd both got what they wanted out of it.

It was over.

CHAPTER NINETEEN

WHEN ANA WOKE this time it was bright outside. She could feel it against her eyelids and didn't want to open her eyes. But she had to. She squinted at the sunlight.

She was lying under a light cover, still with the towel wrapped around her. Caio must have unravelled the towel from her hair, and it was under her head on the pillow.

She was alone. She sensed a distinct change in the air. The spell of last night was broken. She felt it as keenly as a cool wind across her skin. In fact, if she hadn't been in Caio's bedroom, and if her body hadn't been aching all over, she might have fancied that she'd just spent a night with the most lurid dreams she'd ever had.

But it hadn't been a dream. It had been real. And epic and devastating all at once.

Not wanting Caio to find her lying there mooning, Ana got up and groaned when she saw the state of her hair in the mirror. She looked as if she'd been pulled through a bush backwards. She was relieved Caio wasn't witnessing this. As if he needed reminding that he'd be returning to more sleek and sophisticated lovers soon.

She pulled the towel tighter around herself and crept out of the bedroom and back to her own, closing the door softly behind her. She'd barely slept in her bed apart from that one sleepless hour before she'd decided to take a night-time swim in the sea and then Caio had appeared like an avenging sea god.

Ana groaned again when she thought of making love on the beach like two crazed teenagers. What must Caio think of her? Insatiable…wanton.

She had another shower in her own bathroom and tried not to notice the sensitive places on her body. The marks on her skin that told of big hands clasping her hips, holding her still so he could pump powerfully into her body.

When she got out, she dressed in loose black trousers and a dark red sleeveless silk V-neck top. Flat black shoes. She wanted to look mature. Elegant. Put-together. Nothing resembling the hot mess she felt inside.

She went downstairs and the kitchen was empty. Ana breathed out a sigh of relief. She wasn't sure if she'd ever be ready to see Caio again after last night. But then she saw him. He was standing on the terrace dressed in jeans and a dark polo shirt, thick hair still damp from the shower.

He lifted his arm and Ana could see he was drinking from a small coffee cup. Her insides twisted. Something else they had in common. Strong coffee first thing in the morning.

As if sensing her regard, he turned around. He was clean-shaven. His face was carefully devoid of expression. Perhaps because she literally didn't provoke a reaction in him. Even after last night.

She forced a smile, as if this morning-after scenario wasn't going to kill her. 'Morning.'

He said, 'I made coffee. It's still fresh.'

'Cool.'

Brilliant, she'd regressed to being a teenager. She turned around before she could embarrass herself even more and went straight to the coffee machine, helping herself to a shot of thick dark coffee. The hot, rich liquid gave a much-needed shot of adrenalin to her veins.

Caio came in and stood on the other side of the island.

She held up the cup. 'That's good, thanks.'

'How are you feeling…after last night?'

She avoided Caio's eye. *Oh, God, he was going to be nice about it. Considerate.*

Feeling exposed, Ana asked a little waspishly, 'Do you normally ask your lovers how they're feeling the next day?'

'No, because I'm not usually around.'

'And now you feel compelled to because we're stuck on an island?'

'You were a virgin.'

Ana put down her coffee cup, its brief restorative effect turning to bile in her stomach. 'I think I'm probably more aware of that fact than you are, but thanks for the reminder.'

Caio cursed softly and ran a hand through his hair. 'Sorry… I didn't mean it like that.'

Ana said quickly, 'We really don't have to do this whole morning-after thing. I'm fine. Really.'

His voice sounded tight. 'Look, Ana, I wanted to talk to you about what you said last night… I never got a chance to explain, and I wasn't going to, but you deserve to know.'

Ana had picked up a piece of fruit, as much to look busy as to satisfy her non-existent appetite. She put it down again. 'You don't owe me an explanation.'

But he was insistent. 'I do. It's not fair for you to

think that I married you because you reminded me of my mother. It was more complicated than that. I never saw you as weak or a victim, Ana. I married you for all the reasons I outlined, but also for another, much less tangible reason. An instinct. I cared what happened to you.'

'Which is just another way of saying you felt like you had to save me from my situation.'

Caio balled his hand into a fist on the kitchen island. 'Dammit, Ana—no, it's not. I'm no one's saviour. I knew that after my mother went back to my father. I just…saw something in you that transcended all the very concrete and practical reasons for marrying you. Maybe it was chemistry, which I wasn't prepared to admit I felt, because that would have complicated matters.'

Ana pushed down a dangerous bloom of hope. 'You don't have to pretend you fancied me all along to make me feel better, Caio. Please don't patronise me. I know last night was an aberration but, as I said, we both got something out of it and now we can get on with our lives.'

'You sound very…okay with everything.'

'Why shouldn't I be?' Ana forced some more coffee down her throat, hoping it would burn away the growing ache she felt at her core. The pain near her heart. This was excruciating.

'Because last night was…intense.'

Ana affected a nonchalant shrug. 'I don't have anything to compare it to, but I'll take your word for it.'

Caio sounded grim. 'Believe me, it was not usual.'

Ana's heart thumped. 'Like I said, I'll just have to take your word for it.' A reckless devil inside her made

her say, 'I can let you know once I've had some more…
experiences.'

The colour in Caio's face grew darker and after a
minute he got out a very terse-sounding, 'That won't
be necessary.'

For a moment Caio looked almost tortured. Could it
be possible that he was actually…jealous?

But before that flight of fancy could sweep Ana away
there was a strident piercing noise. It was so unexpected
that it took her a moment to identify it as the ringing of
a mobile phone. Caio's phone. Which was now vibrat-
ing on the island between them.

Ana's guts turned to water. This was it. The outside
world was back. What if they were told they had to stay
for longer? That prospect alternately made her feel ridiculously relieved and also sick. Clearly Caio was ready
to draw a line under the whole experience and move on.

He looked at her as he picked up the phone. He listened for a long moment and then said, 'Okay, that's
good news. Thank you for all your hard work.' And
then, after a few more seconds, 'Yes, we'll be ready.
Thank you, Tomás.' He took the phone from his ear.

Ana couldn't speak. She just lifted a brow in query.

'It's over. They got the gang. They mounted a huge
operation using two stand-ins for us. The gang had no
idea we'd managed to escape. Security forces in Rio
and Europe followed the stand-ins, and the gang were
arrested in the act of kidnapping "you" at the airport
in Amsterdam, and "me" in Rio. They didn't want to
tell us how big the operation was until they knew it was
successful, but it had been in the planning for some time
before we heard about it.'

'Oh, wow.'

Ana felt flat. Somehow the fact that a major kidnap

operation had been averted didn't have as much of an impact as the fact that they could now leave the island.

'They're sending a helicopter to get us; it'll be here within the hour.'

Within the hour.

A sense of panic, dangerous and far too exposing, rose like a ball from Ana's liquefied guts. But she just nodded her head and said, 'I should retrieve those clothes from the beach and pack.'

Caio put out a hand. 'No, I'll do it.'

But Ana was already walking out of the kitchen and down the lawn, in a bid to escape. She slipped off her shoes and left them on the grass, and stepped onto the beach in her bare feet.

She spotted Caio's sweats and her night clothes. They looked flimsy in the daytime, and she couldn't quite believe she'd felt compelled to come down here and swim in the dark. A moment of insanity induced by lust.

Caio was right. It had been reckless and dangerous. But she could remember the feeling of needing to connect with some elemental force. And now that elemental force was within her and she would never be the same.

She sensed Caio behind her. The suspicion that he wasn't remotely fazed by last night and the fact that they would be parting ways made her feel desperate, and also devastated. Now she could understand why he'd been reluctant to sleep with her—because he'd known better than her that she would find herself in emotional turmoil.

Except he had no idea that her turmoil had far deeper roots than merely confusing sex with emotion or because he was her first lover. He had no idea she'd been falling for him over the last year. That this was no overnight sensation.

He couldn't know. He couldn't possibly ever know
how devastating this was for her. She'd already exposed
herself so much by seducing him that this would kill
her. And so, as he came alongside her, she affected an
expression of bland neutrality.

CHAPTER TWENTY

A year ago, Cristo Redentor Church, Rio de Janeiro

ANA DIAZ WAS LATE. Approximately ten minutes late. Which was perfectly respectable—expected, even—on a traditional wedding day, but this wasn't a traditional wedding, and Caio could feel a prickling sensation at the back of his neck.

He was acutely aware of the small congregation behind him, whispering and looking at him. Speculating. A sense of exposure crept over him when he thought of the fact that Rodolfo Diaz was a notoriously tricky individual to do business with, and Caio had only done so because he'd known that Diaz had more to lose than he did in their deal.

But now he wondered if he'd missed something. If he'd got it wrong. Perhaps the marriage set-up with his daughter, Ana, was some sort of distraction technique— she'd stand him up at the altar, publicly humiliate him, and wreck Caio's reputation with a view to undermining his business. After all, Diaz knew his weak spots—hence the suggestion of a convenient marriage.

Caio imagined his father gloating. He'd always hated the fact that Caio had left the family and made a fortune all on his own. He'd love to see his youngest son fall flat on his face. And nowhere better than in the middle of high society in Rio de Janeiro.

But just as he was beginning to fear the worst he heard the congregation hush behind him. The surge of relief caught him off guard. He turned around to see Ana on her father's arm in the church's entrance.

She cut a curiously traditional figure, in a long dress that covered her from neck to toe and shoulder to wrist. A veil covered her face. But he could see her long dark hair, drawn back from her face.

She started walking down the aisle. For the first time Caio could appreciate her figure. She was usually wearing something baggy, making him wonder what she was hiding. But even in this less than fashionable wedding dress he could see that she'd been disguising a slimly petite figure with tantalising curves.

He imagined her long dark hair tumbling down her narrow back and a spark of desire made his blood pulse. He immediately tensed against it. This marriage was not about desire. It was about business, pure and simple.

She'd reached him now and he could see her eyes under the veil, huge and dark. Something about the modesty of her dress caught at him. He realised that after years of seeing women parade in front of him in as little as possible there was something erotic about Ana's entire body being covered up.

And then he had to grit his jaw and exert control again. He wouldn't be peeling this dress off his new wife.

She was looking up at him from under her veil and Caio lifted it up and over the back of her head, revealing her face. The purity of her bone structure and the lush natural pout of her mouth gave him a sense in that moment that he might very easily underestimate this woman, and that it would be a mistake to do so.

Then he noticed that she looked irritated. He said, for her ears only, 'Okay?'

She gestured minutely towards where her father stood to one side. 'I'm sorry I'm late. He delayed us…just to prove some macho point to you or something, I'm sure.'

So Caio had been right. Diaz might not have gone so far as to ruin the wedding, but he wasn't above playing games. He had never expected Ana to be in his corner with such a lack of guile. He felt a surprising sense of kinship with her. Even though he barely knew her.

He took her small hand in his and said, 'Let's do this, shall we?'

Now she looked nervous, but determined. 'Okay.' And she turned to face the priest.

It took a long second for Caio to take his eyes off her face and turn to the front…

The memory of their wedding day lingered in Caio's head. He'd thought of it because looking at Ana's profile now, as she stared out to sea, reminded him of that day in the church for some reason.

Her profile looked serene. He knew he should be feeling serene too. He'd just experienced a night of unexpected and unbridled passion and now he was a free man again. His business had never been better, nor his prospects as good.

But he didn't feel serene. He had the same feeling he did when he hadn't prepared well enough for a business meeting and knew he was at a disadvantage or on the back foot. The same feeling he'd had when he'd realised that he was in danger of eroding his success unless he did something drastic.

Marrying Ana had been a drastic move. But it had also been the best decision he'd ever made.

She looked totally impenetrable. Even though they'd spent a year together, and last night had effectively smashed aside the last boundaries of intimacy, right now he felt as if he knew nothing about her. She was as much of a mystery as she'd been when they'd first married.

'What are you thinking about?' The fact that he'd had to ask that question because she wasn't simpering all over him irritated Caio.

Ana glanced at him and then away again. That irritated him too.

'Just about the fact that within a couple of days I'll be on the other side of the world, starting a whole new life.'

Caio felt something hard lodge in his chest. He should be cheering Ana on. He should be offering to make arrangements to rebook her flight. But that rudderless feeling was back. That feeling of needing to do something drastic.

For a man who had carved out a solitary path and made a huge success of it, he *should* be relishing this confirmation that she was okay with what had happened, and that she was happy to proceed with getting on with their separate lives.

He should be. But he wasn't.

He still wanted her.

The thought of her leaving, of not having her again, was…inconceivable. Caio was not used to not getting what he wanted. Yet here he was in this unique situation. Unprecedented. It had always been easy for him to say goodbye to a lover. But not this time.

He turned to face Ana. 'You don't have to go. You could stay.'

Ana went very still. Had she heard right? Or was her imagination playing tricks on her?

She forced herself to look at Caio. 'What did you say?'

He folded his arms over his chest. 'You could stay. You don't have to leave.'

'And do what, exactly?'

'Stay with me.'

Ana's heart thumped. 'We're divorced, Caio. In what capacity would I be staying with you?'

'As my lover.'

Ana hated the betraying bloom of hope deep inside when Caio wasn't really offering anything at all. Just a stay of execution. 'What do you think the gossips would make of that?'

'Since when did you care about society's opinion?'

That stung. Ana had to concede that, while she'd always disdained the world she'd been born into, she'd come to move within it in the past year with more ease than she'd like to admit. Sharing Caio's cynicism about many of the people in their world, she'd learnt not to take it so seriously. And she'd loved it that Caio's attitude to it all was to do his best to get the most out of people, to appeal to their very superficial sense of charity to extract as much money from them as possible and pass it on to worthy causes.

'You've spent a year in a marriage of convenience,' she pointed out. 'In order to shore up your reputation. And now you're willing to jeopardise it all? Just for sex?'

Caio's face flushed. 'This chemistry is…insane, Ana. I've never experienced anything like it. It's more than just sex.'

Ana's heart palpitated. *Exactly.* It was more than just sex. The stubborn bloom of hope was back. 'What exactly are you offering, Caio?'

'A chance to let this play out.'

A chance to let this play out. The bloom of hope faded again.

Ana folded her arms too. 'How long would you see this "playing out"?'

'A week…a month…who knows?'

The old hurt of abandonment and a sense of vulnerability made Ana say, 'What about a year? You managed to keep your hands off me for a whole year, Caio. Clearly I wasn't all that irresistible. Are you sure it's not just the island air going to your head?'

Caio's face tightened. 'I respected you, Ana. I didn't want to blur the lines.'

'So you don't respect the women you sleep with?'

Caio cursed. 'Of course I do. I didn't mean it like that.'

'But it's okay to sleep with me now because we're no longer married. Marriage really is a passion-killer for you, isn't it?'

Angry with herself for feeling torn by Caio's suggestion—tempted, but also devastated anew because it was more than obvious that he wasn't interested in more—Ana was galvanised to move. She picked up the strewn clothes from the beach and began to walk back up to the villa.

Caio was behind her. In the kitchen, Ana put the clothes into the washing machine and turned it on.

He said, 'So that's it, then? You're not interested?'

Ana stopped, but didn't turn to face him. *Not interested?* Her heart twisted. He had no idea. Every cell in her body clamoured at the sound of his voice. Her blood simmered. Between her legs she ached to feel him slide there again, thrusting so deep inside her she couldn't breathe. She knew she'd never experience that again. And it was heartbreaking.

She thought of something and went into the den. She found the picture and picked it up, then took it over to Caio. She held it out.

He said, 'What's this?'

Ana pushed it towards him. 'Look at it.'

He sighed, took it and looked. It was a photo of Luca Fonseca and his wife. She was heavily pregnant and sitting on his lap. They were both oblivious to the camera, looking at each other intently. His hand was on her bump. It was incredibly intimate and it had caught Ana's eye when Estella had been showing them around.

Ana knew she couldn't pretend that she was blasé about what had happened and about what she wanted.

She said, 'That's what I want, Caio. I want forever. In spite of everything I know, and in spite of everything I witnessed. My own mother walked away from me without looking back. I can't put myself through that again. Not for an affair.' She looked at Caio. 'You were right. We shouldn't have slept together. But I don't think you'll have any problem moving on. Now I'm going to pack and wait for the helicopter to come.'

CHAPTER TWENTY-ONE

For a long moment Caio just stood in the same spot, looking at the empty space Ana had left, holding the picture in his hand. He looked down at it again, feeling a little numb. At first he hadn't quite been able to make it out, almost as if it was in another language—as if he literally couldn't understand what he was seeing.

A couple. *Happiness. Intimacy. Family.* And something else he wasn't willing to name.

He couldn't think straight. Ana's words *'I don't think you'll have any problem moving on'* reverberated sickeningly in his head.

The was a massive pressure building up inside him, and he had to move or it would explode. He put the picture down on a table and went back outside, paced up and down.

He'd asked Ana to stay, to continue this affair...and she'd said no. Not something Caio was used to where women were concerned. She'd said, *'I want forever.'* But not with him, evidently.

Not that he wanted forever. Ever since he'd been small and he and his brothers had been dominated and bullied by their father, and he'd seen his mother browbeaten and worse, he'd fostered an aversion to the notion of happy families and marriage. It didn't exist.

But when he'd believed that his mother was going to break away, prove him wrong, Caio had been surprised to find himself thinking that perhaps there could be some hope for a different existence. For choosing happiness.

That hope hadn't lived long. His mother had chosen to go back into a toxic situation, citing love as a reason. It had solidified Caio's beliefs that love and marriage spelled nothing but dysfunction.

Forever. What even *was* that? Ana knew as well as he did that it wasn't possible for people like them.

But then Caio's gut twisted. Maybe it was possible for her. Because she wasn't infected with his cynicism.

The picture of Luca Fonseca and his wife haunted him. He didn't know them well, so he couldn't attest to how authentic their union was, but he had a sick feeling that that picture was real, and if it was real, it upended a lot of Caio's assertions. Shifted the bedrock of his foundation. That he survived better alone. That love and marriage were toxic. That he didn't need anyone by his side.

You've had someone by your side for a year now, a little voice reminded him.

For the first few events it had felt strange, having someone by his side, someone he had to look out for. It had almost felt like an intrusion. But then…it hadn't.

He thought back to one of their first big events in Europe. London. A gala benefit dinner supporting a charity that helped disadvantaged young people to embrace technology and foster new talent in those who didn't have the advantages that someone like Caio had had.

Ana had gone to the restroom and the crowd had started to move into the main ballroom for dinner. There had been no sign of her. Irritation had prickled under

Caio's skin. With hindsight, he could appreciate that his irritation hadn't just been down to the fact that he wasn't a solo operator any more…it had also been down to the fact that Ana had had her makeover that day, and the shock of her much sleeker and more elegant look had unsettled Caio in a way he hadn't liked at all.

As he'd waited for her in that hotel his irritation had mounted, and an insidious thought had entered Caio's head: *she's becoming a distraction*.

And then he'd seen her, and she'd been with a young man. Caio hadn't been prepared for the surge of something hot and volatile inside him. *Jealousy*. It had only been when they'd got closer that he'd realised the young man was actually a teenager and he looked incredibly nervous.

Ana, clearly putting the young boy at ease, had introduced him to Caio as a huge fan, and Caio had felt the volatility drain away. That evening something had shifted between them. He'd stopped feeling her presence was an intrusion. The distraction had remained, but he'd countered that by using their public appearances as an excuse to touch her. Reaching for her hand. Pulling her into his side.

He recognised now that he'd lived for those moments. He'd engineered them by accepting invitations to events that he wasn't even interested in. Yet he'd never admitted that to himself before now. He'd been too much of a coward to acknowledge his growing attraction. To admit that his wife of convenience was impacting on him in a profound way.

It had only been in the past month, since it had become harder and harder to remain immune to her, that he'd resisted touching her for fear of revealing himself.

Last night had blasted apart the illusion that he'd ever

had any sense of control around Ana. He'd lost control a long time ago. What had happened between them in the last twenty-four hours had been a foregone conclusion for months. *Since the moment they'd met.*

Much to his shame and disgust, Caio was forced to admit now that Ana had had to be the one to initiate the seduction. Because he'd been in the grip of a desire so intense he couldn't have contemplated a rejection. So he'd let her come to him, and he'd resisted and resisted until he was sure that he was risking nothing. Except he'd risked everything.

Because for the first time in his life with a woman his emotions were at stake.

Caio stopped pacing as that sank in. As the full enormity of it gripped him.

At that moment he heard a distinctive noise in the distance, and before he could think about what he was doing he acted on an impulse too strong to ignore.

Ana frowned at the sky from her bedroom balcony. Where on earth was the helicopter going? It had been on a steady path towards the island, but suddenly it had banked to the right and now it was going back in the opposite direction.

Not that she'd noted the arrival of it with relief—more a sense of futility and loss. Annoyingly.

She also noticed that the security boats were gone. She was confused. She felt as if she should jump up and down and shout. Wave a bright-coloured shirt in the air. But they knew they were here…what were they doing?

Suddenly a suspicion formed. *Caio.* He was a man used to getting his own way.

Fuelled by a sense of anger, and far more betrayingly

by excitement and hope, Ana left her things on the bed and went downstairs.

She found Caio in the kitchen, putting his phone back into his pocket. He turned around. Ana tried to ignore how her heart hitched.

'Why is the helicopter not landing?'

'I told them to go back to Rio and await further instructions. We're not done here, Ana.'

She'd been right. Anger at his high-handedness made her put her hands on her hips. 'Who do you think you are to make that decision on my behalf?'

Caio mirrored her, putting his hands on his hips. 'The man you chose...no, *begged* to be your first lover.'

Ana flushed with self-consciousness. 'I'm beginning to regret my decision.'

Caio took his hands down and moved closer. 'Are you really?'

Ana took a step back and put a hand out. 'Don't come near me, Caio.'

'Why? Because you can't think straight if I'm near you? Because you're afraid of what you'll do?'

Ana scooted around the kitchen island so that it was between them. She wasn't afraid of him; it was of herself she was terrified. He was right. Damn him.

She realised that Caio looked a little wild. As if his civilised veneer had been cracked open, revealing the elemental man she'd met last night.

'I would have thought you'd be delighted to return to work. To your life in Rio. Your usual lovers.'

'What life would that be, hmm? The life I led before? Where I cut myself off from my family and was dumped by women and friends who'd only accepted me for my family connections? And yet those were the first people who rushed back when I made my first million? Lovers who saw only the status I could offer them, and the expensive trinkets? Lovers who had no interest in who I really was? The life where I took my mother's name, casting aside hundreds of years of legacy, and worked twenty-four-seven to build up a business that needed a marriage of convenience to take it to the next level? A business that will die with me? Rendering everything I've done as futile?'

Surprised at his outburst, Ana said, 'It won't be futile. You've created innovations that will last forever.'

He waved a hand. 'They'll last until someone comes up with a better idea.' Then he continued, 'Or perhaps I should return to the life I've had for the past year, with a wife of convenience who turned out to be not as convenient as I expected?'

Ana swallowed. There was something dangerously exciting about this far more volatile Caio. 'You no longer have a wife. We're divorced, remember?'

Caio glanced down at her hand. 'You haven't stopped wearing your rings.'

Ana blinked and looked down to see the gold band and the very plain round cut diamond engagement ring that Caio had insisted she pick out for herself. She hadn't removed them.

She reached for them now, feeling exposed, but Caio said, 'Don't. Wait.'

CHAPTER TWENTY-TWO

ANA'S FINGERS WERE on the rings. She felt angry with Caio for delaying the inevitable. She pulled them off and put them on the island between them. 'Why would you not want me to take them off? We're no longer married.'

Caio ran his hands through his hair, clearly agitated. He looked at Ana. 'I thought I had it all mapped out—that I knew exactly what I wanted. You would be the perfect accompaniment, taking me to the next level, and in return you'd get your own freedom, and your brother's.' He started to pace back and forth. 'But then it wasn't just that I got used to you by my side. I began to *need* it. I told myself it wasn't that at all. That I just appreciated your opinion and the company you provided. I told myself I wasn't coming to depend on you...' He stopped pacing and looked at her. 'Do you remember when you had that tummy bug in Kuala Lumpur?'

Ana nodded. She'd seen that city through the triple-glazed glass of her bathroom and bedroom as she'd succumbed to a violent but thankfully short-lived stomach bug. It had meant, though, that she hadn't been able to attend one of the events with Caio.

'We'd only attended a few events by then, but when you weren't there...it bothered me. And it bothered me that it bothered me. I didn't like how you'd inserted yourself into my life so seamlessly. How I already felt a reflex to turn to you and see if you were okay. See your reaction to something. To *need* you by my side. I'd been coping fine for years. I didn't need anyone. But suddenly... I did.'

Ana swallowed. Not sure how to respond. She could remember how Caio had been a bit more distant than usual with her for a couple of weeks after that. She'd seen it as a judgement on her far too human frailties. But it hadn't been that at all.

She said, 'I didn't know. At every event I was just concentrating on not tripping over my own feet or saying something stupid.'

'I know. And you did yourself a disservice. You are a natural, warm person, and people gravitated to you because of that. You did more than help me enhance my business, Ana, you made *me* look like a better person.'

Ana's chest felt tight. 'You are a good person, Caio.'

He snorted. 'My focus has been singularly on myself—satisfying passing desires and building my own brand to the exclusion of thinking about anything or anyone else.'

'You thought about me,' Ana pointed out.

And he had. They could have lived very separate existences during their marriage, literally coming together only for public events. After all, that had been the agreement laid out in the marriage contract. But over the months they'd naturally gravitated towards spending more time together outside of those public appearances.

Caio had begun joining her for dinner in the evenings when nothing else was planned. Watching a documentary or a movie with her. And on days in foreign cities when he'd had to work, he'd always arranged for her to be taken on a tour with a private guide.

She said, almost to herself, 'There was that day in Paris...'

Caio looked at her. 'I think that was the start of it. I was finding it harder and harder to leave you to your own devices.'

They'd been in Paris and he'd arranged, as usual, for her to be taken to see the sights with a guide. He'd called her to see how she was getting on, and he'd sounded so wistful about her excursion that she'd joked, 'Why don't you join us?'

And he had. Ana had nearly fallen off her seat in the boat on the Seine when they'd made a stop to let him on. He'd dismissed the private guide and confided a little sheepishly that he'd been to Paris many times, but never seen the sights.

That day, they'd visited the Eiffel Tower, the Musée d'Orsay and the Louvre. And at one point, not thinking, Ana had taken Caio's hand—a moment borne out of excitement and appreciation for everything she was experiencing. She'd soon realised with a hot and cold flash of embarrassment what she'd done, and that it would serve no purpose, and she had pulled away saying, 'Sorry, I forgot for a moment...'

But Caio had held on and she'd looked up at him, her pulse suddenly going crazy. There'd been an arrested expression on his face, as if he too had forgotten, and then his grip had relaxed. The next time she'd pulled away he'd let her go.

That was when Ana had realised that she had to be more careful around him.

She felt dangerously close to exposing herself all over again now.

She shook her head. 'Caio…what's going on? Why are we still here?'

As if talking to himself, Caio said, 'You know, everything might still be okay if last night hadn't happened. You know why I resisted you for so long?'

Ana shook her head. Caio was moving slowly around the kitchen island. She was rooted to the spot.

'Because I knew that you were different. I knew that from the start. And I knew that if I gave in to the temptation to seduce you it would blow everything apart.'

'You didn't want me on our wedding night.'

His gaze narrowed on her face. The island no longer separated them. He was just a few feet away. 'When I saw you in that wedding dress—'

Ana ducked her head. 'That dress was awful. So unfashionable.'

Caio's bare feet came into her line of vision. His fingers tipped her face up. He shook his head. 'I've had fantasies about that dress. On our wedding night it was easy for me to pretend that the erotic charge I'd felt was some kind of aberration. But it didn't go away. It only grew stronger. Why do you think I threw myself into work so much? It was easier to deny my desire if I wasn't with you. But then it got harder to stay away.'

Ana pulled Caio's hand down and stepped back. Anger resurging—at the things he was saying, at the thought that the undercurrents she'd sensed between them hadn't all been in her head, a figment of her imagination.

'Why are you saying this now, Caio? What's the point?'

He looked grim. 'Because last night effectively blew the façade that everything was okay to pieces.'

'What's that supposed to mean?' Ana asked a little shakily.

'It means that this isn't over.'

Ana shook her head. 'Caio, I've already told you—'

'You've told me nothing. All you've done is point to a picture and say that you want *forever*.'

Ana gulped. 'I meant what I said.'

Caio's expression was stark. 'You're telling me you're able to walk away from what we started last night? That if I was to kiss you right now we wouldn't be making love right here within minutes?'

A wave of heat pulsed through her body.

'Are you telling me that was enough for you?' he demanded.

Anger at Caio's insistence on pushing Ana to expose herself utterly made her say angrily, 'No, it's not enough for me. But the problem is that it never will be, Caio. I knew from the moment we kissed that I was ruined. And I know after last night that the thought of another man touching me would make me sick.'

Tears stung Ana's eyes. She'd hoped and prayed that she could at least get off the island with her dignity intact. But now Caio would know everything and—

'Good.'

CHAPTER TWENTY-THREE

GOOD? THE WORD stopped Ana's whirling thoughts dead. She blinked back her emotion. Caio was looking smug. Anger turned to rage, because he was *loving* it that he'd ruined her for anyone else while he would just blithely go back to normal.

Ana lifted up an apple and threw it at him. It bounced off his shoulder.

He frowned. 'Hey, what's that for?'

She picked up another piece of fruit—a clementine. 'You arrogant, smug so-and-so.'

She fired the fruit at him, but he caught it.

She continued. 'You're so egotistical that you want to make sure I'll never think of another man again, while you can just take up where you left off and bask in the knowledge that I'll never forget you.'

She punctuated this by firing another piece of fruit in his direction. This time a plum. It missed by a mile. Caio started advancing on her again. She picked up a banana and held it threateningly.

He said, 'What are you going to do? Shoot me?'

Ana scowled and threw the banana down. She stopped moving back. 'What's your plan, Caio? To make me admit that I still want you? Well, I already have. To take me to bed again until you've got me out of your system? So you can get on with your life? Well, that's not going to happen. Call the helicopter back this minute. I'm ready to go.'

Ana had somehow backed herself into a corner. Caio was still advancing. She had nowhere to run or hide. She put up a hand to stop him, but he swatted it out of his way and scooped her up as if she weighed nothing, sat her on the island and wedged himself firmly between her legs.

Ana couldn't speak.

'That's better,' he said.

Ana opened her mouth, but he put a finger to her lips.

'Now, are you ready to listen to why I said *good*?'

Ana folded her arms. But it was impossible to ignore Caio. His face was inches from hers, and his lean hips were wedged between her thighs. She could smell him and, *Deus*, she wanted to touch him.

He was waiting for her to speak. She threw her arms up. 'Fine. I can't move anyway.'

His mouth twitched, but then he became serious. 'The reason I said *good* is because I feel exactly the same way. You have ruined me forever—but it is a beautiful ruin that I will take over and over again. The thought of ever touching another woman makes me feel panicky and nauseous all at once. From the moment we met, Ana, no other woman has interested me.'

Ana could feel the colour draining from her face. 'But I was wearing leggings…and a T-shirt.'

'And hiding behind your hair.'

Ana couldn't say another word. She just looked at Caio.

He went on. 'As for the thought of another man touching you—that makes me feel violent. And that scares me, because I do not want to resemble my father in any way.'

Ana touched Caio's face. 'You're nothing like your father.'

He turned his head and placed a kiss to the middle of the palm of her hand. She drew it back, still not entirely sure what was going on in spite of the way he was looking at her and the things he was saying. It was too huge. Too much of a sea-change.

As if sensing her trepidation, Caio said, 'You asked me about children, a family…asked me what was the point of my success there's no one to leave it all to. I've always rejected the idea of family because of my own toxic example, and I rejected the notion of legacy because that's what our families are built on—and look at what they've become… But I've come to realise that they might have started out with a very positive idea of legacy, but success and greed twisted them. You were right, Ana. What *is* the point of all this work—of extricating myself from my family and taking my mother's name—if I can't share it with someone else, or some day, hand it down to the next generation. They might not want it, but that's okay.'

Ana found her voice. 'They…? Who is *they*?'

'Our children.'

Suddenly it was too much. It was as if she was in some parallel dimension and Caio was articulating all her most secret fantasies. Except she'd never even allowed herself to indulge in this one.

She pushed at Caio until he moved back, and then slid down off the counter and escaped back to the other side of the island. She needed space. Air.

'What you're saying is… It's too much, Caio. I don't know if I believe you. Only yesterday you were saying that you don't believe in marriage or family. That that was why you wanted a marriage of convenience. Yet now...'

Caio looked at Ana. He saw the distrust in her eyes. On her face. And something else. A yearning. His insides twisted. It was all so clear to him now, but not to her, and he had a sickening sense that no matter what he said she wouldn't believe him. And he couldn't really blame her. After all, he'd done a spectacular job for the last few months—and hours—of living in a state of denial.

He ran a hand through his hair. 'Look, Ana, I know this is hard to grasp, but everything I'm saying has been here...' he touched his chest '...building up.' He cursed silently. It sounded weak to his own ears.

She lifted her chin. 'Last night, *I* seduced *you*. I'll never know if you would have seduced me.'

The hum of desire inside Caio refuted that. 'I was a coward. I wanted you too much to risk trying to seduce you and you rejecting me.'

Ana's eyes widened. '*You* were scared of *me* rejecting *you*.' Her tone was flat. She folded her arms. 'What if last night hadn't happened?'

'I think I would have lasted about a week before following you to Amsterdam and seducing you into coming back to Rio.'

He knew that now. The absence of Ana would have thrown everything into sharp relief.

He said, 'All last night did was accelerate the process.'

Ana shook her head. 'I don't believe you.'

Caio seized on something he'd forgotten about. 'So why did I book to go to a conference in Dublin in ten days' time? A conference that has asked me to deliver the keynote speech every year for the past five years, and this year I said yes.'

Ana looked doubtful.

Caio's guts clenched. 'In case it's not obvious by now… I love you, Ana. And, believe me, no one is more surprised than me that I'm saying those words. But, quite simply, the thought of you leaving, of you being out in the world without me, is terrifying. Why do you think that gang targeted us? They'd been following us for months…they saw something that we weren't even ready to admit to ourselves. They knew I'd do whatever it took to get you back.'

Ana looked at him for a long moment. Her face was pale. Eyes huge. Eventually she said, 'You see, the thing is, Caio, that I've loved you for some time now. In spite of my best instincts and my attempts to stop myself from falling for you because I knew you were all wrong for me. And it wasn't as if you gave me any encouragement. But I fell for you anyway. Maybe you believe you love me for now, after last night…but you're the one who warned me about confusing sex with emotion, Caio. Maybe you need to take your own advice.'

She turned and walked out of the villa, but not before he'd seen the glint of emotion in her eyes.

Not for the first time in twenty-four hours, Caio felt helpless. A hollow ache spread through him. A sense of futility. His dogged cynicism and strong sense of self-preservation mocked him mercilessly. He'd not only convinced himself that he was above such mortal concerns as love and connection…he'd convinced Ana too.

CHAPTER TWENTY-FOUR

ANA STOOD ON the beach looking out to sea. Funny how she kept gravitating to this place. *Caio had told her he loved her.* How she'd managed to walk away from him after he'd said that, she wasn't sure. Her legs still felt like jelly. But she couldn't afford to believe him. The risk was too huge. If her own mother could turn her back on her and walk away, then a man who'd briefly confused passion and sex with emotion could do far worse.

And it would be infinitely more painful this time.

She'd never heal from it and she'd become as cynical and self-protective as him.

That thought made her stop.

It made her think about a young boy growing up—superfluous to requirements, all but ignored by his father and brothers, with a brittle mother living in the shadow of her domineering husband.

She thought of Caio watching that. Absorbing it. Seeing the moment when his mother had decided to take a chance and fight for her own survival only to go back, proving to Caio that any attempt to find one's own emotional happiness was just not worth it. And then his experience at the hands of his first lover.

She knew where his bone-deep cynicism came from.

That was why she couldn't trust that he'd let it go so quickly. No matter how much she wanted to.

The sun was rising into the sky. It was almost exactly twenty-four hours since they'd signed the papers in Rio.

She would have to be strong. She would have to tell Caio that—

She heard a noise behind her and tensed. She started to turn around, but Caio said, 'Don't turn around. Not yet.'

Ana stayed where she was.

For a long moment Caio said nothing, and then, 'I know what you're thinking. That it's too much too soon. That you can't trust that I mean what I say.'

Ana was glad that she was facing away from Caio, that he couldn't see her expression.

'The truth is that this isn't something that's just happened. It started when we first met, Ana. On our wedding day when you walked down the aisle in that dress. And when you said to me that you were sorry for being late.' He continued, 'I know you hated that dress, and I know you felt uncomfortable and unfashionable. But *I* found that dress erotic. I had fantasies about the wedding night we never got to share. Fantasies about stripping that dress off you and baring your body to my gaze.'

He made a small sound—a curt, laughing noise.

'I put those thoughts down to some weird reaction to getting married. But every day you were sinking deeper and deeper into my head and my blood. You fascinated me. Your habits. Your interests. I'd never spent so much time with a woman in a platonic setting. But what I was feeling for you wasn't platonic. And yet... you became my friend too, Ana. The first real friend I ever had. I always shut everyone out. Rejected them before they could reject me. And I know you can appreciate that because you did it too. Except you were lucky—you had Francisco.

'You crept under my skin in such a way that it took me until our divorce, with the prospect of you walking away, for me to fully acknowledge just how integral you'd become to my life. To me. And it took last night and blowing the world to pieces for me to realise that what I feel for you goes so much deeper than transient desire. There's nothing transient about how you make me feel, Ana.'

Ana only realised she was holding her breath when her body forced her to take a huge shuddering breath in, making her light-headed.

Caio said, 'I know what your mother's rejection did to you. I can't even imagine that pain. And yet you're brave, because you're not letting it define you. You know you want more, and you won't rest until you find it. You're infinitely braver than me. I know you, Ana. I know every part of you. I love how you came out of your shell and blossomed into the beautiful woman you are. I love how you've realised that you can navigate our world with more skill and ease than you'd like to admit because otherwise it means that somehow *they've* won. But they haven't won. You've won. Because you navigate society with humanity and compassion—and that's the difference. I love experiencing the world with you. And I can't keep pretending that I don't want forever too. I was done with my emotionally empty existence a long time before I acknowledged it. I'm tired of the cynicism and jadedness. I want more. Joy. Happiness. *You*. Forever.'

Ana's vision was blurry. With every word Caio dismantled the last of her defences. Even if it turned out that this was all an elaborate play to keep her in his bed just for as long as he wanted her then she knew she couldn't refuse. He'd broken her.

'You can turn around now.'

Wiping her eyes, Ana slowly turned around—but Caio wasn't there. It took her a second to realise he was kneeling down, and she had to adjust her eyeline.

She frowned. 'Caio…?'

He was looking incredibly nervous, and was holding her wedding and engagement rings in the palm of his hand. Ana's heart skipped.

'Ana Diaz, will you marry me? For real this time? And not just for a year, but until death us do part. Because anything less won't do for me.'

Ana's legs went from jelly to water. She collapsed onto her knees in front of Caio. He reached for her and she went into his arms in the same breath, the two of them falling back onto the sand, his body cushioning hers, a hard-muscled cushion.

She looked down at him. 'Caio…'

She realised she had a torrent of words to say—voicing all her doubts and insecurities and fears. The enduring vision of her mother walking away. Her father's indifference. Feeling insecure. Vulnerable. But now those things faded away. She felt strong. Invincible. No matter what.

All the words melted on her tongue. Except for one. *'Yes.'*

His eyes widened. His arms tightened around her. 'Ana…?'

She smiled at his shock. At his very uncharacteristic insecurity. 'Yes, Caio. *Yes.* Let's get married again— for real this time.'

Suddenly Ana was on her back on the sand and

Caio was hovering over her, looking intense. 'Ana, I... You...'

She took pity on him and put a finger to his mouth. 'Just kiss me, Caio. We have a lot of catching up to do.'

His gaze went to her mouth, hungry. He lowered his head, Ana wrapped her arms around his neck, and they kissed for a long time, until the tide reached their feet.

Before they left the beach Ana held out her hand and Caio put the rings back onto her finger. The enormity of what had happened here within twenty-four hours caught at her heart. But Caio was right. It hadn't been twenty-four hours—it had been happening for a year.

They walked back into the villa barefoot, clothes dishevelled, hand in hand. At the doorway Ana said, 'What about the helicopter?'

Caio pulled her close. 'It's on standby for whenever we need it. There's no rush, is there?'

Ana looped her arms around his neck and pressed close, revelling in the evidence of his desire for her. 'No rush at all. Take me to bed, Caio.'

Caio scooped Ana into his arms and carried her through the villa to the bedroom. They made love and whispered vows and promises, told each other of all the things they'd keep secret for so long.

And finally, about a week later, when the food ran out, they called for the helicopter to come and get them.

A month later, Civil Register Office, Rio de Janeiro

Ana stood outside the main doors of the register office. She was nervous. Her brother Francisco, whom Caio had flown home for today, took her hands.

'Ana, *why* are you wearing that hideous dress again?'

Ana giggled and hiccupped at the same time, emotion high in her chest. 'It's a private thing.'

Her brother shook his head and put her arm in his. 'Straight people are so weird,' he muttered.

Ana was wearing her wedding dress again. On strict instructions from her fiancé, who had told her in forensic detail how he wanted to dispense with it later.

A flash of gold and yellow caught her eye and she looked down to see the new engagement ring he'd surprised her with when they'd eventually returned to Rio from the island. A square yellow diamond in a gold setting.

He had her gold wedding band, and she had his.

Her hair was up in a loose knot. She wore small diamond earrings. Minimal make-up. Carried a small posy of seasonal flowers.

In the seconds before the doors opened Ana had a flashback to her first wedding day, when she'd stood outside the church doors with her father. She'd never really admitted it to herself before now, but she'd felt an incredible sense of loss that day. The loss of a dream she'd harboured so deeply that she'd been too afraid to acknowledge it. A dream of walking down the aisle towards someone she loved. Who loved her. Towards a life that she'd never experienced but which she still hoped existed.

She hadn't seen Caio in twenty-four hours, because he'd had a business meeting in Sao Paulo and they'd both wanted to observe the tradition of not seeing each other before the wedding.

Except last night Ana had been beset by doubts and fears. She knew how long twenty-four hours could be. After all, their lives had changed in twenty-four hours on that island. What if all it took for Caio to realise he was making a huge mistake was another twenty-four hours?

She hated herself for feeling so insecure.

The doors to the register office suddenly opened and Francisco squeezed her hand. The second Ana's eyes met Caio's all her doubts and fears melted into a pool of heat. Love swelled in her chest, making it tight.

His molten gaze held hers until she reached him, and then he took her hand, acknowledged Francisco briefly, before pulling Ana into his side. Oblivious to the registrar, he said, 'I missed you… I was afraid—'

Ana felt tears prick her eyes. 'I know…me too.'

Caio kissed Ana until an insistent coughing broke through the intense bubble they were in. They came up for air and the registrar began proceedings.

Afterwards, when the rabid press had got their fill of pictures of Caio and Ana's remarriage, and after they'd danced and drunk wine and celebrated, Caio carried a deliciously dishevelled Ana into the bedroom in their apartment.

He put her down on her feet by the bed and stood back. Ana devoured him with her eyes. His white shirt, open at the top. Black trousers. Stubble lining his jaw.

His gaze devoured her right back. Travelling down over her breasts to her waist and hips. To her bare feet.

Ana squirmed slightly. She wanted to be out of the dress so they were skin on skin…but Caio had other ideas.

He came towards her and shook his head. 'I've been waiting for a long time for this moment.'

He turned her around and started undoing the small buttons at the back of the dress. Ana shivered slightly as the cool air touched her skin, followed by Caio's mouth and tongue.

Already breathless, she said plaintively, 'I really don't mind if you just want to rip it off...'

Caio put his hands on her waist and pressed a kiss to the side of her neck. 'Oh, no, meu amor, there will be no ripping...'

His hands came up to cup her breasts under the lacy material. Ana squirmed, pushing her bottom against him. But Caio showed more restraint than her and, as promised, it was a long and slow and deliciously tor-turous process.

When the dress was finally dispensed with, and lying in a pool of silk and lace on the floor, Ana was fever-ish with lust.

Caio seated himself between her legs and entwined his fingers with hers, holding her hands above her head. He thrust deep into her body and she arched against him. She'd never felt so full, so impaled... Their eyes met and Caio started to move, never taking his eyes off hers.

Words trembled on her lips.

Caio pressed a kiss to her mouth and said huskily, 'I know, love. Me too. Forever.'

Pleasure broke Ana into a million pieces, with Caio following just seconds later. He tucked her into his body and she pressed a kiss to his shoulder. She whispered an echo of love against his skin. 'Forever.'

EPILOGUE

Five years later

'ANA DIAZ SALAZAR.'

Everyone clapped as Ana got up from her seat and walked to the podium in her black gown and cap, the golden tassel swinging beside her beaming face. Her hair was glossy and longer now, falling below her shoulders in loose waves.

She wore a cream floaty wrap dress underneath the gown, and high heels. The only jewellery she wore was a pair of diamond drop earrings, her wedding ring and engagement ring. Someone indiscreet behind Caio noted waspily that for a billionaire's wife she wasn't exactly blingy, but she was very pretty.

Caio turned around to the gossipers, smiled benevolently, and said, 'She's the most beautiful woman in the world. She doesn't need adornment.'

The two women nearly fell off their chairs.

Caio turned back to see Ana shaking the hand of the president of the university and accepting her first class honours degree. She smiled for the cameras. And then the moment Caio had hoped they would avoid happened, when their three-year-old daughter Luna woke up abruptly and spotted Ana on the stage.

'Look! Mama!'

Ana saw them and Caio smiled at her minute eye-roll. His heart expanded with love and pride as she rejoined her fellow classmates and they waited for the rest of the ceremony to finish.

After Ana had said emotional goodbyes to friends and professors, and had handed back her ceremonial gown and cap, she went looking for Caio and Luna. He'd taken their daughter outside in case she was too noisy.

She spotted them before they saw her. They were down by the river which ran along the bottom of a beautiful landscaped lawn. The air was laden with the scent of flowers and cut grass. Students posed with families and smiled. Other students, not graduating, sat on the grass and ate lunch, or discussed lectures.

Ana's eyes went back to Caio and Luna. Two dark heads together as he held her safely while she squealed and pointed at the ducks. Ana's hand went to her chest for a minute, to try and contain her emotion as the full impact of the scene she was looking at sank in.

Caio had done this. Given her a chance to pursue her dream. To give her wings. But to keep her rooted at the same time—rooted in his unconditional love and security.

This was what she'd always dreamt of, and it was so much more than she'd ever believed might be possible. And there was more. She put a hand to her belly and the growing bump under her dress. She was almost five months pregnant with their second child. The light flutters of the last couple of weeks were getting stronger daily.

As if sensing her regard, Caio turned his head and found her unerringly. As he always did. He stood up, taking Luna into his arms, and Ana walked down towards them and straight into his arms. *Home.*

He drew her in for a kiss, and Ana relished his scent and the steely strength of his body. She could feel the inevitable spark of desire, still there, as strong as ever.

Reading her mind, Caio smirked at her. 'Wait till I get you home, Mrs Salazar.'

She winked at him. 'Promises, promises...'

Luna launched herself at Ana, wrapping her small arms around her neck, and Ana buried her face in Luna's neck, making her laugh when she nuzzled her. Their daughter had her father's dark golden eyes and dark hair, and it took all their collective wits to keep up with her.

Caio said softly, 'I'm so proud of you.'

Ana's vision blurred a little. 'I'm proud of me too.'

Her husband took her hand and kissed it. 'You should be—you've worked hard.'

Caio took Luna back into his arms and held Ana's hand as he led her through the leafy and idyllic grounds of the university to the waiting car that would take them back to the townhouse he'd bought in Mayfair when he'd suggested moving to London, so that Ana could pursue her dream of studying and getting a degree in an English university.

For the last four years Caio had based his head office in London and had commuted to far flung places only when absolutely necessary. And only when Ana's schedule had allowed her to travel with him.

They hadn't planned on Ana getting pregnant so soon, but inevitably their insane chemistry had led to increasingly lax efforts to protect her against pregnancy—*et voilà*, Luna.

Luna had been very obliging—her due date had been

after Ana's first-year exams. And Caio had taken to fatherhood like a duck to water, regularly taking Luna to work in a papoose, and setting up a creche in his building to facilitate employees with families.

Ana would have been jealous of their bond if it didn't make her so happy that their daughter would experience the kind of father/daughter relationship she and her brother had never had. Nor Caio.

But within the next few weeks they were moving back to Rio, so that Caio could refocus his energies on South America, now that he was firmly established in Europe and North America. Ana had ambitions to set up a publishing company, specialising in nurturing new voices in fiction from all over the world. And, they had an island waiting for them to spend some serious family downtime together.

Caio had surprised Ana on the first anniversary of their second wedding, when he'd taken her back to the island for a holiday and presented her with a piece of paper.

She'd unfolded it, but hadn't understood what she was looking at for a long moment. Eventually she'd choked out, 'You've bought the island from Luca Fonseca? For...*me*?'

Caio had nodded. 'I've had it renamed Ilha Ana. It's yours.'

Ana hadn't been able to speak for a long moment, and then she'd launched herself at Caio. She was pretty sure that what had happened next had resulted in their daughter, born approximately nine months later.

Later that evening, after the graduation, Caio surprised Ana with a celebratory dinner, together with her brother Francisco and his new partner, in one of London's most exclusive restaurants with views over the sparkling city.

When they'd returned to the house and checked on Luna—flat on her back, snoring gently—they went to their own bedroom and Ana, still emotional, turned to Caio.

'Thank you—not just for this evening, but for…everything. The last few years… No one has ever believed in me like you do. I would never have had the nerve to do it all without you.'

Caio tipped Ana's chin up. He looked serious. 'Yes, you would. You're one of the bravest people I know. This was all *you*. I followed you here, my love, and I'd follow you to the ends of the earth.'

Ana shook her head, protesting, but before she could say another word Caio was taking something out of his pocket. A small square velvet box. Ridiculously, he looked nervous.

'Caio…?'

He opened the box to reveal a simple gold ring studded with tiny diamonds. He said, 'It's an eternity ring. Because I will love you and want you for all eternity, Ana Diaz Salazar. Every day I marvel that I kept my distance from you for that whole year, but that was because I knew deep down that the minute I touched you I'd be yours. It took twenty-four hours for me to fall so deep and so hard that my life changed forever. You taught me that being cynical was a very weak protection and that love exists.'

Ana's eyes stung with emotion.

Caio took the ring out of the box, but before he put it on Ana's finger he showed her the inscription on the inside. It said, in beautifully delicate calligraphy, *One Night is Forever. Ana & Caio*. There was a date too—

the date they'd spent that first night on the island. The night they'd been reborn.

Ana said in a choked voice, 'It's beautiful.'

Caio slipped it onto her finger and Ana wound her arms around his neck, pressing close, her curves melting against his hardness.

'I love you, Caio, and I want to spend my one night with you every night. Forever.'

He smiled. 'Forever it is.'

That night melted into many more days and nights, filled with their growing family and a love that only grew more rooted. Their names were added to the urban legend of a very few others that were spoken about in hushed, disbelieving tones—because they were the real thing. Truly in love and happy.

But, wait, that couldn't possibly exist...could it?

* * * * *

REVEALING HER NINE-MONTH SECRET

NATALIE ANDERSON

MILLS & BOON

For my Cheesy Crafts Crew.
You're the best bunch of witchy, wool-magic women…
Thanks for letting this lefty bring nothing but the cheese!

CHAPTER ONE

HOPE HADN'T *QUITE* DIED. Carrie Barrett glanced again at the door. A blind date with her workmate's cousin. Agreeing had been a terrible people-pleaser moment—second only to doing that reading at her sister's wedding. Since that horror fest she'd been trying to train herself out of the habit. But today she'd not just wanted to agree to a favour for someone else, she'd wanted to fit in. She'd even wanted to meet someone new.

It was a full year since she'd been jilted. Six months since she'd travelled from her home to the other side of the world. It was time to at least try and have some *fun*. But her date was late and a lifetime of punctuality meant Carrie was now sitting in a not-quite-fitted summer dress that wasn't even hers, conspicuously alone in the rooftop restaurant of the plushest waterfront hotel in Auckland, New Zealand.

At least she could avoid the waiter's enquiring looks by admiring the gleaming super yachts moored in the marina. The Waitematā harbour was especially stunning at sunset. But, despite the postcard perfection, she couldn't help glancing back to the door as more people arrived.

Please show up. It would be so great if someone would just show up. Just this once.

Her stomach somersaulted as a man walked in just as she willed it. Impressive height. Broad shoulders. Brilliant eyes—their focus landed directly on her. Just for a second.

It wasn't him, of course. Her date would be wearing a

red jacket. This guy was entirely in black and the hold of his head, his all-encompassing gaze and his wholly confident stance sealed his command of the room. His arrival electrified everyone. They all turned, immediately straightening, eyes brightening, literally lip-licking.

Carrie wasn't miraculously immune. Goose bumps shimmied over her skin. Allergic, right? He was high performance personified. She'd been around the type long enough to instantly recognise the aura. Doubtless he'd be ruthlessly driven. As were her law-partner parents and champion-athletics stars sisters. Worst of all, her ex-fiancé too. Carrie *intimately* understood that the fight for success at the highest level meant other things got sacrificed—time and attention always, people often and sometimes someone wanted to win so badly they *cheated*.

Despite knowing this, she wasn't repelled by the new arrival but as transfixed as everyone else. He was a pirate, plundering hearts with the sheer authority of his presence. Even the ultra-professional and discreet maître d' took half a second to recover.

A murmured word and a moment later, the man followed the restaurateur. Only one empty table separated hers from his—now the last empty table. Apparently he felt no discomfort going solo in such a convivial setting. Of course, if he wanted company, he only needed to toss a glance at anyone crowding that bar and he'd be accosted in seconds. But he obviously didn't want, because he chose to sit with his back to them.

Which meant he faced her. Which meant she now had to look anywhere but straight ahead because otherwise she'd be staring right at him. It was as if they were at the same table—stretched apart by only a little distance.

So awkward.

She wanted to surreptitiously slither away. Instead, she watched the door. A woman arrived and another couple of men. They all went to the bar. She drew a disappointed breath and her gaze inadvertently slid over *him* and stopped. Because, just like that, time ended. He was more than a pirate. He had the beauty of an angel and the tempting gleam of a devil. And he was taking in far more than the colour of her hair.

Her cheeks heated as his gaze slowly swept over her features. Utterly fanciful thoughts filled her head. And, worse, her body actually reacted—heating as sensation zinged along her veins, tightening, *softening*. Shocking. Super-embarrassing. Also unstoppable.

The spell was only broken by the arrival of the maître d' at the man's shoulder. Her devilish pirate-angel angled his head to listen to the man but didn't take his eyes off her. But the interruption recalled her brain from its whimsical, sensual flight.

So, so awkward. Had he seen her reaction? Read her mind? But something had started unfurling inside and it couldn't be stopped. He said something in a low voice, and the maître d's eyes widened, but he nodded. Of course. Because this man got what he wanted. Every. Time.

But he wouldn't want *her.* She was way too ordinary. Like attracted like—superstars bonded with other superstars and that was as it should be. Because the less bright got burned to bits when they got too close to stars like him.

'Would madam like to order or wait a while longer for her guest?'

The maître d's question mortified her. She'd been stood up. And she'd not ordered yet because this restaurant was *not* travelling-temp budget-friendly. But a random hit of pride made her refuse to walk out in front of the guy who had it all. The one who was still watching her. There'd be no slithering out without him noticing because he'd *already* noticed. For once, for this worst of moments, she was *not* invisible.

She wasn't his type. But Massimo Donati-Wells listened to the conversation between the maître d' and the strawberry

blonde at the opposite table anyway. He'd already succumbed
to the inexplicable urge to instruct the man not to allow
anyone to be seated at the table between him and the petite
woman with the pouting lips and soft-looking skin. He'd
spotted her when he'd walked in and deliberately sat with
his back to the rest of the room. She'd noticed him and, while
that was hardly unusual, his shockingly instant response to
her hyper-aware stare?

Very, *very* physical. It wasn't unwelcome. It had been a
long few days, and after the satisfaction of securing his latest contract a reward wouldn't go astray. So he sat back and
didn't try to stop the current flowing. The electricity that
had arced the moment he'd locked eyes with her had an ad-
dictive burst.

Her attention again flickered to the door over his shoulder.
She was waiting for someone. A date? His muscles tensed.
Foolish date for being late. Her phone pinged. Massimo un-
ashamedly watched her read the message. She blinked rapidly and her mouth compressed.

'Actually, I will order something, please.' She called the
maître d' back.

Pink-cheeked, the blue-eyed princess was clearly trying
not to run. She was scraping together *pride*. Good for her.

'Um…' She didn't bother to scan the menu. 'A pina colada, please.'

He bit the inside of his cheek so he didn't smile. The beach
cocktail classic wasn't even on the menu at this bar. It was
known for its champagne selection. But the maître d' was
too professional even to blink.

'Of course.'

She *really* wasn't his type. Too fresh. Too soft. The sort
that blushed and probably dreamed of one true love. He selected the sort who played quick and never expected him
to stay. The streetwise sort who were the same as him. But
something kept him staring. Not just her smooth skin and soft

curves, but the defiant courage shimmering in her sapphire eyes—and the vulnerability that underpinned it.

She shouldn't have been stood up. His ribs tightened, making his heart beat more forcefully against the constraints while his imagination slipped its chain and plotted just what she *should* be getting tonight. Touch. Definitely touch. The kind of touch to make her smile, sparkle, *scream*.

And he wanted her to look back at him so he'd feel that jolt of electricity again.

'Mind if I join you?' He called across the slight distance, shocking himself with his inability to resist temptation. 'My guest cancelled on me last minute.'

He'd wanted to dine alone. He'd had people seeking his pleasure and approval all day. This was supposed to have been an evening of peace before flying home tomorrow. And the strawberry-blonde sweetheart wasn't stupid. She pointedly glanced at the single place-setting at his table. Yeah, he'd just lied to her, and she knew it.

'Just a drink until your guest arrives...' he murmured, not used to having to ask anyone a second time.

In her heart-shaped face her smile twisted. 'He's not coming.' She didn't even try to lie.

'Then he's an idiot.' Massimo stood and moved seats before she could say anything more. 'I'm hungry,' he said equably. 'Are you?'

For a second he wondered if she was about to refuse. If he'd misread the arc of attraction that had bewitched him moments ago. If his customary boldness was too much for her. She was, after all, too soft.

But her chin lifted. 'I'm not sure. I can't actually think right now.'

The hit of honesty amused him. 'Let's find out.'

He glanced to his side and the maître d' materialised as if by magic. Massimo murmured his order.

'They serve tapas,' he explained after the man hurried away. 'I ordered some of everything.'

She assessed him with the clearest, bluest eyes he'd ever looked into and, despite the sizzling energy, there wasn't exactly approval shining in them.

'Everything? You must be hungry,' she said, sharpness edging her tone. 'You didn't want some big, juicy steak with a rich sauce and all the trimmings?'

A hint of challenge, of censure. She probably thought him a jerk and maybe he was. But there was another jolt of fire. Massimo wanted more because it warmed him in a way he hadn't felt in an age.

'Sampling lots of things is more fun than being stuck with only the one dish, don't you think?' He played up the arrogance she clearly read in him.

Suspicion firmed in her eyes. 'You mean you like to try *all* the different meats available on the charcuterie board?'

Her tart riposte burned in the best way. 'Absolutely. A nibble here, a nibble there. Sometimes, however,' he acknowledged swiftly, 'It's nice enough just to look.'

Because *she* probably shouldn't be on the board. He'd devour her and, despite her little push-back, he wasn't sure she'd handle it.

'Just looking leaves *you* satisfied?' she queried, disbelief audible. 'Your appetite is fully assuaged by little more than a glance?'

His ribs tightened even more. 'I guess it depends. What about yours?'

She looked at him for a long moment. 'I'm still developing my palate. There's a lot I haven't tried.'

A ball of heat exploded in his loins. Hadn't she? Did she *want* to?

'You're very used to getting your own way,' she added after a moment. 'Do you choose from the board before anyone else gets a chance?'

He smiled. 'You think I would do that?'

'You don't bat an eyelid when ordering absolutely everything on the menu, having walked into a place and taking a seat at a table as if it were your own…'

He saw the moment she realised and her mouth formed an 'O'. It was a very luscious mouth. Massimo's watered.

'*Is* it your own?' She gazed at him intently. 'This hotel?'

'I'm only an investor.' Massimo had made so much money, he spent his days finding things to invest in. Well, fighting off the people who came to him asking for his investment and advice. His private equity empire was renowned for identifying future successful entities, meaning he simply kept making more money. He was not going to lie—he liked it. He liked success, liked living on his own terms. He also liked seducing pretty women who knew the score. This woman didn't.

'*Only*,' she echoed. 'So you only invest in high-end luxury hotels?'

'Actually, I'm currently focussing on renewable energy projects.'

A hint of humour stole into those blue eyes. 'Oh, how worthy.' She nodded. 'Do you hope to create a more sustainable future for your children?'

He stared back at her, appreciating the totally passive-aggressive niggle. No one had dared deal to him in a long while and he badly wanted to strike back with something inflammatory to provoke a reaction from her. The judgement got beneath his skin. 'Actually,' he said silkily. 'I have no intention of having children.'

'Naturally.' She smiled.

He shot her a look. 'Meaning?'

'Meaning, it is a truth universally acknowledged that every wealthy man feels a driving need to warn every female he meets that he's not in the market for either marriage or children.'

He looked at her, his mouth twitching. 'Quite.' He nodded firmly, appreciating her distortion of the famous literary line. 'So glad you readily understand my position.'

'I'm not in the market either, in case you were curious.' Her arrogance was completely faked.

He smirked. 'Which is why you're sitting here waiting for...?'

She eyed him severely but spoilt the look with an eventual smile. 'I was doing a friend a favour.'

'Oh, really? That's what you're going with?'

'It happens to be the truth.' She shrugged. 'But please, fear not, I'm only using you as a foil against public humiliation and for free food.'

'Okay,' he said. 'Glad we're able to be so frank. Equally, glad I'm able to oblige.'

'Indeed.'

'Who was he?' He was stupidly curious now. 'The idiot?'

'I don't even know. It was a set-up. I said yes for a friend but apparently the guy's been caught up at work.' The bitterness in her tone ran deep.

'Oh, workaholics.' He shook his head ruefully. 'Need to steer clear of those.'

A flash of disbelief widened her blue eyes, then her smile blossomed and a little laugh escaped. 'Indeed.'

That laugh was everything. He wanted more. He wanted that laugh in his *bed*.

'What about your date?' she asked.

'There wasn't one. I lied.' The pretence fell away and he was honest.

'Yes.' Her lashes lifted and those blue eyes lanced through him. 'You've experience with that.'

'Doesn't everyone?' Now he was the one who couldn't keep a splinter of bitterness back. 'Both ways.'

'Apparently so.'

The connection between them suddenly flared and he felt a wave of empathy. He knew exactly how awful it was to be lied to.

A waiter arrived with her pina colada and a bottle of wine

for him, severing the surprisingly solemn connection that had formed so suddenly.

'You're English,' he noted when the waiter was gone.

'You're Australian,' she countered with a smile.

Accents were the least of what they were noticing about each other.

'So we're both far from home, but you're the farthest. What brings you all the way to Auckland?' he asked.

He didn't want to know too much. He didn't want to get invested. He never did with women. He knew relationships ended up too intense. Too devastating. He just wanted to touch. But at the same time, for the first time, he wanted to know what it was that had made her look so alone.

'Adventure.' She sipped her drink. 'You?'

'Business. I'm heading back to Sydney first flight in the morning.'

Carrie looked into his eyes and saw the challenge lurking. He expected her to call him out on that and she wasn't able to resist. Because he was oh-so-not-very-smoothly letting her know he was here for only one more night. It was a form of arrogant weaponry, his arsenal against the threat of a woman wanting *more*.

Of course, this was a guy who *needed* defence, he was that attractive. And of course he *would* want children one day, once he met the right woman. *She* wasn't that woman— that was what had made her laugh. The ridiculousness of it. She was so far from his league, she'd been amused he'd felt the need to mention it.

'Gosh, what a shame you're not here for longer,' she said. 'I can't put my trap-you-into-marriage plan into action.'

He inclined his head. 'I find I'm devastated.'

'Indeed?' She stifled a laugh.

She usually didn't flirt so badly with anyone. She didn't flirt at all. But this was silly *easy*. That he'd commandeered the spare seat at her table and saved her from the indignity of dining alone, when all the staff knew she'd been waiting for a date. That he didn't seem to be able to take his eyes off her. That beneath that outrageous arrogance there was a core that called to something equally deep within her own soul.

'I'm Massimo.' He extended his hand across the table. 'Thank you for graciously allowing me to dine with you.'

'I'm Carrie. I'm not sure that you gave me much choice.' She put her hand in his.

A jolt sizzled along her skin at the contact. His fingers tightened.

'Allow me to correct that.' He looked across at her with total seriousness in his stunning eyes. 'Would you like me to stay or would you prefer to be left alone? I'll do whatever you wish.'

Whatever she wished? Carrie's breath vanished. Palm to palm, feeling that sizzle up her arm, she never wanted him to let go.

Any anxiety was vanquished by his touch and the vibrancy of his green eyes. Richly emphasised by lush lashes, the colour was striking enough from a distance. Up close, it was mesmerising. No wonder he needed to warn women away.

But, while he was confident, there was more to him than money-man arrogance. More depth, more humanity than the stereotype she'd pinned on him. No caricature, he was flesh and blood, hot and *hurt*. Quite how she knew that, she wasn't sure. But she was certain of its truth. In this one moment, Massimo needed her as much as she needed him. Just for company at dinner.

'You can stay,' she said flatly.

'Thank you.'

Massimo released her hand as the maître d' approached, flanked by two waiters. All three carried wooden platters that they placed on the table. She diverted herself from the shocking intensity of her feelings by taking in the vast array. There was fresh oysters, each kept cool in its open shell with a spoonful of champagne granita. There was a dish of baked brie, as well as a trinity of boards—cheese, charcuterie and chocolate.

'There's a lot of food here,' she said.

'We can take our time.' He shrugged. 'But is there something to tempt that elusive appetite of yours?'

She took in the other offerings. Olives. Ceviche. Vegan tartlets and tempura vegetables. Even salted potato crisps. There was something to tempt almost anyone.

'What are you doing in Auckland, Carrie?' Massimo couldn't resist the urge to find out more about her. He wanted to know everything.

'Working as a temp,' she said. 'Office administrator. I plan to head somewhere warmer soon.'

'Sydney?' he immediately suggested with a smile.

'Too big.' She dismissed it just as instantly with a laugh. 'I want smaller and more isolated.'

He glanced at her cocktail. 'Fiji? The Cook Islands?'

She nodded, her enthusiasm building. 'Paradise.'

His brows lifted. 'You think?'

'Don't you?'

The topic was light and breezy and he didn't quite believe everything she was saying. But then, he didn't believe everything anyone said.

'An island holiday wouldn't be paradise, it would be boring,' he said blandly.

'*Boring?*' She laughed. 'You disappoint. I thought you'd have a better imagination.'

Massimo's imagination was firing up most unhelpfully right now. 'How would you fill your days?'

'A walk early in the morning. Then a swim. Fresh fruit to awaken the palate…'

Fresh fruit and awakenings of palate made him laugh. 'You've thought about this.'

'Often.' She nodded with perfect seriousness before stunning him with a wide smile.

'Are we talking meditation and yoga poses along the shoreline?' he teased. 'Shots for your social media?'

'Walking is meditative,' she agreed. 'But no socials. They don't keep one *present*. I would read. A book a day.'

'If it doesn't inform me on investments, then I'm not reading it,' he said blithely.

'No novels? No history? No philosophy?' She shot him a look as he shuddered theatrically. 'No *poetry*? Reading can inform your soul.'

'You assume I have a soul.'

'I do believe you're human,' she countered dryly. 'Therefore, have imagination. And I bet yours is good.' She cocked her head. 'So I don't believe you about the books.'

His gaze intensified on her. 'Why do you think I have a good imagination?'

'Because success takes more than brains and business acumen. It takes vision and creativity.'

'And you understand this…?'

'Because I've been around other successful people.'

He paused. The edge to her tone suggested she wasn't that thrilled to have known these successful people. She classed them as belonging to a group other than her. 'Yet you don't seem to want to stick around them. You want to escape to an isolated island.'

She stiffened. 'I'm not escaping. I'm enriching my life with *adventure*.'

'Are you?' He shook his head. 'Or are you enriching your life with someone *else's* dreams and adventures in their books?'

'So you're an adrenalin junkie rather than a beach-read, relaxation holiday sort, or—?' She suddenly broke off as she realised the even worse truth. 'No. I've got it wrong. You don't holiday at all.' She sat back and looked at him as if he were a lost cause. '*You're* a fully paid-up member of workaholics not-so-anonymous.'

'Well,' he drawled not-so-apologetically. 'The demands on my very expensive time are too great.'

'And of course you prioritise the demands that *pay* over those that are personal.' Bitterness underlined her scorn. 'What do you do exactly—spend your days deciding which exciting new companies you should invest your pots of gold into?'

'That's not far off the mark, actually.'

'And everyone wants to be your friend because you A, have the gold, and B, can pick the winners?'

'Hence my wariness when it comes to women...' He shot her a smug glance.

Her laugh was reluctant. 'Yes, you're clearly such a wall-flower. While I'm clearly a gold-digger.' She shook her head. 'Super-successful people make great personal sacrifices.'

'Now you think I don't have balance in my life?'

'I'm sure of it.'

He pressed his hand to his chest in mockery of being wounded. But, in truth, his heart was pounding too hard for comfort. 'Contrary to your judgement, I *do* know how to relax.' He leaned closer. 'But I can assure you, copious amounts of sand *aren't* part of a good time.'

'But there might be good sustainability projects in the islands for the future of those children you're not having.' She parodied his worthiness.

'Perhaps I should investigate.' He smiled. 'I like a challenge.'

'Reading on the beach all day *can* be a challenge,' she informed him with *faux* earnestness. 'The angle of the sun, ensuring you're not getting burned...' She shook her head at him sadly. 'But *you* can't get past the need to accumulate, to score that thrill—high risk and high reward, high speed, need to win at all costs...'

'There's nothing wrong with chasing the best rewards.' He shrugged. He'd make no apology for driving for success. It was how he'd survived. 'But you shouldn't read on the beach all day. You'll get sunburned.'

Her lips twisted in a little smile. 'I promise to cover up.'

Fierce heat hit him low down. 'People shouldn't make promises,' he muttered, trying to joke but failing. 'They tend not to keep them.'

Her blue gaze shone at him. Her voice was soft. 'Actually, on that we agree.'

That thread pulled, tugging him closer to her. It was moored to an elemental weight within him, something raw that he recognised she also had deep inside. Something sore.

'Here's to no promises, then,' he said quietly.

'No promises.' She lifted her glass, the bright cocktail at odds with the sombre note in her voice. 'No lies.'

How was it that one *look* had sparked madness to life? Carrie had turned into someone she didn't recognise—her awkwardness melted, she laughed easily and joked lightly. Yet humour barely hid the chemistry pushing them closer— beneath the frothy flippancy, that killer electrical current pulsed with tempting, decadent danger.

With the grazing platters between them, there were no interruptions from the staff. After she'd finished her cocktail, Massimo leisurely filled her glass with the warming red wine at required intervals. There was no natural conclusion of each course, so time, that had ended the moment when she'd first enmeshed her gaze with his, now raced, spinning on an invisible loom. Long stretches disappeared between breath, look and teasing banter, soft, silly arguments that neither of them really meant yet weren't entirely untrue. Hours evaporated into the atmosphere, unrealised, unseen, so easily sucked away.

It was the clatter of crystal in the kitchen that brought her back to reality. Glancing around, Carrie realised they were the only two diners remaining. The staff had cleaned and put away everything from the other tables. Even the bar at the other end of the rooftop terrace was now quiet. Yet there was still food on their platters, still wine in their bottle. They'd barely begun. A glance at Massimo's expensive watch showed the hands well on the other side of midnight. She had work tomorrow. He had a flight home. This flirt would never lead to anything more.

It wouldn't have *anyway*—even if he'd lived in town. Massimo was way beyond her earthly plane, up in the stratosphere somewhere. Superstars didn't stick with mortals like her. She'd learned that the hard way. But that meant it didn't matter what she said or did right now. Because there was *only* now. It was stupidly easy to talk, tease him and say things she'd not normally mutter aloud. Growing up in a house of success stories, with people who couldn't understand why she didn't set her expectations higher, who didn't have time for dinner because they were too busy training, too busy pushing, and for whom spending time together wasn't a priority…it hadn't just been lonely. It had been hard.

Don't interrupt my focus… Don't be a fool…

And Massimo was one of them, wasn't he? A driven workaholic who prioritised performance over the personal. Carrie should have broken out in hives already. But she hadn't, because he wasn't working now. Now, humanity lurked in his eyes. Hot, hurt, lonely. Surely she was wrong? Surely this guy lacked nothing?

'I ought to get going,' she murmured.

She didn't want to. Beneath that easy fun, regardless of their differing lifestyle goals, they'd connected. It was just lust, right? They had stellar chemistry despite being so strikingly different. It was new to her. And shockingly powerful.

Massimo reluctantly nodded. He could suggest she come back for a drink. She would understand the implication… she would say yes and he could, would, win. But as much as he ached for it—because he ached for it so *unbearably*—he found this wasn't a game. Not tonight. This was imbued with something other than the usual quest of catch and release and short-lived, decadent hedonism. Oddly, this was more precious. He'd enjoyed simply talking to her. Talking frippery and teasing nonsense. Yet they'd both known something serious simmered underneath at the same time.

He was *not* taking advantage. She *wasn't* his type. She was not a carefree, experienced woman who understood someone like him. She'd been hurt—tonight was the least of it, he suspected. She was emotionally vulnerable, right? Which meant she was out of bounds. Because high emotion wasn't something he could manage.

Besides, the intensity of the driving urge to pull her close…the compelling need to brand her as his, somehow… That sharp ache wasn't just foreign, it was too strong. He would resist simply to prove he could. Because it was a near-run thing.

But he accompanied her in the lift down to the dark street, where a taxi waited to take her away. Carrie faced him, her old awkwardness filling her fast. 'Thank you for dinner,' she mumbled.

It sounded inadequate. Worse, she knew she sounded *forlorn*.

This *wasn't* a pick-up. He'd merely been amusing himself. He'd felt sorry for her and had been filling in time during a boring business-trip dinner. The ease with which they'd laughed was now lost in a jelly-like slop of mortification. She couldn't get out of here soon enough because otherwise she was going to do something stupid. But he reached out and took her hand and that electricity sparked again. He looked into her face but said nothing. For a second, he didn't seem able to move, as if he didn't want to let go of her hand.

But then he did.

She quickly climbed into the taxi. He leaned down to the open window, only it was too dark for her to read his expression.

'Bye, Carrie.' The stark thread in his voice pulled taut an answering thread within—like a leash tethering them at the very core. It tugged up temptation. But it was too late.

As he stepped back, the street light illuminated his face. The bleak, unbearable expression of loneliness shocked then echoed within her. It gave name to the seriousness that hadn't been absent but unacknowledged until now.

Desolation.

The taxi was already carrying her away. She twisted in her seat to keep her gaze on him, wanting to catch a glimmer of his lighter charm. Wanting to know she'd been mistaken. But the last impression she had of him was of pain.

For a few minutes she could hardly think and then slowly a sense greater than regret filled her. Urgently she leant forward to speak to the driver. 'Please, would you mind turning around?'

She would just drive by. He'd have gone back into the hotel. But, illuminated by the lights along the waterfront, was a tall, lone figure. Hands deep in his pockets, he faced the inky, almost invisible sea. He glanced round at the sound of the car. Then he glanced again. His gaze held and suddenly, swiftly, he walked over as it approached the kerb, ready to open the door as soon as it pulled up.

Wordlessly, he held out his hand to her.

CHAPTER TWO

HE DIDN'T LET go of her hand. In the darkness it was still impossible to read his expression. But his grip tightened, he tugged her closer and she *knew*. Astonishing as it was, he wanted her.

'You came back.' His husky whisper was almost wonderstruck.

'I didn't want tonight to be over,' she confessed.

'I'm…' He cupped her face and released a ragged breath. 'My mind has failed. I just want to kiss you.'

'Oh.' She breathed a ragged breath of her own at the sizzling jolt from the touch, intent and that hint of amazement. A beat of delight of her own. 'Good.'

That sizzling current of electricity hummed higher and louder. She didn't want to shut it off. She leaned closer, already addicted to the intimate tease of his fingers on the side of her neck. A cascade of sensations shimmered down her body as his touch lit her deepest, darkest places. She wanted this. She wanted *more*.

His lips hit hers. Finally. It was like coming home and shooting for the moon at the same time—perfect and fierce. That current of energy arced and she closed her eyes at the blinding white brilliance of starburst and pleasure. His mouth was soft and firm, taking and giving, and she opened instantly, leaning, learning, *aching*. His hands were everywhere, pressing her closer as his kiss deepened. It was not plundering but perfect. The demanding pressure of his body pressed full length against hers heated her so much more than physically and she grabbed him hard. Combustion was so close. She was hot and breathless in seconds. There was only one way this could go.

He tore his lips from hers, barely able to breathe. 'Come with me.'

'Yes.'

He didn't let go of her hand. He walked her along the marina, towards the water. Towards the dark. He stopped at far end of the wooden walkway and she stared at the yacht gleaming in the silvery moonlight.

'Are you staying on *that*?' she asked. 'Not the hotel?'

His smile flashed. He really was a pirate. 'That okay or do you get seasick?'

'Well, we're not actually going anywhere, are we?'

'We're definitely going somewhere,' he muttered and led her up the gangway. He placed his free hand on a small flat screen, and after a faint whirring sound the door lock clicked.

'Very high-tech.' She breathed, paying attention and yet not. She needed to touch him again and it was crazy.

'It's not mine,' he said as the door slid open and he led her inside.

'I bet you're an investor,' she teased.

He turned that stunning smile on her. Peripherally she absorbed the stunning interior of the yacht but, honestly, she couldn't drag her attention from him.

'Would you like a drink?' he offered but completely ignored the sparkling bar behind him. Keeping her hand tightly in his, he stepped into her space and placed his other hand on her waist before she could even think of an answer.

That jolt again. Heart racing, blood zinging, she spread her hand back on his chest, glad that he too seemed as eager as she was for this contact. His heat burned through his black shirt. He was real, not a fantasy of her wildest dreams. This *wasn't* a dream and suddenly she was driven to be honest.

He needed to know—not only because it would be unfair

not to tell him, but because instinctively she knew he'd accommodate her wishes.

'I've never done this before,' she said huskily. 'Any of this.'

His eyes widened and he cocked his head. *'Any?'*

Her mouth dried, but somehow she still wasn't scared. It was still okay to tell him her secret. 'Not any. None. *Nada.*'

His heart kicked beneath her fingers. 'Then perhaps we shouldn't…'

Verbally he was leaving it up to her, but she read the intensity in his eyes and felt that current flowing back and forth between them. The electrical impulse made her heart pound in sync with his. She'd never experienced anything like that kiss and perhaps never would again. Which was why there was no hesitation. 'But perhaps we should.'

His pulse picked up, even as he nodded. 'What if anything and everything is on offer?' he asked huskily, still careful with her. 'What if you get to pick and choose? You can have as little as you like, or you can have the lot. And you can change your mind any time.'

Desire unravelled at the prospect of him putting himself forward so completely for *her* pleasure. Suddenly she struggled to breathe at all. 'That doesn't seem fair. What about what you want?'

A smile stole into his heated gaze. 'I'm confident you'll choose well.'

Oh? She wrinkled her nose. 'Because that's been your experience?'

'No,' he said. 'Because chemistry like this can't be contained.'

His sudden solemn note surprised her. 'Isn't it always like this?'

He lifted his hand, softly torturing that intensely sensitive skin on her neck again. 'Has it been like this for you before?'

'No, but—'

'Me neither.'

That was pure charm, wasn't it?

But he held her hip and gently pressed against her so she felt the length of him against her belly. His very hard length. 'This part of me can't lie.'

She shook her head. 'That's a physical response to...'

He leaned closer, crushing her hand against his chest. His heart raced the gallop of hers. 'Chemistry this strong is scary.'

She gazed up into his intense green eyes. 'Scary?'

His grip on her hip tightened. 'I don't want to let you down. You were meant to meet someone else tonight.'

'I've never even spoken to him. Maybe I was meant to meet you instead. Maybe this is the universe granting me one special night. I mean, you're leaving in the morning. You're not in the marriage market. Most importantly, you're not my type.'

He smiled but the expression in his eyes was still serious. 'No, I'm not.'

Yet something in him called to something true deep within her and she knew he felt the same. They shared a commonality. She didn't know what, or why, but somehow she knew there was *recognition*. And because of that a boldness she'd never imagined feeling swept over her. She was going to take this moment because, if she didn't, she'd always regret it.

'You don't need to protect me,' she said softly. 'You need to please me.'

'You deserve much more than one special night,' he said.

Didn't everyone? Didn't he? But, the fact was, life didn't work that way. It wasn't fair. Carrie knew that.

'There's only *now*,' she said. 'That's all there ever is.'

She'd come back to him. He knew it had taken a boldness she didn't usually feel—certainly not if she'd never done this before. Whoever had made her doubt herself ought to be shot, and that guy who'd let her down tonight was a fool. But Massimo had never been more grateful. Because, while she wasn't his type, she was the fantasy he'd never dared dream of and he'd never wanted a woman as much. Damn it if he didn't admire her courage. If he wasn't amused by the way she talked back to him. If he wasn't humbled by her return.

So he moved. Fast. Scooping her into his arms, he strode to the master bedroom and set her down before desperately activating the electronics. She chuckled as the vast curtains closed and the room was softly lit. Then the world was shut out and there was only the two of them, and he was pleasing her if it was the last thing he'd ever do.

Because she'd come back. She was his. Just for tonight. And now he would take his time. She stood still as he walked towards her. Nerves and anticipation were apparent in her blue eyes, but there was certainty too—and lush, sensual appreciation as he unfastened the buttons of his shirt. He didn't know how she'd got to this night, never having had sex before. But he was shockingly pleased he now got to be the one to show her how. And why.

She was made for pleasure. He loved the lift of her chin as she met him, the warm softness of her willing, pliant body. He kissed her, consumed in the fire in seconds, desperately trying to slow down but failing. His hands worked, racing ahead of his intentions. The dress slid from her shoulders into a satiny puddle on the floor and for a split-second all he could do was stare.

'You're sensational,' he rasped. He cupped her breasts in his hands, loving the way they spilled over the top of her simple satin bra. He felt her self-conscious shiver and glanced up to tease her. 'Not going to argue with me?'

'I've decided to believe your flattery. It's my fantasy night.'

'It's not flattery.' Suddenly he didn't want to pretend this was nothing. He didn't want her to either. He wanted her to believe him. And he wanted her to be *sure* of what she was doing. 'And it's not a fantasy. Don't forget this is *real*.'

Overwhelmingly real, and the intensity still scared him

if he stopped to consider it. So he didn't stop. She was so hungry for his kisses, he couldn't.

She pressed against him, her softness moulding to his hardness, filling the gaps, heating him in places and in ways he'd not known needed warming. As she leaned into his lush, slow kisses he felt a deepening intimacy, a deepening connection that he'd not anticipated. His control of the situation rapidly slid away from him. He lifted her to the bed and could barely keep his hands steady enough to gently remove her bra and matching navy panties.

'You've got no idea how badly I want you.' He all but ripped the rest of his clothes off. 'I'm trying really hard to slow down.'

Because he wanted this to be so good for her. Trouble was, his hunger was almost out of control, and the look in her eyes as she stared at his bared body wasn't helping.

Shock. Appreciation. Anticipation. He knew how she felt. He wanted to taste *all* of her, not just zero in on the ripest treasures like some sex-starved youth. He wanted to trace the soft skin at the backs of her knees and gently press his teeth to test the delicate flesh of her inner thighs. Damn it, yes, he just wanted to lick her in the most intimate part of all, to taste and tease until she was totally ripe and ready for the rest of him. And she didn't help his control. Instead she encouraged him to race, instinctively parting her legs, circling her hips, compelling him closer to that very part until he couldn't resist discovering all her sweet secrets.

Growling in feral pleasure, he discovered how slippery and how hot she was. Her sighs drove him out of his mind. Goose bumps rippled over his skin as the effort to delay pleasure almost broke him. He'd wanted to go slow, to impress with finesse. But there was no bloody finesse. There was only hunger in his exploration and an incredible, unexpected joy.

Because she was with him at every step. Having his hands on her, having her spread before him, made him feel like the wealthiest man in the world, rich in bountiful softness and heat, and that snug, secret part that he was first to explore. He was going to have *all* of her, like the selfish glutton he was.

The sight of her pleasure, the sounds as she released the shackles of shyness, undid him. Self-restraint obliterated, she grasped his hair and rocked her hips hard, utterly abandoned in her pursuit of the satisfaction she instinctively knew he could give. He knew it too. He'd recognised it the second he'd seen her sitting alone in that restaurant. Electricity and chemistry, the basic building blocks of life, that raw *want*, had smacked into both of them.

Carrie couldn't cope with the sensations piling over her. His grip was hard as he held her bucking hips so he could keep tormenting her with his tongue. He wouldn't let her escape. And she didn't want to, she just wanted the *peak*—the finish she knew he was holding just out of her reach. She relished the sight of him halfway down the massive bed, intently focused on teasing her swift response, craving it as much as she did. The game in his gaze had sparked her own playfulness, overpowering her initial shyness of such intimacy. Nothing felt more natural, easy, right and utterly *infuriating*.

'Don't stop,' she begged, arching again and again.

'Hmm?' He smiled up at her.

His enjoyment of her torment only turned her on more.

'Don't stop,' she repeated on her held breath.

But he did. His fingers ceased their deliciously wicked strumming. The teasing smile on his angelically, sinfully, beautiful face stirred a fire within her.

'Don't stop.' But it was an order that time.

His smoky green gaze was so full of wicked intent, it drove her wild. But she couldn't move as she watched him lower his mouth and sucked, his fingers and tongue striking up their fast play again. And, just like that, she lost herself.

'Don't stop. Don't stop. Don't stop.' She chanted the command, the plea, sobbing until she didn't even know what the words meant.

The last thing she saw before squeezing her eyes shut

were the muscles rippling in his wide, bronzed shoulders and the wild burst of fire in his eyes. And she screamed as pleasure tumbled through her. Uncivil sensation. All emotion in her abandonment.

When she opened her eyes she saw his. The stunning green was now only the narrowest ring around the wide black pupils. Dark and dangerous. Utterly inviting. But he was watching, waiting. And he was wonderful.

'Don't stop now,' she said softly.

He swallowed hard. 'If you give me this, I can't give it back.'

'You're giving me something else in return. Something I get to keep.'

His lush lashes fluttered. 'What's that?'

'A perfect memory.'

'Perfect?' His eyebrows arched. 'Stop. I'll get performance anxiety.'

'You know it's already perfect!' She half-laughed, but it was true. 'I just want you.'

'I'm...' he drew in a breath '...honoured.'

He rummaged in the sleek drawer beside the bed. 'Hell, I hope...' He straightened, an almost boyish smile of relief on his face. 'Thank God.'

His hands shook as he tore open the square packet. She saw him breathing carefully as he rolled the condom down his rigid length. He glanced over at her and stifled a moan that sounded almost despairing. 'I want you so much, I'm afraid I might fail you.'

That *he* wanted *her* was mind-blowing in itself, but she knew how desperately he wanted to *please* her. This heart-stopping man was no pirate. He had depth and, for all the playful banter and pretence, an honesty of intention that touched her far more than physically.

'I want you to take pleasure in me too,' she admitted. 'I think... I think it's impossible not to.' Because just one kiss had felt ridiculously good. Every touch since had been designed to send her insane. 'It's chemistry.'

He moved, bracing his entire length above her in a show of strength and muscled beauty. She couldn't help staring at his straining erection. That part of him looked magnificent. And big.

'Don't worry.' He nudged her thigh with his hand and gently strummed between her legs. 'I've got you so hot and slippery, I'll slide in.'

She gaped at his raw, sensual claim, but his smile widened as he pressed his finger into her.

'See?'

He turned her on even more, filling her with his fingers, pressing his thumb against her sensitive nub. She groaned and then his mouth was on hers. She strained, loving the sensations as he teased her, realising he was readying her for more. He kissed down her neck, inhaling her scent, gliding lips over her skin as if he couldn't get enough of her. She gasped as he pushed her close to that edge again. She wanted it. But she wanted it *all*. She wanted not just his hand, but his...

'Talk to me, Carrie,' he murmured, an intimate invitation.

Seriously?

'And say what?' She panted.

His soft laugh was more of a choke. She giggled too but she was shockingly desperate for him to hurry and claim all she'd offered.

'Is this a final consent question or something? Because I want it, okay? You're good to go. Full steam ahead.'

He laughed again. 'Oh, Carrie, you're good for my soul.'

'Your ego, you mean.' She had just enough breath to tease. 'You said you didn't have a soul.'

'Maybe I was wrong.'

She cupped the side of his face with her hand and smiled into his stunning eyes. 'Of course you were.'

He didn't just have soul. He had humour, heart and all

the good human things, most especially generosity, and she trusted him utterly.

He pushed her legs wider, settling his hips between her slick thighs. The hard ridge of his erection pressed big and heavy, and she couldn't do anything other than look into his eyes. She couldn't even breathe. He didn't let go hold of her hand. They were palm to palm, chest to breast, hip to hip. He was taut, intense, and so deliciously careful as he slowly pushed against her, then into her.

'Just like that.' He groaned, his tension building as he watched her close. 'Okay?'

The eroticism of his possession…his body in hers, his fingers laced through hers… She shook, almost giddy with the intensity, pleasure literally shafting through her. She smiled at him. She couldn't not. She couldn't hold anything back.

His concentrated expression broke apart, his answering smile radiating. She breathed out. This was so much simpler than she'd ever imagined it would be. It was easy. And intimate—not in a scary way but a hot, funny, sweet way.

She wriggled, lifting her hips to meet the slow rhythm of his. 'Just like that?'

His assenting growl satisfied that deeply buried part of her. That yearning for recognition, for connection. But then he moved. And then it wasn't so funny, it wasn't so sweet. It was *scorching*. And she moved with him, unrestrained in the fierceness. Between the blinding flashes of her own erotic annihilation, she saw the moment that he caved beneath the unbearable need to release all he had left. She felt the final thrust of his powerful body, the rasping catch of his cry, the power he could no longer control. The force of pleasure flowed between them in an utterly unstoppable form.

And he didn't let go of her hand.

'I can't…' *Think.*

Words…what were they?

She was spent—she'd never felt as limp or as dazed. Yet

warmth trickled through her. It was as if she had a new base-line temperature, as if her engine now ran on new fuel—bliss.

He lifted, shifting to lie beside her. But he pulled her into his arms, pressing her head to rest on his chest. His fingers skimmed across her back, his touch light, as if he knew how highly sensitised her skin still was. How raw her soul was. How it needed soothing touch. He traced down her arm, catching her fingers with his once more. And then...

He didn't let go of her hand.

CHAPTER THREE

Fiji. A six-month contract. Visa and accommodation sorted. Sun. Sand. And, yes, *escape*. Carrie couldn't wait to fly out next week. It was going to be brilliant. Walking towards her temporary office job in central Auckland, she glimpsed the marina in the distance, filled with luxury boats. Her heart twisted but she steadied her wistfulness with her secret, often muttered, refrain—at least she'd had that one special night.

She had no regrets. *None*. It was done. And she was okay.

She'd not rung the number Massimo had left for her before heading to his flight that morning just over a month ago. Okay, in occasional weaker moments she'd mentally composed a few text messages, but she'd not let herself send them. It had been a perfect moment, but a *moment* was all it was, and would ever be. She wasn't spoiling it by asking for more only to have him eventually say no. Because that *would* have happened.

But, even though she knew that, her confidence had lifted from the encounter. She'd asked for what she'd wanted once—with him—and she'd since asked again with something else. She'd applied for a job she'd never thought she'd actually get, figuring she had nothing to lose…and the result?

Fiji. A six-month contract. Visa and accommodation sorted.

All she needed now was to shake off the stomach upset that had plagued her these last few days. But as she passed the coffee stand outside her office she gagged so violently she knew she had to go home. She couldn't spread anything in the office and she needed to get well enough to travel next week.

She stopped at a pharmacy on her way home to get something to settle her stomach. 'Any chance you're pregnant?' the pharmacist asked quietly when she'd explained her symptoms.

'No chance.' Carrie laughed. There'd never been a chance in her life.

Uh...actually, there had.

Her smile faded as she suddenly remembered. In a millisecond, hot sweat slicked over her body and that nausea returned.

'Here, take a seat.' The pharmacist sent her a sympathetic smile. 'Breathe. It'll be okay.'

It wasn't okay. It wasn't possible—*surely*?

Carrie purchased the test the pharmacist fetched and got home as quickly as she could. She was so shaken up she had to read the instructions three times before they made sense. He'd used protection. He'd definitely used protection. She remembered his relief at finding some on that outrageously opulent boat. More moments from that night crowded her mind. Searing pleasure. The multiple times he'd made her scream with satisfaction. Then a rush of something else flooded her. Pure protectiveness.

Because the result....

Pregnant. Pregnant. Pregnant.

She lost hours muttering it in shock. Then performed the mental gymnastics of *what the hell was she going to do*? How was she going to tell him? How might he react? How she was going to cope? What were her parents going to say?

They were going to judge this as a failure, of course. And he was going to be appalled. This was so not in his plan.

But there was one positive certainty in her mind. She *wanted* this baby. She was having this baby. This miracle, this lapse of fate, was *hers*. And she would be and do everything she could for this child. Because this child deserved all the love in the world.

She needed to tell him in person, to *see* his reaction. But she couldn't fly to Australia and turn up on his doorstep. For one thing, she couldn't afford it. For another, she didn't know where he lived. She only had a number for him so, no matter what, she was going to have to call first.

Feeling sick all over again, she reached for her phone and checked the time. She'd lost most of the day in a haze of rumination and confusion, but it would be early afternoon in Sydney. That was assuming he was even in Sydney. Or that he'd even answer. But she had to try. A video call would work—so she would still see him—and that was what she'd do. Panicked choices flooded her mind and she moved before she could ruminate and end up uncertain of anything. She just had to act. Telling him was imperative.

Moments later, his face filled her phone screen. For a few seconds she could only stare—her heart had stopped…she couldn't breathe. It should have been impossible but those perfect angles of his face, and the bronzed skin that offset those stunningly vibrant green eyes that were now wide, were even more handsome.

'Carrie?' Pure astonishment sounded then he glanced to the side of the screen. 'I need a moment.'

He muttered something unintelligible to someone unseen, then she heard a door close.

'This is a surprise. You—' He paused, frowning directly into the screen. 'Is everything okay?'

She hadn't expected to see him ever again and now she was. Her bursting heart pounded into her throat. How did she plan to tell him?

'I'm pregnant.'

For a second she thought the screen had frozen because he didn't even blink. But then she heard the audio.

'That's not possible.'

'Well, obviously it is,' she floundered. 'Because I'm pregnant.'

The screen hadn't frozen, because an awfully cold expression hardened his face. 'No. I used protection. You know I did.'

Yes. But…did she have to point out the obvious? 'Apparently protection doesn't always work.'

'No.' He repeated that damning, revealing, rejection. 'That's not been my experience to date.'

'And, as you know, I don't have any other experience to date.' Her grip on her emotions slipped. 'I'm telling you, I'm pregnant.'

'No.' Massimo stared, simply nonplussed. 'That's *not* possible.'

How had his day gone from fantastic to fatal in one split-second? She was a stranger to him now, growing paler by the second until she had a positively greenish tint, and it wasn't some filter on the phone. He couldn't comprehend what she was saying.

Pregnant? *No.*

His reaction was visceral, violent, an outright rejection because it *was* impossible. He wasn't having children. He'd *not* got her pregnant. He would never get a woman pregnant. Never take that risk. He'd used protection. Every time. So he didn't believe her. He couldn't.

This had to be something else. This had to be a trick. What was she planning? What was the point of this? For all their banter that night, had she played the innocent but actually been the player? Did she think she could take him for a ride?

'I did a test earlier today.' She sounded adamant. And angry.

He didn't believe her for a second. It was far too improbable. *Impossible.* A million questions flooded his mind. He shook his head. 'It's not possible.' People lied—all people, all the time. 'Do you take me for a fool?'

'A fool?' She stared at him as if he'd just grown horns and fangs. 'Don't you *believe* me?'

It hadn't occurred to Carrie that he wouldn't believe her. That he'd turn so cold. She'd not imagined he'd speak quite so harshly—not just judging her but *hating* her.

'Why don't you believe me?' This was worse than anything. Even worse than when her sister had revealed her betrayal. 'Should I get the test and prove it to you?'

'You're going to need several tests.'

Her jaw dropped. What did that even mean? A test to prove she was pregnant? A test to prove *he* was the father?

'How could you think I'd make this up? That I would lie to you?' She struggled to understand his thinking. 'I might have been the ultimate loser the night we met, but I'm not so desperate that I'd… I'd…' She couldn't even figure out what nefarious plan it was that he thought she was capable of.

'I'm…' He clenched his jaw.

'You're what?' Her anger billowed.

He lifted his chin. 'Very wealthy.'

She stared at him for another moment as her shocked brain took an eternity to process what he was implying.

'You *jerk*.' Her mouth was so dry and her throat so tight, it was nigh impossible for sound actually to emerge. But just enough did. 'You think I'm making this up because I want your *money*?' She stared at him. 'What an appalling accusation, to assume that I would…' Emotion temporarily robbed her of speech. Furious and hurt, she stared at him, utterly appalled. 'I'm having a *baby*. Your baby.'

He actually shuddered. She jerked, almost dropping the phone.

Because the expression in his eyes wasn't about *money*. He had too much of that to be bothered. This was the worst news in the world to him because he didn't want a baby. He didn't want her.

'Okay.' She broke. 'I've told you. That's all I'm obligated to do. You've chosen not to believe me. You don't have to.'

He just stared at her. To her horror, beads of sweat formed on his forehead and the colour leached from his skin. As belief dawned in his eyes, he looked as unwell as she felt. And it wasn't just belief she saw in him. It was *horror*.

Even through the churning nausea of her own despair she saw that change. His jaw was so clamped he was either stuck for something to say or desperately trying to hold back a stream of expletives. She suspected it was the latter.

He shot a look away from the screen. 'I need time to process this.'

'Yep,' she said, desperate to end the call before she vomited.

He was horrified. She was mortified.

'I'll be on the first flight I can.' His words were clipped. 'I'll message you the details.'

He ended the call. He couldn't go fast enough for her nor for himself. She leaned against the wall, her strength evaporating.

It had been a shock for her but it hadn't been the worst thing in the world. That was the thing—she was already past the horror and through to the disbelieving wonder. There was *such* wonder. This was unexpected. But this baby wasn't *unwanted* by her.

The same wasn't true for Massimo. He couldn't have looked more horrified. He'd been so outraged, he'd not believed her—he'd been furious at the thought. Then he'd realised she was telling the truth and he'd not just shut down, he'd been repulsed.

Devastated, Carrie kept replaying the moment he'd believed her. He'd all but shuddered with revulsion. Any last warmth had been snuffed by the nightmare she'd presented him with. He didn't want the baby. He certainly didn't want her. Which meant she was going to be on her own.

Her family would make her feel as if she'd failed, but there wasn't anything terribly new in that. She could handle it. But she wouldn't have her child striving to meet their impossible standards—or then being neglected of attention if she or he wasn't their kind of superstar. So somehow she would make it work. Other people did. They solo-parented all the world over. She could too. Because she *wasn't* a failure. She was just kind of normal.

But right now everything hurt. She curled into a ball on her sofa, trying to stop the incessant replay of that moment but failing. He'd accused her of lying. He'd looked at her with disbelief and disgust. That he'd believed that of her... Had everything she'd felt that night been false? The betrayal *hurt*. She closed her eyes, desperate to wipe the sight of his reaction from her mind, exhausted by the effort of it all.

She woke some time in the pre-dawn hours. It wasn't a crippling, searing pain but a dull ache down low. One she felt every damn month. Fresh tears stung as her sad little heart tore. She still felt sick but figured that was from shame. God, it was so typical that she'd made such a colossal, embarrassing mistake.

Except she hadn't. The test yesterday had been positive. Maybe she'd done it wrong. But she knew she hadn't. She knew, in her bones, that she'd been pregnant. Now she wasn't. And the hurt she'd felt only hours before had nothing on this.

At least *he* didn't have to worry any more.

She couldn't bear to tell him to his face tomorrow. He wouldn't be able to hide his relief, while she wouldn't be able to hide her devastation. Hopefully he'd not yet left for the airport.

She didn't make a video call this time. She sent a simple single text.

Just got my period. Sorry to have concerned you.

She switched off her phone the second she'd sent it. Now they never, *ever* had to see each other again.

CHAPTER FOUR

Seven months later

'BULA VINAKA!' CARRIE smiled at the street vendor and savoured the scent of fresh sliced pineapple, hoping the juicy mix of sweet and acidic would be the invigorating kick she desperately needed. Breakfast hadn't happened. She'd slept badly, only to wake late, and had literally run to work. Fortunately, her boss, Sereana, had suggested they grab a snack before their first meeting.

Around her the market crowd moved amorphously. She pushed back on the lingering discomfort that had robbed her of rest and breathed in the vibrancy. Her contract extension was almost over and she was determined to enjoy every final moment she had in Fiji. She turned, taking in the verdant, vital atmosphere, and a tall figure crossed her vision in the distance. Clad in black, the guy moved with the confidence of someone who owned it all.

Recognition sparked, making her do a double take. Memories flooded, muddying her mind. She'd worked hard to suppress all thoughts of Massimo these last few months, but suddenly she *saw* him.

Surely not? Fiji would be the *last* place he'd appear—he wasn't a beach holiday kind of guy, remember? But Carrie's tired mind tricked her regardless, super-imposing other attributes onto that distant hewn physique—arrogance, sensuality, *challenge*.

She gritted her teeth. She was in the most beautiful place in the world and life was wonderful. She'd moved on from that one night all those months ago, and the mortifying mistake she'd made those few weeks later. But her sun-dazzled eyes kept tracking the figure. Laughter, excitement and energy hummed from the group surrounding him. She blinked away the black spots of sun blindness. Even though he had his back to her, she saw the way his hair fell slightly long and remembered the feel of it between her fingers.

She needed him to turn. Would she see those disturbingly green eyes? Would she see a sensual mouth? If he stepped closer, would she hear a voice that whispered wicked invitation and wilful temptation? All those months ago she'd been so seduced by him, she'd abandoned all caution, all reticence, for a single night of silken ecstasy only to...

A sharp pain lanced, shocking her back to the present. Winded, she pressed her hand to her stomach. How the mind could wreak havoc on the body. The stabbing sensation was a visceral reminder of the desolate emptiness she'd been trying to ignore for so long.

She'd recovered from that heartbreak. She was living her best life here—free and adventurous, bathing in the warm, brilliant waters of the Pacific. Her confusion was because she was tired. But she couldn't resist stepping closer—even as another sharp pain stole her breath.

'That's interesting.' He addressed the man beside him. 'Why are...?'

Shock deadened her senses, muting both him and the pain still squeezing her to the point where she couldn't breathe. That *voice*. The low tone that invited such confidence and tempted the listener to share their deepest secrets.

Massimo hadn't just spoken to her. He'd offered the sort of attention that had simply stupefied her mind and left her able only to say *yes*. And she had. Like all the women who'd come before her. And doubtless all those who'd come after.

Now his brief laugh was deep and infectious. Despite

the distance, it was as if he had his head intimately close to hers, his arm around her waist, his lips brushing her highly sensitised skin…

Pain tore through her muscles, forcing her to the present again. She gasped as it seared from her insides and radiated out with increasingly harsh intensity. She stared, helpless in the power of it, as that dark head turned in her direction. His green-eyed gaze arrowed on her.

Massimo.

'Carrie?' Sereana materialised, blocking him from Carrie's view. 'Are you okay?' Her boss looked as alarmed as she sounded.

Carrie crumpled as the cramp intensified. It was as if she'd been grabbed by a ginormous shark that was trying to tear her in two. 'Maybe I ate something…'

Her vision tunnelled as she tumbled to the ground.

'Carrie?'

Not Sereana.

She opened her eyes and stared straight into his. 'Massimo?'

It couldn't really be him. She was hallucinating, surely? But she felt strong arms close about her. She felt herself being lifted and pressed to his broad, hard chest. He was hot and she could hear the thud of his racing heart. Or maybe it was only her own.

If this were just a dream, fine. She closed her eyes and kept them closed. She would sleep and this awful agony would stop. She really needed it to stop.

'*Carrie!*'

CHAPTER FIVE

'CAN I GET an update on Carrie Barrett's condition please?'

Massimo paced across the office floor while he waited for the hospital receptionist to answer.

'She's listed as serious. I'm sorry, sir, I can't say anything more.'

He closed his eyes. For the first time in almost a week, she'd not been classed as *critical*. Relief warred with frustration. He still didn't know what the hell was wrong with her. Patient privacy rules meant he wasn't cleared to receive information and her doctors had ruled she couldn't have visitors or take calls. He wasn't family. They had no relationship. He was just the guy who'd caught her when she'd collapsed.

It had been terrifying.

She'd not regained consciousness in those horrific minutes when he'd held her as his driver had taken them to the nearest hospital. Medics had met him in the car park. He'd not got inside, and in the confusion he hadn't been able to find out who was the woman she'd been with. Now he was unable to find out anything more than the one-word answer. And he couldn't just leave. He needed to know she was okay. He'd been needing to know that for months. Because of the guilt still roiling in his belly.

The receptionist now recognised his voice and the next day she answered before he'd finished asking.

'She's stable, sir.'

Massimo breathed out. Stable was better than serious. Whatever it was, Carrie was obviously on the mend. Equally obviously, she didn't want him to know more. Because she'd seen him. She'd said his name. But she hadn't contacted him or authorised the hospital to allow him to receive information about her. And maybe, after what had happened, that was understandable. He couldn't bear to remember the last time they'd spoke. Not that shocking video call nor the harrowing message he'd received less than twelve hours later.

Yeah, that guilt still burned. He hadn't just reacted badly to her news on the call, he'd been appalling. And he'd not explained. How could he have said anything to her then? Why add to her obvious distress with his own nightmares of maternal mortality? He knew the facts. What had happened to his mother was rare. But that hadn't stopped his immediate, uncontrollable horror. He hadn't wanted Carrie in any danger.

But the situation had resolved itself. Rapidly. Awfully. Her message had been the end. He should have been able to let it go. Let all thoughts of *her* go. That was obviously what she'd wanted, given she'd cut off her phone. Instead his thoughts had festered. Was it his fault? Had he upset her so much? Was she okay?

So he couldn't just leave her now. He still didn't want her in any danger. How much her condition mattered! It was that lingering guilt, right?

Not entirely, no. He couldn't forget *her*. Hell, she was why he was in Fiji at all. Her joyful dreams of heading to a Pacific island paradise had got to him. He'd not taken her teasing suggestion that he invest there seriously at the time. But a couple of months later he'd still been unable to shake the thought and he'd begun a genuine investigation for work. Now he was feeling raw enough to admit the ridiculous truth. He'd been tempting fate—wanting to find her, unable to forget her. Hell, he still dreamed about her every damn night, and had since the start. It was horrendous.

And she didn't want to see him.

So Massimo had respected her wishes. He'd forced himself to fly home. He couldn't waste more time on something so ludicrously personal. He never had before and he was not going to succumb to obsession in the way of his father. But from Sydney he still made the daily call, indulging that stupid need for the few minutes it took. The need to know how she was. Where she was.

Each day he got the same response. *Stable. Stable. Stable.* Always followed by the kicker, 'I'm sorry, sir, no visitors or calls allowed.'

It was almost another three weeks before everything changed. Because it wasn't the usual receptionist.

'Barrett?' the telephonist echoed vaguely as he tapped on the computer. 'Barrett. They're both doing well.'

Well was good, but... Massimo froze. 'Both?'

'Uh...' The stand-in receptionist sounded hesitant.

But Massimo wasn't losing this nugget of information now. 'Both Barretts?' he confirmed confidently, as if this was exactly what he'd expected. 'Not just Carrie?'

'Yes, both are stable. I'm afraid I can't give any more information, sir.'

'Of course. I understand.'

But he didn't. At all.

He replayed that moment in the market, when he'd been on a tour with some interested advisors. Everything had happened so quickly. She was already on the ground when he'd got to her. He'd not had time to pay close attention to anything other than getting her help. She'd been in a loose summer dress. Maybe she'd been a little softer than she'd been all those months ago, but she hadn't looked obviously *pregnant*.

Now he pulled up the very last message he'd received from Carrie Barrett before her phone had been disconnected. The message that had haunted him every day of the seven months since it had landed.

Just got my period. So sorry to have concerned you.

He'd been awash with regret and guilt the first time he'd read it. But this time? Fury filled him. Because it had been a lie. An absolute, unforgivable lie.

Two weeks later Massimo leaned against the car, his gaze fixed on the automatic doors. He'd been here all day. Yesterday. The day before. He'd be here tomorrow too, if necessary. On the ground he'd chased the rumour and found it was true.

Both stable.

Rage had gripped him so tightly, he'd almost stormed straight into that hospital and swept the child into his arms, ready to eviscerate Carrie with his fury. At the same time sweep *her* into his arms. He wanted to run his hands all over her to ensure she was fine. He needed certainty that both she and the baby were okay. He needed that more than his next damn breath. And that need made him even angrier. He did not want to be so consumed by thoughts of *her*. But how much she must have suffered. To have been in hospital, so long. *Critical…*

But allowing emotion to overwhelm him wasn't going to get him what he wanted. He needed control—not to be locked out, not to be lied to.

It was the *worst*. This meant *family*, meant commitment, meant everything beyond his capability. But he had to ensure their security. So he would. Because Massimo refused to fail. He'd got *himself* under control. And he'd planned. Meticulously.

Carrie rolled her shoulders to loosen the sundress from her skin. The last few weeks had been a blur of confusion, of kindness from people she barely knew and of overwhelming emotion. She just needed five minutes alone before leaving the hospital for good. While she felt physically stronger, mentally she'd only recently emerged from a fog of disbelief. But she had to face what—and who—she'd been avoiding.

Massimo.

She actually thought she'd seen him that day in the market. She'd been in such pain, she'd hallucinated, her mind playing tricks as her body had been compelled to give up its secret. It had been an embarrassingly wishful 'rescue me' fantasy. She'd 'casually' asked Sereana what had happened at the market because she couldn't remember clearly. Sereana had explained that a couple of men had swept her up and brought her to the hospital in a private car, but that she had got left behind and had made her own way there. She'd not known who they were and had not seen them again.

Of course it hadn't been Massimo. Carrie shivered at the prospect of telling him her news now, knowing exactly how much he'd not wanted this.

She walked out of the hospital towards the flame tree marking the edge of the grounds. Its branches were smothered in scarlet flowers, signalling the height of a strong summer. Returning to England and her parents' judgement wasn't an option. As soon as she got to Sereana's house, she'd book her ticket to Australia. She had to do what was right. She'd taken too long already.

'Carrie?'

Great. Now she was hearing him—a conjuring up in her stressed, sleep-deprived state because she'd been thinking of him. Because she was finally well enough to know she couldn't put seeing him off any longer and actually had to do something about it. Because until now she'd had to focus on…

'Carrie.'

She turned, startled.

Massimo Donati-Wells was standing only a few feet away.

Her brain cut out. He *wasn't* a hallucination. He was here. With a raw edge to his voice and ferociousness in his stance. Time ended, just as it had the first night she'd met him. Only now his moss-coloured eyes were icy, his cheekbones like blades, his lethal energy coiled.

She couldn't breathe, unwilling to accept or even define the surfeit of feelings rampaging through her. Equally unable to deny them. Shockingly, one in particular ballooned—an effervescent bubble that couldn't be contained. *Pleasure*.

For a sliver of a second she saw heat flare in his green gaze, a mirror of the yearning burn sparking within her. A fleeting wisp of dangerous, dangerous *hope* soared. But the bubble burst and released true terror. Because Massimo was *not* smiling.

Tell him.

Her lips parted but nothing emerged. There was no breath in her boneless body, no thought in her cotton-wool brain. She could only stare as memories surfaced from that locked box deep inside. They spilled out of order like fragments of shattered glass—some too perfect, others too devastating, all too painful to piece together.

Despite her determination to bury all thoughts of him, every night her subconscious battled her mental rigor. Every night it won. He appeared in the dreams she dreaded—the dreams that made her restless and hot—despite the overhead fan and her single layer of cotton covering, despite her heart-break, despite her massive new responsibilities.

Tell him.

But she remembered the last time she'd done that. She'd tried for months to wipe it from her memory. She didn't want to see that expression again now.

You have no choice.

This was the last thing he wanted. *She* was the last thing he wanted. And as for…

Now.

Guilt burned the back of her throat. How could she easily segue into, *Wow, how convenient you're here. I've been meaning to get in touch…there's something I need to tell you…*

How, when he towered, commanding attention, leaner than she remembered? How, when he looked impossibly cool in that shirt, apparently unaffected by humidity or heat or heightened emotion?

There *was* no emotion. Why would there be? They'd had a one-night stand. That was all. He was a master of them. The brilliant billionaire—sleek and successful, oblivious to heat or other pressure, utterly in control. But that sharpness hadn't been there the night they'd met. Nor had there been such an uncompromising set to his jaw.

She should have got in contact with him by now. She should have phoned. But she'd wanted to deal with him in person because she'd been afraid he wasn't going to believe, or understand. It had taken *her* weeks to understand. Dread poured into her veins, dripping into a bottomless pool of despair.

'You lied to me.' The charming warmth was gone.

He wasn't the man she'd allowed to seduce her in a night so searing she'd not wanted it to end. But the ramifications were unending.

Her voice still wouldn't work. She was unable to utter even an inanity, let alone the truth. He shoved his hands into his pockets. His stance grew increasingly rigid. She could see his fists despite that perfectly cut fabric. No blood beat around her icy body as the horrific realisation hit.

'Are you not going to answer?' His over-enunciated demand excoriated her like a shower of small, sharp stones. 'Can't you tell me the truth even when I'm standing right in front of you?'

'Mass...' She couldn't even say his whole name. Her throat was thick, her brain sluggish. Her words were rusty and weren't the ones she needed to say.

He jerked his head in a negating gesture. 'Liar.' His whisper didn't just cut, it poisoned. An almost inaudible accusation that dripped with scorn. 'You're a *liar*.'

She deserved his anger. She did. But she'd *not* lied. She

needed to explain but she didn't even know where to begin. The truth was so preposterous it had taken her weeks to believe—even when she'd had the proof right in front of her.

'How *could* you?' The fury in him frothed over. 'Stop stalling, Carrie.' He stepped closer and sliced open her worst nightmare. 'You know I'm here for my child. Why are you alone? What have you done with her?'

Massimo had thought he'd moved past anger. He'd thought he'd worked through the white-hot, visceral fury that had scoured him relentlessly over the last two weeks. He'd been so arrogant, he'd thought he was now comfortably cruising in the lane of ice-cold control and that he had been for days as he'd made the final, crucial preparations of his perfect plan.

Wrong. So damned wrong.

One glance into her clear blue eyes, one look at her soft lips and elfin chin, one whiff of her floral sensuality, one tiny moment in the same space as her and he was tossed back into the maelstrom of rage that had been shredding him for days.

How could someone so deceitful be so angelically beautiful? With one look, with barely one word, she had destroyed his equanimity. He, who managed difficult people and tense contract negotiations, apparently couldn't stand two seconds in her company without falling victim to his emotions. The instant surge of rage was almost impossible to control.

Rage *was* the emotion. There was *nothing* else. Certainly not some damned flare of… *No.* She'd betrayed him completely and he did not *want* her. He wanted only to do what was necessary, what was *right*.

The teal dress hid her curves but highlighted the clarity of her eyes. They'd widened while the rest of her petite features had become pinched. Pallor dulled her radiance as fear stripped away her customary soft, smiling welcome.

'Where is she?' he asked tensely.

'In the hospital.'

'And you've abandoned her?'

'No!'

'Then why are you out here alone? Take me to her.' Her shocked expression infuriated him and that supposed control slipped. 'I know she's mine.'

Her eyes widened. 'How...?'

'Do you expect me to believe that, within a day of gifting your virginity to me, you were off having unprotected sex with an assortment of other men?' he snapped. 'Maybe you did. Maybe that was all part of your plan.'

Her jaw dropped. 'What plan? There was no plan.'

Pure deceit dripped from her tongue. He drew a sharp breath as his anger railed against the tight bonds he fought to secure it with. There'd been too many liars in his life already, liars who'd razed his world to the ground. That wasn't happening again.

'You expect me to believe that?' He tightened his fists in his pockets, pushed close to losing control. He had to shove every other muscle into a kind of stasis.

How could he be surprised that Carrie Barrett could lie right to his face without even blinking or blushing? She'd been lying for months. He had to restrain himself from pacing closer, from shouting out the frustration that had amassed since he'd found out the appalling truth. He'd play this as coolly as he'd planned.

But just looking at her derailed his thoughts. The bright sundress didn't suit her sleepless, worry-ravaged visage. She didn't look as if she'd been living it up on the beach. Any tan she'd managed to acquire had faded during these weeks in hospital. Tiredness muted her. She looked vulnerable and that made him feel guilty. No. *She* was the guilty one.

'Did you lie about everything?' His control slipped again. 'About your virginity? Maybe you're *that* good an actress.'

Fierce rejection flooded his body even as he spoke. He didn't know why he was torturing himself but seeing her in the flesh brought forth all the memories he'd been failing to suppress. Right now his bloody brain replayed the moment when he'd claimed first possession—when he'd stared so closely into her blue eyes and watched so carefully for her response. He'd never drawn such deep pleasure in bringing a lover to that peak, again and again. She'd been so eager, so gorgeous, she'd turned him inside out in seconds.

They'd only had one night. He rarely had more with a woman—a deliberate choice to avoid emotional entanglement. But he'd not slept with another woman since Carrie. It had been the best part of a *year*. Never had he gone without for so long. Appallingly, even now in the face of her lies, with the full extent of her betrayal revealed, his body still wanted hers. As if hauling her against him could possibly salve the wounds she'd inflicted!

Fool.

He'd waited these last two weeks—pacing while preparing, hoping against hope that she would initiate contact, that she would seek him out and show some skerrick of integrity. She hadn't. Her true character had been revealed. She'd chosen this path and, now he knew what he was up against, *he* had to do all that was necessary. Which meant sticking to *his* plan. The ends absolutely justified the means.

A bruised mix of accusation and hurt shadowed her eyes. She drew a steadying breath and he knew she was about to brave it. The gesture stirred another unwanted memory. The night they'd met she'd been let down but she'd lifted her head and ordered that cocktail, determined not to show her humiliation even though it had been obvious. Just as her emotion was obvious now. Why had she wanted to hide from him? What was her agenda?

Massimo wanted the truth, no matter the price—moral or otherwise. 'Don't bother trying to lie more. You know I can see through your bravado,' he said bitterly. It was far too late for that.

'I was going to tell you.' She finally spoke. A whispery confession that still wasn't the truth.

He had to hold his muscles so rigid he couldn't even roll

his eyes. He didn't want to hear more of her lies, but as for honesty? He realised too late that there was nothing she could say that would make this okay.

She stepped towards him, her words tumbling faster. 'You have to understand—'

'*How?*' Fury got the better of him and he viciously hurled the word at her. 'How am I *ever* supposed to do that? You told me you were pregnant. Then you told me you weren't. No, wait—you didn't even bother to tell me, you just sent a message and disappeared. You went completely offline, unable to be contacted. Turns out you moved to some remote Pacific island to enjoy your pregnancy alone and have your baby in secret. Weeks later you *still* haven't told me. How can I ever understand any of that? What the hell is going on, Carrie?'

She laced her fingers together and slowly shook her head in continued denial, her heartbreakingly blue eyes beseeching. 'I didn't...'

He waited, his muscles burning.

'I didn't know...'

She only managed one more word before her voice petered out again.

'Didn't know what—how to get in touch with me?' Impatiently he stepped closer. 'I gave you my *personal* number.'

She gaped at him for a second and sudden defiance flashed in her eyes. 'Should I consider myself honoured?'

'Absolutely.' He glared at her. He rarely gave that number to anyone. 'Why didn't you call?' he snapped. 'You know I wanted to do right by you.'

A stricken look flickered in her face.

'You've had *months*!' he erupted, retaliating against the tug in his chest at her expression. 'And there are no excuses. Nothing you can say can adequately explain what you've done.'

He hated that he sounded wounded. He didn't want her to know how badly her actions had bothered him—he didn't even want to admit that to himself. He'd claw back his self-control and focus on the only thing that mattered—the welfare of the baby she'd hidden from him. Children had never been in his plan and still weren't. But, while fate had other ideas, he wasn't having Carrie steal his remaining choices. She could think what she liked of him. That was *her* problem, not his.

'Are you going to take her from me?' she asked brokenly.

Her. His daughter.

Massimo stared at her, struggling with the burning sensation deep in his gut. Rage warred with empathy. Her widened eyes were almost feverishly bright. Terror emanated from her in an oppressive, desperate wave that he couldn't turn his back on. He gritted his teeth and mustered every speck of control, of unwilling compassion, that he could.

'You might think it's acceptable to take a child from a parent without so much as a word. I, however, do not,' he muttered hoarsely.

The breath she released blew like a stormy gust but it cleared none of the tense air between them. His pulse raced, tumultuous and unpredictable—as his feelings concerning her apparently were. They surged like tumble weed. He didn't want *feelings*. They weren't conducive to his plan. Emotions—intense emotions—destroyed everything. They had before.

Stay on track. Stay calm.

He wanted to turn from her fear but couldn't. It was so thick, it encapsulated her—as if she were stuck in a smeared glass dome that he itched to smash so he could free her, see her properly. But *he* was who she was afraid of.

It rankled more than it should have. Of course, she *should* be afraid. She should wonder what he might do now. Who would blame him for this anger considering what she'd done? But *why* had she done it?

There was the rub. There was the unanswered question.

He didn't want to care. She was just the lying, secretive mother of the child he'd not wanted. And there was the *real* problem. The *last* thing he wanted was to be left solely responsible for the baby. She needed his assets, but not him personally. He didn't have the skills to parent. He'd not had the example. And honestly? He didn't have the desire. Relationships were not something he managed. Emotional intimacy? No, not something he was capable of. But that child would know the *truth* of her parentage. Massimo would provide all he *could*.

Stability and security mattered. But right now nothing mattered as much as the truth. 'Why did you lie about losing the baby?'

She was very still now. 'I didn't lie.'

Massimo briefly closed his eyes in frustrated disbelief at her quiet, determined reply because it rang so damned true. And then to his fury she went one further.

'I've never lied to you.'

CHAPTER SIX

CARRIE WINCED AS Massimo opened his eyes and shot her a look of such condemnation that she should have instantly been eviscerated.

'This is a waste of time. We need to leave.' He growled.

Her heart thundered. 'To—?'

'Get out of this heat,' he interrupted, his energy unleashed. 'You look like you're about to pass out.'

But she planted herself in front of him. 'I *didn't* lie.'

She'd just not told him some things. Yes, some very *important* things, but she'd wanted to tell him in person. In those first days she'd been too unwell to think, let alone act. More recently she'd coped only by focussing moment by moment. 'It all happened so fast—'

'Pregnancies aren't all that fast,' he interrupted before she could fully explain. Those lines of condemnation deepened. 'You could have found five minutes to call...'

He was so angry, he was unable to listen let alone believe. The warm, attentive man from all those months ago was the mirage. The *reality* of Massimo was right in front of her. The one she'd seen on that video call. The one who'd believed the very worst of her. Untrusting. Uncaring. Implacable. Impatient. Her fear had been so very justified. He was going to be ruthless and relentless in pursuing what he wanted. And he wasn't going to give her a chance.

And, at the same time as her fear exploded, guilt crashed in on a tsunami that smashed what little confidence she had left. Because she had messed up. If he'd only give her a few seconds to explain. But that was her own fault too, wasn't it? She'd had weeks to do that and she hadn't. *That* was on her.

It was no excuse, but the physical weakness had wrecked her in ways she was still coming to terms with, and Massimo appearing so unexpectedly had shocked her into an unthinking, reactionary response.

'I'm sorry,' she said desolately. 'I should have got in touch. I promise I was going to. *Please* let me explain.'

His jaw clamped and he jerked his chin—assent full of resentment.

It was going to sound preposterous. Why she'd not reached out already—not to him or to any family or friends, beyond the few she'd made here.

'When I messaged you, I truly believed I'd got my period,' she explained flatly. 'I didn't know I was still pregnant until I went into labour at the market here a few weeks ago.'

The morning she'd thought she'd seen him. That unforgettably hot day when she and Sereana had stopped for a snack before a meeting.

Massimo didn't move. She began to wonder if he'd even heard her. She was about to repeat herself when he finally spoke.

'Is *that* what you're going with?' Contempt tarred the bitterest laugh she'd ever heard. 'How do you expect me to believe that?'

'I can't make you believe anything.' She drew deep, summoning dignity to suppress the tears stinging her eyes. 'But it's the truth.'

'How could you not know? Not in all those months of pregnancy?' He put his hands on his hips and glared at her. 'Didn't you gain weight? *Show?*'

'Not initially.' Her skin burned. It was *obvious* she'd gained some weight. 'And then I thought I was just enjoying the food here. I wasn't focused on trying to stay fit or anything.'

She'd avoided scales and mirrors for a long while, as coconut *brûlée* had become a favourite treat. Okay, there'd been some comfort eating. She was human and she'd been hurt and she'd wanted to forget things. And she'd had minor erratic bleeding, but she'd figured her system was taking a while to regulate again after the loss. Honestly, most of the time she'd tried hard not to think about it.

'I know how unbelievable it sounds. *I* still can't believe it and I'm the one who's—' She broke off as she saw him tense. 'No one is more aware of how stupid this makes me seem. But why would I do this? Why *wouldn't* I tell you?'

'That's what I've been wondering.' Hot fury flashed in his eyes. He hated her right now.

'You're Massimo Donati-Wells, Australian billionaire genius. If I'm the awful woman you obviously think me, wouldn't I want you to know? Wouldn't I be out to get everything I could from you?'

'For all I know you might still be,' he countered crisply. 'This might be part of your plan to extract exactly that.'

'I don't want anything from you,' she snapped. 'Would I choose to collapse in a public market? Would I choose to give birth unknowing and utterly unprepared? I didn't know anything—not even how to change a nappy, let alone feed and properly care for a tiny baby. It was terrifying.'

He was somehow nearer, somehow taller, somehow even angrier—grinding out his condemnation. 'If you hadn't run away in the first place, that *never* would have happened.'

She'd been dreading explaining her pathetic mistake to anyone. Who would believe that even *she* had been that stupid and naive? Then again, she'd believed her ex-fiancé when he'd said he wanted to wait until they were married to have sex when all the while he'd been off having sex with…

Don't think about that now.

She'd been so confused when she'd first woken—more than two days after Ana's delivery. Apparently she wasn't the first woman to have claimed she 'didn't know she was pregnant'. When she'd first regained consciousness and expressed her total shock, one of the doctors had sat beside her with patronising kindness, repeatedly telling her she wasn't to feel ashamed at being an unwed mother, and that she didn't need to make up such an outlandish tale. She could just admit the truth…

But she *genuinely* hadn't known she was pregnant. She'd *grieved* all those months ago. And she'd grieved over Massimo. She'd run away from Auckland that very night because she hadn't wanted to face him, had been afraid that, if she did, he'd see how desperately she'd wanted their unplanned child when he so desperately *hadn't*.

Massimo stared into her eyes, a frown in his. 'When you thought you'd miscarried, you didn't see a doctor for confirmation?'

'It was so early on I didn't think I needed to,' she mumbled.

She'd not wanted to be baldly told the truth by some doctor she didn't know. She'd just wanted to escape. She'd come to Fiji early and told herself it was all going to be okay… eventually.

'Why didn't you care for yourself enough to get checked out?' he asked roughly.

Massimo's question threw her. He wasn't judging her for not realising she'd still been pregnant, but…

Why didn't you care for yourself enough…?

Now she felt worse. Not only did no one else really care, *she* hadn't cared for *herself*. And there was no answer she could give him.

'I was already on a flight from Sydney when I got that message, but when I landed, you'd vanished.'

Another layer of guilt piled on. Because, yes, she'd run away. Truthfully, she still didn't want him to know how much he'd impacted on her decision to go. She'd fallen beneath his spell. But now? He couldn't think less of her anyway.

'I didn't want to burden you with my emotions,' she said shakily. 'We barely knew each other.'

'Even so, you didn't think I'd have supported you?'

He made it sound as if *he'd* actually cared. That stoked her anger.

'You didn't want the baby, Massimo,' she said. 'You *know* you didn't. You were so shocked and appalled, you couldn't get off that call quickly enough.'

His expression shuttered. 'I wanted to know *you* were okay but you blew me off. I would have paid for the doctors if I'd known you were struggling. I would have taken you to see one myself.'

Sure, he was courteous, and he'd wanted to ensure her physical well-being. He was decent enough guy. But all she'd been to him was a novelty one-night stand. He'd not wanted anything more. Certainly not a literally life-long connection. Because he didn't deny her first truth. He hadn't wanted their child.

He muttered an oath beneath his breath and she felt his shift in thinking—from anger to wary concern.

'Even if I believe you about the pregnancy—and I'm not saying I do—it's been seven weeks since you gave birth. Why haven't you been in touch since? I phoned that hospital every day. You must know that.'

'What?' She gaped at him. 'No one told me you'd called. How did you know I was in hospital?

'Seriously?' He gaped at her. 'I *took* you there.'

Her vision tunnelled. 'You really were at the market?'

He gaped, raw fury firing his words. 'You called my name.'

'I thought I'd hallucinated you,' she whispered. 'I thought that was a dream. Because after…after…'

It had been days before she'd regained consciousness, then she'd been overwhelmed by caring for Ana. The doctors had been concerned by her agitation, her supposed confusion and refusal to admit she'd been pregnant. They'd not even let Sereana visit her for several days. 'No one mentioned any calls,' she said. 'Surely they would have passed on your messages?'

His jaw clamped. 'I didn't leave a message. I didn't leave my name.'

'Why not?' She was stunned.

'I didn't think I needed to.' He growled. 'You'd seen me at the market.'

'But I didn't think that was real.'

He hesitated. 'I didn't realise you were that confused at the time. But why didn't you call me in the days after?'

'I got rid of my phone in New Zealand. I didn't have your number here. Besides, it wasn't something I could tell you on a call. Not this time.'

'Yet you've not booked a flight.'

'How do you know?' She felt angry and confused. 'Have you been spying on me?'

'You've hardly given me reason to trust you,' he justified. But his body tensed. 'People lie.'

'*I* didn't,' she said, drawing in a hard breath. 'I just didn't tell you.'

'Isn't that the same thing?'

She shook her head. 'I was scared.'

His mouth tightened. 'You trusted me enough to sleep with me when you hadn't with anyone else.'

'That was different.'

That had just been about her, and *she* was used to rejection. It had been a risk she'd taken for herself. But Massimo had already rejected their baby once and she'd not wanted to see that rejection again. Because, while rejection for herself hurt enough, seeing her baby rejected, not valued—not happening. She wasn't having what had happened to her happen to her daughter. And he'd already rejected their baby once.

She saw his ferocity return and stepped in before he could ask. 'Maybe I should have got medical care all those months ago,' she admitted. 'But I didn't want to face it. Or you. I'm not proud of that. Ana's birth was shocking, and my world went *crazy*. She was little and needed support and I…' She couldn't even remember those first few nights.

'You shouldn't have been alone.'

'I wasn't,' she hastened to reassure him. 'We had the best care. My friend Sereana has been a huge support. Everyone here has been generous and caring. They've been wonderful.'

Far from reassured, he looked angrier. 'Well, now I guess it's my turn to be generous and caring and *wonderful*,' he said sarcastically. 'I already told you I'm here for the baby. And, as at this point in her life, *you're* part of the package, so that means you're coming too. Now.'

At this point in her life?

Did that mean that at some point in the future he expected Carrie *wouldn't* be part of the package?

Fear transformed into fight and Carrie—who usually wouldn't argue with anyone, who would simply smile and say, *Sure!* To whatever was requested because she was such a damned people-pleaser—now stood her ground. Even as she shook while doing so.

'No,' she said harshly. 'I'm not leaving with you.'

Not without knowing where, why and for how long. Not without some *say* in it.

'No?'

Carrie stiffened her legs to stop them trembling. 'I have friends here.'

'And you think they'll rescue you from my evil clutches?' He shook his head sceptically. 'Are they aware that you've denied your child's father *everything*—right down to knowledge of her existence?'

Nausea roiled in her stomach. 'They'll assume I have my reasons for not wanting to be with you.'

She'd made a massive mistake but she couldn't cede *all* control to him. He'd interpreted everything awfully and her own bitter hurt cut deep. Worse, another tension still strained. Another source of crackling energy that was so wrong. Because, even when icily furious, Massimo was gorgeous and her stupid, *stupid* body didn't want to resist him.

'What are they?' he asked softly. 'How terrible will you make them—make *me*—out to be?' His expression tightened. 'What did I do to make you *this* determined to cut me from the child's life?'

She'd never intended to cut him from Ana's life, but his reaction now... He still wouldn't believe her...

'You don't *want* her!' she snapped angrily. 'You didn't believe me all those months ago. And you *still* think I just want your money.'

What had *she* done to make him that mistrustful of her?

'Yeah?' Fury flashed in his eyes as he snapped back. 'Because I do have money, Carrie. I have unlimited resources. My lawyers will make a compelling case for full custody. You'll be labelled as a mother who was so neglectful she didn't even *know* she was pregnant, who then didn't bother to even try to get in touch with the father, who didn't have a home to bring her child to from hospital... How can you think you'll win?'

She wouldn't. Not when he stacked it like that. Her behaviour sounded appalling and unworthy. But there was no mention of the post-birth complications, the illness, the exhaustion and extenuating circumstances.

But she wasn't about to use her health to manipulate him into pitying her. All those months ago she'd had no idea how powerful he really was. Now she knew more—he was a billionaire boy-wonder who'd made his first millions by 'playing' with investments as a teen. He'd formed his own private equity company specialising in structuring deals for start-ups, then for firms needing to expand. Frankly, she didn't understand it entirely. But the several spotlight articles she'd read had stressed his work ethic. Detail on his personal life had been scant in those articles. But photos of him out with a bunch of different women littered Sydney city-life blogs. *That* hadn't surprised her at all.

She understood he was driven, not just to achieve, but to *accumulate*. To win at all costs. She needed to break through to him.

'You said you weren't going to take her from me,' she said.

There was a moment of electric silence. She stared into his furious green eyes, reading the swirl of emotion that he couldn't suppress.

'And I'm not,' he said eventually. 'But compromise takes two and I'll take what I'm *owed*. So come with me now, or I'll call the police and kick up such merry hell you won't know what's hit you. *Nothing* will stand in the way of what I want. Certainly not you.'

Some *compromise*. It was an unadulterated, vicious ultimatum.

So, she had to push. 'And what is it, exactly, that you want?'

He paused again. 'I want what's best for the child. I want to work through this *with* you. There's no need for this to be acrimonious. The least you can give me right now is time. I think I deserve just a little of that, given how much I've already missed out on.' Massimo growled. 'You need time. You look tired.'

His brusque assessment diminished her. She must have mistaken the flicker of heat in his eyes when she'd first seen him. It was mortifying that she was still so wishful for his attention. That she was still so blown away by him that she'd read anger as lust.

Pull it together. The only person who mattered now was Ana.

'I assume you have room in a hotel somewhere?' she asked.

He lifted his head like a gleaming warrior sensing victory. Triumph flashed in his mossy eyes. 'Room for all of us, yes.'

'Which hotel? Ana and I can meet you there.'

'Do you honestly think I'm going to let you out of my

sight?' His brief laugh was mirthless. 'I wouldn't put it past you to vanish again.'

How little he trusted her. But she didn't trust him either. He assumed. He judged. And he wanted to control. But Massimo Donati-Wells wasn't going to get everything his own way. Because Carrie had a purpose bigger than herself. She had her daughter to protect.

'Then let's go.' Folding her arms across her chest, she held herself tightly. 'You need to meet Ana.'

CHAPTER SEVEN

MASSIMO STRODE TOWARDS the hospital entrance, hyper-conscious of Carrie silent alongside him. She was so close and yet so damned distant.

I was scared.

Why? Had she sensed the danger within him? Did she somehow know he wasn't capable of sticking as a father? Was that why she'd just spun him such a tale? Yet, impossible as her story was, part of him believed her. It incensed him that she'd faced any of this alone. That she'd not sought help all those months ago, suffering needless stress. Putting herself and the child at *risk*. It was unforgivable.

Plus the fact that his damned body couldn't care less whether she'd lied to him or not. All it wanted was for him to lie *with* her. For the first time, the afternoon heat bothered him. He wanted to peel off the shirt sticking to his back. Even though she'd agreed to come with him his tension now worsened. He'd not envisaged *this* moment—seeing the baby. Figuring out how he was going to be a father.

Carrie hadn't been wrong. He didn't want children. He never had. His family weren't meant to, after all. They weren't good at caring for them. Massimo was a prime example of both those truths. He was the child that his mother had struggled to conceive and hadn't been able to stay for; the child his father had initially neglected and ultimately abandoned. How the hell was he going to be a decent parent when he'd come from that?

He followed Carrie down the corridor. She greeted the staff by name and they responded with wide smiles. Her awareness and appreciation of them seemed genuine, and they certainly responded to her.

'Dr Taito,' she murmured as they arrived on the maternity ward.

'Carrie.'

Doctor.

Massimo stopped walking. So did the white-coat-clad woman.

Carrie realised and then turned reluctantly. 'Doctor, this is Massimo. Ana's father.'

The doctor stiffened and turned to cast a measuring eye over him. 'I'm sure you're looking forward to meeting your daughter, Massimo.'

His jaw ached from being held so tightly. 'Yes.'

The doctor glanced at Carrie. 'Sereana is waiting with her.'

Carrie smiled awkwardly and moved past. But, as Massimo went to follow, the doctor stopped him with a clinical hand on his arm and a cold stare.

'Carrie had a very tough time,' she said. 'She needs rest.'

Massimo stared back. 'Do you have a moment to talk more?'

The doctor nodded brusquely. 'Absolutely.'

Carrie awkwardly watched Massimo talking quietly with the doctor and wished she had bat ears. She'd not realised they were going to stop outside the room and continue a hushed conversation *without* her, but she couldn't go back and butt in.

Sereana and one of the nurses were now on either side of her, full of excitement about Ana's imminent discharge from the hospital and the surprise arrival of Massimo. Avid curiosity sparkled in their eyes and their smiles were broad. She could hardly create a *scene*. They'd already guessed he was Ana's father. One look at him now, and they were as delighted as if this were a fairy-tale ending to the drama. But it wasn't like that at all.

Moments later Massimo walked in without the doctor. To Carrie's horror, he flashed a full wattage smile at Sereana and spoke before Carrie had a chance to say anything.

'You must be Sereana. I understand I have much to thank you for. I'm very sorry I wasn't able to be here sooner.'

Had the doctor just given him a personality transplant? Now he was all polite charm, the fury completely masked. Predictably, Sereana's eyes widened and, while her mouth opened, no words emerged. Massimo had that effect.

Carrie's heart sank. He'd won already. She only half-listened as Massimo thanked Sereana again and explained that he was now here to take care of everything. Sereana was so stunned by him, she didn't realise he'd smoothly manoeuvred her into leaving sooner than she'd intended. Honestly, Carrie knew it was for the best. She and Massimo needed to work through this on their own.

'I can't thank you enough. You've been so kind to me.' Carrie hugged her friend goodbye. 'I'm so sorry—'

'You've nothing to apologise for!' Sereana interrupted. 'And you kept working on the schedule even when you were laid up in bed!'

Working on their upcoming athletics event had been the one thing Carrie *could* do to say thank you. 'I'll take the laptop with me so I can keep going.'

'I think you have other things to focus on.' Sereana's gaze arrowed to Massimo again.

'I *want* to finish it,' Carrie said quickly.

But Sereana was focused on everything else. 'I'm so glad he's come for you,' she murmured as she hugged her again. 'You should have sent for him *so* much sooner!'

Carrie agreed, but not for the reasons her friend was obviously assuming. But the delighted relief in Sereana's eyes was obvious. Carrie hadn't realised she'd been such a cause of concern for her friend, but of course she had. More than that, maybe she'd been a burden. So she smiled and hid her private concerns. She'd sort everything out just with Massimo.

Once they were alone, Massimo crossed the room, but she caught his quick glance into Ana's cot before he stood by her luggage.

'Is this everything?' His voice sounded husky.

Carrie didn't immediately reply. Tiny and utterly perfect, Ana had completely stolen her heart the second she'd clapped eyes on her. But Massimo hadn't glanced at the baby for more than a millisecond. Carrie's fear mushroomed into something unwieldy and out of control. She knew too well what it was like to be overlooked by the people who should love you unconditionally. She wanted *family* always to come first—ahead of work or other ambition. She wanted Ana to be as valued as she should be. Because Carrie hadn't been and she knew how much it hurt.

'Do you want to hold her?' she asked quietly. And, yes, it was a test.

Massimo stiffened. 'My finally meeting her, weeks late, is not a moment for public viewing.' He nodded towards the open curtain through which she could see the staff standing at their work station, from where they were not so surreptitiously staring.

Chastened, hot emotion engulfed Carrie.

'You bring her. I'll carry the bags. Is that all the luggage there is?' Again, he shot her bag a disparaging glance.

'I travel light and I was going to buy more for Ana once I—'

'It's fine. I've already bought what's required.' He cut her off.

His expression was so shuttered, she didn't ask what he meant by 'required'. Instead, she carefully lifted Ana.

The hospital farewells were a blur. Once outside, Carrie fumbled to figure how to click the safety harness in the baby seat already installed in Massimo's waiting car. Apparently, she needed a specialist engineering degree. With a stifled growl, Massimo brushed her fumbling fingers aside and swiftly made the contraption click. But then for a timeless moment he paused, his gaze fixed on the baby. Because, in the gentle movement, Ana stirred and her sweet eyes opened.

Carrie had believed that lots of babies had bluish eyes when first born. That their true colour settled a few months in. But Ana's eye colour was strikingly vibrant and—Carrie hoped—fixed. Because her beautiful little eyes were the exact mossy shade of her father's.

Undeniably his eyes. Undeniably *his* child.

Massimo turned and his gaze clashed with Carrie's. His green eyes now almost glowed with an edge that silenced her. Hot and terrifyingly intense. She saw protectiveness. *Possessiveness.*

Carrie's throat constricted. Her heart constricted. Her whole body went on hold—afraid and yet hoping so *hard* for some kind of acceptance. But he said nothing, and Carrie was too choked to.

They drove for only ten minutes then stopped at an island transport service. A helicopter was parked on the pad, its engine already roaring. Butterflies were instantly on a rotor beneath Carrie's ribs. A helicopter felt precarious. Everything was happening too fast and was too far from her control.

Massimo helped unfasten the baby seat and Carrie lifted it. He touched the small of her back with a lightly guiding hand, sensing her reluctance.

'I wouldn't be getting in if I didn't think it was safe,' he said softly. 'I like living. I have a lot to live for.'

Up close she saw it wasn't one of the usual island-hopping helicopters. This one was larger. Its midnight exterior gleamed while the interior was sleek. Once in, Carrie perched on the luxurious leather seat while Massimo secured Ana's baby seat and then took the seat opposite. There were no heads sets so she guessed the cabin must be soundproofed.

'Carrie.' He regarded her intensely as she felt them ascend. 'Breathe.'

She should be looking at her daughter, or at least the view as they left Suva, but she couldn't break free from Massimo's gaze. There was such intensity and judgement. But, as his gaze held hers, it morphed into wordless reassurance. She wasn't alone in this. Not any more. He was going nowhere. And, while that was concerning in some ways, it also gave her something to depend on.

And then there was something else again.

Her body contracted in reaction. She always yearned for that spark. Fear transformed into slow-building exhilaration. Into energy. She got a full charge from just one long look.

He was *here* and suddenly she was flooded with...

Ana snuffled. The small noise short-circuited the electricity arcing between them. Carrie immediately turned to check on her, hugely relieved to sever the connection, half-disappointed at the same time. Her heart melted at the sight of her daughter's sweet face with her perfect, petite lashes resting on her cheek. She had Massimo's hair colouring too—tiny jet lashes, and downy wisps of dark hair on her head. Carrie stroked her soft cheek in the lightest graze of reassurance. 'Hey, sweetheart.'

With a little turn of her tiny head, Ana blinked slowly a couple of times before her eyes closed and she slept again. A wave of protectiveness surged through Carrie, another of such gratitude that she'd made it.

When Carrie looked back, Massimo was intently focused on the view out of the window. There was no look between them now—no shared acknowledgment of the heart-melting adorableness of their baby with her full, pink cheeks. That rush of exhilaration was obliterated. It hurt to breathe deeply. Rejection? Being ignored? She'd do anything to spare her child those wounds. His reticence to engage with Ana was only because he wanted privacy, right?

Carrie could scarcely concentrate as they soared over the water. Islands dotted the brilliant blue waters beneath them like emerald and gold jewels—breathtakingly, unbelievably beautiful. Eventually they neared one small island, the sort upon which was only one exclusive resort. Privacy would *definitely* be ensured here.

The sandy beach encircling the island was a stunning creamy gold while the forest area rising in the centre was verdant and lush. Tucked in the plantings on the left stood a group of jaw-dropping buildings, the central villa a vision.

'This is Karakarawa Island,' Massimo said when they landed.

He hopped out of the helicopter and then turned, holding out his hand to offer her support.

His grip was firm and the immediate sizzle sent her straight back to that night. To heat, laughter and the most sensual experience ever. In the mêlée of memories, she barely noticed a man lift her bags and head along the path. But she did see a middle-aged woman in a crisp, white uniform approaching them with a deferential smile.

Wary, Carrie tensed and tugged her hand from Massimo's.

'Leah will take the baby in while I show you around,' Massimo said firmly.

Carrie watched the woman unclasp Ana's baby seat with expert ease.

'Leah is a fully qualified paediatric nurse,' Massimo added.

The woman smiled at Carrie. 'We'll be waiting in the nursery for you.'

Her Australian accent was obvious. Carrie's heart raced. Had Massimo brought Leah to Fiji with him? A nanny to whom he could entrust Ana's care—did that mean he could return to Australia with Ana but *without* Carrie?

'I won't be a moment.' Carrie anxiously watched Leah carry Ana away. She couldn't ignore the presence of the vital, ruthless man beside her.

'Leah's room is room right next to the nursery,' Massimo said. 'She also has a monitor, so she'll be there when the baby wakes in the night.'

'I'll tend to Ana at night. She needs me.'

His jaw tightened. 'But *you* need undisturbed sleep.'

Their eyes met. She refused to bend on this. But, as she stared at him, other things suddenly entered her mind. *Undisturbed sleep?* Heat scalded as inappropriate thoughts sneaked into her mind like inappropriate bandits. She actually envisioned being with him again.

Idiot! She dropped her gaze. Lingering lust was the last thing she needed. There was too much to sort out to add such distraction to the mix. Berating herself, she barely listened to Massimo as he led her along the neatly trimmed path towards the stunning building, pointing out amenities as they went. But after a moment she realised there was no one else in sight—no one using the beach shades or swimming in the pool, no one having an afternoon drink at the bar... It was extremely, *oddly* quiet.

'Where are the other guests?' she asked as they entered the large main building.

'There aren't any.'

'Did you hire the whole resort?'

A sharp glint shone in his eyes before he blinked back to bland.

'Massimo?' She stopped dead. 'Do you *own* this resort?''

A muscle in his jaw flexed, making his cheek bones impossibly sharper. 'I do now.'

So, it was a recent purchase. Back in Auckland, when they'd met, they'd sparred over the merits of island holidays. She'd been Team Beach while he'd declared them boring. He was all business.

'Are you telling me you bought this island 'specially for...?' She couldn't quite finish the thought. It was preposterous.

'It guarantees privacy and ensures we have everything we need while we're here.'

Who on earth just went and bought an *island*—one with

a luxury accommodation complex, swimming pool and all sorts of indulgent amenities?

'How long do you anticipate we'll stay?' She was standing still but she couldn't seem to catch her breath.

'As long as it takes for us to be in agreement regarding the child's future.'

In agreement? Her skin felt too small. They came from different sides of the world and were light years apart in wealth and status. *How* could she hold her own against him? Any agreement would simply be what *he* wanted.

'There's a skeleton staff on the island.' He continued his tour of his newly purchased paradise. 'Apart from Leah, their accommodation is on the other side of the pool. There's plenty of water, plenty of food. There's a satellite phone, also Wi-Fi.'

The last thing Carrie wanted was to go online. It was easier to avoid her family if she didn't. She *definitely* planned to tell them about Ana face to face. Presented with the delicate perfection of her baby, they couldn't *possibly* think she was any kind of mistake. But she couldn't resist provoking Massimo now.

'So I can email an SOS?' she drawled.

'Because you're so good at asking for help when you most need it?' He shot her a look. 'Go right ahead. I'm not afraid of people knowing where you are, who you're with and why. *I* have nothing to hide.'

He led her up to a vast, shaded wooden deck with a stunning view over the beach. They walked up the stairs towards the open doors and into a large, airy room. 'This is the nursery.'

She paused on the threshold. There was space in here for a *dozen* babies. There was a beautiful cot with hand-stitched cotton coverings and a hand-crafted mobile hanging near a carved rocking chair. Alongside the incredible pieces of artisan carpentry, there was a medical-grade neonatal bassinet and accompanying supplies. That shocked her. The room was totally over-equipped. He'd provided things she wouldn't even have *thought* of, let alone had the money to purchase. It had all just been done, here and organised, *including* round-the-clock care for Ana. Did he need *her* to be here at all?

Leah placed a freshly changed Ana into the cot. 'I'll return later.' She politely smiled and left the room.

Carrie walked straight to Ana. She was happily gazing up at the gorgeous mobile. Carrie's heart puckered as she waited for Massimo to join her beside their baby.

'You've provided so much,' Carrie eventually mumbled. 'Ana doesn't need…'

'I didn't have the luxury of knowing what might be necessary, so I bought everything with me from Australia,' he said coolly.

Including that hyper-efficient nanny. Carrie swallowed and glanced across at him. 'How long have you been here?'

'A week.'

'You didn't see me sooner?'

'I wasn't on your visitor list, remember? I've been waiting at the hospital for Ana to be discharged,' he said grimly.

'You were waiting outside the whole week?'

'I watched the door while working from the car. Don't worry. I can do a lot via phone. And I had things to arrange. Especially when it became evident that you weren't about to get in touch.'

He'd been ruthlessly cool-headed as he'd worked out his plan.

But she'd intended to get in touch. As soon as she got Ana to Sereana's, she'd been going to book the flight. One look at Massimo's hardened face told her there was no point trying to convince him of that. Too little, too late.

'Your room is in the wing on the other side of this. You can't miss it.' He stepped backwards. 'There are some essentials supplied for you too. I'll leave you to get settled.'

'Don't you want to hold Ana now we're alone?' Her throat tightened.

A muscle flicked in his jaw. 'Later. I have an urgent matter to attend to.'

Her blood iced and she felt it as pure rejection. Why was he determined to be in Ana's life if he wasn't interested in getting to *know* her? The memory of his reaction to news of her pregnancy flashed in her mind. He didn't want children. He didn't want Ana.

'We'll dine in an hour. Leah will care for Ana while we discuss everything.' Massimo dictated the agenda as if this were merely another business deal.

No doubt Leah was completely capable, but Carrie didn't want her caring for Ana round the clock. But she couldn't say anything until she had herself under control. And it wasn't just anxiety and anger causing her problems.

Every time she looked at Massimo she was hurtled back to that best night of her life. It didn't seem to matter that he'd broken her heart. That he'd disappointed her with his coolness towards their daughter. Carrie's body simply still craved his.

That chemistry was, in fact, stronger than ever. Surely it was just hormones? Maybe it was also some prehistoric instinct to be attracted to the father of her baby—to thirst for his attention because her inner cave woman sought security.

Her brain fought back. She'd figure out her future and that of her daughter's without succumbing to the seductive spell he cast without even knowing—let alone wanting to.

'Am I a prisoner here?' she called as he reached the deck.

He paused and glanced back. Time stretched as his gaze pinned her for too long. 'No.'

The upward inflexion of his smouldering answer sounded more challenging than reassuring. Because how, exactly, would she get off this island? It was accessible only by helicopter or boat. The pilots of both were on Massimo's payroll. As were all the others comprising the 'skeleton staff'. Her joke about emailing an SOS suddenly wasn't that funny.

'So, if I wanted to leave, you'd summon the helicopter?' she pressed.

'Of course.' His sudden smile was arrogantly smug. 'You can leave any time you like.'

There was a pregnant pause before she realised.

'But not Ana,' she said huskily.

He walked out without replying.

Shortly after Leah returned, and Carrie forced herself to focus on finding out about the woman. It didn't take long for her to feel more relaxed about leaving Ana in her care, at least for a little while. She was insanely well-qualified but, more importantly, she was *kind*.

As Carrie sat in the rocking chair to nurse Ana, she gazed from her daughter to the view. From here she could see there was gym equipment set up on the farthest side of the pool, on the edge of the beach. Massimo now walked towards it, clad only in shorts. Moments later he hung suspended from the high bar. His skin glinted in the late-afternoon sun, his muscles rippling as he performed slow, super-controlled pull-up after pull-up—his strength was staggering.

This was the more urgent matter? He'd chosen to do some exercise instead of holding his child for the first time.

She ignored the unwelcome heat igniting within and raged. The selfishness of him! He was too used to having his own way. Was that the real reason for his insistence that she and Ana stay with him now? Was he playing with their lives in a fit of self-centred, controlling *petulance*? She stared, stunned as he worked out with single-minded force.

And she was *furious*.

CHAPTER EIGHT

I'VE NEVER DONE this before. Any of this.

It didn't matter how hard he pushed himself Massimo couldn't burn enough energy, couldn't slough the heat trapped beneath his skin, couldn't escape the memories that tortured him more than ever. He strode from the sand up the stairs to his own villa and stalked straight into the shower, desperate to forget.

He couldn't.

Who knew why their chemistry was so strong? He'd dated more conventionally beautiful women—svelte models, sparkling graduates, society princesses. He'd never wanted any of them the way he'd wanted her. The way he *still* wanted her. At the time he'd been arrogant enough to think *he'd* been treating *her*, but the gift had been his and he'd devoured it. When he'd seen the unknown number flash up on his phone about a month later, he'd answered it immediately. He'd been delighted she'd finally reached out because he'd been so close to breaking down his own resistance and returning to Auckland to see her.

Her tear-stained face and taut anxiety had pierced through the screen, heralding her most unwelcome news. *Pregnant?* He hadn't just flinched, he'd been so repelled he'd outright rejected her claim. Because he'd been careful. He was always careful. Because it was the last thing he ever wanted. She'd not just seen all that horror, she'd borne the brunt of his anger because he'd lashed out. Scornfully accusing her of...

Guilt made him gag. Had his rude treatment of her impacted on what had happened that night? Had she started bleeding because she'd been so upset, because of *him*? He'd lived with that sickening suspicion for months. And for her not to have got in touch with him since the baby's birth was impossible not to take personally.

Today her doctor hadn't offered many details but had given him a very clear steer that Carrie had suffered a lot in Ana's delivery. That she'd taken a long time to regain strength. That she needed care and rest now.

Massimo's anger billowed. All this trauma could and *should* have been avoided. If she hadn't run away, he could have helped her. She could've had medical care and known the pregnancy had held. He could have flown family over for her if she'd wanted him to. He still could, if she wanted. If she trusted him enough even to *tell* him about her family.

But he couldn't blame her for not doing so. He'd let her down.

After his own lonely childhood and the betrayal he'd suffered in his teens, he didn't want emotional encumbrance. Life was more *efficient* and easier without it. He liked his work and the liberty of his solo lifestyle. He'd never wanted the responsibility of someone else's happiness. His father had loved his mother too much. Had wanted too much. Had expected too much. So had she. And people lied, they let one another down, they left—all that was inevitable.

Honestly, he'd been happy—fantastic, in fact—since his life had been stripped of familial duty. He'd taken pleasure in the pursuit of business success, in the physical satisfaction of sex…and little else. He didn't *need* anything else. Only now that duty had roared right back in on an unstoppable freight train—in the form of a strawberry-blonde and her sweet-cheeked, green-eyed baby. A baby he could scarcely bear to look at. She was too small. Too perfect.

And her mother?

The cold shower did nothing to ease his anger or the thrum

of frustration coursing through his hot blood. Carrie was the whole reason he'd come to Fiji in the first place of course. She'd put the idea in his head with her passionate argument for paradisiacal beach holidays, and her smart-mouthed suggestion he might find a suitable sustainability project to support here…for the future of those children he'd sworn he'd never have.

The joke was on him. But he had it together now, right? His plan had been perfectly executed and he had everything exactly as he wanted—both her and the baby safe and secure on this island. Now they could work it all out.

Her astonishment over his purchase of the island, the way she'd queried her ability to leave… Had he wanted to punish her? Imprison her? Exert his control?

Yes. He'd wanted to assuage the outrage of her secrecy. He'd wanted to flex his power. He still did. He had to keep a close eye on her and he refused to feel guilty about coercing her into coming with him today. She didn't appear to have any sort of plan. The irresponsibility of her decisions appalled him. It was time she learned running away didn't work.

But that cold shower still hadn't done its job. *How* could he still want her when she'd hidden so much from him? He buttoned his shirt wrong. He ripped it off and slid on a tee shirt. He walked down to the dining deck to the stunning view and complete privacy he'd requested. At least here she couldn't avoid the conversations they needed to have.

He gritted his teeth as she walked towards him. She still wore the teal dress and white canvas shoes. She was still stunning. Basic instinct, wasn't it—and basic stupidity—to want more of the forbidden? Like a child being told he couldn't have any more sweets, he only wanted to scoff every last one. That was what denial did—made him unable to think of anything else. Made him addicted. Made him *obsessed*.

And *that* was where he drew the line. Because he was not going to give way to such a destructive inclination. His father's obsessive love had ultimately led to Massimo's abandonment. Massimo wasn't doing that to his baby. He was damn well going to stay in control, compromise and come to a perfectly satisfactory solution that they could both tolerate. He'd keep both Ana and Carrie safe and secure.

'Does Leah have everything in hand in the nursery?' he asked when it became evident she wasn't about to offer polite chit-chat.

'For the moment.' Her features tightened as she served some aromatic spiced fish onto her plate. 'What do you want to do?' she asked, not picking up her fork to eat. 'I'm figuring that you've organised all this already, so no doubt your plans go much further.'

'We get married.'

'You don't want children.' She barely skipped a beat. 'I'm quite sure you don't want a wife either.'

He sipped his drink, needing a moment to recalibrate. There was a lot she didn't know about him.

'You were appalled,' she added softly. 'You know you were.'

'I was shocked,' he said stiffly, not controlled enough to explain his deeply personal pain right now. 'I was careful. I've never had such an incident before.' But he hadn't been as careful as usual, either. He'd been desperate and he'd relied on condoms that might've been a century old, for all he knew. 'I was more experienced,' he conceded. 'I let you down. I apologise for that.'

Her blue gaze was frank. 'It wasn't either of our faults,' she said. 'And Ana is here now.'

'Yes.' He gritted his teeth. 'So, we marry.'

She actually rolled her eyes. 'That's not necessary.'

'You don't think?'

'This isn't Victorian England. A myriad of diverse relationships is accepted now. There's no stigma about having a child out of wedlock.'

'Perhaps, but there are still valid—I'd say *vital*—reasons requiring us to marry.'

She stiffened.

'Don't get me wrong,' he muttered. 'I don't actually want to marry you either. This is far from ideal.' He'd *never* wanted to marry but he'd do this because he had to. Because it wouldn't be a traditional type of marriage anyway. 'But I'll put up with it for the sake of the baby. You can too. Or don't you want to do what's best?'

Her blue eyes sharpened. 'I don't think that our being married is in any way best for *Ana*.'

Carrie hadn't left enough time to change or even check out her own accommodation before hurrying to dinner. She'd been too busy being furious with him and then tending to Ana. Now he looked appallingly handsome in that fresh tee and trousers. She had to avoid looking at him but, looking around her, she couldn't cope with the sheer romance of the environment. Everything was geared towards luxurious intimacy. The crisp linen-clad dining table stood on a secluded private deck. The view stretched beyond the leafy grounds to the pale golden sands and endless ombre-blue waters. In the far distance, other islands rose from the shades of blue, while the evening sky was scalded in pinks and golds as the sun began to set.

It was the kind of thing conjured by Hollywood—a perfect island paradise. In an alternative reality, she would have adored it. A reality in which she hadn't just been confronted by the most grim wedding proposal ever. It wasn't even a proposal. It was an order.

'What is best for her, then, in your opinion?' he prompted, forcing her to face him again.

'We could go…' She trailed off, partially lost in those green eyes.

Fiji wasn't practical for him businesswise. New Zealand was neither her home nor his. She'd never been to Australia.

She had no family there, no friends. But it was *his* home, and where his business was. She didn't even have a permanent job. So the answer was obvious.

'You have no plans to return to England?'

'Not at this stage.'

He took another sip of his wine. The tension in his jaw eased. Had he thought she was going to flee to the United Kingdom without even getting in touch with him? She regretted her silence more than ever. Truthfully, she'd liked him so much that she hadn't been ready to face him again. Not that she could tell him that *now*. She had to get over herself. Quickly. Lust could be controlled. Fairy-tale fantasy nights could be forgotten.

'Is there no family you want to come and support you?' He rolled his shoulders. 'I'm happy to fly someone else here if you'd like that.'

She inwardly shrivelled.

'Have you *told* your parents?' His frown deepened. 'Are there even parents to tell?'

He knew so little about her and she knew as little about him. They'd had one night—with no confessions, no sense of the commitment that came with confidences.

'My parents live in England,' she said awkwardly. 'I have two sisters there too. I'm the middle child. And, no, I don't want any of them flying out to help save me from my own stupidity.'

'So they don't know?'

She looked at him. 'I couldn't manage to tell *you*. I was hardly about to tell them. Or anyone.'

'Are you ashamed?'

'Not of Ana. Never Ana.' In that sense, Carrie didn't care about anyone any more. Ana was the most precious thing in her life. 'But *how* it happened,' she admitted. 'How *I* didn't know... I understand why people don't believe me. *I* can't believe it of *myself*.'

He watched her. 'Your own family wouldn't believe you?'

She shrugged, swallowing back the self-pity.

'They wouldn't come and help you if you asked them to?' he asked quietly.

'They're very busy. They have big lives.'

'Big, busy lives doing what?' he echoed thoughtfully.

'You've not heard of the Barrett sisters? They're international athletics champions. Maddie is heptathlon, Rosalyn is pole vault.'

'Athletics?' He stared at her.

'They're amazing,' Carrie said, still staunchly supportive despite everything. 'Like, seriously amazing. Very glamorous too. Social media sponsorships and everything. They're just stunning.'

'And your parents?'

'Lawyers. My father was an amateur athletics champion in his day. Maddie is almost finished her law degree now—she's going into the firm part-time while she's still competing.'

'They definitely all sound busy. While you're on the other side of the world, desperately escaping to your Pacific island paradise.'

She *had* moved across to the other side of the world to escape. Yet disappointment clung to her like a damp cloud that wouldn't evaporate no matter how hot the sun. The betrayal of those she'd thought she was closest to still stung.

'Why is that?' he asked when she said nothing. 'What did they do?'

It was more what they *hadn't* done. As a child, they hadn't given her the attention she'd longed for. Even when she'd tried to be someone they needed, it still hadn't been enough. She'd thought she'd found her place with Gabe. But when he'd met her family—the better versions—he'd fallen for Maddie. Her sister, who'd always won everything. The sister Carrie had given up a term of study to support while she'd been competing on the European circuit. Maddie, who felt no guilt about 'falling in love' because 'it just happened'.

Gabe had admitted that he'd grown bored with Carrie

anyway. She'd been sidelined completely. And Carrie had just accepted it all. She'd even done that damned reading.

'You should call them,' he said when she didn't answer.

'Maybe later,' she muttered. 'Once we've made a solid plan.'

She glanced up and caught his intent gaze. Time stopped again. Heat twisted as treacherous desire uncoiled in the hum of that wretched chemistry. How could she react to him like this from one look?

'If you don't want their help then would you object to settling in Australia?' he asked huskily. 'You know I can ensure Ana's needs are met. And yours.' He cleared his throat. 'Financially.'

'We still don't need to get married for that.'

She needed to maintain a *practical* perspective. To focus on what was best for Ana. There was no denying Massimo could provide so much that Carrie couldn't. He thought nothing of buying an entire Pacific island paradise, and financial security mattered. But Carrie was determined to be around to provide the *unconditional* love.

'Actually, marriage will strengthen your immigration case,' he said.

A hard ball of self-preservation in her solar plexus propelled her to say no. Not only to protect herself, but her daughter. Ana, who he still hadn't looked at properly. Ana, who needed better.

'If you're the father on Ana's certificate, then her entry ought to be assured,' she said. 'So I can go in on another type of visa.'

'Are you willing to take the risk of rejection?' He paused for effect. 'What if you're denied entry—could you stand there and watch me carry her straight through Customs without you?'

Her stomach dropped. It was a horrifying image. 'That wouldn't happen.'

'Worse things have. Wouldn't it be better to be certain?' he asked softly.

He had her in a corner but she wasn't willing to concede. 'So you're okay for us to lie to achieve certainty?'

'What's the lie?' he challenged. 'We slept together. We have a relationship of sorts. Who's to say a marriage between us isn't legitimate? We can define it however we want. The details are no one else's business.'

'But you don't want to be married to me for long.'

'We'll be married for as long as is necessary.'

'But we wouldn't be sleeping together. We wouldn't be—'

'You don't want to sleep with me again?' he interrupted, a wry smile curving his lips.

Battling the blush slithering across her skin like an alien contagion, she replied as best she could. 'I think that one night was enough, don't you?'

The infuriating man smirked and her embarrassment morphed into something else. Something hotter and more intense. *Rage, right?*

'Won't you find it difficult to remain celibate the entire time we're married?' he queried.

'Because I've been so sexually active up til now?' she scoffed tartly. 'I won't find it *hard*. How about you?'

His eyes glinted.

'I don't want a succession of other women in Ana's life,' she added determinedly.

'I don't want a series of random men passing through her life either,' he said smoothly. 'But I do want you to get permanent residency so we can all reside in the same country.'

She drew a breath. 'How long does it take to get residency?'

The merest pause. 'I understand it can take three to four years.'

Her jaw dropped. *Years?* 'We have to be married *that* long?'

'I believe so.' He studied her with that smirk hovering. 'Will that be a problem?'

'What do you think?'

She knew he was right about a lot of things. He was too astute, too well-researched. She wouldn't get a visa any other way—she didn't have some special skill there was a shortage of…she didn't have loads of money to invest in the country. Her only chance was on a partner visa. So she needed to come up with another solution. This was too challenging.

'I need time to think everything through.'

'Take your time, Carrie.' Sitting back, he toyed with the stem of his wine glass. 'This is neutral territory.'

Neutral? Hardly. This was his island. And his terminology showed he viewed this as a kind of war. What did he expect her to surrender? She had a horrible, hot premonition that it was going to be too much.

'We can stay here for as long as you need,' he added, as if he were being nothing but accommodating.

As long as was needed until she said *yes*.

CHAPTER NINE

CARRIE STARED UP at the delicate awning covering her massive bed. She'd been staring at it for the last seven hours. Cocooned in the luxuriously cool cotton sheets, with Ana nearby and a plan of sorts for the immediate future, she *should* have slept peacefully. Instead she'd been tormented by unbidden memories and rekindled desire as inappropriate thoughts circled in a constant agony. So it was a relief when Ana woke early.

Carrie whispered to Leah that she didn't need her help. Fully focusing on her daughter would keep her present and grounded. But as she fed and changed her child she still couldn't shake Massimo from her head. He had literally everything—looks, intellect, ambition and money. Yet, while he'd gone to such lengths in preparing this place, he'd not held Ana, not spoken to her. He'd not asked Carrie about her at dinner, nor come to the nursery to say goodnight. It didn't make sense when he'd basically kidnapped them and brought them to a place from which there was no easy escape.

But she remembered the way he'd looked at Ana in the hospital in the helicopter. Except he'd battened down that emotion—resisting the obvious urge to reach out. Was he determined to stay distanced? If so, why?

Carrie pulled on her blue sundress and, cradling Ana, crossed onto the sand and strolled down to the water. She breathed deep, drawing in the beauty and optimism of the fresh day. Surely they could work out a sustainable solution? She watched the sun slowly bring colour to the vast sky, feeling the water glide back and forth across her feet with the gentle tide.

'Carrie?'

Her pulse skipped. So easily he knocked her equilibrium. She turned and lost her breath. His black board shorts and white tee shirt highlighted his long limbs, his strong, sleek physique. But the second he saw Ana in her arms his expression hardened.

'Shouldn't she go indoors before it gets too hot?' He glanced back to the buildings.

'Her *name* is Ana.'

A flash flood of disappointment toppled her two seconds of serenity. Was this simply about pride and possession—some 'alpha overlord' need to claim ownership and control even when he didn't actually want either of them?

'Is it?' he countered. 'Her birth hasn't been registered yet. She doesn't have a full name, certainly not *mine*. You don't think I would have liked input into that?'

Honestly, to Carrie he didn't appear to want any kind of input into Ana's life. But she swallowed the bitterness down. It was early and his words had unveiled the deep chasm still separating them—anger and mistrust still burned.

She drew a steadying breath and tried to explain. 'You met my friend Sereana yesterday. She helped me through my recovery after the birth. I wanted to honour her.'

Massimo blamed her for the difficulties of Ana's delivery. He'd already argued that, had she faced him so much earlier when she'd thought she'd miscarried, then that frantic confusion would never have happened. He was probably right. But that didn't mean that her choice to honour her friend wasn't valid. She hoped he would understand.

'But I haven't chosen a middle name or anything,' Carrie said softly, trying to meet him halfway, hoping this revealed true interest—not ownership. 'She could take your surname if that's what you want.' Her heart sank at his continued silence. 'Is there a particular name you'd prefer?' Was there someone *he* wished to honour?

He gazed across the azure waters, his jaw tense. He finally glanced at her. 'Ana is a pretty name and it's appropriate to honour your friend. The lawyers will file the registration.'

'Lawyers?'

'I've engaged one on your behalf. You need advice and it needs to be independent of my own.' He pulled his phone from his pocket.

Mere moments after he sent a message, Leah appeared.

'Carrie needs a rest,' he said curtly. 'Please take Ana back to the nursery.'

Carrie didn't need a rest. Further more, she was perfectly capable of taking Ana to the nursery herself. Heaven forbid Massimo should do it.

'You resent Leah?' He misread her frown as she watched Leah carry Ana inside. 'You know if I'd really wanted you out of the picture you would be by now. But I'm not completely without humanity. I know a baby needs a consistent carer.'

She didn't think he was completely without humanity but his term 'consistent carer' was deliberately emotionless.

'You mean her mother?' she clarified dryly. 'Or maybe even her father?'

He shot her a look. 'A baby needs stability and security. Ideally with one primary person. Other people can be introduced over time but they don't have to be the biological parents.'

'Mansplain away, why don't you?' she said tartly. 'But we're *both* here and we can *share* the responsibility for *Ana*'s stability and security. And doesn't it take a village anyway?' She stepped towards him. 'I don't understand you. If you're not all that interested in her why are you bothering to do all—?'

'What makes you think I'm not interested in her?'

'You won't hold her,' Carrie blurted, unable to hold back

now. 'You won't spend any time with her. You just sent her indoors within seconds of seeing her—'

'Because I don't want her getting sunburned or over-heated. *You* should get indoors too.'

He made it sound as if he was all concern. But he wasn't.

'You know, you could just pay me off completely,' Carrie said. 'I'll take her and care for her on my own. You don't need to develop a conscience if you don't want to.'

'Not happening.' He gritted his teeth. 'I don't trust other people to do important things. Not without my oversight.'

'You don't trust *me* to make important decisions for her?' She would *always* put Ana first.

'Do you blame me for not trusting you yet?' he asked. 'I like to get the job done myself, then I can be sure it has been done.'

'So this is about *control*, not caring!' she snapped. 'You're not interested in *her*. The second you saw that I was holding her, you frowned.'

'I frowned the second I saw your face and how tired *you* still are,' he contradicted fiercely. 'You look like you haven't slept at all.'

Derailed, she stared at him.

'I want the best for our baby,' he said in exasperation. 'Ana needs a mother who's healthy and not looking as if she's about to collapse any second. Rest and recovery *has* to be your priority. You need a break.'

'I don't need a break from *her*.'

She'd not been able to care for Ana in those first days. She'd been so unwell it had taken almost a week for her to return to full consciousness, let alone be *competent*. She still felt guilty about that even when she'd not been at fault.

Now she worried that, if she didn't have time to forge her importance in her own child's life, she might be easily ex-cised from it. He already had a super nanny in position. And Carrie didn't just want to matter, she *needed* to.

The horrible truth was she'd left her own family back in

England and they weren't very bothered. They'd been too busy to notice the gap she'd left. It felt as if all the effort she'd put into supporting them hadn't just been unrecognised but unappreciated. She wanted Ana to feel her mother loved and valued her—utterly.

'This has been far harder on you than it needed to be,' he said. 'You're so pale…you look terrible.'

Massimo gritted his teeth because, while the first was true, the second was a lie. She was stunning and he was working hard to stop his primal reaction to her proximity. But the tightening of his muscles…

'Maybe I just need a little sunshine.' Hurt bloomed in her eyes.

She was the sunshine. He'd been unable to resist coming to the water when he'd seen her in the distance. But, when she'd faced him, the drawn look in her face had concerned him. Now he regretted saying anything because she looked even more pale.

His fault. Again. Because, truthfully, this was all his fault. He'd barely slept as he'd considered what she'd been through, and what the doctor had told him yesterday—cautioning him to take care of her. And taking care of her didn't mean tumbling her to the sand and kissing every inch of her gorgeously soft skin.

As she tilted her face towards the sky he couldn't stop staring, could barely resist the desire to reach out and touch. He drew a breath. The last thing she needed was him complicating matters with his unresolved urges. As for her questioning his interest in Ana? That hurt. Because she was right. She'd seen through to his limitations.

Intensity ruined lives. Love, he'd learned from his father, was all-consuming and ultimately destructive. Massimo knew he shared some traits with the man—intense focus, for one thing. So he turned his obsessiveness to work instead. While there was physical release in sex, he'd never allow an emotional connection to form—not one that might over-power everything else. But he couldn't abandon Ana—emotionally or otherwise. He wasn't going to let history repeat itself. He knew too intensely how much it hurt a child. It had devastated him. Which meant he had to find some kind of middle ground.

'Look, we both know I didn't want children, but now Ana's here and I want the best for her.' He tried to explain. 'I want her to know who her family is. I want her to know where and how she belongs in this world. She deserves to have that knowledge and security.'

Because he'd not had it. He'd had only secrets and ultimately betrayal. He wasn't having Ana suffer that. So, not only did he understand Carrie's desire to name Ana in tribute to her friend, he respected it.

The curiosity in Carrie's gaze was impossible to deny.

'Surprises in the family aren't great,' he added reluctantly. 'Ana should know who both her parents are. Where she fits in. She should understand her places and her people.'

The fact that Carrie hadn't told anyone in her family yet concerned him. That she thought they wouldn't believe her and wouldn't want to help her. That made his skin tighten. Because Carrie wasn't like him—she wasn't hardened, independent and tough—she was kind and sweet and she should have better support than that. Didn't her family see that in her?

'But she needs to know *you*, not just who you are,' Carrie said. 'Doesn't that mean *you* need to spend time with her and not just send her inside with the nanny?'

He clenched his jaw, annoyed that his actions had been so misinterpreted. 'That nanny is vital. I don't want you to be overwhelmed or isolated. I'm trying to do the right thing for *you* too. And, for what it's worth, I had a great nanny.'

Her eyes widened. 'You did?'

'Yes. She was lovely.'

She'd been Massimo's only support until he'd turned seven and been sent away to boarding school. He'd been so naïve, he'd thought she'd be waiting for him in the holidays, but he'd never seen her again. His father had dismissed her as an unnecessary expense now he'd been school age—not understanding Massimo's needs at all. Not understanding his devastation. Certainly not caring.

'Frankly, I haven't had time to adjust to the concept of fatherhood myself,' he admitted huskily.

'I didn't get time to adjust either,' Carrie tossed back. 'She just arrived and I had to get on with it as soon as I was well enough. For *her*. *She* is the priority.'

'I know that.' His tension built. 'But I have no idea—'

'And you think I did?' Carrie said quietly. 'Just *start*. Spend time with her, not money. Get better from there.'

He hated that she was schooling him. That she was right—in part. But she didn't understand where he was coming from and he had no intention of discussing anything so deeply *personal*. The truth was, he wasn't supposed to have been born at all. His parents had been unable to conceive and in the end his mother had secretly gone with an alternative. Massimo had learned years later that said alternative was a serial cheater who'd taken advantage of his mother's desperation. Who'd never actually been interested in being a *dad*.

Massimo's actual father hadn't been interested either. He'd only agreed to try for his wife's sake and after her death he'd barely engaged with Massimo—apparently too bereaved to cope. Years later, when he'd found out the truth, it had enabled him to do what he'd always wanted—abandon Massimo completely.

'Now that we're here, I can do exactly that,' he said stiffly, pushing back on the memories. 'But let's agree we operate with wildly different expectations. I expected you to be in touch with me sooner. You expect more from me as a father. Perhaps we both need to make adjustments.' He sighed. 'Fighting isn't going to make this easier. We need to give each other a chance to catch a breath.'

Carrie stared at Massimo. Catching her breath around him

was an impossible ask. But he was offering an olive branch and they were aligned in wanting the best for Ana. He wanted her to be well, and she appreciated that.

Maybe she'd been impatient with him because of her own family baggage. He didn't know anything about that. And, given he'd been raised by a nanny, maybe there were other things she didn't know. Maybe he had issues of his own to work through.

'Okay.'

'Okay.' He smiled at her.

Carrie's skin tingled. When he smiled like that his eyes lit up—making their striking colour even more contrasting. It made her want to smile back. To lean in. To let him…

No.

It would be like deliberately throwing herself into a fire. And if she succumbed to this weakness she might lose control not just of her heart, but of what would happen with her daughter. She had to put Ana first.

'You know, we don't need to stay here all that long, do we?' She fidgeted. 'I mean, we agree that we both want what's best for Ana, so we could just go to Australia now. We don't need to stay here to figure out the finer details.' She worried her lower lip when he didn't respond. 'I know you've gone to all this trouble…'

'Indeed I have,' he said softly. 'What is it about the place that you don't like?'

'Nothing. It's beautiful. But—'

'Then why not rest here for a few more days?' He stepped closer. 'You *are* tired. The doctor said…'

'Said what?' She stilled, defensiveness flaring.

'That you'd been through a lot. And you need rest.'

Great, so he was being nice to her on doctor's orders. She'd misread the concern in his eyes for something else. It was mortifying.

'When we head to Sydney, it might get a little busy,' he said. 'People will be interested in you.'

'No, they won't.'

His eyes narrowed slightly. 'I'm wealthy. Therefore, stupid as it is, they'll want to know who you are. Especially when we arrive with a baby.'

They were going take one look at her and know he was only with her *because* of the baby. 'They don't scare me.' She shrugged, defiantly refusing to care any more about what others thought of her and about not living up to anyone's expectations or immediately failing.

'No? People don't scare you?' he jeered softly. 'Someone who's dreamed her whole life about escaping to a remote paradise island to read books on the beach?'

She stared at him. 'If they want to know, then maybe we should go face them and get it over with.'

'Are you scared to be alone here with *me*?'

She shot him a look. 'You're still unbelievably arrogant.'

'Doesn't mean I'm not right.' He gazed into her eyes. 'You know you scare me.'

'No, *chemistry* scared you. But that's long gone.'

He stilled before abruptly turning towards the building. 'Well, what scares me most right now is seeing you sunburned. At least put on some sunscreen.'

As she walked with him towards the deck outside her suite of rooms, he glanced at her dress. 'Didn't any of the clothes suit?'

She shot him a mystified look. 'What clothes?'

'I had supplies for you delivered. Haven't you looked at them?' He stepped inside to her bedroom and went to the cupboard next to the bathroom. Except it wasn't a cupboard. It was a whole other room, and on the long garment racks hung dresses, skirts, blouses and casual tee shirts, even shoes still in boxes, neatly stacked. Who needed shoes when the sand outside was so fine it was like walking on talcum powder?

'I didn't look in here last night. I was busy with Ana.' Now she stared in amazement at the display. 'Did you order all this?'

'The standard selection, sure.'

She eyed him warily. 'This is the "standard selection"?'

'The department store's standard selection.' He nodded carelessly. 'That's what the assistant said she'd pull together. A capsule wardrobe or something?'

This wasn't a capsule. This was colossal. And of course he'd not *personally* selected every item—Carrie mocked herself for the half-second she'd thought he had. He'd simply given a personal shopper his credit card details and told her to get on to it. The woman had probably had a ball. She'd certainly done a good job. There was everything Carrie could think of and then so much more as well—even swimsuits.

Carrie opened another drawer and discovered pretty silk and lace. She quickly shut it. 'I can't accept all this.'

'Well, it's here if you want it, or you can keep wearing your favourite sundress twenty-four-seven.' He shrugged.

She knew money wasn't a big deal to him but it was to her. And accepting this didn't feel quite right. She didn't want to *owe* him.

'There's a beauty room you're more than welcome to use,' he added negligently. 'Leah will summon the staff. Just ask her.'

Carrie couldn't cope. 'Are beauticians classed as skeleton staff?'

'Actually, yes,' he said. 'I didn't want any of the resort workers to be made redundant when I took over the complex, even though we're not having paying guests for the foreseeable future.'

She swallowed. 'I don't know what to say,' she muttered. 'This is all…'

'Just stuff.' He nodded. 'Enjoy it. Rest. Feel better. Meanwhile I'm going to—'

'Attend to a more important matter?' she asked tartly before thinking better of it. 'Out by the pool?'

His fallen-angel eyes suddenly gleamed and that sinful smile flashed. 'Perhaps. Why? Do you enjoy watching?'

CHAPTER TEN

CARRIE TURNED HER back on his soft laughter and walked to the nursery. She *refused* to watch him working out again. She'd play with Ana. But Ana was currently sleeping soundly in her cot.

'She's just gone down.' Leah glanced up from her cross-word puzzle. 'She should sleep for a while yet.'

Carrie nodded as she stared down, melting at the cheru-bic beauty of her baby sleeping. But after a while the temp-tation for some self-care sneaked in. A massage…? Besides, she justified, it would be a way of *not* watching Massimo.

'Massimo said there were some staff on the island for the beauty room?'

Leah set aside her crossword and smiled. 'Oh, there is. Give me a couple of minutes.'

Ten minutes later Carrie was blinking hard to believe she was standing in such a stunning space. The beauty room was in a small villa further along the beach. There was a large, deep spa bath on the deck that had views of the water, while inside there were polished wooden floors. Sheer fab-rics wafted in the breeze generated by smoothly whirring ceiling fans. Fresh-cut flowers floated in gorgeous water bowls and a gorgeous scent filled the air.

'Would you like a massage first?' asked Naomi, the beau-tician, anticipation gleaming in her eyes. 'Then we can do a mani-pedi, your hair, a facial—'

'In other words, *everything*!' Carrie giggled nervously. 'That sounds amazing. Thank you.'

Awkwardly she changed into the soft robe. She'd only gone to budget walk-in beauty bars before and had never had a *massage*. But Naomi's friendliness soon put her at ease. And, as the woman gently rubbed her back and shoulders, the luscious botanic scent somehow thinned her thoughts until she heard only the sound of the gentle waves. It was warm and calm and everything was safe. *Ana* was safe. Slowly Carrie's eyes closed.

'Bula Carrie?'

Carrie drowsily blinked at the soft greeting, confused by the colour of the sheer curtains floating in the balmy breeze. Where was she? More to the point, *where was Ana*?

It was Naomi who'd gently roused her and who answered her unspoken question now. 'Leah is just bringing Ana and I have some refreshment for you.'

'Oh, I'm so sorry.' Carrie sat up. 'How long have I been asleep?'

Naomi just laughed. 'You need rest. Don't move, we'll bring everything to you.' She smiled at her. 'New mothers need to be cared for.'

Leah arrived with Ana and Carrie fed her. Refreshed from the nap, she talked to the two women and together they cooed over Ana. Then Leah took her for a walk while Naomi got to work on Carrie with a facial, manicure and on her hair.

Carrie melted. It was *luxurious*. Every inch of her body was cleansed, massaged and cared for. Blissfully indulging herself, she chatted with Naomi, learning about her family, her ambitions and her pleasure in Massimo's plans for the resort.

Two hours later she stared in amazement at her reflection. Her hair had been trimmed and was shining. Somehow the circles beneath her eyes had faded and her skin glowed even though she wasn't even wearing any make-up.

'I brought over one of the dresses from your room.' Naomi winked at her in the mirror. 'There are some lovely things in there.'

Carrie looked doubtfully at the pale lemon dress Naomi had selected. It looked clingy but she didn't want to disappoint the woman who'd done so much for her. The silky fabric slithered over her body, so soft it was almost sensual. Again she blinked at her reflection. Both the style and colour looked better than she'd imagined they would. She slid her feet into the sleek sandals Naomi produced with a flourish.

'Much better.' Naomi positively beamed.

For a tiny moment Carrie hesitated, but it would be a shame for the clothing to remain unworn. Could she trust his motives? Was she a prisoner in a gilded cage or was he simply demonstrating how comfortable he could make her life to convince her to say yes?

You're not the reason why he brought you here.

He was doing all this for *Ana*. And Carrie couldn't be dependent on him for *everything*. She would need her own space away from him to continue to develop her own sense of self-worth—that was why she'd come travelling in the first place, wasn't it?

She couldn't risk losing her identity and drowning in his, and that was a very real possibility, because his was that forceful. *He* loomed that large in life. Yet she felt more alive than she'd felt in months. And that was him too, wasn't it? Something within her sparked into life when he was around. That first night, she'd laughed and teased easily and had been frankly fearless in what she'd said. Now he provoked her again.

Mulling over her confusing thoughts, Carrie went to see Ana. As she quietly walked onto the deck of the nursery wing she saw Massimo standing beside her cot. Carrie immediately froze, not wanting to intrude. But she wasn't able to look away either. He was only in swimming shorts. But his physical magnificence wasn't what arrested her. It was that *expression*. Still and silent, he gazed down intently at their baby. Fascination, curiosity and wariness flickered across his face—all the feelings that perfectly echoed her own. Ana was so tiny, so perfect, and it was *terrifying* to have complete responsibility for someone so precious.

She didn't want to spoil his private moment but, as she gingerly stepped backwards, he glanced up. She froze, ensnared anew. Because now, having seen her, his green eyes were stormy—gleaming with defiance and a defensiveness she didn't understand.

Every one of Massimo's muscles screamed with the restraint he exerted over them. He would *not* stride over to her. He would *not* pull her into his arms. He would *not* kiss her. She'd barely recovered from major surgery and he was not going to pounce on her with uncontrolled passion. Leaving her this morning had been hard enough, but *now*?

Now he was overwhelmed with feelings for the tiny creature who'd been gazing up at him every bit as intently as he'd been gazing at her. *Now* he'd glanced up and caught sight of the beautiful woman who'd brought that baby into this world. All he wanted was to bury everything exploding inside him, to blow away this cascade of all-encompassing emotion in the fiery oblivion of sex. He'd take Carrie. *Now*. Get physical. Feel better. Forget.

As if that was going to work! It wasn't how it had worked between them all those months ago and it sure as hell wasn't an option now. He wouldn't use her like that. And he wouldn't give in to that damned overwhelming *temptation*. He would get himself under control.

His muscles howled. He'd just worked out—again—desperate to ease their frenetic twitch. The whole thing had been a waste of time. He'd been drawn to see Ana because Carrie was right—he'd been avoiding their baby. He'd thought he could sneak in and out, but he'd been standing here for the last twenty minutes, barely coping with the ache consuming him. Ana was so very, very sweet, he could scarcely breathe. She was too small. Too fragile. Frankly he still couldn't believe she was even *real*. He had no damned idea how he was supposed to interact with her. As for *holding* her? He'd break her, right? And he'd be lost.

Who was he kidding? He was already lost, a hostage to fate and fortune. What impacted Ana, impacted him. She was his child, so precious, so vulnerable, he was terrified even to touch her. He didn't have a damned clue how to. He needed an immediate software update—the fatherhood download. Because he felt the burden of responsibility, the fear of failing her, when he knew *nothing*.

Yesterday he'd desperately tried not to notice the natural way Carrie cared for her. It felt intrusive, too intimate to watch. He'd been unable to look away and still couldn't. But his paralysis wasn't for lack of want, it was for lack of *skill*.

He'd thought he ought to stay in his own lane, play to his own strengths…but Carrie had called him out on that. She'd pushed him to do better. And he *wanted* to do better. Only now she'd caught him—frozen. Frankly, useless. Now he couldn't stare at Ana any more because he was staring at Carrie instead. That was worse. And impossible to stop.

His pulse roared. Her hair framed her face, loose and glossy, the strawberry strands gleaming. Her crushed-rose-bud-coloured lips looked pillowy. There'd always been a softness to her that he was unable to resist—not then and not now.

'You look lovely,' he croaked.

She brushed her hand down the side of her dress. 'It's amazing what a beauty treatment will do.'

'It's not the treatment.' There was a glow within her that wasn't superficial.

An adorably sheepish pink mottled her cheeks. 'I fell asleep.'

That admission soothed him a little. 'That's good.'

She needed rest. He knew she'd had fantastic care, that those people had done everything possible and more to ensure her wellbeing. But he was still angry. Still guilty. His heart pounded harder because now he had to confront the feelings. The fears. Escaping into sex wasn't an option. 'You lost a lot of blood.'

He chilled, remembering the time years ago when he'd lost blood. It hadn't been life threatening, but it had spilled a terrible secret of its own.

'I'm better. Everything's healed pretty well now.' A hint of embarrassment shimmered in her eyes.

The doctor had crisply informed him yesterday that 'marital relations' could resume. With care. That she could swim. With care. That she'd be fine. With care. Care that Massimo wasn't sure he was capable of.

Carrie walked to the other side of Ana's cot and looked down at the gently stirring baby.

'She has your eyes.' There was a catch in her voice.

'Not my eyes,' Massimo muttered huskily, glancing across the cot to explain to Carrie. 'My mother's.'

'Oh.'

His were the eyes that reminded his father of his loss, his heartache—and because of that he could hardly bear to look at Massimo at all. He'd never let Massimo forget that he'd lost the love of his life because of *him*. She'd made the ultimate sacrifice and Massimo had tried so hard to be worthy of it, naively hoping he might help his father heal...

He never had. And when that final terrible truth had emerged... Massimo had told no one the true circumstances surrounding his conception or the impact of that devastating discovery years later. But this once he felt pressure to explain a little. Carrie ought to understand why he'd reacted as strongly as he had to the chaotic circumstances of Ana's birth and something about why he didn't want children. He wanted her to know he wasn't a total monster.

Carrie was guileless and sweet and the disappointment in her eyes as she'd accused him of being uninterested in Ana had scalded him more than anything his father had screamed at him in the past.

'She died just after giving birth to me.' He forced the basics out.

Her eyes widened. 'I'm so sorry.'

Her words were awash with sympathy he didn't want, and he knew she was waiting for him to tell her more, but he couldn't do details. Not on this.

'I never wanted to put anyone in the position of...' He shrugged.

'*That's* why you don't want children?' Those rosebud lips parted. 'Childbirth worries you?'

It didn't just worry him, it terrified him. 'Utterly. With good reason.'

She swallowed. 'But I'm okay. Truly.'

Was she?

He glanced down at Ana again. 'I never had a mother. And I have no idea how to be a father.'

'You're not close to your own?'

'Never really have been.' His father had been too mired in grief to see him for years, then twisted by bitterness and blame—until one final betrayal had led to absolute abandonment.

'I'm sorry to hear that too.' She hesitated. 'But then I guess you might know a few things *not* to do,' she muttered cautiously. 'That's how I'm trying to work it—not to do some of the things my parents did.'

His curiosity spiked. Despite himself, he had the deep desire to know more about her. 'Such as?'

That sheepish colour mottled her cheeks again. 'I know I've already made mistakes and I'm sure I'll make more.' She shot him a small, wary smile. 'But I'm going to make sure she knows how loved she is. I'm going to tell her and show her. Every single day, so she's never in doubt...'

Carrie was aware Massimo was regarding her even more intently than usual. She ached to know the details she had no right to ask. He'd lost so much—no mother to cradle him, not close to his father. He'd mentioned that nanny… No wonder he'd been angry that Carrie hadn't seen a doctor, that she hadn't been prepared for the birth. That would have made him horribly anxious even after the fact. He wouldn't want his daughter suffering in the way that he had by losing a parent so young…and knowledge was power, wasn't it? Knowledge gave assurance, control. So for him to have been shut out of all information…

'I should have phoned you,' she muttered. 'I promised myself I would but then the days just—'

'It's okay, Carrie,' he interrupted in a low voice. 'The sheer shock, all those emotions and hormones… I understand. And I believe you about not knowing. About everything.'

At the clear ring of forgiveness, she felt hot tears sting her eyes.

'And I am really very sorry about how I reacted when you called me to tell me you were pregnant.' A stricken expression tightened his face. 'I worried that I upset you so much that…'

'You thought it caused my mistaken miscarriage?' She shook her head vehemently. 'No. *No.*'

Suddenly she saw the guilt in *his* eyes, the horror, and her heart tore. His mother had died giving birth to him and then he'd worried all that time that somehow he'd been responsible for her miscarrying his child. That had been a terrible thing to bear.

'No. The doctor here said it's common for some women to get spotting all through their pregnancies. Ana was a healthy weight. It was just how it was for me. And I just thought that it was erratic. It wasn't anything you did. Or that I did. When I went into labour, Ana was the wrong way round so the only way she could get out was with a caesarean. My haemorrhage was just bad luck.'

He gazed at her, swallowing, as if it were hard to speak. 'I'm still sorry.'

'So am I,' she whispered. 'Because you were right, I should have seen a doctor so much sooner. But I think we need to put that all behind us now.'

Another long pause.

'Just like that?'

She drew in a breath and braved it. 'Yes?'

The tension in his eyes slowly ebbed and he smiled. And *just like that* she was seduced again and hope blossomed. Maybe this *was* going to be okay. Maybe this was going to...

Ana mewled. Both Carrie and Massimo startled.

'She'll be hungry.' Carrie quickly stepped away from the cot so that Massimo could stay. 'I wasn't well enough to feed her myself at first so I supplement with a bottle.'

Massimo didn't pick Ana up but he did place a gentle hand on her stomach while Carrie checked the bottle that Leah had left ready.

Carrie breathed though the twisting pull of hope and fear of rejection. 'Do you want to feed her?' Her offer was belated, awkward, possibly unwanted.

His lips twisted. 'I might watch and learn this time.'

Carrie nodded. Compromise could work, couldn't it?

'I didn't know what I was doing.' She sat with Ana in the rocking chair, babbling to ease her own tension. 'I watched the nurses. But new and difficult things get easier with practice, right? I've always had to practise things a lot.'

'Oh? I thought you were a fast learner.'

There was a teasing lightness in his tone and she knew he intended to remind her of that night. She glanced at him balefully. It wasn't fair of him to switch into that charming man again. Not when she'd finally thought they might be *friends*.

'You know, there's a wide spectrum between failing and excelling.' He sat in the chair Leah had used earlier. 'There's doing okay. Good enough.'

'You don't really believe that.' She half-laughed. 'I bet you've never failed at anything.'

His eyebrows shot up. 'That's flattering but completely wrong. Though you're right about practice,' he added softly. 'It builds confidence.'

She glanced at him askance. Had she misheard that *suggestion* in his tone? He didn't think she ought to practice *that*, again, did he?

Amusement suddenly danced in his eyes but his tone switched back to bland. 'When I first went into business, I had no idea what I was doing. I couldn't believe people were asking me to invest their life savings for them.'

She couldn't imagine him suffering doubts. 'Did you make the right calls?'

'Mostly. Miraculously, none of my mistakes were too massive. The more decisions I made, the better I got at making them. Although...' he suddenly looked impish '... I wonder if I might be too used to making decisions *unilaterally*.'

'Autocratic, you mean? Dictatorial?' She smiled, enjoying the easy tumble back into banter. 'I guess you're used to having to. When you're the boss, you're the one people look to for answers.' She lifted her chin and reminded him. 'But, Massimo, you're not the boss of *me*.'

'Apparently not.' That amused glint in his eye was now laced with challenge.

The tension between them changed. Antagonism melted as attraction resurged. The chains she'd desperately locked around her desire inside loosened. They might just have made a tentative peace but now she realised her true problems had just proliferated.

CHAPTER ELEVEN

NOT BEING IN CHARGE. Not being in control—of himself and of everything? Yeah. Massimo wasn't used to it. But he hadn't spent most of his life overcoming expectations and challenges to abandon the attempt now. Carrie had set him a challenge and he'd meet it. He'd learn how to handle Ana.

He'd *also* learn to handle his own urges which were worsening by the hour. The desire to seduce Carrie was so wrong. She'd been through the wringer and they had too much to work out for him to wreck the situation any more with something as weak as lust. Except that was the problem. This lust wasn't weak. It was overpowering his *reason*. And that was alarming.

He needed structure. A timetable. He worked out and then worked remotely, taking meetings online late into the evening. He kept up with business well enough. But he was distracted.

He spent time with Ana. He worked alongside Leah, determined to master at least the basics. But he couldn't control his hyper-awareness of Carrie. He watched her in the distance as she paddled along the shoreline, fighting the urge to follow her, to lean close and breathe in her scent, to touch her silky skin and press into her sweet softness.

He lay awake hours into the night, reminding himself why he had to keep his distance. She was still physically vulnerable. And what little she'd told him about her family was an additional warning—she wanted to ensure Ana was loved.

Valued. The inference was easy to make. Carrie hadn't felt that. Which made her more emotionally vulnerable than he'd realised. He couldn't give her the kind of romance or love he suspected she craved. But he *needed* her to marry him. He needed to solidify her immigration status and create that security for Ana.

Confusing her with no-holds-barred sex? *Not an option.* But it took everything in him to resist.

Carrie discovered Massimo's paradise island *was* still a prison, just a different kind. Where she should be relaxed, she felt nothing but restrained, unable to act on the desires eating her up inside. Inappropriate. *Unwanted.*

She *should* be happy, right? She should feel upbeat and positive, excited even, that she and Massimo had resolved some things and now had a basis upon which to move forward. But a powerful instinct still held her back from saying yes to marriage.

They'd been on the island another two nights and, while they'd settled into a regular routine, her base level anxiety hadn't lowered. Instead it was steadily rising and she was plagued by restlessness. Resisting the urges of her own body, enduring the ache not just for his touch but his *time*, was a slow torture—watching him in the distance, maintaining polite conversation every evening at dinner.

Get a grip.

Right now he was down on the beach and Carrie was *not* reading the novel she had open on her knee. He'd just done some massive workout in the gym and then Leah had brought Ana over to him. Watching him take the baby so carefully, the size of Ana in his muscled arms, seeing him relaxed, unguarded and laughing... The way he looked at Ana, his expression unreserved and open, frankly adoring.

A knot tightened inside. Was she actually jealous of her beautiful little baby?

His torso was tanned and gleaming and his muscles

primed. Carrie was primed too. Just watching him had her horrifically aroused and aching for the press of his body. But worse than the chemistry was the mushiness of her heart. The scarred protective layer had been stripped by the sight of him showering Ana with his attention. Raw lust was slowly transforming into something scarier.

Nope. She was not falling for him. She refused.

She'd not given in to her longings for him before—she wouldn't now. They were only worse because hormones were at play and she'd been through a tough time. Her feelings for him weren't *real*. But he'd said he believed her. It had been so long since she'd had *anyone* believe in her, and she couldn't tear her gaze away as he carried Ana from the beach to the deck where she waited. Tall and muscled carrying tiny and sweet.

'I can't get used to how little she is,' he murmured. 'She's the most perfect thing.'

'On the planet,' Carrie agreed. But Massimo and Ana together? It was the most perfect thing in the universe.

'Time disappears,' he added. 'I don't even know where the day drifts.'

Pleasure flooded Carrie. Her baby girl had wormed her way into his heart and now he was as besotted as she. Her child had a father who would do anything for her. Who would always *adore* her. That flicker of jealousy died completely because she wanted her child to have *everything* she'd never had. Now she was just grateful.

Another day floated by. Never had she felt like such a princess... She didn't have to cook, didn't have to think about work, didn't even have to make her own bed. Except she didn't have to do public appearances, so this was *way* better than being some poor put-upon royal. It was an utterly spoilt, charmed life but it came with a catch—the total threat to her heart.

Massimo was too easy to say yes to. Too impossible to say no to.

Sitting at the table on her deck in the shade, she pulled out her laptop and got to work. Avoidance. Distraction. Helping someone else had to help her too.

'What are you doing?'

She didn't glance up. In her peripheral vision she could see he was in those wretchedly flattering swimming trunks again. And nothing else. Again.

'Spreadsheet,' she muttered.

'You shouldn't be working. You still need to rest.'

'I am resting. While working.' She glanced up at him. 'I'm not an invalid. I had a baby. Weeks ago now.'

'The point of us staying here is for rest and recuperation, but you look more tired than when we first arrived.' Massimo crouched beside her. 'Are you not sleeping?'

The gently asked question made her slide further beneath his spell. She glanced at him and discovered he was too close. She swallowed as his mossy green gaze burned through to her secrets.

'I'm not either.'

She *felt* rather than heard his low admission. The raw, underlying emotions hit hard—lust, but resentment too. Desire so strong but just as strongly unwanted. It was better to stay level-headed, slightly distanced. To focus on Ana and only on Ana. Because Ana was the only reason they were here at all. But her body wasn't listening. Her body just wanted his. His time, his attention, his touch.

'Leah told me we're supposed to sleep when Ana does,' he said. 'Instead, you're working. You're not even reading your novels.' He put his hand on hers. 'You know, you don't owe Sereana. She wouldn't expect you to work right now.'

'I do owe her,' Carrie said. 'But that's not the only reason I'm doing this.' She risked a glance at him. 'I *like* what I'm doing.'

'Spreadsheets?'

'Why sound so sceptical? You like figures.'

'True.' He chuckled. 'What's in your spreadsheets?'

Talking about work was less dangerous than playing with innuendo. She could focus on her project, not the fact that he was gorgeous.

'I'm a sports administrator. You know, the one who organises training grounds and the schedules for competitions. I work out the progression for the draws, health and safety... It probably sounds boring.'

'No. You got into it because of your sisters?'

'Yeah.' Since she was ten she'd quietly got on with the tasks her family were too busy for. Finding her place—her purpose—had been paramount. 'My family were all very busy. I wasn't a competitor. I found I was better at organising everything for them. I even took a term off my degree to support Maddie on the European circuit a couple of years ago. She said she desperately needed me, but basically I'm just a really good side-line supporter.'

A small smile flitted into his eyes. 'Who's your side-line supporter?'

She laughed, not going to let him show how her parents' words had hurt. 'I'm not good enough to compete.'

'Not good enough?' His eyebrows lifted.

'They're all about *winning*.'

'So if you're not going to win...?'

'Then you don't race.' She nodded. 'I couldn't please them.'

'You should please only *yourself*, Carrie.'

It wasn't that easy when family was involved. 'Did you never want parental approval?' She stilled, suddenly remembering. He'd lost his mother. Wasn't close to his father. So, maybe not. 'Sorry,' she muttered.

'No, it's okay. I could never get my father's approval. It wouldn't matter what I did.'

Not even when he'd become so successful so young? 'I'm sorry. I know that sucks.'

Massimo's gaze had lowered to her mouth. Now he cleared his throat. 'Why don't we go for a walk? A change of scene might be good.'

'A change of scene?' She laughed. 'You think you can find a better one?' She gestured towards the beach. 'You can't be bored already?'

'I'm far from bored. That's the problem. Get your walking shoes on. I'll meet you on the beach in ten. Maybe some activity will help us both sleep better.'

He'd said it innocuously enough but she was thinking about the *wrong* kind of activity. Her pulse and mood lifted. They'd not spent much time together. The beach was in full view of the staff and they really only interacted at dinner. That distance had somehow been mutually agreed upon in silence. But they could be friends—if she could ever get her body to agree to the prospect of a platonic relationship.

Fifteen minutes later she followed him along an inland path. Wide leaves of the emerald and jade trees offered shade as they climbed to the highest peak on the perfect patch of paradise. From here they could look down at the resort and she could see the lighter waters of the reef encircling almost all of their island. Other islands dotted the deepening blue in the distance. But it was behind her, just below the summit on the eastern side, that the immediate treasure was found. A tiny, private pool nestled into the rocks.

'Wow...' She gazed at it, stunned. The trees were so lush they gave the grotto privacy and shelter—from the sun, from sight. 'Even *you* have to admit this is not boring.'

'Not boring at all.' He smiled.

'Admit it, you love a beach holiday. I saw you paddle boarding at dawn this morning,' she added. 'And working out on the gym.'

He waggled his eyebrows. 'Voyeur...'

She caught his eye and blushed. 'Don't let it go to your head. There aren't many other people to watch around here...'

His laugh was low. He whipped his tee over his head.

Carrie gaped. 'What are you doing?'

'Providing you with more visual entertainment.' He shrugged. 'Isn't this better than your spreadsheet?' He waded into the small pool and laughed at her expression. 'I got hot from the walk. Didn't you?'

Not from the walk, she hadn't. But she had a swimsuit on beneath her loose dress and the doctor had given her the all-clear for swimming before she'd left hospital last week. For other more intimate activities too. Not that they were on offer.

She hesitated, increasingly irked by the laughter in his eyes as he floated lazily, frankly showing off his sleek muscles.

'Fine.' She gritted her teeth and slipped her dress off.

The water was just that one degree below perfect, chilled enough to make her shiver yet love it at the same time. It was so lush. It was the second-most pleasurable experience of her life. And it was so, so stunning.

'I've never been anywhere as beautiful as this.'

Massimo waded to the side of the pool and grabbed the thermal-lined bag he'd had slung over his shoulder while they'd walked. To Carrie's delight he pulled out precious, delicious things. Chilled squares of dark chocolate and salted nuts revitalised her. She almost moaned. How could the simplest of things taste so good?

'You were prepared.' She sighed in pleasure.

'I can organise a few things too. And I didn't want you to end up more tired than you already were.'

Carrie froze—both shocked and captivated as he touched her. Slowly he rubbed his thumb against her lip and when he lifted it away she saw a small smear of dark chocolate on his skin. She watched, melting, as he licked it off. They shouldn't. They both knew they shouldn't. But it was like that magical night back in Auckland. The chemistry was too strong and she couldn't resist.

'Massimo,' she whispered.

Whether it was to warn him away or will him closer, she'd

never know, because from the first brush of his lips there was no stopping. No slowing. There was just that sizzling arc of electricity that shorted out her reason. She trembled and his answering groan melted any last nugget of doubt. Golden heat radiated beyond her skin—too pure to be contained.

It didn't matter if this was going to complicate things. Her body wasn't interested in the arguments of her rational mind. Her body overruled *everything*. This was too good. He was the one thing she wanted more than anything. And how could it be wrong when they'd made something so wonderful together? The biology between them was perfect, the chemistry completely explosive and the physics elemental— the gravitational pull a force impossible to withstand. As sure as a stone sinking to the bottom of the sea, she would succumb to it.

But she saw the conflict in his eyes as he gazed into hers. He shook his head and she thought he was going to pull away completely. But then he was back, there was a hungrier press of lips and then the sheer, utter delight of his touch. His hands stroked over her swimsuit, touching parts that didn't just ache but burned for him. Shaking uncontrollably, she moaned her need—her utter, desperate, intense need. And he met it, with the most delightful, far too gentle, reverent touch.

And that was all it took. Almost nothing. He caught her scream of ecstasy with his lips. For a moment she felt the heavenly press of him right against her. Only the flimsy barriers of bathing suits separated them.

'No.' He suddenly broke away from her. 'No. This isn't happening.'

Shocked, she blinked. He was out of the water already. She stared at him, bereft. Why had he shut down? Why wouldn't he look at her?

'Massimo?' She was shaking again, but this time on the verge of tears.

'I'm sorry, Carrie. That shouldn't have happened.'

'Um… I wanted it to happen.' Her heart pounded. 'I want more to happen.'

And she *wanted* him inside her. Surely he wanted that too—when *he'd* been the one to instigate it? She'd felt how much he wanted it. Distractedly, he grabbed the chocolate wrapper and shoved it back in his bag so they'd leave no trace of their presence here.

Her tears evaporated as anger intensified. Why was he so determined to reject what he actually wanted—*her*? He was clearly frustrated but refused to take satisfaction from her. Why had he given it to her, then? Had he just been indulging her? She didn't believe that. She could *see* how much his body wanted her. There was no hiding *that*. So why was he fighting so hard to stop himself from being with her? What did he think was so awful that would happen if he did?

'It's obvious you want me,' she said, shaky but determined. 'Apparently you'd rather sit in a bath of sea snakes than let yourself sleep with me.' She was so hurt. 'What makes me so unworthy?'

'I don't want to hurt you any more than I already have,' he said roughly. 'Hell, Carrie. I took your virginity in a one-night stand. You got pregnant. You then suffered the heart-ache of a miscarriage, only to discover months later when you went into a crippling labour that you were still pregnant and about to give birth to a slightly premature baby. You lost so much blood, you were lucky to survive. *All* my fault. Every last bit of it.'

'Did I have no say in that night?' she retorted. 'Wasn't I the one who said yes? Wasn't I the one who asked you for several repeats that night? Or was I just some passive creature who lay there and let you do whatever you wanted and make all the decisions? Because that's not how I remember it happening, Massimo.'

A vision of that night swept over her. She'd not been herself. And, even with everything, she'd not regretted it. Not until this very moment when she realised how much *he* regretted it.

He shook his head. 'We need to leave before I do something we both regret.'

'You already regret everything'

'No. I just don't want to hurt you more.' He growled.

'Too late,' she said. 'You just made me feel desperate. Like it was all one-sided. Like I'm the only one who wanted that and you were only *indulging* me.'

It was excruciating. Apparently he could take it or leave it. Whereas she was borderline obsessed. But, though he stood stock-still, his breathing quickened.

'I wasn't *that* prepared,' he said gruffly. 'We can't take the risk of you getting pregnant again.'

Her heart pounded. 'But I...'

He closed his eyes and she trailed off, hurt by the visual rejection. She chose not to tell him she was on the pill now to regulate her crazy periods. Or that she would have caressed him the way he had her... Because he didn't even want that. He was still in control, his release incomplete—and unwanted.

'I don't want you offering yourself to me to assuage any lingering guilt over what happened,' he said.

'That *wasn't* what I was doing.' Embarrassment burned her skin. 'I want you. Or I did, until you started saying stupid things.'

'I have *wrecked* your life, Carrie.'

'I don't see it that way.' She was shocked by the guilt in his tone. 'This hasn't made my life worse. Different, yes. But honestly? Ana has made it so much better.' She looked at him. 'But that's not the same for you. *You're* the one whose life's been wrecked.'

'No.' He shook his head. 'Ana is a gift. But...' He rolled his shoulders uncomfortably. 'We still can't do this. You're too vulnerable.'

'In what way?'

A muscle flicked in his jaw. 'You've only just been through a traumatic experience, and I am much more experienced than you.'

She frowned, still not getting it. 'You mean sexually?' She blinked. 'What are you afraid is going to happen? That if we sleep together again I'm going to want to marry you for *real*?' She thrust her hands on her hips, annoyance flaring. 'You're the one who proposed to *me*.'

'We can't let this get more complicated.'

'It can't get any more complicated than it already is.'

His arrogance felled her as she realised just what he was afraid of. He almost looked sheepish. Too late. She was furious.

'Newsflash, Massimo—I'm not going to *fall in love with you*. It's just sex. We've done it before and I can take it or leave it any time. It's not that amazing.'

There was a dangerous glint in his eye now that probably should have made her pause. She didn't.

'What are you afraid might happen? That I might get so addicted to sex with you I won't want our marriage to ever end?' She laughed. 'You're such a jerk. You do *not* need to worry that I'm going to deny you your divorce in the future!'

His expression hardened. 'So you've no concerns about us getting married now?'

'None at all,' she declared recklessly. 'Bring it on, Massimo. Marry me as soon as you can manage it!'

CHAPTER TWELVE

THERE WAS NO taking it back now. For once Carrie had too much pride. Besides, she'd pretty much known it would be inevitable that she would say yes to him. She'd do anything to remain central in Ana's life and she wanted her daughter to have the best—both parents in her life. But the satisfaction in squaring off with him, in calling him out on his ridiculously egotistical concerns... She'd show him.

'Here are my rules,' she said determinedly. 'We marry. But only in name. We *won't* sleep together. When we finally get the permanent leave to remain, we separate.' It was going to take years but surely she could handle it if they were physically distant within their household? 'Eventually we share custody. I'll stay in whatever city you want.'

'But for now we live together,' he insisted. 'We're *married.*'

'Defined how we want, as you first suggested. Until my residency is through.'

His jaw clenched but he nodded slowly. 'Done.'

She glared at him. She wasn't finished yet. 'Don't lie to me. Don't cheat on me. Don't make promises you can't fulfil.'

'We really don't know each other, do we?' He looked as angry as she felt.

'I guess we can be good at maintaining some distance even on tiny islands.'

'If we're going to successfully maintain a *marriage* for a few years, then we'd better change that.' He huffed a harsh breath and put his hands on his hips. 'Got any burning questions for me?'

For a split second she was shockingly distracted by his chest—her body still rebelling at the plan for them not to sleep together.

'Or do you want to start?' he asked when she remained speechless. 'So who lied? Or cheated? Or made promises they couldn't keep? What are the reasons for that specific list?'

Emotion exhausted her. From the heights of ecstasy, to brutal disappointment, to fiery rage—she'd run through it all in the last ten minutes alone. So she was in no place to hold back now. 'My fiancé nailed all three.'

'*Fiancé?*' He gaped.

'Why do you think I didn't want to marry? There's a little more to the story of my unstoppably successful sisters.' She gritted her teeth. 'My *ex*-fiancé is now married to Maddie. My older sister.'

'Your fiancé married your *sister*?' Massimo's features sharpened. 'How is…? How did…? *What* fiancé?'

Carrie stomped to the side of the path and sat in the shade. If they were to survive a few years of a fake marriage for visa purposes, they were going to need to be civil, and he'd have to know something of her sad love life.

'I met Gabe at university. I was working on reception at the gym part-time and he came in regularly,' she explained briefly. 'He was charming, and we got talking, and I was a fool and fell for him. He studied law and I wanted to help him, you know? I like to help. I'm good at it. So I introduced him to my father and Dad offered him a summer placement.'

'At the family firm?'

She nodded. 'Gabe didn't have accommodation in the city so my parents invited him to stay with us.'

Massimo looked confused. 'Move in with you?'

'I wasn't there,' she said. 'I was working a couple of jobs on the coast for the summer. I was saving. I wanted to pay for my dress then I could pick it myself, you know?' She shook her head with a little laugh. 'Anyway, while I was away working to save for the wedding of my dreams, Gabe and Maddie couldn't help themselves.'

He took a moment. 'That must have hurt.'

She nodded slowly. 'It *sucked*.'

His frown deepened. 'You hadn't slept with him.'

She rolled her eyes. Honestly, was sex all that mattered? 'He wanted to wait til we were married. But I guess he didn't feel the same about Maddie. They were having an affair for weeks before they told me. They even consulted my family on *how* to tell me. So everyone knew for ages before I did. Everyone supported them. It was…'

'Horrible,' Massimo muttered. 'They betrayed you.'

'I love supporting them. But I would've loved *their* support too,' she said. 'Why didn't they have my back?'

'They should have,' he said. 'He was a fool, Carrie.'

She shook her head. 'No, he just wanted the prettier, smarter, skinner, sportier one.' She grimaced at her own self-pity. 'I wasn't enough for him.'

'He said that?'

She nodded slowly. 'He realised I wasn't ambitious enough for him. Or exciting enough. He'd got bored.'

Massimo was very still. 'Did you go to the wedding?'

'I did a reading.'

Massimo's thunderstruck expression actually made her giggle.

'I wasn't a bridesmaid,' she explained. 'Only my younger sister, Rosie, was. Maddie figured I wouldn't want to wear a dress with spaghetti straps because she knows I wouldn't want to show my upper arms.'

'You're showing your upper arms now. They're very nice upper arms.'

'Thank you. I don't think they're that awful either, but I guess she did.' Carrie shrugged. 'I wore a jacket and read about love and loyalty and smiled as if it didn't hurt at all.'

'And your parents let all that happen?'

'Didn't I want them to be happy?' She echoed their words. 'They thought I shouldn't mind too much because it was obvious to everyone that Gabe felt more brotherly towards me anyway.'

'Carrie—'

'It wasn't completely untrue.' She'd realised it now. 'There wasn't that spark I felt with…' Suddenly awkward, she glanced at him.

'You didn't want to make a scene in the church? Go all-out drama?'

She grinned ruefully. 'What would've been the point?'

'It might've been cathartic.'

She shook her head.

'So you said nothing and ran away.'

'Chose to travel the world, actually,' she corrected with a tilt of her chin. 'Spent all my dress money on the air ticket.'

'Far better investment.' However, he didn't smile. 'You never told them how much they'd all hurt you? Not even your parents?'

'Sometimes it's better to walk away, don't you think? There's no point fighting for something you can't ever win.'

'Doesn't mean you let them off with bad behaviour. You've called me out on it. Why not them?'

Don't interrupt my focus… Don't interrupt their training…

She'd always felt as if her concerns weren't important enough to interrupt any of them. But Massimo had wanted her to talk and he'd paid attention when she had. And he'd challenged her. He also took her seriously. And that first night he'd *wanted* distraction—he'd welcomed it as much as she had. They'd had *fun* together.

'When *are* you going to tell them about Ana?' he asked.

She sighed. 'I don't want to. I don't want their pity. *"Poor Carrie. Did you hear she had a fling and got herself knocked up and now she's a single mother and no one will ever want her now?"*'

'Is that what you think—?'

'No. I don't think that,' she interrupted him. 'I don't have *any* regrets. But that I didn't realise I was pregnant? It just adds to a long list of humiliating failures that I'm never going to live down. I just...' She shrugged. 'I've never excelled in anything the way they have.'

'Maybe you're good at different things.'

'It all depends on what's valued, right?'

'*Ana* is valued,' he pointed out. 'You ensure that. So you should tell them about her. And you should let them know they hurt you. Don't make it easy for them to get away with it. Stand up and say how you feel. Say what you want.'

He made it sound easy. And with him it had been. But with her family?

'It wouldn't make any difference,' she said.

Massimo glanced towards the sea then back at her. 'So Gabe is why you didn't want to say yes to marriage sooner?'

She braced. 'I thought he loved me and that I loved him. I was wrong on both counts. But I don't want to be hurt or humiliated like that ever again.' She swallowed. 'But this is different, right? This isn't like that at all.'

He slowly nodded. 'I won't make promises I won't keep. I won't lie. And I certainly won't cheat—I wouldn't do that to you. Or Ana. When we separate, I don't want it to hurt her.' His tone held more than a ring of authenticity. It had pain.

She knew his mother had died but had someone else betrayed him?

'Nor do I,' she said. 'She comes first, Massimo. Always. Okay?'

He gazed into her eyes for a long moment. 'That's important to you, isn't it?'

'It's everything.'

'I'll organise the wedding right away. It won't take much to arrange.'

'Right away?' She paused. 'Do you want us to get married *here*?'

'You did just challenge me to *bring it on*.' He suddenly grinned. 'So, yeah, here. As soon as possible. Are you going to argue with me?'

She *could* list a bunch of reasons why it wasn't a good idea. Except none of the objections popping in her head were insurmountable, and some rear-guard reaction to delay the inevitable was pointless. She'd said yes. She'd said what she wanted. For Ana. So she'd face it.

'Sunrise or sunset?' she asked.

Surprise lit his eyes and he leaned in. 'Which would you prefer?

'Ana will be in a good mood at sunrise,' she said pragmatically. 'One of us will be pacing with her at sunset when she's tired and grizzly. It will be easier to get through it without interruptions from her in the morning.'

'Sunrise it is.'

His easy practicality quelled her flaring nerves. They weren't going to have a wedding night. She'd ruled out sex after his arrogant declaration she was 'too vulnerable' for him to sleep with her. If they married early in the morning, it would turn into another simple day spent caring for Ana. Nothing special. This would be a passionless arrangement. She could deal with that. For sure.

We won't sleep together.

Massimo needed space and time away from her to think. Learning about her ex and her sister only confirmed what he'd known the night they'd met—she wasn't his type. Carrie needed and wanted someone to love. She was emotionally generous—kind and caring, with an enthusiastic effervescence, and she was eternally supportive, even to her own detriment. She'd put her own study on hold to support the sister who'd then gone on to betray her. She'd worked hard for Sereana even when she'd been so sick.

And she wanted Ana to be put *first*.

She was a fighter for others. But she didn't often ask for what *she* wanted. Maybe she'd learned not to, if her family had been so busy pushing their own achievements and not recognising hers because they hadn't involved certificates or medals.

Except she'd asked for all kinds of things from *him*. That night. Just now by the rock pool. He couldn't believe he'd pulled away. He didn't know where he'd found the strength. But, agonising as it had been at the time, it was the right thing to do.

We won't sleep together.

That was good. He could never, ever give her all she really needed. Though she'd been insulted, he'd been right—she *was* too vulnerable to handle his limitations. While he could do sex without emotional involvement, he didn't think she could, and it wasn't because of her inexperience. It was because she poured all her emotion into *everything* she did. She had *integrity*. And to him that was priceless.

But he also knew that ultimately they'd want different things. Ultimately she *should* meet someone who could give her everything.

His stomach churned. She didn't like to let people down and he wouldn't let her down. He knew she worked hard because she thought she had to *earn* value. Because some jerk had told her she was boring. She was feisty and she was funny, and Massimo was filled with a horrifically Neanderthal pleasure in knowing that the jerk had never discovered just how *not* boring Carrie was. And not just in bed.

She deserved far more than he could ever offer. But she was stuck with him for the immediate future. He wished he could make it better.

The wedding of my dreams.

This was hardly going to be that. But maybe he could somehow make it a little special. He could make the effort for her—give her something of what she put in for other people.

Carrie shouldn't have been surprised to discover Massimo had their whole wedding planned only two hours after she'd accepted his proposal in a pique.

Just after lunch the next day—at the exact time on the schedule that he'd outlined to her the night before—she heard the helicopter coming in to land. But it wasn't only the lawyer and the celebrant she'd expected who were on board. Another man emerged, carrying a bunch of camera equipment. And then Sereana appeared, burdened by several garment bags.

Carrie's heart soared and she pressed her hand on Massimo's arm. 'You invited Sereana?'

That hadn't been on the schedule.

'You need an attendant.' His gaze was very warm, very green. 'Who better than Ana's namesake?'

Carrie beamed. 'Thank you.'

Massimo pressed his lips together in a tight smile and quickly strode ahead to greet the others.

After a bubbling few moments showing Sereana her villa, Carrie met Massimo and the lawyer, Jai. If the lawyer thought it odd that they were so carefully preparing for their separation, he didn't give it away. There was a sheaf of paperwork to be filled in—including Carrie's consent for a DNA test from Ana.

'It's only to ensure the visa application is as strong as possible,' Massimo said.

'I know.'

'Are you sure you don't want further independent advice?' Massimo frowned at her across the table.

'I trust you,' Carrie muttered.

Something flickered in his eyes and his mouth twitched. 'So soon?'

'I know you wouldn't want to harm Ana in any way. So you won't harm me.' But she bit her lip as she pointed to one line in the lengthy contract. 'That is too much.'

His hot, intense gaze held hers for two seconds too long. 'That settlement is barely enough to ensure Ana has the best when she is with you. You need to be safe and secure so that she is.'

It was all about Ana. All for Ana. And that was everything she wanted. Except that chemistry wouldn't wash away.

As soon as she'd signed the documents, she walked back to Sereana's villa, avidly curious about those garment bags. Her friend was stretched out on a lounger, a vibrant cocktail in hand and a broad smile on her face. 'I've met the marvellous Naomi already. She's going to do my hair. I'm in heaven, right? Because she's an angel.'

'*You're* the angel!' Carrie laughed. 'Tell me what was in all your bags!'

Were her stupidly hopeful suspicions correct?

'Only the few wedding dresses I could get in town with less than twenty-four hours' notice.' Sereana chuckled. 'Massimo said not to worry about the expense, so I didn't.'

Until Sereana had emerged with those bags, Carrie had barely thought about what she was going to wear for the ceremony at dawn tomorrow. But now it *mattered*. She wanted to look good. Frankly, suddenly she wanted to *own* this whole thing.

Sereana didn't know the truth about Carrie's relationship with Massimo, and the resort staff weren't aware it wasn't a 'real' wedding either, and, at dinner on the eve of the ceremony, everyone joined them in the large dining deck. Laughter rang out, as Massimo was in full charm mode. Seated in the centre beside him, Carrie laughed too. And, even though she knew it wasn't real, it didn't feel fraudulent. It was fun.

We won't sleep together.

She'd stipulated that and she'd be fine with it. This would be enough.

Early the next morning Sereana and Naomi, vivacious in their respective green and pink sundresses, helped Carrie get ready. Carrie knew it mightn't have the meaning of other wedding ceremonies, but this was still *her* day. Her commitment to a future for Ana, for Massimo and for herself. And, while the marriage wouldn't last, she was going to wholly commit to it now. She wasn't going to be an unwilling participant only doing it to keep the peace. She was doing it because she truly believed it was the best course of action in this circumstance. Because she'd *chosen* to. She wasn't being forced into anything—not by him, or by fate.

'He's going to die when he sees you,' Sereana said, deftly sewing in a last tuck on the feathery light dress that Carrie had chosen from the four her friend had brought with her.

'Thank you for the confidence boost.'

'You don't need it,' Sereana said.

Carrie looked in the mirror and barely recognised herself. Sereana was right. Carrie was in her dream destination, in a dress more beautiful than she could ever have imagined, with the most beautiful baby on earth, about to marry the most fascinating man on earth. *He'd be her friend going forward, right?*

She wasn't a prisoner, but a woman who wanted everything she'd signed up for.

CHAPTER THIRTEEN

MASSIMO HAD NEVER been lost for words. His ability to smooth awkward social moments had always been effortless. Now it wasn't just that he couldn't think what to say, he'd lost the physical ability to create sound at all. His throat was clogged, his mouth parched, and his tight lungs rendered breathing impossible. He felt hot, tense and uncomfortably helpless— he wasn't coping. He'd never failed to cope with anything. But watching Carrie walk down the fine sand to where he stood right by the shore was killing him.

Her long silk slip was covered by a loose gossamer-light layer of lace, creamy and hinting at such softness. She was luminous—demure yet devastatingly sensual. He couldn't stop staring, even as doing so destroyed him. Her blue eyes were as clear as the water beside them, while her hair gleamed like a rose-gold crown, and suddenly his made-to-measure linen shirt felt too small. Tongue-tied and breaking into a sweat, he was unable to tear his gaze away. And he was suddenly afraid. The temptation to take her hand—to stop her from disappearing, to keep her ethereal beauty beside him—was crippling. As for the ache to kiss her…

Why had he agreed that they wouldn't sleep together? What had he been *thinking*? He hadn't, of course. He'd been hot-headed, wanting to win, because she somehow pushed all his buttons and made him want to fight.

But as the sun sent streaks of light across the sky, and petite waves lapped at the shore, he didn't want to fight any more. He'd just drown in her eyes. He had before. Sinkingly, he knew he would again. The clogged sensation in his throat descended to his chest where his ribs weren't strong enough to contain his pounding heart.

They were only doing this for Ana. So surely he could control the physical attraction to Carrie? But all thoughts of parenting arrangements and future plans for a separate lifestyle fled from his head as she drew nearer. All he wanted was the oblivion he knew he'd find in her arms. He shouldn't have resisted the other day. Why had he thought he *could*? He didn't want to restrain anything any more. Had that rash decision not to act made their chemistry stronger than ever?

The maxim said you always wanted what you couldn't have. Maybe it was that simple and that easily resolved. If he took her back to bed, it would ease, right?

But the sexual tension tearing him apart was augmented by a sense of foreboding. He knew their marriage should make scant difference to anything. It was only to obtain a simple piece of paper for a practical purpose. It was not anything portentous. Yet he could scarcely breathe through the intensity of the damned ceremony. And why had it got to him so much when, beside him, Carrie seemed a picture of unbothered serenity? Couldn't she feel the desire screaming from his cramping muscles?

Yeah. He wanted her more than was rational or healthy. So he forced his glance away.

He saw Sereana, and Jai his lawyer, saw Ana sleeping in the nanny's arms. He saw them all. Then he chose to ignore their knowing smiles.

Carrie had to listen hard to hear over the drumming in her ears, had to breathe deeply to echo the vows that felt more permanent and more meaningful than she'd expected, had to blink and look away from the stunning decorations they'd surprised her with.

And, while she tried so hard not to stare at Massimo, it was impossible not to. That white linen shirt made his skin all the more bronzed and in turn highlighted his eyes. He enthralled her. The barely leashed energy emanating from him was incredibly intense but she couldn't trust her ability to decode the emotional source. Was it anger or something else entirely? She wanted to be alone with him so she could ask. So she could... *No. There'll be none of that, remember?* Thankfully the officiating went relatively quickly.

Vows? Check.

Rings?

She was thrown when Jai presented a small woven basket to them both. There weren't two but *three* rings nestling on the layer of soft fabric inside. First Massimo slid a solid gold band on her finger, then a ring with an enormous ocean-blue stone in the centre. She put the remaining ring onto his finger. He flipped his wrist to keep hold of her hand. Distracted by that enormous stone, by the pulse in her heart skipping fast and faster, she let him.

'Carrie?'

A quiet call to complete the ceremony.

Vows. Ring. *Kiss.*

It was time for the kiss. *Awkward.*

She lifted her chin. A peck would do, right?

His grip on her hand tightened. A tug pulled her closer. It wasn't a peck. Carrie's eyes closed as he gave her the gentlest reverential kiss—a promise of something richer, sweeter, more nuanced than any before. She lifted her hand to his chest, unable to restrain the rush of desire, of reciprocation. The kiss changed. Deepened. Provocative and lush, it was a gift that took at the same time.

Her fingers curled into his shirt. She wanted to shred the soft linen to feel his skin against hers. Distantly she heard cheering, a little laughter and applause. Too late, she remembered there were witnesses—an *audience*, in fact, because this was a *performance*. It hadn't served any other purpose, or meant anything more to him. And they weren't doing lust. They'd agreed on that. Yet she knew in her bones that to be false. The chemistry was undeniable and had not yet burned out.

'Do we need all these photos?' she asked quietly as she held Ana, posing for what felt like aeons after the ceremony.

'For immigration,' Massimo explained. 'We need everything documented and looking legitimate.'

Did that have to mean images of her all but swooning in his arms? With crushed petals at their feet, releasing an intoxicating romantic perfume and blurring her reality? With Ana gurgling in delight as Massimo teased them both into giggling?

Finally, Massimo went to the photographer, checking the images to ensure they were enough. Carrie sought out Sereana for some respite but, to her disappointment, her friend had already changed and was now waiting by the helicopter pad.

'Are you not staying longer?' Carrie asked. 'Not even for breakfast?'

'You newlyweds need to be alone.' Sereana's infectious laugh rang across the grounds. 'I'll come back another time. Massimo has offered the resort for my family and I whenever we want.'

It wasn't only Sereana who left. The lawyer, officiant and photographer all went with her. And, then to Carrie's surprise, relief descended. The show was over. Ana's future was secure. It was all going to be okay, right?

'Leah still has Ana, so you can get changed if you'd like.' Massimo watched her approach the dining table, where he was drinking coffee.

'Do I need to?' She rather loved her dress. She liked the way it swished around her legs and the lace overlay felt cool. 'I could wear this all day.'

'Sure, stay in it,' he said tightly. 'You're remarkably relaxed.'

'What I am,' she suddenly realised, 'Is ravenous.'

She'd been too busy to eat breakfast before but, now

the vows were done, she needed…a displacement activity. Something to stop her looking to where he sat in the shade, watching her.

'Are you?' His voice sounded oddly tight again.

'Yeah.' She selected a croissant, tearing the fresh, warm folds of golden pastry with her fingers. 'It's good that's done. I don't know why I was worried. It's going to be fine.'

Massimo refilled his coffee cup, only almost to empty it in one gulp. How he could drink it scalding hot like that? Maybe he wasn't as easy about their marriage as he made out but, with their pre-marital agreement already signed, it wouldn't be for ever. *That* thought vanquished both her hunger and her relief. She abandoned the rest of the croissant.

'Are you satisfied already?' he asked.

There was a dangerous edge to his question that made her feel a sudden need to escape.

'Where's Leah?' She glanced around. 'I can take Ana now.'

'I think Leah planned to settle her for a nap.'

'Oh.' Carrie's pulse skittered. 'Then I might paddle before it gets too hot.'

After that she'd get out of her dress and the day would carry on as if it were like any other they'd had here. Resting. Reading. Dipping in the water. Cradling Ana.

Without waiting for Massimo's reply, she walked down to the water. She'd avoid her feelings for him. Avoid *him* altogether. It was too huge for her to handle. How could she ever comprehend the absurdly shocking fact that the man was her *husband*?

'Carrie.'

He'd followed her.

She turned. The look in his eyes reset her again. Electricity crackled, drowning her recently resurrected anxiety. And, of all the volatile, mercurial emotions he inspired in her, desire was the most constant.

'Are you running away?' he asked.

'Not a strong enough swimmer, sadly.' She waved at the islands in the distance. 'So I'm resigned to my fate.'

'What fate do you think that is?' He gave a half-smile as he stepped closer.

His tease reminded her of how he'd been the night they'd met. Charming and playful. Yet there was that tension underlying their spark. Neither of them could escape. Not then. And they were bound together differently now. This couldn't be like that reckless, carefree night. Desperate for distraction, she stared at the rings adorning her finger. The stunning solitaire gleamed more brilliantly than the mid-morning sun.

'It's a blue diamond,' he muttered. 'If it's not the right size, we can get it altered when we get to Sydney.'

It fit her perfectly. As had the clothes. From only that one night, he'd gathered all kinds of information about her. Maybe he could accurately guess a woman's size from one glance. The thought didn't make her feel great.

'Did you get it in Suva?' she asked.

'No, I brought all the rings with me.'

She was shocked enough to draw a breath but at the same time wasn't surprised. 'You were that sure I would say yes?'

'I made the plan.'

And she'd fallen into step with it.

'Do your plans ever fail?'

'All the time. I just adapt.'

She didn't believe him. He worked to ensure he won. Always. A wave of melancholy washed through her. 'How are you going to outdo this next time?' she asked. 'When you get married for real?'

'*We're* married for real,' he said quietly. 'I have no plans to marry a second time.'

'But our marriage *will* end.'

He shrugged. 'Then I'll go back to being single.'

'So you can play the field?'

'Is that so awful?'

'You don't ever want to settle down?'

He shook his head. 'Now I have an heir to inherit all the things. This whole situation is surprisingly convenient.'

'You think?'

He stared at her, the facade of teasing humour dropped. 'No. It's frustrating as hell.'

She stood still. 'What do you want to do about that?'

'What do I want to do?' he echoed in a furious whisper. 'I want to peel that dress off you. Very slowly. Very carefully. And then—' He broke off to drag in a ragged breath. 'I am so sick of fighting it. I am so sick of trying not to...'

'Not to what?'

'Touch you.'

The desire neither of them wanted yet neither could resist took control.

'Then *why* insist on trying?'

Emotion flared in his eyes. 'Because we're not sleeping together.' But he held out his hand.

And, with a boldness she'd felt only around him, Carrie took it and tugged *him* closer to her. 'Who said anything about sleeping?'

Carrie lost herself in the kiss. The drive to dive into his arms was irresistible. She'd never imagined that, the next time she touched him like this, she would be his *wife*.

It doesn't mean anything. It's just for immigration purposes. It's pure practicality.

But he shot her a look of such hot possessiveness that she nearly crisped to a cinder on the spot. He made her feel wanted in a way no one had ever made her feel wanted. But it was a falsity, wasn't it? Because it was Ana he wanted. Security for their baby. Not really her. But in this moment Ana wasn't here. She was safe with Leah. And Massimo had followed Carrie down to the water. Now they faced each other on the edge of the world. Alone. And what she wanted was reflected in his eyes. In this instant there was only them and, on this one, most basic of levels, they were equal in terms of desire. So she let him sweep her off her feet. She let him carry her up to the privacy of his spacious villa. She would let him do everything this moment. And he knew it.

But, as he peeled the filmy fabric from her skin, the glide of his hands over her body was too gentle.

'You're recovering well,' he muttered. That tightness, that ragged jerk of his breath, told her so much.

'Yes.' She was healthy and strong and he didn't need to worry. She was only going to break if he *didn't* give her the release she'd been craving so long. She reached for him with hungry hands. 'Massimo.'

He shook his head, shuddering as she touched him. He lifted her on to his big bed.

'I want everything. Fast, slow, now!' He half-laughed, half-choked. 'There are no half-measures for me. Not with you.'

'Good.' Because that was what she wanted too. 'So hurry up.'

His kiss was catastrophic for her control. Her response the same for his. Together they toppled into a fast, furious, panting, desperate need for completion.

'It's been so long.' He growled as he braced above her.

But at those words she turned her face away. How long was 'so long' for him? She didn't want to think of him with anyone else. Certainly not right now. But he gently turned her face back round and his green eyes saw right through her.

'There hasn't been anyone since you,' he muttered fiercely as he reclaimed possession of her. 'Not in months and months and months.' His mutter became a growl. 'And I am not going to last as long as I'd like because you're so hot. So soft.'

Shaking, she sighed in pure pleasure. The vulnerability in this was too exquisite, too precious, not to share and reciprocate. 'There hasn't been anyone *but* you.'

He closed his eyes. 'I'm glad. I know that makes me...'

'Human.'

She was human too. She was unbearably glad there'd been no one else for him. At the very least, they had this, and this was magic. He weaved his fingers through her hair to tilt her face towards his.

'More.' He demanded. He devoured. 'More.'

CHAPTER FOURTEEN

MASSIMO RECLINED ON the sun lounger, holding his sleeping daughter in his arms as he surveyed the scene from behind the safety of his aviators. He'd never considered the meditative powers of a sleeping infant before, but he'd never remained so still for so long in his life. Usually he was a perpetual-motion machine, moving from one thing to the next, to the next, and the next. Holding tiny Ana, he couldn't do that. It had led to a lax attitude to his work—he'd barely thought about it.

Rather, it was Carrie who fascinated him. He couldn't stop staring as she languorously stretched out in the pool. Maybe she'd been right to accuse him of arrogance in assuming that she'd want more from him emotionally if they slept together again. Maybe he'd been wrong after all. She'd adamantly insisted she wasn't going to fall for him, and right now she seemed as happy as him to keep conversation light and the nights very, very long. She accepted that their marriage would end in the medium term. But a stray thought lifted as something in his gut tensed.

Maybe this arrangement could last longer than the length of time required to satisfy immigration requirements. Arranged marriages worked all the world over, so why not theirs? Essentially that was what it was—a practical union based in practical need, not the vagaries of emotion. They could provide Ana with a stable home, two parents who were there for her—the things he wanted his gorgeous baby to have. The things he hadn't had.

Carrie had been engaged once before. She'd cared enough about another man to say yes to him and she'd not wanted to do that again. Massimo had assured her this was different. It was because it was an *arrangement*. They could keep it this easy. Not emotionally intense. Not destructive. They could keep it safe for all of them. But a twinge of discomfort pulled between his shoulder blades.

'Why the frown?' Carrie called softly from the water.

'Ana's stirring.' He swung his legs down and stood. He waded in to let Ana feel the water, staying at the shaded end of the pool. She gurgled as he gently sprinkled her.

'She's a mermaid.' Carrie swam closer.

'Like her mother.'

Truthfully Carrie was more of a siren, summoning him to his sensual destruction. And he couldn't get enough of it. He figured it would settle down when they returned to Australia. He'd be busy back at work and she'd have her own projects. She'd already promised to keep supporting Sereana remotely. But life *would* be different for her. His wealth engendered a certain public interest and she was going to have to navigate that. It would be intense—at least initially. He just knew she wasn't going to be keen. The tension in his shoulders tightened more.

He didn't want to go back to Sydney yet. He wanted to play in the water and share knowing smiles with Carrie as they cared for Ana. They were a *unit* and he'd never been part of such a thing before. He wanted to savour it. And, as much as he wanted to take Carrie to bed this second, he wasn't going to summon Leah to mind Ana. He was going to wait. Not even when Carrie climbed out of the pool and lay on the lounger, and he had to gaze at her beautiful curves, did he give in to the temptation. She needed rest.

'I've never been anywhere as beautiful as this.' Her

drowsy gaze tracked him as he paced slowly around the pool, keeping Ana content.

Wanting Carrie while not wanting this precious moment with both her and Ana to end was the sweetest torture. So in the hour that he cradled the baby and watched Carrie sleep he planned exactly what he was going to do once he was finally alone with her tonight.

That evening he uncovered the hot tub on his private deck, feeling Carrie's full attention on him as he worked. The low flame from a brazier illuminated her face, casting her in a golden glow. Her hair was swept up into a messy knot while the rings he'd given her sparkled intermittently as they caught the light.

'Is it ready?' Her husky voice betrayed her need.

He'd already seen the smoke in her eyes and felt the electricity all though the dinner he'd deliberately lingered over. But that tension tightened. He needed to prepare her properly. And she needed to prepare her family.

'My assistant is going to send a media release out before we leave Fiji,' he said as she stepped into the heated water. 'There'll be attention when we land in Sydney. You might want to inform your family. They'll get some calls.'

'Media calls?' Her startled expression turned comical. 'But my family live on the other side of the world.'

'I have business interests all over the world, and this isn't expected from me. They're going to make a meal of it.'

He sat across from her in the water and watched as the smoke in her eyes evaporated.

'So I have to…'

'You're going to have to tell them at some point,' he reasoned. 'You have a child. You're *married*.' Protectiveness rose inside as reluctance blanched her face. 'You're afraid of their reaction?'

'I know I shouldn't let it get to me. I know it's not rational.'

'They're your family. Rational doesn't factor into it. And when you've been hurt…' He shrugged.

She looked at him steadily. 'I guess I could phone them now,' she said valiantly. 'The time difference works. And I'm relaxed. I couldn't be anywhere more beautiful…'

Honestly, the last thing he wanted this second was for her to phone her parents, but it was also something she *needed* to get done.

'It's perfect timing,' he lied.

She laughed. 'No, it isn't.'

'There's never going to be a perfect time,' he pointed out.

She stared at him for a long moment, then snatched up his phone from the deck. He unlocked it and then she tapped in the number.

'Carolyn!' Her mother's voice carried clear in the still night the second Carrie had greeted her. 'Oh, it's such good timing that you've called. Maddie is here with Gabe. They've got marvellous news.'

Massimo narrowed his eyes—would that be the betraying sister and ex?

'Have they? That sounds exciting.' Carrie managed a smile.

It turned out Maddie had a new job *and* she and Gabe were expecting. Massimo winced at her mother's utter lack of sensitivity, but Carrie kept the smile and congratulated them. Minutes passed as Carrie listened to more detail, more drama, before her mother seamlessly moved on to a description of her other sister's last event and then segued into an update of her latest case.

To Massimo's increasing displeasure, she hadn't even asked Carrie how she was, let alone given her any chance to share her *own* news. Her mother didn't seem able to *listen*. Massimo raised his brows meaningfully.

Her gaze still locked on him, Carrie took a breath.

'Look, I'm sorry to interrupt, but I really do need to tell you a couple of things.' She finally cut off her mother's endless update. 'I've met someone. I met him a while back, actually.'

'Oh, that's nice,' her mother said glibly. 'That reminds me, I forgot to tell you about—'

'Mum, I got married,' Carried interrupted bluntly.

'What?'

'Here. In Fiji. I got married.'

Finally, there was a pause. Albeit brief. 'But you wanted to get married in Isherwood Hall.'

Carrie's jaw dropped. 'That's where Maddie and Gabe got married.'

Her older sister and her ex again... Massimo frowned. Why hadn't this woman asked her daughter just *who* it was she'd married? Why wasn't she interested in what was *important*—her own daughter's happiness?

'Exactly,' her mother gushed. 'It was beautiful. You've wanted to get married there since you were a little girl.'

The wedding of her dreams? Massimo moved through the water to put his hands on Carrie's shoulders. Her eyes were heartachingly shiny but she sent him a half-smile. 'Well, I had a lovely ceremony on the beach at dawn. It was very special. And there's more.' She drew another breath. 'I had a baby a few weeks ago.'

'What?' Her mother's voice leapt an octave. 'Don't be silly. We saw that picture of you just recently.'

Carrie frowned. 'What picture?'

'With the athletes at that meet in Fiji. Did you run the race or were you just on the admin side again?'

Were you just...again...?

Massimo clenched his jaw to stop himself saying something unforgivable. But he felt Carrie straighten beneath his hands.

'My daughter's name is Ana,' she said, suddenly calm, suddenly strong, as she looked at him. 'My husband's name is Massimo Donati-Wells. He's quite well-known over here. You might get some people asking about it.'

'Massimo Dona-*what*? Never heard of him.'

Amusement flashed in her eyes then. With a grin, Massimo leaned closer and rested his forehead against hers. To his delight she leaned back, her blue gaze still locked on his. He liked the connection. He didn't want her to be alone in this. She needed a sideline supporter.

'I just wanted to let you know before you found out from someone else,' she said. 'I have to go now. It's very late over here. I'll send photos in the morning.'

'But, Carrie...' Her mother sounded confused. 'Are you sure you don't want to talk to Maddie?'

'No, I really need to go.'

There was a silence after she ended the call.

'I'm sorry, Carrie,' he said.

'I always hope it might be different. But it never is. They're just...'

'Self-centred?' He shook his head in amazement. 'But what was the photo she meant?'

'I've no idea. Something on social media? My sisters are all over it.'

He took the phone from her and did a quick social media search.

'Oh.' Carrie stared as he turned the phone so they could both see the result. 'I didn't know Sereana had posted that. Or that my family would have been interested in seeing it.'

No wonder her mother had laughed at the idea she'd had a baby. In the photo, a group of athletes stood smiling at the camera. Carrie was on the far left of the line-up next to Sereana. Her silky hair was shining and she looked care-free and happy.

Massimo's throat thickened. Her radiant face looked only a little softer about the edges and her sundress hung simply. She didn't look pregnant at all—certainly not as if she was about to give birth. But she had—just *three days* after this photo was taken.

'Where *did* you hide her?' His words sounded raspy.

'I've no idea. I thought the backaches were tweaks from sleeping in a different bed.' She smiled sheepishly. 'My waist was a bit thicker. Like, my jeans were a struggle to do up. But I thought that was just a few extra comfort-eating kilos. It wasn't all centred in a lump out front, you know?'

It sure hadn't been. His skin prickled. Comfort-eating because she'd *needed* comfort. Because she'd been sad and alone. Because he'd been a jerk when she'd called him.

'I'm sorry I didn't believe you when you first told me,' he said huskily.

Not only had her family not listened to her, neither had he.

'I don't blame you,' she said stoically. 'It's pretty unusual.'

But he hated thinking how alone she'd been. He knew she'd not spoken up more because she'd never had *anyone* really listen to her. Her family were too busy and clearly didn't value what she had to offer. While he'd shut her down because he'd been *unable* to listen because of his own fears. So she'd had to deal with everything alone.

How he'd treated her haunted him. It wasn't her fault—his reaction hadn't really been *anything* to do with her. It hadn't been because he'd not valued her in that way. He wanted her to know that.

'*You'd* done nothing to make me mistrustful,' he muttered. 'I was that way long before I met you.'

He didn't trust anyone. He hadn't for a long time. People died or lied or left. Always.

She stilled. 'Why?'

He couldn't look away from the gentle question in her eyes. She was alone too, yet she still reached out, offering support. She knew he hurt and she wanted to help. But that wasn't why he wanted to tell her. He wanted to *explain* his own shoddy behaviour to her. Not to excuse it, but so she could understand it hadn't been about her.

'I always believed Mum was the love of my father's life,' he said gruffly, turning to sit beside her in the warm water. 'She was *everything* to him, and when she died he effectively died too. Emotionally. He was so lost in grief he couldn't really function, and certainly couldn't look at me.'

'Your eyes?' she muttered softly.

He grimaced. 'My nanny tried to tell me it wasn't *me*. It was that he loved my mother so much that he couldn't cope with her loss.'

'Massimo…'

He didn't want to feel love like that. To be so enthralled by someone that life was destroyed when that person left.

'But it *was* me. He hadn't wanted me. He'd wanted her. *Only* her. When I was a kid he told me he'd only agreed to try for a baby because it was what *she'd* wanted, and that he'd hated how unhappy she was every month when she found she wasn't pregnant. That all those years of trying ruined their happy marriage.'

'He actually *said* that to you?'

'Because it was my fault she was dead. Only a couple of hours after I was born, she had a massive stroke and died.'

He had only one photo of her holding him, when he was only minutes old. It was his most treasured possession. His father had destroyed the rest in a rage just over a decade later. It was why he'd wanted all those photos from their wedding day for Ana. Massimo wanted her to know her mother adored her. And her father.

'She'd been his world and she was gone, and that was because of me. So I had a nanny until I was sent to boarding school. Dad hadn't wanted to retain the nanny for my holidays, so then there was a succession of them. A temporary carer for each break. Some interested. Most not.'

'There was no stability for you,' she said. 'No one you could trust.'

He sighed heavily. 'Anyway, I used to get sore throats as a kid, and eventually I needed an operation. As part of the pre-op procedures, they tested my blood type. Dad said it wasn't necessary because both he and my mother were quite a rare blood type. The *same* blood type.'

'Massimo…'

'Yeah. Turns out I'm a blood type that's impossible for my parents to have produced together. Which means my father…'

She drew in a steadying breath. 'Is not your biological father.'

'My mother lied to get pregnant,' he mumbled. 'She had an affair.'

He had to look away from Carrie. The look in her eyes was troubled and too tender and he wanted to tumble into her in *every* way. Not this time. He gazed up at the stars instead. There were so many, they reminded him he was a mere speck.

'I found him through a DNA search,' he finally said. 'Apparently they were acquaintances. The guy admitted he'd always wanted her but he didn't want *me*. I was never meant to have found out.'

'And your father—when he found out?'

'I was thirteen when he walked out of that hospital and didn't come back.'

'What?' The water splashed as she twisted to face him fully. 'When you were having that operation?'

Alone and unwanted, the world he knew in ruins… Everything he'd believed in had been destroyed—his father's rejection of his mother. That such an intense love could be rejected so completely had stunned him. After that, nothing could have been certain or safe.

'It was hard enough when I reminded her of what he'd lost, but when I became proof that the woman he'd loved had actually betrayed him…'

'Massimo…'

He tried to smile but he couldn't. 'Her death had devastated him, but discovering that? He'd rejected her completely. And, by extension, me—completely. I wasn't his son. He wanted nothing more to do with me.' Massimo hadn't been able to trust anything or anyone after that. 'He sent me to several different boarding schools overseas after that. A new one each year, ostensibly to learn more languages and get the very best education.'

'That was so much change for you.' She frowned. 'Constant change.'

'I actually thought if I could become successful he might be interested in seeing me again. Stupid, huh? That I could prove myself worthy enough to be back in his life.'

His father had been a partner in a multi-national finance firm. Massimo had gone out alone. Taking on higher risk because he had nothing to lose.

'I thought that if I succeeded in his area he'd realise he'd had some influence on me...that I *was* his son in a way.'

Her expression melted. 'But that didn't happen?'

'The only positive he acknowledged was that my business success enabled him to stop supporting me financially.' He sighed.

He'd never been enough to cause his father to push beyond that anger.

'I'm so sorry, Massimo,' Carrie said quietly.

'My mother ruined her marriage to get me. Then I took her life from her.' His whole being was a destructive force. 'If I hadn't been conceived, if I hadn't been born, then she'd still be alive and they would still be happy.'

'It was a terrible *tragedy* that took her,' Carrie said. 'And it was terrible that he took it out on you.'

'He loved too hard. And he was hurt,' Massimo replied tautly.

'But that didn't mean he had to hurt you. *None* of this was your fault. He should have been there for you. He should have loved you for who you are. Just *you*.' She frowned. 'And, if he loved her so much, why couldn't he find a way to forgive her? She must have felt so desperate.'

'Which is why it's foolish to love, right?' Massimo said stiffly. 'People sacrifice too much to accommodate someone else. They compromise. Then it turns to resentment and regret, and inevitably someone lies. Someone leaves.'

'*Not* inevitably. People make it work all the time. Maybe they just communicate more,' Carrie argued. 'They discuss their dreams, take turns and grow in the same path so there's no resentment. Only reward.'

He couldn't help a small smile. 'Ever the optimist.'

Despite the heartbreak her own family caused her. But what she'd described was what she wanted—the kind of thing he couldn't do.

She swallowed. 'Will you tell him about Ana?'

The fierce need to protect Ana locked his muscles. 'You think I should?'

'Not necessarily.' A sad expression flickered across her face. 'Sometimes you need to know when to let go. When you've tried so hard...why continually put yourself up for repeated rejection? I guess it's a balance about being open to reconciliation but protecting yourself at the same time.'

Did she feel rejected repeatedly? That she was never enough?

'So that's why you're on the other side of the world—protecting yourself from your family's constant self-centredness?' he asked.

'I stay in touch but on my terms.' She nodded. 'But maybe you're right. Maybe I should have told them how it really made me feel all this time. I still didn't—not even just now.'

'You did make her shut up and listen eventually,' he said wryly.

'Only because my news was so shocking.' She cupped his face. 'But what your father did, that's a whole other level. I'm so sorry, Massimo.'

He couldn't listen. He didn't want her pity, he wanted her body. It was the perfect antidote. He pulled her onto his lap. 'It's okay.'

'It's not.' She breathed and leaned closer. 'You're hurt.'

'So are you.' He skimmed his hands over her waist beneath the water. 'So let's feel better together. Let's forget.'

But her sweet lips twisted. 'You *can't* forget. It'll still be there.' She placed her hand over his heart. 'It's always there, whether you can bear to admit it or not.'

'Shh.' He didn't want to hear it. He only wanted the physical relief to be found with her.

She wrapped her legs around his waist and gazed into his eyes but for once he couldn't keep looking at her. She saw too much. So he buried his face into the side of her neck, breathing her scent, tasting her soft, warm skin. And somehow that was worse.

'You don't feel better by forgetting,' she whispered. 'You feel better by *sharing.*'

She was wrong. Sex was an escape. It was mindless. It was only about the release of tension and the chemical high of orgasms. The pain beating beneath her hand was something he could ignore most of the time. But now she'd mentioned it, now she touched it, she'd made it real. And now he couldn't push past it.

'Carrie.' He tensed.

'I know.' She didn't release him. Instead she embraced him more. Soft and warm and passionate. She moved with him. She wouldn't let him be alone. Be isolated. Not with her.

'Let me take it,' she muttered.

'No.' But he grabbed her thighs, holding her where he needed her. He could hardly resist—not what she was doing or offering. 'You have enough.'

'Then I'll share mine too.'

A surge of energy roared within—the hurt, the longing. It was like a crust of protection had been torn from him, revealing the ache beneath. He reached right round her to haul her closer still, needing the balm of her satiny skin and the snug heat of her welcome. More than that, he needed her strength as she coiled more tightly around him, even as he savagely drove into her.

He growled. This wasn't sex, this pulsing, raw emotion. He didn't want to frighten her with his physicality, but the depth of feeling it betrayed frightened the hell out of him. The howling ache of pain, of need, pushed him to drive harder, deeper still. But she didn't flinch. She didn't try to soothe him with words any more, only with actions, with an embrace like no other. Because there was desperation in her embrace too. In the way she clung, her legs wrapped around him, tightly accepting the raging conflict within him. Hurt transformed into action. The need to drive harder. To get closer still.

'I can take it,' she assured him huskily, and it was all he needed.

His hands tightened on her as the storm overtook him. From intimacy, to surging emotion, to a sudden need for stillness. The need to look straight into her eyes and see the safe harbour she offered. He paused on the brink—locked in stasis, of yearning so intense he thought he might die.

'Carrie.' His voice cracked.

'I'm here.'

His orgasm was as cerebral as it was physical. More emotional than anything. And he was lost.

CHAPTER FIFTEEN

How did you produce a baby that beautiful?

CARRIE ANSWERED HER mother's text message by sending a photo of Massimo. Her mother's reply was instant.

How did YOU meet HIM?!!!

Because it was unbelievable, right? That someone like him could have wanted someone like her.

But he didn't want her as much now. Since that night in the hot tub two nights ago, Massimo had stepped back. Apparently a large deal required urgent attention, so he was preoccupied, frowning at his screen as he worked in the shade up on his deck for hours. She didn't disturb him and he didn't come to her for distraction. She knew he had massive business responsibilities, that he had a lot of people counting on him. She could rationalise the changes in his behaviour. But she could also over-think and doubt everything.

It was too abrupt. Too near to that night under the stars when they'd become too close for his comfort. She knew he was a man used to being in control and it wasn't something he wanted to relinquish. That he'd come apart so completely in her arms had filled her with wonder at first, but his silence since... Didn't he trust that she'd never abuse that intimacy? But he'd suffered so much in his life—such unfair blame, such hurtful secrets exposed, such abandonment. No wonder he never trusted anyone.

On the third day of his self-imposed isolation, he came to her room. He stood on the threshold, his fists in his pockets. 'We need to go back to Sydney.'

Her heart crushed at his clipped tone but she didn't argue. She'd known that everything would change once he'd got what he'd wanted. And all he'd wanted, *really*, was Ana's security. She understood now why he'd wanted that so very much. The fantasy was over and she was going to have to figure out how to cope in his real world. It was so different from hers.

Two days later she followed him as he carried Ana through the customs facilities reserved for ultra-wealthy travellers who required ultimate privacy.

'We make a good team, Carrie,' he said. 'Our partnership is legitimate.'

But he meant in the *business* sense more than the married sense. And it wasn't true. She didn't fly in private jets. She didn't fit into this lifestyle, with sleekly groomed assistants offering to accommodate her every whim. With uniformed drivers chauffeuring them to his sophisticated Sydney apartment. She didn't know how to deal with them or his other employees or friends or ex-lovers…and she was bound to meet a few of those soon, wasn't she?

Insecurity raged. Most of all because he was so remote. The playful guy who'd stolen time for fun with her, who'd talked intimately with her, had vanished. In the real world, that guy rarely showed. And he didn't reach for her.

Massimo's Shock Marriage!
Billionaire's Baby Stunner!

The headlines in the Sydney gossip columns screamed. But it was the *baby* who was the stunner, not the bride. The conjecture was endless—when and where and how they'd met, rumours of his island retreat. The constant questions drained the last of her bleeding-out confidence.

Massimo was at work all day and at his tablet or on more business calls all evening until she went to bed. Alone. The workaholic was in his element. That was *fine*. She'd been prepared for that. He had other priorities—of course he did. People always did. She had to get her head round Sydney, round a new routine with Ana and Leah and round ideas for her own future career. She wasn't worried. Much. Only all the time. Because he didn't hold her gaze the same. He didn't tease her.

He didn't take the *time*. For Ana, yes—an hour before he left for work, and he made the effort to be back in the evening for her bath. But other than that he'd all but disappeared into his work.

It hurt. Had their time together just been an island holiday interlude for him? Had she imagined the intense intimacy they'd shared? Doubt nibbled all belief in her decisions.

She stared at her reflection, wondering whether the dress she'd chosen was appropriate, whether she should have tied up her hair, whether she was going to be able to make polite conversation at all. They had to go to some fund-raising event—her first outing as his wife. But he'd not yet arrived home and they were supposed to have left ten minutes ago.

'You're ready?' Massimo walked in and barely glanced at her.

'Yes.'

Anger flickered in her veins at his briskness. She was *trying* but he didn't seem to be. But she couldn't summon the courage to call him out on it. Her world felt too precarious—as if there were seismic danger just beneath the surface and it would take nothing to set it off. Simply put, she was too scared she would lose *everything*.

Massimo couldn't stand to look at her. She was stunning in that sleeveless black dress, and he just wanted to walk her backwards until she was against the wall, where he'd part her legs and ravish her hard.

No. He had to retain in control. Perspective. *Distance.* He'd lost all of it that night in Fiji after she'd phoned her parents and he'd told her everything. He'd been engulfed by a firestorm of emotion that had felt insanely good.

Until the next day. He'd woken up. Completely.

He shouldn't have told her about his parents. Dredging it up, discussing it, had made him think more about it than he'd ever let himself before. And he couldn't stop comparing his parents' relationship to theirs. He didn't want Carrie to be unable to ask for what she really wanted from him, or be afraid of *hurting* him if she asked for more than he could give. Because she'd seen his hurt. And he'd never let anyone see that before. He hated that she knew he was vulnerable. And what was missing within him was never going to be fixed.

Carrie needed laughter, light and love and she *deserved* those things. But she was stuck, married to him, and he couldn't give her any of them for long—certainly not *love*. Because his family's kind of love wasn't healthy. It was desperate, controlling and destructive.

So he reshaped his plan. He pulled away because she was too true, too soft. He couldn't let her fall for him but she would. They'd have to stop sleeping together, separate sooner. He just had to get through now. Going out was the only way he could resist the ache to take her in a storm of lust this second.

Carrie tried to smile but the intimidation factor was off the scale. The other guests at the exhibition were works of art themselves. All beautiful specimens of humanity. But it wasn't just their looks. They were superstars like her sisters, like Massimo too. She paled next to them. She'd slowly disappear and become invisible to them. to him too. But right now they all turned and stared.

'*You're* Massimo's new wife?'

Carrie wasn't quite sure how to interpret the woman's emphasis, but she determinedly smiled back. '*Only* wife, as far as I'm aware.'

'I helped him pull together your wardrobe,' the woman informed her with a speculative gleam. 'I'm Janelle. I own the department store he favours. He was very particular in what he wanted you to have. I've never known Massimo to take such an interest in dressing a woman…'

'He's usually interested only in undressing them.' The man next to Janelle made the obvious unfunny joke. 'But how lovely to have him provide you with a completely new wardrobe.'

Their words were veiled in amusement, in a light, joking tone, but the looks were sly, the speculation that he was with her only because of Ana obvious.

Of course it was obvious. They all knew he would never have married her if it hadn't been for Ana and Carrie knew that better than anyone. But suddenly she was too angry to feel inferior about it. Not tonight. Never.

'Oh, yes,' she agreed. 'I'm terribly lucky.'

'And it's most unusual for him to abandon his empire for so long.' They glanced at her sideways.

'Well, I did have his baby,' Carrie said, boldly referencing the thing they were so shocked about.

'Very clever of you, I must say.' Janelle smiled.

'Well…' Recklessly Carrie matched the woman's tone. 'I did want to bag a wealthy husband.'

'Carrie?' Massimo suddenly materialised right beside her. The man must have had ears like a bat.

'It's all right, darling.' She turned and smiled sharply. 'Your charming friend Janelle was just admiring my cleverness in conceiving your child. Naturally, I'm in complete agreement. Now, I'm going for some air.' She handed him her drink and walked out.

'What did you just say to my wife?'

Behind her Massimo was the embodiment of arctic fury.

But Carrie kept walking. She made it onto the balcony. She was winded by their attack but her breath was truly stolen by her own audacity. What the hell was wrong with her? She'd just created a *scene*. She didn't do drama—not even when her sister had taken up with her fiancé with her family's full approval. But it had been impossible not to react to that remark.

A heartbeat later, Massimo joined her on the balcony, fire swirling in his eyes.

'I'm not going to apologise,' she said. In truth she was seconds away from grovelling and stammering, *Sorry!* 'I've had enough, Massimo. I'm not going to be treated like an idiot. Or underestimated. Or put up with people just being plain rude to my face.'

'Quite right.' The air crackled with energy he was barely containing. 'I completely agree, and just told them the same. Less politely.'

'You what? But they're—'

'Rude. As you said.'

She took a breath. She'd just wrecked their first social 'showing'. She wasn't the stunning, socially adept superstar wife they all expected him to have. Not the wife he *needed*. 'How did they react?'

'Don't know. Don't care. Came after you.' He stared down at her and visibly tried to steady his breathing. 'Is it okay if I come nearer?'

'Why are you asking?' she asked. 'Are you afraid I might do you harm?'

'Just want to give you the option.'

'Make me feel as if I have some control?'

'You do,' he said. 'I think you have it all, Carrie.'

To her horror, her eyes suddenly filled with tears. Because he didn't mean that in the way she wanted him to.

'I'm sorry.' Fire still raged in his eyes. 'I didn't think they'd be so blatant.'

Of course they thought he was only with her because of

the baby. It was true. The last few days had proven it—he'd had enough of anything intimate with her.

With an indecipherable mutter, Massimo pulled her into his arms and pressed his mouth to hers. And she, sad creature that she was, leaned in and took it all. Because that electricity shocked her to life. Their chemistry resulted in the kind of kiss *not* supposed to occur in public situations. The kind of kiss she'd desperately, desperately, missed and so badly needed.

But it was only moments before he tore away from her. 'We need to get out of here. Now.'

She almost stumbled as he grabbed her hand and marched her to the stairwell. 'Aren't we going to say goodbye?'

'No.'

Her pulse roared as she registered his intention. And it was totally fine by her.

They were silent in the car. Silent in the lift. Silent until they'd both stepped inside the apartment and he'd carefully closed their bedroom door so they wouldn't wake Ana or the nanny. And then...

Massimo turned to her, wildness filling his head and heart. He smashed his mouth over hers—demanding more than he ever had before, stripped right back to raw sexuality. There was no veneer of polite hesitation, of careful courtesy, and her acquiescence wasn't needed because she was the same—stripped right back to raw emotion, needing him so much she was shaking. He *had* to answer that need. He couldn't leave her trembling, alone and aching. Not his brave, honest, generous lover.

With voracious urgency he dropped to his knees, worshipping the woman he wanted more than his next breath. He was completely lost to the power of his desire, not just for her, but to please her. He peeled aside her panties. He'd make her come. Now. Hard. On his tongue. Because giving her pleasure was the one thing he could do for her. He could make her feel good. He could make her forget everything else. Most especially, that hurt.

And he did. He held her tight as she buckled beneath his onslaught. As she screamed her sudden release. But it wasn't enough. He pulled her to the floor and plunged to the hilt into her heat. Rocking his hips, he drove the rhythm he knew she loved. Her hands gripped him hard, her fingers pinching and pushing to hurry him. He wasn't having it. Not until she was on the edge again. Not until she was arching uncontrollably, her hair tumbling, her skin flushed and gleaming, her cries quickening.

Only then did he let himself go again, surging into her soft, searing, sweet-as-heaven body and finding his own satisfaction. His own breath was stolen and his heart raced. He was almost dizzy with both relief and the sudden renewal of desire. He lifted his head and stared down at her beauty.

Again. Again. Again. It would *never* be enough.

He saw the shock in her eyes—the widening, then the *wonder*. Belatedly, he realised his mistake. She was confusing this passion, this addiction to mutual pleasure, for *feelings*. The depth of which he didn't have. He *couldn't*.

But he couldn't pull back, couldn't make himself let go of the melting pleasure to be found in her arms. *All* control was gone. Which meant tonight had to be the last time.

'Please, please, please…' Carrie begged him again and again and again.

Only it wasn't begging. It was *asking* for what she wanted. What she needed.

Love me. Love me. Love me.

He filled her again. He took her right to where she wanted to go. But it wasn't enough. He held her. He touched her. But it wasn't enough, even after the next orgasm shattered her and left her limp. Even when her lips were salty from the sweat dampening her face, her pretty dress was shredded and she simply couldn't move. It wasn't enough.

Even when he set about making her come apart all over again, it wasn't enough. It would *never* be enough.

CHAPTER SIXTEEN

'MASSIMO...'

He didn't reply.

'Massi—'

'Don't, Carrie.' He turned his head to look at her and this time the expression in his eyes was sombre. 'Don't.'

He'd taken her to heaven and she—wanton, reckless, desperate lover that she was—hadn't just *let* him, she'd spurred him on, breathlessly demanding he hurry. She'd been such a willing participant in her own destruction. The assumption of that woman tonight—that Massimo was only with her because of their baby—was true. *How very clever of Carrie!* Wrong.

'Don't silence me,' she said. 'Not now.'

Not when she'd finally found the confidence to speak on something so important.

He flinched. 'Carrie—'

'I want more,' she said.

She wanted it all. She didn't just want the spectacular sex and the security of his name. She wanted his *love*. And she wasn't going to get it. So she needed to end it now. Not because it wasn't going to last but because it wasn't *enough*. She'd given him everything and, if she stayed, if she let this continue as it was, there would be nothing left of herself. She'd be swallowed whole while remaining incomplete. What a fool she'd been to think she could somehow have her cake and eat it too.

'I want honesty and truth and openness,' she said. 'And that needs to start with me. So here goes.' She sucked in a breath. 'I love you, Massimo. I'm utterly in love with you.'

She knew it would destroy everything, yet it was such a relief to admit it. She was so completely, utterly and irrevocably in love with him.

'It's just sex,' Massimo answered.

His default setting was blanket denial—as with when she'd told him she was pregnant all those months ago. He didn't believe her. She knew he had trust issues—but surely he trusted her word now?

She shook her head. 'We just shared *so* much more than that. Lust, yes, absolutely. But don't you get why it was so frantic?' She stared at his frozen face, willing him to go with her on this. 'That need was love, Massimo. I opened up and let you in. That's what you wanted. That's what you took. I wanted it too.'

'It's just physical for me.' He pushed away from her. 'It was frantic because it's been a while. It's a biological urge and response. That's all.'

His words welted her heart.

'That's not true.' Her breathing quickened. 'You can't get enough.' Her chin lifted with the last of her courage. 'Same as me.'

'Because it's a *temporary* high,' he said. 'I *warned* you.' His eyes closed. 'It won't last.'

But he'd also told her that chemistry like this couldn't be contained.

'You do not get to deny or debase what that was.' Her anger surged. 'And, while I love sex *with* you, you are not *only* sex to me. I'm being as honest, as clear, as I can. Letting you see right through me to my heart. To what matters. To *all* that matters. And you're...'

Unable to say anything. Because—she realised with horror—it wasn't that he didn't *believe* her. It was because he couldn't give her the answer she so desperately wanted. Because he'd already told her and *she* was the one not listening. He'd told her not to settle for second best. Not to let herself be undervalued any more. To make a scene if necessary, not to stay silent. That she was stronger than that.

But she wasn't. She was not strong enough. Because the truth was *he* didn't want to settle for her. *He* didn't love *her*. She wasn't enough for him. She wasn't wanted by him for anything more than sex. Which meant she had to push him away. Because *he* was her paradise. And her paradise had become her prison. Her life, her heart, was now irrevocably bound with his. Because with Ana they were a tightly woven group that couldn't be separated.

But they could be loosened.

She ached to breathe freely. She was going to have to live with it somehow. And she would, because of her daughter. But she was *not* settling. She was not staying silent. Not this time. Not any more, ever again.

'You know, that night back in Auckland, you were my treat,' she said sadly. 'My indulgence just for me. No real risk. I *knew* you were leaving. I *knew* you weren't meant for me. And because of that I wasn't going to fall in love with you. That was never a threat. You weren't supposed to be a *threat*.'

Even though she'd known he was so far out of her league, she'd rolled with the *chemistry*. She'd run with the fantasy of it. Only it had all fallen apart because, when confronted with the reality of him all those months later in Fiji—when faced with the tough things, when they'd reconnected, when she'd got to know his depths—was when she'd *really* fallen.

'I didn't want to see you again. That first night was dangerous enough. That's why I never phoned. I *knew* this would happen.' Even though she'd tried to save pride and denied that it would. Now there was no pride left.

He was still frozen. This was not what he wanted to hear. Of course it wasn't.

'Carrie…'

She bowed her head. 'You don't feel the same way.'

'I can't.' He stared at her grimly. 'I don't want this, Carrie. I'm not capable—'

'You don't want *me*,' she argued, hurt by his easy excuses. 'You're not a robot, Massimo. You love Ana.'

He drew a sharp breath. 'That's different.'

'Yes, but at the same time it isn't,' she said. 'You can love when you want to. You *let* yourself love her. You let her in. I think you didn't have a choice about that, really, because it's Ana.' She breathed harder. 'But you won't let yourself love me. You won't let me in *because* it's me. One day with someone else there'll be no choice. You won't be able to say no.'

'That's not going to happen. Ever.'

He really believed he didn't want love in his life.

'You really think that you can *control* it?'

'Yes.'

'I can't stay here any more.' She climbed out of bed and pulled on the nearest pair of jeans. They were his and they fell straight off.

He stood and snatched them from her. 'Where do you think you can go right now?'

'Anywhere. I've fallen in love with you and that's not what you want. And I can't stay here to be—'

'Well, you can't run away.' His anger rose. 'Ana anchors you here. She always will. And she tethers us together. You can't just *escape* from this.'

'No, but I can *cope*,' she snapped. 'And distance from *you* is essential for me to do that. Some space. Take my passport, if you want. Take Ana's. You know I'll never leave *her*. But *we* don't have to stay together.' She glared at him. 'You can't have your cake and eat it, Massimo. *I'm* not that convenient. I'm not going to make it easy. Not this time. Not any more.'

'What more do I have to do to make you happy?' His temper shredded. 'I bought that bloody island for you.'

'I never asked you to buy me anything. You just did that because you *could*. Because it's power and control for you. I don't give a damn about islands or clothes or *things*. I care about *you*. The person you are when you let your guard down.' She gazed at him, desolation filling her so fast. 'But you shouldn't have to *try* to make me happy. You know you don't really want me to stay, and I *can't* be here with you like this. It's not fair, Massimo. You need to let me go.'

Abruptly he turned and pulled on his jeans. 'Then let's enact these changes tonight.' He now displayed nothing but business-like precision.

She watched as the war within him was lost—so quickly. He didn't want to fight for her. So she'd won. And she was *devastated*. She couldn't swallow…could hardly speak. 'I'll go to—'

'*I'll* leave,' he snapped. 'You're not going anywhere.'

'No, that's not fair.' She breathed raggedly. 'This is your home. *I* need somewhere else. I'll find somewhere to rent.' She winced. 'I'm sorry I've cost you so much.'

'Money is irrelevant.'

She hadn't meant money—not entirely. She'd meant time and resources. But now he was icy and proactive.

'We would have had separate residences eventually anyway. The other apartments are already vacant. It's no problem for me to go to mine now while you stay here with Ana. When it's my turn to spend time with her, you'll go to your personal apartment. It's only a brief walk from here. That way it's less disruptive to Ana and we don't need to duplicate all of her things. We can eventually, of course, but it will be good for her to remain in familiar surroundings initially. It's easier for Leah too.'

'That's…' Carrie swallowed. 'That's a good idea.'

But she was stunned. Not only had Massimo worked out an action plan for when they were no longer together, he'd *already done* all the preparation. Those apartments were ready *now*. Which meant he'd been mulling this for a while, whereas she'd only had a lightning strike realisation minutes ago. When she'd fully opened up, only to be shot down by him. Bitterness trickled. 'And you say I'm the one who runs away? You've got your escape plan hatched perfectly.'

He shot her a glance. 'It was only a matter of time.'

Yet he was the one who'd insisted on them living together in the first place. He'd spent time with her, making her laugh, making her feel good, making her fall for him. Until she'd got too close. He was so cruel.

'Self-fulfilling prophecies, don't you think?' Disappointment flooded her. And anger. So much anger. 'You *expected* me to end it. You *made* me want to. Because you're too cowardly to envisage an alternative altogether. You can't possibly believe that this could have lasted. You refused to *ever* seriously entertain the idea.'

His face stiffened. 'Actually, you're wrong. I did wonder if this could last longer. But that would only be possible if it remained as it was.'

As some convenient arrangement.

'So it's my fault for speaking up? For asking for more? For wanting to name what's *really* between us?'

It was the one thing he'd encouraged her to do.

Devastated, she watched him throw a few things into a carry-all. His automatic movements just proved his lack of care. Yet, if she hadn't said anything, he would have been happy to keep sleeping with her. He'd been *using* her.

Silence would have kept this easy. Silence would have betrayed her. She couldn't stay silent any more.

'I can't give you *everything*.' Her voice rose. 'Why should I give and give when you don't want it all from me? When you don't want to give *me* everything in return?' She caught the sudden look of fury from him. 'I'm not talking about tangibles, Massimo. I'm talking about more precious things—time, consideration, to be thought of *first*. To be your number one…'

That was all she wanted. To be someone's number one. And, while the love he showed for Ana redeemed him, it ripped her heart into pieces. Because it showed how he could love. Just not her.

'Why should I hurt myself wishing that one day you might? The convenience of me was a plus, but it doesn't really matter. I know you'll be a good father for Ana. But you don't have to be a good husband for me. Not any more. You like sex? You're free to get it from someone else. My blessings.'

He threw her look of such fury, she actually stepped back.

'You ask for too much!' He growled.

'You told me I should say how I felt. Or didn't you think I'd apply that advice directly to you?'

'But because you didn't get the answer you wanted, you just want to run away.'

'From you, yes.'

'Good. Because I *cannot* be the man you want me to be. I am *not* the man you think you love.'

What did he even mean by that? 'Of course you are,' she said. And for one last, devastating time she was compelled to admit the truth. 'I love you, Massimo. *All* of you. Flaws and all. *Fears* and all.'

But he didn't even see her any more. He just scooped up the bag and stalked out of the apartment.

Carrie stared after him, shattered. She'd just offered him everything. But it wasn't enough. *She* wasn't enough.

CHAPTER SEVENTEEN

Massimo swallowed a painkiller and winced. He hadn't had a sore throat like this in years. The childhood complaint had come back to haunt him when he needed it least.

Week two of the new arrangement.

He'd known it wouldn't last. He'd known she would leave. When she didn't get what she wanted, when she was overwhelmed, she tried to escape. But *he* was the one who'd gone. *He'd* clawed back his control and not allowed emotion to overrule reason. He'd been strong enough to do what was sensible. Only it hadn't really been strength. It had been self-preservation. He'd had to get out of there before the tumultuous emotion toppled his equilibrium entirely. Control? Not so much.

He missed Ana unbearably. But Leah sent him through photos and little movies on the days he was apart from her.

He missed Carrie. Awfully. So awfully, he couldn't stand to think of her. Yet he couldn't stop. Why hadn't it been enough that he'd supported her when she'd dealt with those people at the fund-raiser? He'd been in her corner. He'd reached out to her. He'd wanted her to do what she wanted. And he'd wanted to make her feel good. Why couldn't that have been enough? Why had she then wanted to *name* what she felt? Why had she asked him for more?

Promises. Declarations. They meant nothing. Nothing could be that *certain* or that *intense*. Now, he'd not got far enough away. The fool in him wanted to go back, to try to seduce her back into that convenient marriage. He could smooth everything over and get that easy life back. But even if he succeeded it would only end the same way. Because, while they might work on that superficial level for a while, it wouldn't be long before the fissures ripped open again. Before she wanted more than he could give. And, if they ignored that, resentment would set in. Everything would rot. So it was better to finish it now before the damage became too great. They could be distant but civil, and co-parent Ana.

This way he'd not hurt her *too* much. Because what she'd said, that declaration, wasn't true. It was the confusion he'd feared would happen because of her inexperience. She only *thought* she was in love with him. She barely knew him.

But she was constantly stuck in his head. He thought of her the instant he woke and all through the day. Of course, he'd already spent all night dreaming of her. The only time he had any respite was when he forced his concentration upon mundane concerns. That quickly grew exhausting. *Carrie* was all-consuming.

It was everything he'd never wanted. He was his father—allowing his life to be ruined by feelings for a woman. His anger turned to the man who'd taught him everything so damned badly. Nolan Wells had blamed Massimo for the loss of the love of his life and had been glad when bitter facts had released him from the duty he'd never wanted. Massimo's throat really hurt now, reminding him of that surgery. The horror immediately after when his father had walked out and left him alone as he'd literally vomited blood.

'Are you going to tell him about Ana?'

He'd been appalled by Carrie's question. He wanted Ana to have what he hadn't had—protection and the security of knowing who her family was. Never to be abandoned by a parent—blood or not. As Carrie had said then, why go for repeated rejection?

Nolan Wells wouldn't accept Ana as his grandchild. He wouldn't even be interested. But somehow, two weeks after walking out on Carrie, Massimo found himself on a flight north. And he found his mother's widower on the local golf course. He'd known he would—Nolan had always loved golf.

'Massimo.' The man straightened and glanced at his watch. 'This is a surprise.'

'I wanted to invite you to Sydney to meet someone,' Massimo said. 'If you're interested.'

'Who's that?'

'Ana. My daughter.'

Nolan angled his head to look at the photo Massimo had unlocked on his phone.

Ana in her cot, looking straight up at the camera. Looking straight-up adorable.

Nolan's expression stayed impassive. 'She has your mother's eyes.'

The ones Nolan couldn't bear to look at. The ones that reminded him both of happiness and the heartbreak of betrayal.

'Does that mean you don't want to meet her?' Massimo asked.

'I don't see the point, do you?' Nolan asked. 'She's not my granddaughter.'

Massimo shouldn't have been surprised or hurt. But he felt the surge of rage. 'You really think that?' he challenged him.

Why hadn't Nolan found the strength—the love—to forgive her?

Your poor father. So devastated. That was what everyone had said when he'd been a child—the nanny and the headmaster of the boarding school. But it wasn't true.

'You didn't love my mother at all.' Massimo shook his head.

'I loved her utterly,' Nolan said. 'But she betrayed me.'

'Why had she needed to?' Massimo asked unevenly.

'We agreed to leave it to fate,' Nolan said stiffly. 'If it was meant to happen, it would have.'

'So she knew you wouldn't accept a child that you didn't believe was your own. She knew you wouldn't compromise.'

'Why would I want to wreck my life looking after some-one else's brat?' Nolan shook his head. 'As it was, she changed. She wasn't there when I wanted her.'

Because it had all been about *him*. What he'd wanted—at his convenience.

Massimo turned and walked away before his rage exploded. What he'd been taught to believe had been a deep and desperate love that had lasted beyond even death hadn't actually been love at all. It had been selfish and controlling and it sure wasn't healthy.

And his father had *used* his grief. It had enabled him to do as he wanted. Everything he'd not wanted to deal with he'd allowed others to take on—such as his son. Even when he'd believed Massimo was his own blood, he'd not wanted to be bothered. There was no *love* in that. There was only self-indulgence.

And, if he'd really loved Massimo's mother, why hadn't he got past the initial hurt of discovering the truth about Massimo? Why hadn't he tried to understand it? Wouldn't he have found the strength to forgive her? Wouldn't he have had the insight to understand why she'd done what she had? Wouldn't he have loved her son regardless? Because her son was the one part of her that lived on.

Why had he taken it out on Massimo? Why had he not even given him a chance? Because Nolan hadn't wanted Massimo from the beginning and it had been a completely convenient escape from him. Massimo's feelings for Ana crystallised everything. Because Ana was *Carrie's* child, and Massimo would do anything to protect her, even if biology proved she wasn't his. Which meant Nolan hadn't cared for Massimo's mother the way Massimo cared for Carrie.

And Nolan hadn't been devastated. Massimo remembered the golf trips, the work travel… His father had just wanted to escape all emotional *responsibility* and he'd used grief, then betrayal, as his excuses. He'd been liberated to live the life he wanted. He wasn't just selfish. He was incapable of love.

The lie that Massimo had been fed was about what love was at all.

Did Massimo want that freedom to do whatever he wanted? He'd had it—all his adult life he'd had it. But where was the woman to tease, the child to snatch up and cuddle? Where was the laughter, the joy in sharing those moments? In sharing them with *Carrie*.

When Massimo returned to his office a large yellow envelope stood out amongst the mail on his desk.

Private and confidential.

The sender stamp showed it was from the lawyer. He'd need to contact the guy and talk about how they could safely progress Carrie's residency status. But for now Massimo ripped the edge and tipped the envelope up. Several official documents scattered out. Their wedding certificate. Ana's birth certificate. The results of the DNA test. A glance at each showed what he already knew. Carrie was his wife. Ana was named for Sereana. And Ana was his daughter. Mere pieces of paper that were meaningless. Only serving to smooth the process of keeping Carrie in the country.

But he stared at the letter confirming his paternity. No, it wouldn't have mattered what that damned DNA test showed. Ana was Carrie's child and as such she was precious to him. But there was more than that. He'd had only a week with her in Fiji, but Massimo *knew* Ana, and he adored her. He loved the snuffling noises she made in her sleep…the way she made a small fist, like a prize fighter, the softness of her hair, her unutterably sweet smile.

Massimo wanted to be there when she took her first steps and said her first words. He wanted her to turn to him when she was tearful. He wanted to make her laugh. He didn't want to miss a thing and he couldn't wait to see how she grew as a person. He wanted to be right alongside her—to encourage, guide and just love. He loved *her*—Carrie's child—as who she was, as she was, as she would be. He couldn't love her more and there was nothing she could do to make him love her less. What he felt was infinite, yet utterly complete, and he had no problem admitting any of that.

That was love, wasn't it? Unconditional, unending, freely given and, now he'd realised it, utterly liberating. It was the kind of love *he'd* never been given.

Maybe his mother would have done, but she'd died before she could. His father—incapable. But, in seeing the destructive ashes of his parents' relationship, Massimo had learned to keep people distant and intimacy frankly transactional. It had been safer to stay alone.

Carrie was the only person ever to tell him she loved him and he hadn't believed her. He'd been too stunned. Too scared. Afraid that, once she really knew him, she'd want to leave him. Everyone else had, right? He'd thought he didn't have whatever it was he needed to keep people close—that he was missing something. He realised now that he wasn't. All that was wrong with him was fear. Because Carrie had offered him the one thing he'd been too afraid to admit he'd ever want.

I love you, Massimo. All of you. Flaws and all. Fears and all.

He'd taken only what had felt safe. Had limited them to sex. But he'd been unable to resist stealing more. The marriage that had been for convenience was so much more. He'd *wanted* to marry her. He just hadn't wanted to admit it. There were so many things about his feelings for Carrie that he hadn't wanted to admit.

He pulled out his phone and looked again at the photo his assistant had released to the media. They were on the beach just after the wedding. Carrie held Ana in her arms as she laughed up at him. It was a picture so perfect, it couldn't possibly be real. It couldn't possibly last.

Yet it was real. He'd not just seen it, he'd lived it. And as for lasting? He'd not had faith in her but he'd had even less in himself. He'd not believed anyone could love him for long because no one ever had.

Sometimes faith was believing in something unseen. Sometimes it was believing in something that hadn't yet happened—the faith was believing that it *would*. Massimo's faith—his trust—had long been in the inevitable *failure* of relationships. Ultimately in abandonment. People lied, they died or they left. The love he'd been shown was destructive and it hadn't lasted. But what he'd been taught was love hadn't been at all. Love was so much more and so much *easier*. Especially when you just gave in—accepting it, *admitting* it.

Why had he feared a future with Carrie? Feared growing old alongside her, sharing in the joy of raising Ana and the possible marvel of giving her a sibling—one they'd adore just as much, just as easily? Why had he allowed the hurts of so long ago—of other people—scar and influence him? He'd been blind to his real choices, the real likelihoods. He'd been blind to what was *real* faith, trust and love.

He paced impatiently. He wasn't going use past hurt to hide from future hope now. Carrie had run away from what hurt her, but she still had hope. She was an optimist, and she was brave, and she'd *tried* with him. She'd shown such courage in telling him her feelings. he advice he'd given her, he needed to take himself. To let her know how afraid he was, what a damned fool he'd been, what he really felt. He'd wanted to provide security and protection for Ana because *he'd* longed for security and protection. Carrie wanted Ana to be put first—for their daughter to know she was the priority. Because Carrie never had been.

Until now. Now she was utterly, and always would be, *his* priority. He just had to prove it to her.

CHAPTER EIGHTEEN

On the nights when Massimo had his time with Ana, Carrie left the apartment extra early so there was no chance of her departure overlapping with his arrival. Massimo would never be late for his daughter. Knowing how much he cared for Ana was both balm and bitter poison. She had to protect the remnants of her crushed heart, needing time and space for healing to begin. Though it was almost three weeks since he'd left and it felt like any healing had hardly started.

But she forced her focus forward. She was doing it for Ana. Not just surviving, thriving. It was important that Ana see her mother valuing *herself*. Even if she didn't get all she yearned for, it was better than accepting less. Massimo had done so much for her, but in truth only because he'd had to, not because he'd wanted to. She wouldn't have seen him again if it hadn't been for Ana. The chemistry still between them wasn't enough. And it wasn't enough for her to sneak under his guard and be near to him because of that. He needed to *let* her in—to do more than allow her in his life, but actually *want* her in his life in that way.

She'd desperately wanted him to open up and admit that she was the one that he would give up almost anything to be with. Only he hadn't. She'd gambled, asked and lost. But she'd spoken up. And that was the real start.

So the twice-weekly night away from Ana was the time to work on her future. She couldn't dwell on her memories of Massimo. Couldn't reflect on the way he cradled Ana with such tender care or on the love that shone in his eyes as he looked at her. She loved that he loved their child but was so hurt that he didn't love *her*.

And so much of what he'd said was right. She couldn't escape. Couldn't run away. She had to deal with her reality, as hard as it was. And she could. Because she'd found dignity in having spoken her truth. Even though it hadn't worked out the way she'd wanted it to, she'd done it.

She'd registered with an agency and had been contracted for a few hours a week to supplement what she could still do for Sereana. So she had something outside herself and her own heartache to focus on. She enjoyed it. She was good at it, and she had plans to develop her sports event-scheduling app.

It was necessary for her self-worth and an independent future. Sure, she wasn't going to need the money, but she needed the satisfaction and purpose. She was good at arranging, at being the sounding board for decisions, for taking away the tasks that were a waste of other people's time. Not because their time was more precious than hers but, because *she* was skilled, it took her less time. She could do the detail that others couldn't see.

Her apartment was barely three minutes' walk. It was plush but impersonal. She'd not bothered to make it her own. It was too big for the two nights a week she stayed, but that was Massimo—providing far too much of some things while withholding the thing she wanted most. Himself.

She didn't know where he stayed the five nights she was alone with Ana. It wasn't at this apartment. It wasn't her business. But she was all ache. In weak moments she regretted her stand. If she'd stayed silent she could still have been with him now, except it would've been a slow torture. He didn't love her and it would have ended eventually. Better to have taken control of it herself. To have stood up for herself.

Today, the door man came over as soon as he saw her. 'I'm sorry, Carrie.' He addressed her informally, as she'd asked him to a couple of weeks ago. 'The apartment is having work done and it's taken longer than anticipated. You can't stay here tonight. Massimo has left this for you, and I have a taxi waiting.'

'Oh?' Frowning, she took the envelope from him.

She opened it as the doorman gave the taxi driver the address. Inside was a key card and a typed note listing a room number. Nothing personal, just the problem solved in true money-fixes-all style. Doubtless there'd be some new outfit there for her to wear tomorrow. Massimo always thought of everything. She drew a deep breath. Okay. She'd have the night at a hotel. Maybe she'd drink her way through the entire damned mini-bar and order everything on the menu.

Only he'd done the 'everything on the menu' thing for her once already, and she wasn't in the least hungry. As soon as she got to the hotel she went straight to the lift. It soared to the top floor. Opening the door, she took another deep breath. It wasn't just a room, it was an entire suite, and the view across the city…

She glimpsed it only briefly because then she noticed the table—it was smothered in dishes. Did she have the wrong room? She'd phone Reception, because there'd clearly been a mistake. But, before she could, someone knocked at the door. Probably a porter come to say she had the wrong key card. So she opened the door without checking the peephole.

Instant regret. Instant freeze.

Massimo Donati-Wells. Tall, dark and damning her wretched heart to hell in one swift second. It had been almost three weeks since he'd walked out. Since they'd shared breathing space. Since *everything*. Now he was at her door in a sharply tailored suit, but it was the stormy look in his eyes that cut her to ribbons.

'You don't have to let me in if you don't want to,' he said unevenly.

Her legs lacked strength. All of her lacked strength. As if she could say no to him!

'Carrie.'

His step forward gave her enough impetus to step back. She couldn't bear his touch. She was nowhere near over him. She needed space or she would give him everything. She couldn't do that.

Massimo stepped inside and closed the door behind him. Another swift glance into her distraught face sent his heart sprinting. Had he made a massive mistake?

'You're supposed to be with Ana,' she said. 'Is something wrong?'

'No,' he reassured her. 'Leah's with her. She's safe and well. This is…' He dragged in a breath.

He could hardly think for the relief of seeing her again. For the anxiety—pending the outcome of this meeting. He had to fight the urge to pull her into his arms and kiss her as if his life depended on it. Which, frankly, it did.

'What?' She bit her lip worriedly. 'Is there anything wrong with the apartment, or is this just part of some plan?'

Yeah, his plan was falling apart already.

'I had to go away for work.' He cleared his throat. 'Actually, I had to make it impossible to come and see you.'

'Because I'm so terrifying?' Her face was pale.

It took everything not to reach for her. But she deserved more than that. She deserved the words, the truth, first.

'I went and saw my father.'

Her eyes dilated. 'You what?'

'I asked if he wanted to meet Ana. It didn't go well.' He sighed. This wasn't working out anything like how he'd planned, and he couldn't explain it easily. 'I didn't want to be like him. I didn't ever want to love someone so much that losing them would be that devastating. But that's not what's happened. Really, he used the loss of my mother as an excuse to live selfishly. He wouldn't compromise for her. Or for me. He didn't *love* either of us.

'What I thought was love…?' He shook his head. He wasn't making sense. She wasn't understanding him. She was just staring at him.

'I thought it was my fault,' he muttered helplessly. 'That Mum wanting me so much led to her infidelity and then to her death. He couldn't bear to look at me. He didn't want me. I thought it was something in *me*.' He rolled his shoulders. 'And I guess I shut down. I thought I had it all under control so I wouldn't be like him. I wouldn't be hurt. Relationships were recreational. Just a good time, right?'

He stared into her eyes. 'Sex was all I gave. All I wanted to give. Until you.'

Carrie couldn't let hope unfurl. She glanced around the suite to avoid looking in his eyes. The flowers in the vases were reminiscent of the arrangements in Fiji. On the table she saw coconut rice, spiced fish, sweet pineapple. The dishes had been deliberately chosen—things she liked. He wanted to please her.

'I want to give you everything,' he said quietly.

She began to tremble.

'I miss Ana,' he added. 'I miss *you*. And I want you to have all of me. If you want.'

She half-flinched, half-held herself back. But he took a step towards her.

'I'm *not* like him. You were right, I'm just me. Carrie, I've been hurt. I'm a bit damaged. I have some work to do and I am screwing this up. But I am here for you, and I will *always* be here for you because, married or not, I want *you*. Only you. Always you, and I want to be *with* you—in everything, every day. And it wouldn't matter if I was or wasn't Ana's father. I would still love her because she is herself and she is wonderful and she is also *yours*. She is a vital, precious part of you, and I adore *you*. *You* are who I want with me in this. With me in everything.'

She couldn't move or speak or even start to believe the wonderful, magical things he was saying. The things she wanted so very much. Now he was so close, she could feel his heat and the soft, warm breath of his whisper.

'I'm so sorry, Carrie.' His murmur hurt. 'I wasn't honest. Not with myself or you, and I hurt you a lot.'

But she shook her head. 'I'm not the woman anyone expects you to be with.'

'In what way?'

'I'm not...'

He waited.

'You're successful.' She swallowed. 'And handsome. And everything. Just everything.'

'And the one woman in the world I can't resist is you.'

'That's just sex. Chemistry.'

'Turning my cowardice on me, Carrie? You know damn well it isn't.' He grabbed her waist and pulled her flush against him. 'You can't deny what it really is. You're too warm, too loyal, too brave. *I'm* the coward here. I wanted to resist, Carrie. *I* was too scared to understand what love even is, let alone accept it. But you? You're a fighter. You fought for Ana. You fought for me. I want to fight for *us*.'

She couldn't let herself believe him. She *couldn't*. She pushed on his chest. 'But you'll get bored. Eventually you'll want someone else.'

He stilled, his expression turning solemn, but he didn't release her. 'I am willing to spend the rest of my life working on your self-esteem, Carrie. Because it breaks my heart that you can't believe that *you're enough* for me.'

She felt hot and cold and horrible, and tears filled her eyes because that was her fear uttered aloud.

'You are, sweetheart.' He cupped her face in his hand. 'You always have been. Always will be. Enough. Just as you are. Funny and smart and generous and *so* genuine.'

His green eyes gleamed with strength and surety. 'I thought I had everything, Carrie. Every success, right? But these last weeks have proved I had nothing of real value.' His hands were so gentle on her now, stroking the side of her neck in that way she simply couldn't resist. 'I didn't think I could ever emotionally commit. Or would ever want to. I didn't want to invest because I didn't want to lose. I couldn't bear it if you abandoned me. But I have to offer you all I can. I'm yours, always yours, if you want me. I want everything with you.'

'But if it weren't for Ana…' she whispered.

'I would have found you in Fiji anyway,' he whispered back, the most gorgeously rueful smile creasing the corners of his eyes. 'Why couldn't I resist investigating investment opportunities on a Pacific paradise? I couldn't get you out of my head. I left you my number. I *wanted* you to contact me,' he said. 'To ask. But you didn't. And I didn't either. I didn't want to accept how much of an impact you had on me. But suddenly there I am, in Fiji. Glancing around in case I spotted you. It was my *third* trip, Carrie.'

'Third?' Her heart skidded.

'It was so easy that night in Auckland. Intense but easy. I didn't want to let you go home alone after dinner but I thought it was for the best. Something in me was scared even then. Subconsciously I knew you were special. And then you came back to me at the marina and it was magic.' His smile was twisted with sadness and hope. 'Come back to me again, Carrie. Come back…but this time stay for always.'

His insistence, his touch, the emotion shining in his eyes…

'Okay.' She collapsed against him.

'Will you ever believe how much I love you?' he murmured between kisses that jump-started everything. 'How much I want you? *Nothing* matters more than having you in my life.'

She closed her eyes, sure she was dreaming. 'Promise?'

'Always, and again and again. I'll tell you. I'll show you. I'll love you and I'll never leave you. You're *my* number one, Carrie, and I want you and Ana in the centre of my life. I want you to stay there.'

'Yes, please.' Now her tears fell. Now her body shook. Now she knew. 'Don't let me go.'

'Never.'

They moved together—magic, intense—tumbling to the floor in hot, fast, sweet desperation. Feeling him tremble at the lightest touch, she realised that, like him, she needed security. She'd secretly longed not for someone who would just ask her to stay, but someone who'd really see her, value her and *want* her right there with him. Here he was. Her anchor. Her everything. And he was so wonderful.

'I love you, Massimo,' she sobbed.

With every piece of her she loved him—hard—until she felt emotion tear him apart in a release more passionate, more intense, than any they'd shared before. They kissed and touched, coming together hotly and fiercely until they could barely breathe. They lay tangled for a long, long while.

'I think we should go back to the island soon,' he murmured contentedly. 'We need more of a honeymoon.'

'Yes, please.' She laced her fingers through his. 'But do you think we can go home to Ana now?'

Her arms ached for their daughter. For them to start anew *together*—their whole little family. She saw the softening in his eyes. The understanding. The *love*. He sat up and scrambled for their clothes so fast, she laughed.

'I can't wait to see her,' he admitted with a goofy smile. 'And I'm *never* sleeping apart from you again.'

'Just like that?' she teased.

He held out his hand to help her to her feet. 'Just like that.'

EPILOGUE

Three years later

MASSIMO STRETCHED LANGUOROUSLY, appreciating the warmth invading his body. It was more than the sun penetrating his skin, it was love steam-cleaning his soul. He watched Carrie the gorgeous, clad in a bikini and some floaty fabric, scoop up their daughter and for a second he wondered if his heart might actually burst.

But then his daughter giggled. Ana had been yawning for the last ten minutes as she too was tired from swimming in the clear water with him these last two hours. Leah stepped forward from where she'd been reading to take her to the nursery, leaving Massimo and Carrie alone in the secluded, shady nook on their private beach.

Massimo loved his life. He especially loved afternoon nap time. He knew this level of contentment was rare. Nowadays he felt rested in a way he'd neither experienced, nor even imagined possible, only a few years ago. And his happy heart beat faster as Carrie strolled towards where he lay sprawled back on the warm sand, mirth sparkling in her eyes.

'Massimo Donati-Wells,' she addressed him with mock civility. 'Are you lazing on the beach doing *nothing*?'

'Not doing nothing,' he replied extremely lazily, yet with a huskiness that betrayed the depths of his emotions. 'I'm plotting.'

'Nefarious takeover plans? Corporate raiding? Some high-profile merger?' Even as she teased there was a softness in her expression.

'Definitely a merger. There's a distinct possibility of a takeover as well.'

The shimmer in her eyes brightened.

He sat up to take her hand, then tugged on it as he lay back again. He didn't have to tug hard—she tumbled to the sand beside him. It was a slow, laughing tumble that she'd totally expected. Because, no, it wasn't the first time he'd made that move. He pushed back the floaty covering so he could touch her. His need to feel her skin against his was almost a torture.

'How is it possible that you're seven months' pregnant?' he whispered in wonder. He knew her and yet she was still such a wondrous mystery to him.

Her shoulders lifted and even she shook her head in bemusement. 'It's just the way I seem to carry them.'

There were small tell-tale signs that did betray her to those closely observant. And right now Massimo was very, very close and very, very observant. He reverentially explored each sign—kissing along that softer line of her jaw, smoothing his palms over her radiant skin, carefully pushing aside the small stretchy bikini so he could ever so gently press his teeth into the deeper blush of her nipples. The curve to her belly, the one that had always been there, wasn't much bigger than usual yet it was little more than two months until her due date.

'You're incredible,' he muttered.

Enchanting. Bewitching. Loving. Generous. Funny. Sharp.

She was so many wonderful things and he was about to lazily make love to his wife for as long as possible. Although in truth it wasn't going to be *that* long, because she felled him. The attraction burned even hotter than in those heady days when they'd first married, when they'd first realised and admitted their love.

But, while there was peace in being with her right in this present moment, there was the paradox of desperation as well. Desire pushed him to move faster even when he wanted to take all the time there was in existence to simply savour this moment. *Every* moment.

Carrie rubbed the backs of her fingers along Massimo's stubbly jawline. She loved him most like this—a little tired, a lot relaxed, with all the love shining from his eyes.

Vulnerable together. Content together. No distraction. No distance. Nothing *but* them. Their family and friends were nearby and they would dine and laugh together later. But this moment? This was theirs alone.

Their son was due soon and Carrie couldn't wait to meet him. Massimo had already started talking about another child after him. He, who'd once been so determined not to have children at *all*, now wanted a large family. And he wanted to share in all the experiences life could offer. He'd pushed back on the hours he worked, striving to better balance their world. He supported her endeavours at work—becoming *her* champion, the supporter she'd lacked for so long. It wasn't perfect, of course. But in that imperfect way, with mistakes and laughter, it absolutely was.

They spent long stretches of time in Fiji. Eventually school terms or work schedules might limit their time there for a while, but she was at peace with that. Because she understood that his love for her knew no limits. Just as her love for him was profoundly complete. Paradise, she'd discovered, wasn't a place. Nor was it an escape. It was simply being with *him*—in the time and space they shared.

Here. Now. Together.

* * * * *

COMING SOON!

We really hope you enjoyed reading this book.
If you're looking for more romance, be sure to
head to the shops when new books are
available on

Thursday 28th April

To see which titles are coming soon, please visit

millsandboon.co.uk/nextmonth

MILLS & BOON

MILLS & BOON ®

Coming next month

CROWNING HIS LOST PRINCESS
Caitlin Crews

"I don't understand this…sitting around in pretty rooms and *talking*," Delaney seethed at him, her blue eyes shooting sparks when they met his. "I like to be outside. I like dirt under my feet. I like a day that ends with me having to scrub soil out from beneath my fingernails."

She glared at the walls as if they had betrayed her.

Then at him, as if he was doing so even now.

For a moment he almost felt as if he had—but that was ridiculous.

"When you are recognized as the true Crown Princess of Ile d'Montagne, the whole island will be your garden," he told her. Trying to soothe her. He wanted to lift a hand to his own chest and massage the brand that wasn't there, but *soothing* was for others, not him. He ignored the too-hot sensation. "You can work in the dirt of your ancestors to your heart's content."

Delaney shot a look at him, pure blue fire. "Even if I did agree to do such a crazy thing, you still wouldn't get what you want. It doesn't matter what blood is in my veins. I am a farm girl, born and bred. I will never look the part of the Princess you imagine. Never."

She sounded almost as final as he had, but Cayetano allowed himself a smile, because that wasn't a flat refusal. It sounded more like a *maybe* to him.

He could work with *maybe*.

In point of fact, he couldn't wait.

He rose then. And he made his way toward her, watching the way her eyes widened. The way her lips parted. There was an unmistakable flush on her cheeks as he drew near, and he could see her pulse beat at her neck.

Cayetano was the warlord of these mountains and would soon enough be the King of this island. And he had been prepared to ignore the fire in him, the fever. The ways he wanted her that had intruded into his work, his sleep. But here and now, he granted himself permission to want this woman. *His* woman. Because he could see that she wanted him.

With that and her *maybe,* he knew he'd already won.

"Let me worry about how you look," he said as he came to a stop before her, enjoying the way she had to look up to hold his gaze. It made her seem softer. He could see the hectic need all over her, matching his own. "There is something far more interesting for you to concentrate on."

Delaney made a noise of frustration. "The barbaric nature of ancient laws and customs?"

"Or this."

And then Cayetano followed the urge that had been with him since he'd seen her standing in a dirt-filled yard with a battered kerchief on her head and kissed her.

He expected her to be sweet. He expected to enjoy himself.

He expected to want her all the more, to tempt his own feverish need with a little taste of her.

But he was totally unprepared for the punch of it. Of a simple kiss—a kiss to show her there was more here than righting old wrongs and reclaiming lost thrones. A kiss to share a little bit of the fire that had been burning in him since he'd first laid eyes on her.

It was a blaze and it took him over.

It was a dark, drugging heat.

It was a mad blaze of passion.

It was a delirium—and he wanted more.

Continue reading
CROWNING HIS LOST PRINCESS
Caitlin Crews

Available next month
www.millsandboon.co.uk

MILLS & BOON

THE HEART OF ROMANCE

A ROMANCE FOR EVERY READER

MODERN

Prepare to be swept off your feet by sophisticated, sexy and seductive heroes, in some of the world's most glamourous and romantic locations, where power and passion collide.

HISTORICAL

Escape with historical heroes from time gone by. Whether your passion is for wicked Regency Rakes, muscled Vikings or rugged Highlanders, awak the romance of the past.

MEDICAL

Set your pulse racing with dedicated, delectable doctors in the high-pressure world of medicine, where emotions run high and passion, comfort an love are the best medicine.

True Love

Celebrate true love with tender stories of heartfelt romance, from the rush of falling in love to the joy a new baby can bring, and a focus on the emotional heart of a relationship.

Desire

Indulge in secrets and scandal, intense drama and plenty of sizzling hot action with powerful and passionate heroes who have it all: wealth, status good looks…everything but the right woman.

HEROES

Experience all the excitement of a gripping thriller, with an intense romance at its heart. Resourceful, true-to-life women and strong, fearless m face danger and desire - a killer combination!

To see which titles are coming soon, please visit

millsandboon.co.uk/nextmonth